MW00907652

A Canoer of
Shorelines

ANNE M.
SMITH-NOCHASAK

 FriesenPress

Suite 300 - 990 Fort St
Victoria, BC, V8V 3K2
Canada

www.friesenpress.com

Copyright © 2021 by Anne M. Smith-Nochasak
First Edition — 2021

All rights reserved.

"Let me live in a house by the side of the road
And be a friend to man."

This quotation is from *The House by the Side of the Road* by Sam Walter Foss
(1858-1911), and is therefore not included in the author's copyright.

No part of this publication may be reproduced in any form, or by any
means, electronic or mechanical, including photocopying, recording, or any
information browsing, storage, or retrieval system, without permission in
writing from FriesenPress.

ISBN
978-1-5255-9878-4 (Hardcover)
978-1-5255-9877-7 (Paperback)
978-1-5255-9879-1 (eBook)

1. FICTION, SMALL TOWN & RURAL

Distributed to the trade by The Ingram Book Company

To Noah

Kajaktutik amma Kajaliutik
and a canoer of shorelines, too

Thank you for the adventures and the joy.

INTRODUCTION
TO THE DREAM

I have had a powerful dream. I have told and retold this dream, but now I am going to write it down, here at Wasaya, before the lines blur and the images slip away. I want to set this dream down before it fades into fiction, shadowed by time and distance.

I will write it as it was, when I awoke in Ontario, having been in Meadowbrook, 2,000 miles away. Here at Wasaya, I write this down.

I swung my car into the driveway at Meadowbrook Acres on a sultry July morning, weary from a long drive after another busy contract in North Ontario. My son dozed in the passenger seat while Saima and Mikijuk pressed against the windows, panting and eager for squirrels and ground-hogs. I slowed and leaned back. The grass was long but the sky was clear and there would be time for coffee and stretching out on the verandah before assuming the tasks of summertime. The grass was still green and rich in the July morning, and speckled with dandelions.

The grass shifted.

The back lawn by the verandah began to pulse, and little snakes of bright reds and blues emerged, rippling and slithering. I turned to reassure my son, but it was my brother, not him, in the passenger seat now. "We have to get inside," I said.

I stumbled out on the driver's side, the snakeless side, and Saima bounded out. Mikijuk and my son, Nathaniel, had faded from the dream, and now my brother was there. Dreams are like that; characters fade in and out to serve the plot.

I smoothed Saima's thick, creamy coat, and it darkened to pointy little black scales. Shiny. Her mouth stretched open to reveal a pink maw. No dog tongue, just two fangs. She arched her mouth wide, displaying the pink emptiness with two sharp fangs.

I backed away. "We have to get inside," I repeated, sprinting across the lawn, lifting sandaled feet high.

The snakes, however, were gone now. Charles followed me, chuckling.

I fumbled with the lock on the side door, yanked it open. "Whatever you do," I insisted, "do not let the dogs into the house." I punched in the security code while Charles ambled into the kitchen.

Now I was entering the kitchen and there was Charles, the kitchen door wide open, shiny black-scaled dog bounding in. "I told you not to let the dogs in!" I screamed.

Charles grinned. "Whoops," he said.

I rushed into the dining room, but the dog was not there. There was movement on the den floor and I cringed. The fat, sluggish body of a great brown snake, thick like a python, was undulating its way under the sofa. The end of the tail dragged in, jerking back and forth, as it burrowed completely under the sofa in the den.

Now I was in the vehicle, jabbing the key at the ignition. I believe that Charles was standing on the verandah. I did not look for or think of Nathaniel and Mikijuk. I would not look for Saima. I would not think of her.

Oh, my dear Saima. What have they done to you?

~

I surfaced to a bleak April morning in North Ontario, snow banks edging back to reveal the trash and sleek grass and matted dog hair and shit. I reached for the phone and punched in Elena's number. "What does it mean?" I demanded.

There was a pause, and then a sigh. I could almost hear her tongue sliding over her teeth. I knew that she was frowning, lips twisting together, eyes squinting as she thought. I had known Elena face to face in my Iqaluit days, but she had become, like so many friends, a telephone voice, and then a name on a Christmas card, and finally a memory.

I move too often. I stop moving and I miss the moving.

"It means," Elena pronounced at last, "that a snake is going to get into your house."

I drew my feet up and tucked them under the couch cushion. I snapped them out and laid them on the cushion. Snakes go under things. I stood and paced, well away from the cushion and the couch.

"I have to caulk the seams," I declared.

"No," Elena explained. "You must not *let* a snake into your house."

"And I'll fill the cracks along the foundation."

Elena sighed again. "You aren't getting it. Listen. One of your brothers will let the snake in."

"Jesus, Elena. Why in the hell would they do that? They both know how I feel about snakes."

"Calm down." When Elena uses that quiet voice her students stop chatting and fidgeting; they fold their hands and lower their eyes and wait. Elena does not approve of hysterics or bad language. "It's the one in the dream. The one who opened the door. He knew what he was doing. He betrayed you. He is the one who will betray you." Elena's voice softened further, becoming barely audible. "The betrayal goes back to your mother," she mused, "because that's where she died, wasn't it? In that room. Yes. And it is huge. A great betrayal.

"Watch for him," she warned. "You trust him. And he will betray you."

I saw my middle-aged brother stuffing a garter snake through a tiny hole in the screen, the snake inflating, pythonesque. Ridiculous. Isn't it?

"It is about you and your mother," she repeated. The warm Newfoundland tones echoed in the satellite connection with Iqaluit. "My dear. Watch for him. He is going to do you great harm if you let him. All about you and him and your poor mother's house.

"Don't let him bring a snake into your house," she intoned.

~

I reveled in this interpretation. I always knew that I was the victim, and now I had the dream to prove it. I stood alone, fists tight against a plotting universe. The anger was justified. I had to hold fast.

~

Yet this morning, with the sun glinting on Wasaya Cove, the breeze stirring the wind chimes, the dogs stretching and sprawling under the porch and across the rug, the fists relax. I do not want to fight. I do not want to accuse.

I do not want to run.

I want to sit on my porch, hear the wind sigh in the pines, watch my hand-washed clothes flutter on the line, and glance up at the hand-painted loon sign beside my door.

"Welcome," it says. It is a gift from my friend Laila. She has never moved from the village where we were born. She has gone to the town and looked at the town and then returned, content. She has stayed. She has carved out her life in the village, and has become a wise woman. She is like the sampler that I saw, in a time and place lost, of a little house stitched against the side of a hill and a road running by. *Let me live in a house by the side of the road, and be a friend to man.* (Sam Walter Foss, *The House by the Side of the Road*)

The world has flowed by her door, and she has recognized and embraced it.

She has lived in a house by the side of the road and been a friend to me.

I have scrambled after the world, and it has slipped through my fingers.

I do not regret my adventures, not really, not the ones of my youth or the ones shared with my son.

I do regret that time has moved on, and he has grown and moved on to his own adventures, and all our adventures are in memory.

We were rooted in the wind, or perhaps I rooted him in the wind, for I could not settle.

He is home now, home in the north where he was born, past all the houses and toys in packing crates, to the first house, the house that we built when he was new.

I want to call Meadowbrook Acres home, but I cannot. I have paced there and raged there. I have stripped open the memories there and wrapped them away again. I have festered in the dark and found fuel for my rage and for my wanderings.

I have been dulled by medication, but now my mind is clear.

I want to peel back the layers of memory now, all of them, and expose them to the light. I want to raise them up, but not in celebration, for there is darkness there, too, which must not be celebrated.

I want to raise them up in benediction, for there is a divine spark in each human moment to be blessed. These are real people I lift up, people who may have gossiped and hated, but have also dreamed and loved. They carry you in their hearts, whether they understand you or not.

Laila knows.

Elena, my brother was not a betrayer, not truly. I saw him crossing the kitchen. I knew where he was going. We always unlocked that door and let the dog in that way, ever since we were children.

I knew where he was going, and I did not stop him. I lift him up now, and I lift up me.

May the Creator take the fire that burns within my blood and make it ashes on the wind, as I tell my story and release it with a blessing.

Chapter 1

LANDMARK

Meadowbrook Acres has stood on the bend above the river through all the summers of Julie's childhood. You look along the broad fields, up the clean line of sturdy maples, and there on the turn is the long white house with neat corners, sagging woodhouse and woodpile trickling down to the great red barn. The barn looms above the orchard, and it sees all. It knows you. You are almost there, it says; real summer is beginning.

You raise your head and when you are five, you see the barn sway forward, just a little, just for you. When you are ten, you see the barn and know that the Park is now almost within your grasp. When you are fifteen, you notice that the barn has shrunk.

And then you are eighteen, and you forget the barn.

Now you are thirty-two, and have decided to recapture the time when you were happy. You will recapture it on your terms, though, and it will not slip away. You have a plan.

~

Julie slows on the flats just past the river and eases her aging SUV to the narrow shoulder of the road. She turns off the ignition and rubs her palms against her jeans. She has never stopped here before. Then again, she has never planned to live, physically live, at Meadowbrook Acres before. Her six-year-old self hurried from the verandah to the barn in the cool of daybreak many, many times, soft nickers of greeting lifting in the semi-darkness. Now, her adult body and adult dreams will in fact inhabit the long white house. She will rise each morning, looking across to the barn from the back verandah, sipping coffee, and planning her day. She will be home, home on Meadowbrook Acres, not driving past on her way to her own life. Meadowbrook Acres will be her life now, and she will watch the envying cars roll by. Her stomach clenches. *They will drive by; they will see her. They will see that she does not belong. They will see a grown woman playing at living at Meadowbrook Acres. They will shake their heads. She failed there, they will be saying; she failed there, and she will fail here.*

She lifts up her eyes, and sees the farm rise still and silent before her. The summer's hay hangs thin and restless on its stalks; brush has sprouted in the low areas and along the roadside. A few gnarled remnants of the once great maples cling along the ditch. The maple and ash in the front yard have dwarfed the house; they will split away, crumpling down through the roof, crushing the upper floor. The house slouches forlorn in grey paint with white trim, a child hunched with its head down, wrapped in a dress ill-chosen by parents. The house ends severely where the woodhouse used to be, and the ground tilts away over the empty site of the great red barn. The bare sky gapes above the twisted ruins of the apples trees. Meadowbrook Acres is old now, brittle-boned and shriveled.

It could be any abandoned old farm on any country road, but perhaps Meadowbrook Acres is still there. Julie has to hope that it is, because that is the plan. She is going to set her life on its true course, and for that, she needs Meadowbrook Acres.

She shifts into gear and eases up the hill and into the turn. She swings left at the driveway, and without warning trucks are hurtling around the bend. She bounces over the ruts at the end of the driveway. She sees the garden patch thick with thistles, the lawns lumpy and patchy, the driveway lost in weeds and potholes. The barn should be open, a light breeze fanning over the fresh hay. Instead there are weeds and patches of crab grass, sloping away to stark green unshielded woods. So this is how one comes home to Meadowbrook.

The landlord is waiting in a dusty blue car, door hanging open in the August afternoon. As Julie's car shudders down the driveway, he hauls himself from the driver's seat and musters a strained grin. "We haven't had a tenant since winter," he apologizes. "They were really good though, did the house up nice—paint, wallpaper, flower pots on the front porch, kept a nice garden."

"And the apple trees?" The remark slides past her lips and will not be hauled back behind her tongue. Now she sounds critical, but inside she is not. Already, Julie's palm itches to grasp a pruning saw, to shake lime over the miserable lawn, to wield hammer and saw to rebuild the barn, if that is what it takes. Meadowbrook Acres lies dormant, awaiting her touch. She will be the one to restore Meadowbrook Acres.

The landlord sighs, following her gaze down to the orchard. His shoulders slump; he rubs a hand across the grey hair at the base of his neck. "Well. There you are. You can't do everything. Some things you just have to let go."

"And the barn? There was always a big red barn. Was it gone, when you got the place?" Julie sees the landlord slump further, and wishes she did not have to ask. However, she must: *If it were your barn, how did you let it go? If they were your trees, why did you not protect them? And why would you paint it grey, when its colour was white?* She knows she is about to ask these questions, too.

The landlord studies the empty field, sweeping down to the woods. "There was always a barn," he mutters. "My grandfather built it, for forty head of cattle. And that orchard—oh, the Gravensteins and McIntoshes we picked, and the Golden Delicious, and the old Northern Spy tree, that's its stump there. Astrakhans, this time of year," he adds.

"You grew up here? You inherited all this?" *How could you let it come down to this? Why did you not fight with your last breath to preserve it?* The landlord turns to survey the house now. "Inherited. My great-grandfather built this place, and my grandfather built it up. My father maintained it. My mother lived here until the day she died. And then we all inherited. And *she* wanted it. She had great plans for a summer home. It was going to be something. So she tore down the barn, my sister did, ripped off the woodhouse, and built that back porch thing, so she could sit and look over the fields without the woodhouse or barn getting in the way. Yes. Don't let history block your view. And then, oh yes, best of all, and then she announced that it was too much, too hard, and she was going to sell. I had to buy it then."

"Oh." Julie nods and bobs her head, because there is really nothing else to say or do. She wants to sweep out that back porch, put plants along the sill, find a wicker rocker and a quilted blanket, and dream away the autumn evenings while sheep graze in the meadow, winding their way toward a great barn. She will deal with the woodhouse later; for now, neat rows of firewood can line the lower driveway. "The house looks very nice," she offers, because she must make some reply.

"She painted it grey," he announces. "It was white."

"It was always so fresh and white."

The landlord stares.

"You know the park? Kejimkujik? Kedge, my father always called it. Anyway, every August we'd go to Kedge, and I'd always look for this place on the way out from Halifax. It was my sign that we were near. It was my landmark," she says.

Now he is the one bobbing and nodding. "The Park. Yeah. That's a good place to go in the summer. Pretty quiet now, though. So many rules. Rules for everything. Park here. Don't park there. Unload here, and then move your car there. Can't have two, oh no. Don't touch this or the hemlocks will all die. Everything is supposed to be so natural, but then they have generators and an internet café. Maybe electricity in some sites soon."

Now Julie is the one staring. "Internet cafes? In Kedge? I don't know, it just doesn't sound like camping."

"So, your father. Would he remember the lodge then?"

"Yes," she says. "A big lodge on the lake, with cabins, and a boat from that landing where they put the canoes. They tore it down, though, when it became a national park. Not in keeping with the park goals or something."

"Generators," he sighs, "and internet cafes."

"Could I see the house now?" Julie asks.

~

There were strawberries, her father would explain each year, acres of strawberries and fields of corn. Before that, it was sheep. They started with cattle, though. You can bet that those kids didn't get two weeks' camping in any park. They would be working every day. Mowing the lawns with a hand mower would seem like a day off to them. That was the way in those days.

Julie and her brother, wedged in the back among pool noodles and sleeping bags, learned to ignore this annual litany. Meadowbrook Acres is now past, and then that big right turn at the corner, and past houses and stores, and a restaurant, and a ball field, and houses and churches and garages and way up along the flats the perfect convenience store with groceries and camping gear all in park portions for park needs. Then you were sitting up straight because the Park was just a moment away.

The farm that Julie remembers was still. There were no hints of the grinding apparatus of a thriving farm. They're retired now, her father explained. But they were certainly busy in their day.

It seems those hard-working, vacationless kids had other ideas for their lives. Acres of strawberries were not in their futures.

Meadowbrook Acres was big and clean, strong as a gateway should be. That was what mattered.

Julie at five loved the Park. She could trundle off to the swings and still be in sight of the campsite. There would be fried chicken and potato salad the first day, packed in a cooler from Waverley, and Kool-Aid anytime. There were sandy afternoons at beaches, with ice cream, and sleepy mornings stuffed down in the canoe with promises of marshmallows at the campfire that night. Julie at ten looked forward to finding new playmates at the Park, and exploring her environment during nature walks. Julie at fifteen hoped to meet a boy who would understand her at the Park. They would walk along the beach at sunset, sharing poetry. In the twilight, he would turn to her. Their lips would brush. They would be a moment, outside time, forever.

He would probably be sixteen.

Julie at eighteen was glad that she had a summer job in Halifax, and was free of the Park. It is one thing to charge down the campground roads on your bike when you are ten, shrieking and laughing with your new friends. It is another altogether to be walking along that same road, a sophisticated seventeen, hoping to attract a sophisticated eighteen-year-old male into your orbit, a sensitive soul who would appreciate intelligence and poetry. Suddenly, a whooping, shrieking mob of ten-year-olds hurtles past, suctioning away your sophistication and dreams. You step around ringette games, and know that if you were the superintendent here, shirts would be mandatory for hairy-bellied, beer-belching dads.

Your parents hover and smile in the background, and the Kedge magic is officially gone.

Fifteen years have passed, and Julie has grown up and grown away. She has kept her thick black hair in a short bob ever since she became a teacher, eight years ago. She is well-toned and tanned, clad in dress jeans and a cotton T-shirt, an experienced young teacher on holiday. She looks confident.

She is, in reality, still adrift at thirty-two, university and waitressing days in the city long past. She stumbled upon teaching as a viable lifestyle—working with kids, exciting settings, opportunities for adventure. A solid career, but a flexible one. Now, with three Reserve contracts and a lot of substitute work, not to mention a failed relationship with Doug, behind her, she is still trying to find a starting point that will define her life. She is a slightly experienced and unemployed young teacher who is not confident at all.

~

The landlord does not notice these details, although Julie is sure that they quiver in the air around her. He is slouching up the lawn toward the back verandah, fumbling with keys. He is past mid-fifties, she guesses, studying the balding head with its fringe of grey-black hair. He is about five foot ten and fit for his age, no paunch creeping over his belt. His shoulders, though, are rounded. He is in his place, in his own home, reclaimed from the porch builder, but Julie can see no joy in it for him.

They step through the dark porch into a large kitchen. Tall, multi-paned farm windows open the room to the west and east. An old-style built-in cabinet dominates the far corner, juxtaposed by electric range, fridge, and washer.

He gestures to an opening. "There's a pantry, kind of a storeroom, I guess. The furnace is downstairs through that door at the back."

One side of the pantry is walled off, and the basement steps backtrack along it. A step leads to a corresponding door in the kitchen; there must be steps running above the basement ones, leading perhaps to an attic. The door is padlocked.

"Family treasures?" Julie asks.

"Yeah." He rubs his fringe of hair. "I put all the family stuff in the attic up there. It was all over the house, before." He strides into the main house, a series of open rooms intersected by archways. "There's the dining room, a den, good light there, and the living room. For Christmas, times like that."

Julie wanders through the downstairs, trying to look like she knows what she is looking for. Her eyes come to rest on the stairs in the front hall. They are plain, with a functional white bannister. The fireplace opposite is basic brick with dried-out, cracked mortar. She had imagined grey flagstones, bold and sleek, pungent with recent coals. It is the bannister, however, that disappoints. She had expected polished wood, massive and overwhelming. It is instead frail, meandering along the stairs incomplete.

He follows her gaze. "In those days," he says, "they put all the money in the barn."

Forty head of cattle trump aesthetics. Cows bring money. Farmwives do not have time to polish massive and overwhelming bannisters.

"Now in here," he announces as he pushes open a heavy door at the foot of the stairs, "was the formal parlour. You know, for receiving the minister, laying out bodies, things like that. Then my grandparents needed it for a bedroom, with the seven kids, you see. My grandfather, now, he died in this room. Well, my parents turned it into a guest room, but my sister turned it back into a little formal parlour with all the family stuff—furniture, pictures, and all. Yeah. Kind of nice." He pauses, frowning. "Well, tenants, you see. And I had to rent it. Anyway, it's a nice little bedroom again. Has a bed, too. It's the coolest room in summer, and it has a little washroom built in. You might like this one for yourself."

They laid out dead bodies here. The open casket rested on chairs. With face powdered, lips stiff, eyes beatifically closed, they contemplated eternity. Grandfather, though, sprawled against his pillows, mouth gaping open for air, eyes rolling, perhaps his wife weeping as she reached for his hand, perhaps keening and reaching as grim aunts pushed her from the room and hovered, checking off the signs of his impending death. She is not sure that she will rest well here.

However, it is cool, and the sunny den through the second door is inviting.

The upstairs has three bedrooms and a large bathroom, once a bedroom. There is a broad hallway cornering around the stairs, and a walk-in closet at one end. It is sweltering in the August heat.

"I will warn you," he begins. Julie braces. Perhaps they prepared the bodies up here. "These high ceilings take a lot of oil in the winter. The rent's just $400, but you'll spend more than that on oil in January. A lot more, maybe. You might want to close some of these rooms off."

Julie is first relieved, and then the dark echoes of unemployment set in. Being an emergency supply teacher while living under your parents' snug roof is one thing; fending off massive oil bills while supply teaching in a new place is another. She sees herself shivering on a mat in the kitchen, the house barricaded, fingers extended to the one small heater she allows herself. She ate yesterday.

"Can't close off the whole upstairs, though, or the bathroom pipes up there will freeze. Maybe shut off the bedrooms, put plastic on that whole front door there."

That front door? That heavy door with ancient panes of glass bordering it? It needs a heavy curtain to block the drafts, not plastic. Other windows will need quaint but lined curtains, and there must be little scatter mats to accent those softwood floors. Julie will arrive home from a busy day, sigh, turn up the heat just a little, draw the curtains, and light a few small lamps. There will be work, work enough, she knows. Five days monthly will be devoted to the oil account. Another five or six days for rent and food. That's half-time work, but it could happen. This is Meadowbrook Acres, and it will come alive under her careful nurturing.

"I guess you'll want to do a financial check," she says.

The sad brown eyes light up. "You want it? Good. That's OK. I think you'd be good here. I mean, you seem right for the place, like you know what it's worth and what it means."

He hurries off down the stairs, muttering about papers in the car. Julie peers into the large front bedroom at the end of the hall and shudders. Not this one. It is so dark. She will close this one off.

As they sign papers in the kitchen, she asks about the big front room upstairs. The landlord, Samuel, seems almost jubilant now, relaxed and light-hearted. "That was my room, mine and my brother's," he says. "It was my great-grandmother's, at one time. She was a holy terror, that one. They say she cut her teeth on Spanish doubloons." He laughs. "Yep. I can generally tell about people, and I think you're just what this place needs. Level-headed, you know."

Oh, he really does not know. She's run from Ontario and back to Waverley, and now she's arrived with all her necessary belongings just in case her childhood memory house opened its doors to her. She has no money for oil, and no real job, and the pipes will freeze and water will gush all over the dear little parlour. She is vulnerable and unprepared. Yet, he is renting to her.

She wonders at his trusting nature. He probably thought he knew his sister, and look how that turned out. He must have broken his heart, perhaps many times, renting out his family home just to afford to keep it in the family, unable to live there, seeing his home deteriorate and fade as strangers carved their lives into its walls. Yet, he is so excited now, so eager.

She vows to sub in the deepest corners of hell, should they be offered, to meet those oil bills. To disappoint the so-vulnerable Samuel would be an act of viciousness and cruelty.

She has her deposit and first month's rent ready; wages are more readily saved when living under one's parents' warm roof, eating their food, when they cannot bear to accept rent. *We want to help, Julie. And it's so much less lonely, knowing you're coming home.* Now she is independent again, thanks to her dependence on them. She felt guilty then and she feels guilty now, but she is here. She is staying at Meadowbrook Acres.

She is paid up until September 16th, and her savings will carry her until October 16th. If it is warm. It must stay warm. And there must be work. There will be.

He is delighted to hear that she wants to stay here tonight. It makes perfect sense to him that she wants to "get organized." Someone to whom home and family are so important does not need to hear that she cannot bear another night in her parents' house, that she told them days ago that she had rented a place and that she was going today to "get organized." That might bring on a need for a financial check. That would break Samuel's spirit. He would have to rent to strangers with money, not Julie, who loves Meadowbrook. That must not happen.

As he spins down the driveway, horn tooting in what he undoubtedly thinks is a comradely salute, she is dragging her backpack and sleeping bag from the back of her SUV.

She is thirty-two today, and her life is beginning yet again.

ASHTRAYS,
WIMPLES, AND THE
BLESSED VIRGIN

his first memory rises and will not stop. It comes here at Wasaya
Cove, the lake beyond shimmering in the heat, the breeze fitful in
the trees.

I have returned to my cabin at Wasaya with a tank of propane.

This morning, the bannock was sizzling in the pan and I was a True
Northerner, content in the rising heat haze and the loons and black tea.
My mind was clear and the town far away and unimportant. Then the
flame flared, sputtered, spit, and died. I paced and stared at the lake. I
had to go out now. I had to smile and shop and tell people that I was
getting the place into shape. My contentment crumpled. I hauled my
tank into the canoe, paddled to the landing, collected my dogs, and
braced for the drive into town.

There was laughter from the cottage deck nearest the landing. There
was a meeting there, a meeting of like minds and environmental spirits
and I wished that I could be one of them. They were having a true

cottage day, sitting on the deck on a muggy, sweltering day, justified in one another's presence.

And I was slinking by, empty propane tank rolling in the bow, dogs frolicking in anticipation, an anomaly.

~

I have returned with ice for the cooler, a fresh tank of propane, and snacks. I sit on my porch, and I am a cottage dweller in my own right, having my own cottage day.

The lake draws me. The colour of the light on the water and the shimmer of humidity pull me, south and east, and I stand on the warped verandah, watching the garage at Meadowbrook Acres through its own shimmer of humidity, the garage wavering because that is what it does when rain is coming. Tomorrow there will be a puff of breeze, and a moment of coolness. There will be a pause and the wind will gust, and then the rain will fall or pass by.

I stand sweating in red shorts and sleeveless blouse, round legs poured into ankle socks and scuffed brown shoes. I am eight, and I am a strawberry picker. My day is done, and I can play.

My father remains on the Strawberry Hill, tending the customers. This was in the early days of U-pick. In those days, they called it Pick-them-yourself, which sounded somehow defiant: *Well, pick them yourself, then, and see how you like that.* And so it became U-pick: short, simple words for a world that thrives on short and simple solutions. Clean and simple: U-pick.

I am watching for the McLeans.

The McLeans moved to Boston a generation ago, but return each summer. Their daughters are stylish and sophisticated. *They wear make-up when they are twelve.* They are magical. They are the essence of summer.

The McLeans are Good Catholics. The daughters were fresh and slim as they stepped into the cool of St. Philip's Church last Sunday morning. I lumbered in ahead of them, my round body crammed into a red satiny dress with short puff sleeves crusted with lace. It cut at the arms, at the neck, at the waist. The dress was bursting with my eight-year-old body, and I dared not turn or bend. A half bonnet of stiff petals crackled against my ears, squashed over my gnarled ringlets.

Anne Marie McLean, age twelve, had a waist. She had slim arms, tanned legs, sandals with heels, a light jacket on her shoulders, knee-length shorts, and *lipstick* for God's sake. And her nails! Fingers and toes with neat, gleaming ovals. Her hair swept back to a clasp at the base of her neck. Not one strand faltered. A scarf draped over her perfect hair was loosely knotted at the throat and it did not slip. She was Sophistication come to Earth to attend Mass, and I wallowed in her presence.

We were Good Catholics, too, on my mother's side. We were very Catholic, clacking rosary beads and dipping fingertips in Holy Water. My father was unbaptized, even in the church of his birth, but I did not think he would go to Hell because we had better be very sick, or the snow plow at least two days away, before we could miss Mass. They had a dispensation from the bishop himself to marry in the Catholic Church. Imagine that in 1946. My mother was a Good Catholic, but my unbaptized, unsacramental father was our Enforcer of Church Doctrine.

I shuffle on the verandah, left foot scuffing the fly bites on my right, scraping the scabs. I know that my brothers are climbing in the hay mow, but I stand on the verandah, watching for the McLeans. They will go first to the Strawberry Hill, and then they will come here.

And now, oh wonder of wonders, night of nights. It is Father, in his black cassock and white collar, rolling down our driveway, Sister Elizabeth Leo and Sister Mary Paul serene in the backseat. A different pair of sisters comes from Halifax each summer to teach us scattered Catholics our catechism. They are patient and have gentle voices. It is a Holy Time.

In the background there is a clattering and scraping as chairs are shoved back and ashtrays are flung beneath the sink. There is a glimpse

19

of slim legs flashing up the stairs, shorts riding over thighs, as my mother and her younger sister, my dear Aunt Claudette, run gasping out of sight.

Now Father is standing on our driveway flanked by the Sisters, so much black fabric and Roman collar and wimple dazzling in the evening. My mother and Aunt Claudette pop through the screen door, breathless and delighted, now in swishing flowered skirts skimming just below the knee. There is a hint of hidden shorts in their eyes.

Tonight it is our turn to be honoured by the Immaculate Mother of God, tucked head-down under Father's right arm. Tonight we will pray the rosary, led by Father. We will pray with Father and the Sisters and the McLeans.

Now the McLean car is rolling down the Strawberry Hill, swinging onto the road, and turning into our driveway. Tim McLean, thirteen, perches on the right fender, legs swinging. The car has *fins*, can you believe that? Oh, to have a sleek American car with fins, and ride with legs dangling casual and free. Tim McLean slides down into the dust and heat, unhurried and unrumpled. His sisters rise slim and cool from the backseat, and then his parents emerge. Mrs. McLean minces across the lawn in spike heels and a flowered print dress, a very Catholic cut. Mr. McLean's sports jacket is open, and he stands, shoulders back, hands loose in his pockets, a very Catholic father.

My brothers emerge from the barn, tugging at socks, rubbing at the chaff that clings along the backs of their necks. They straighten, tucking shirts and wiping palms, and then they approach the verandah, nodding to Mr. McLean and to Father, murmuring greetings to the Sisters.

It is a perfect Catholic moment as we troop through the kitchen, across the dining room, and into the living room where we put the tree in December.

On this muggy July evening, the Immaculate Mary whose praises we sing will adorn our mantle.

The Father rocks his way down to the floor, one knee and then the other, twisting a little and then settling. Sisters Elizabeth Leo and

Mary Paul glide to the floor, flanking him. Mother and Aunt Claudette drop to the floor behind them, while Mrs. McLean floats down in one motion, a little to one side of the Sisters. Mr. McLean shuffles off to one side, and my brothers and I wriggle into place beside the young McLeans. Their knees are not scabbed.

Rosaries flash and click—from where did they come? Did Mother keep a secret cache behind the candles on the mantel for moments like this? Father intones the Creed and we garble the words a pace behind him. We launch into the Joyful Mysteries, spinning through the Annunciation in record time.

Afterward there is coffee for the grown-ups in china cups with painted flowers. It is instant coffee—instant is still new, a novelty. There is Kool-Aid for us, more amazing powders stirred into water. There are store-bought cookies, because who can cook in this heat and the strawberries keep us busy. Besides, who could produce neat little maple leaves, with icing perfectly flat between them, in the old wood stove? Store-bought cookies show consideration for your guests.

It is cooling, growing darker, and my father is among us now. He greets the Father and the Sisters with a respectful nod, and then retires to the back verandah with Mr. McLean. The moment grows secular now, not because my father has arrived, but because the Catholic moment has passed. The Immaculate Mother is tucked back in her case, lips pressed together as she fingers her aching heart.

Finally, everyone is milling in the kitchen and then McLeans and clergy are trickling out to their cars. The McLeans get to leave with Father and the Sisters. They will drive behind him all through the village. Imagine that.

Mother and Aunt Claudette strip away the flowered skirts and retrieve the ashtrays, gasping with laughter. They are Good Catholics, but with a touch of secular practicality.

After all, my mother got the bishop to give her a dispensation.

While we prayed the Joyful Mysteries the living room was all in light; yet that room was, at other times, dark to me. The Christmas tree

21

gleamed from a dusky corner, and I was afraid in that room. There were claws and eyes behind the ornate flowers of the rug; crouching figures lurked behind the whatnot. There were dark, full drapes and black horse-hair-covered furniture. "Like a great weight setting over you," Charles's wife pronounced, forty years later.

You might think it strange that we did not have those little niches and shrines that defined so many Catholic homes in that time. We did have our plaster Guardian Angels by our beds, our rosaries during Advent and Lent, those little Catholic touches that marked the Latin Mass days.

But you do not Catholicize Grandma Mary's house. If you impose too much Catholicism, she will resist. She has her ways.

My mother was a good Catholic, but she was a quiet Catholic, keeping her Catholic niche very private.

When my father died, she retreated to her bedroom, asking Samuel's wife to accompany her. There they prayed the rosary while my brothers and I, uninvited to the moment, ate soup in the kitchen. We were becoming occasional Catholics, with occasional relapses to the Mysteries and the devotions, and this moment called for participation by consistent Catholics, who lived in the Mysteries and devotions.

Perhaps, however, it was more because we were the great-grandchildren of Grandma Mary. She was tough privateer stock, Protestant to the core. They say she cut her teeth on Spanish doubloons, but I do not know if that is true. She was a Holy Terror, an Iron Hand.

My mother needed to be surrounded by unadulterated Catholicism at this moment, to be comforted in all the faith of her own childhood. We, her children, had just enough privateer blood to reproach her.

Chapter 2

WELCOME PLANT

In the end, Julie opts for the ex-front parlour, Grandfather's body notwithstanding. It is cooler, and it does have a bed. It is nice to have the toilet and sink just a few steps away. The upstairs hallway after dark is a little too oppressive, a long, winding walk to the bathroom past the shadowy recesses. It is too bad that the bathtub is up there, but she can work daylight baths into her schedule. She can race home in the fading light, then dash up the stairs and wallow in lukewarm water before sprinting downstairs to dress. Perhaps she will adjust with time.

Julie spreads her sleeping bag on the mattress and switches off the lamp. The house is grim in the night; the ceilings stretch high, shifting and creaking above her. She nestles down in her sleeping bag, face to the wall. A light pulses just behind her shoulder and she rolls over. There is only darkness, thick and close. She rolls back to the wall. The light pulses, a glimmer in the open bedroom door. She rolls over. The doorway is dark, gaping, and the hall beyond still. She rolls back. Pulse. Turn. Darkness. Roll back. Again and again.

Julie hitches around on the bed and faces the doorway. The little panes framing the front door flicker; the light pulses on the stairwell, and then darkness returns. She strains for the sound of an engine, the rumble of thunder, but the night is silent.

At three in the morning, she dozes off, propped against the wall facing the door.

At five o'clock, the logging trucks start rolling by, wailing through the flats, grinding and shaking around the turn, and then howling their way down the hill on their way to the pulp and paper plant.

Julie considers moving upstairs. She would be farther from the light, but it would still be near. Perhaps the source would be on her level. That is a thought. Realistically, if the house caught fire, she does not think she would be able to charge straight through the pulsing light. She is not superstitious, but darkness does not draw out her most scientific thoughts.

Julie then considers getting a cat. She pictures a slim, chocolate-pointed Siamese cat, oblivious to flickering and pulsing lights. It would slink along the bookshelves, slithering in the shadows, unblinking eyes shimmering in the light. No, a cat would not improve the atmosphere.

She cannot bear to have a dog. Not yet.

Julie attempts to refresh herself in the plain old tub, the heat already sticky at 8 a.m., but the light is now sunlight, and there is bird song. Now the scientific thoughts surface. It was heat lightning, plain and simple heat lightning, flashing in the window and reflecting off that antique mirror in the stairway.

Of course. Julie relaxes. This is where she will make her stand, become happy, and stay happy.

~

Julie is sipping instant coffee on the back verandah when the sedan rolls past the house and parks by the garage. The driver studies her for a long moment, and finally eases her way out of the car. She rummages in the backseat, and then turns and plods up to the verandah, holding a squat, potted plant before her. It looks tough. It will have to be. Julie has no idea what kind it is or what to do to keep it alive.

The woman extends a card, balancing the plant with one hand. "Welcome to the community," she says in a soft drawl that is both formal and honest. "I'm Laila, and this is from our church community. We always bring a little something to welcome the new people, and here is my number, and our church secretary Vera's number, in case you want anything or have any questions, or just want some company."

Julie gropes for a place for her mug and then sets it on the verandah floor. She pulls herself to her feet, hands reaching to take the plant.

Laila smiles as Julie gushes over the thick leaves and the greenness. "You'll want to hang that in the den," she says. "It's too hot out here and too shady out front. There should still be a hook in there, I'd imagine." She glances at the door.

"Why, sure," Julie enthuses. "Let's, um, do that, right now." She gestures in the general direction of the kitchen door.

Laila walks through the kitchen, eyes moving over the clutter. She nods. "Looks like you're camping," she says. "Been a lot of camping done out of this kitchen." She continues through the door and heads straight for the den. She locates the hook over the east window and is soon back in the kitchen rummaging under the sink.

"Looks like nobody touched the watering can," she declares, lifting the plain green container. She pauses, her eyes on Julie. "Don't mind me, now. I used to watch the place winters for Rachel when she was up there working. It's just sort of interesting, isn't it, the way things change and don't change?" She raises the watering can by way of explanation.

Julie is nodding and making vague hand movements. Laila smiles. "Oh, now, there I go. Don't you worry. I'll just set up your plant with a little water and be out of your hair in no time. You got things to do, I'm sure."

Julie fumbles into gear. "Oh, no! That's fine. Really. It's just—I was wondering—coffee? It's instant," she adds.

"Water's fine." Julie wonders whether she means for herself or for the plant.

Laila applies the water to the plant in little sips. "Samuel is mighty happy you took the place," she says. "He hasn't had much luck with tenants. First ones kind of let the place go, and there were some others, but the last ones was real nice. They had to move—work, you know— and he couldn't find anyone decent after that. Didn't want to take a chance, you know. So you're a teacher?"

Julie nods. "Substituting. For now. How about a muffin, and coffee? Instant?" She gestures to the red maple kitchen table. Samuel's table. Entrusted to her.

Laila smiles again. "Just cold water's fine," she croons.

They sit at the old red maple table in the kitchen, and Julie nibbles at a muffin while Laila sips from a glass of water. Soon Julie knows that Laila grew up just down the road, has known the Hardys all her life, and picked strawberries here as a teenager. She hears that Rachel is Samuel's sister, who had all kinds of ideas for the place but couldn't seem to slow down and enjoy them, instead kept rushing from change to change, and finally said that she could never feel at home here. She used to live here summers with her son, coming down from teaching in different places in Ontario, always changing jobs, changing the place. Then one day she decided to sell, and that was devastating for Samuel. He either had to buy or lose contact with the place that meant everything to him.

"When the family sold it to her, they thought she'd never sell, so it would always stay their heritage, too. Oh, there must have been some hard feelings on both sides, I'd expect; he couldn't afford to buy, and he couldn't afford not to, you see. He knew if he bought it, he'd have to rent it, and there would be strangers there, but in a way it would still be there for him. Now Rachel, on the other hand, said she was getting too caught up in land and houses and everybody's ideas for her. She used to come down and camp summers at the Park with her boy then, but after a while she bought a sort of cabin, up on a lake near the Park. Nice and private, easy to care for, she said. Well, next thing he's spend- ing summers with his father, up north where he was from, and she's rattling around out there feeling guilty for selling this place, and guilty for buying that place, and then she stopped coming a year or so back."

"She sold that place, too?"

"Well, no. We never heard of it being sold. And everything's still there. Just the canoe's gone, and the car's gone. Now, every summer she stowed her canoe in the cabin when she was heading back to Ontario— she had a steady job, a good one, with the public board and everything by now—and then she'd swim down the lake to her car and drive back to Ontario. Well, we'd hear from her once in a while. 'I'm just getting on the ferry for St. John.' 'I'm back now. Lawns need work again!' But not this time. And no answer when we called. Now when we went up to check the cabin, Tom and me, like we usually did when she left, there was no canoe in the cabin, no canoe chained along the shore like when she went for the day or overnight. Everything closed up as usual, but no canoe."

Julie is boiling more water for coffee in a little pot on the stove. "Sounds like someone stole the canoe." She does not add, "or the car," for then Rachel would be on the lake bottom between the canoe site and the car site. "But maybe she hid it in the woods or something."

Laila closes her eyes and swings her head left and right. "No. No, she did not. We checked the shore pretty carefully, and that canoe would be easy to find—bright blue, you see. No, she took it with her, I'm thinking. Because she left a note. On the kitchen table."

Oh. A note. Julie braces against the memories of so many notes and not notes in her brief career.

"She did not drown. No. And she didn't do something, neither. We would've known, see? Samuel would've said. It would've been in the papers. No. Samuel just got all drawn in and bitter. More hurt than anything. Kind of made you think Rachel's at it again. And we even called her school, and they said they didn't have anyone by that name working there. Not any 'I'm sorry, but did you know her well because.' And then there was the note."

Julie frowns, sipping her coffee. "The note?" she prompts. Although none of this is her business, it seems the most natural of questions in this delicate but somehow natural conversation.

Laila refills her glass at the sink, studying the west window. "That Japanese quince is going to need some work," she mutters. She returns to the table, and sits for a while. "Well, it was on the table at the cabin," she continues at last. "Tom and me knew where she'd kept the key; we went by each September, like I said. It was nice there, the leaves just starting to turn and all. Well, there it was, just a little paper, and it was to Nathaniel—that's her son—and she was wishing him peace and fulfilment on his journey, and she hoped he wished her the same on hers. We got in touch with him, up north, and he didn't seem surprised at all. Seemed to think it was all perfectly natural, and then he said he had to go now."

"She doesn't sound very reliable, somehow. Maybe she's off, you know, doing something, somewhere, so they know but don't want to discuss it." Like we are. In detail.

"Oh, it was mighty hard on Samuel, though. He wouldn't talk about it. And it was mighty hard on her friends. I guess we thought we was part of that journey. She just took the canoe and the dogs—she would never go anywhere without those dogs—and she's out there some-where, maybe up north, maybe close by, and she's bound to be with those dogs. I just can't understand why she couldn't share it. She always talked over everything. But this time, she just—left—without a word. It's hard, not knowing."

Julie suspects that Rachel is indeed close, at the bottom of the lake or in a mental institution, with or without those dogs.

Great-Grandmother was a Holy Terror. Grandfather died in her new bedroom, and was probably laid out by the fireplace, where she would put her Christmas tree. Rachel Hardy stripped down the barn for forty head of cattle, and is unaccounted for. Meadowbrook Acres is more than a sentimental landmark on the roadway to summer.

The plant squats in its pot in the den, its leaves oily and heavy.

Julie hopes that her second night will be better than her first.

Chapter 3

BINS

After Laila departs, Julie applies herself to the bins that she stowed in the old dining room the night before. It is a hollow room, dark in spite of the tall, curtainless west window, the faded bricks that back the fireplace protruding weakly into the space. Soon the laptop is up and running. Samuel, the trusting landlord, has left her in charge of switching over the hydro account. Two bins of books are placed in the den, where one day bookcases will be warmed by the east and south exposure, and the welcome plant will be glossy and cheering. The clothes bin is sorted onto the bed, and the towels and toiletries take their place on the small stand by the sink. The remaining items join the clothes on the bed. The few dishes look cheap and rough in the kitchen cabinet.

There are six bins, and one backpack. Julie in Ontario had ten bins of books and teaching resources. She had furniture and blankets and art and sets of dishes and pots and pans and pans. She had an iron and a microwave and a television. She had a coffee maker and a teapot. She had all the things that people rummage in drawers and pull out because it is just what they needed. She has left much behind, in second-hand stores and Sally Anns, in yard sales, and in garbage cans in North Bay. If she had stayed on the Reserve, there would have been many gifts to pass on—stoneware bread pans to the Elder who taught her how to make bannock, books for Simon, a spare blanket to the young couple with the new baby. Then her possessions would have had homes. Now, they are simply abandoned.

It doesn't matter. And yet, it does.

Six bins and one backpack is not much to show for thirty-two years. Julie, at thirty-two, should have a career, a pension plan, and a bungalow. She should be greeting a husband over morning coffee, and taking her kids to swimming lessons in the summer. She should, at least, have a full set of pots and pans, proper dishes, and a hobby. She should knit a blanket in the evenings, perhaps for Laila.

She is forever packing, discarding, replacing, and starting again. This time, though, she has a plan that will work.

She is renting a discarded farmhouse and she does not have a job. Still, it will work. She has learned from experience. Experience must not be under-estimated.

She tinkers with her resume until lunchtime, oil bills hovering beneath every entry. She is busy; she could call herself self-employed. Mainly, she is tired of resumes.

Warmed tinned beans and crackers seem an inappropriate lunch for these windows. There should be bowls of steaming fresh vegetables, fresh-baked bread, feet drumming on the verandah, screen door slamming, and laughter in the wings. There should be tractors starting up and shutting down in the barnyard, and freshly washed clothes billowing on the line. Instead, there are tinned beans in a camp bowl, a packet of crackers flat on the table. Julie steps back from herself and sees a slim, neat brunette hunched over a red maple table, methodically scooping and chewing in the silence. She feels a fleeting sympathy for this dejected and friendless one, playing grown-up at an oversized tea table.

Julie had had excitement, she had had friends, and she had had goals and plans. She had packed up and flown by Sesna over miles of wilderness to her first teaching job. While circling the Reserve, she had seen a small school bus pelting out to the airstrip. This was her welcome committee; they had known that she was the new teacher because the pilot circled the community twice. There were no phones in the houses; all business, all intimate and confidential calls, were placed from the payphone outside the OPP residence/office. She had to queue up to order groceries. There was adventure, and learning needs not covered in her courses.

The kids would probably shock most of her teachers' college contemporaries, if the lack of resources did not send them marching back to the plane. The children realized that they were a stepping stone in someone's career, to be used and discarded and forgotten. Therefore, they planned to shock, to probe out the weaknesses and find if a heart beat there for them, a heart that would care for them and be there for them and accept them and love them as all children, especially stepping-stone children, deserve to be loved. Only then would something called curriculum begin to matter. Love us first as we are, they were pleading, in all our rejection, in all our brokenness. Love that in us, and be with us. Then, we can begin.

It made sense to Julie that the children would drive out the weak and selfish, would push them away before they could be hurt and disappointed again. For only the teachers who loved them, who did not abandon them during the trial, could be trusted. So she shed her tears in her apartment, at night, and loved them more. However much she was hurt, they had been hurt more.

And she stayed. She stayed three years. She made them cupcakes. She cried with them as she read *Sadako and the One Thousand Paper Cranes* to them. She walked with them on the road in the evenings. At Christmas she would find odds and ends from her apartment and desk, taped up in torn corners of construction paper. Offerings. Borrowings. *I held this for a while, and because it was yours it was special to me. But here it is, back.*

You are letting them steal from you, said the principal.

But it always comes back, Julie pointed out.

Nevertheless, said the principal, *stealing is stealing.*

It's more like sharing, Julie decided. The principal sighed.

Three years later, with another weak performance review from the office but firm handshakes from every parent, Julie found herself at the airstrip saying goodbye. They had had one last cupcake party, and the kids teased the tears from her face. There were promises and farewells. She was a good teacher, the parents said. Maybe things would have gone better with the new principal in the fall, but they could understand. Change could be good.

Julie was restless in her new contract, which was also a fly-in community, but had phones. She did not apply for renewal after her first year. She liked her students, but could not seem to let herself draw close to them. She was afraid, in a way, to reach across to them and be so vulnerable again. They remained aloof, but not unkind, sensing a hurt that was unfamiliar in a teacher. The year slipped past, and Julie moved on.

The third contract brought Musko and Doug into her life. First came Musko, or Black Bear, with his heavy black fur, massive paws, flopped-over ears, and square face. Musko followed her and studied her from a distance all fall. *He is a good dog,* the kids said. *You should take him; he likes you.* Julie was not so sure. Musko, however, was. At Christmas her first year, his observations were complete; he settled down on the porch and assumed the role of her dog.

Doug took a little more time. He arrived on the Reserve in late January, a little green from his flight but enthusiastic and eager to teach high school science to anyone willing to be taught. His students grew accustomed to his energy, and he became a sort of pet to them. They would tolerate his enthusiasm, and respond with a gentle smile to the tricks he would perform. They would also learn enough to get the credits they needed. Julie, meanwhile, was working in the resource program this time, instead of having her own classroom. She found motivating and supporting her students very satisfying, but found Doug's overbearing positive attitude a little unnerving at times. Initially, she was somewhat embarrassed by his shouts of encouragement; his "C'mon! Think! Think! You know you can!" sounded insincere, and just a little insulting. However, like his students, she came to accept this as just the way he was and, like them, grew a little fond and protective of him.

Musko remained ambivalent, studying Doug throughout the winter, plodding behind him and Julie as they skied. He glowered on the mat as they chatted over coffee, and growled if Doug brushed a hand to Julie's face or shoulder. It was March before he tolerated Doug, and April before he laid his head on Doug's lap and agreed to have his ears rubbed.

Thus, Doug joined Musko's pack, and received his trust.

Julie was comfortable with the transition when the relationship between her and Doug became physical, and they began discreetly making love in the evenings on Julie's couch in May. Now, Julie realized, she was in a Relationship. She was fond of Doug. She liked being with him and making love with him. Sometimes she felt that she was playing grown-up, but most days she felt that this was the natural progression of life.

Thus it was that Julie did not go home to Waverley that summer, but went canoeing in Algonquin Park with Doug and Musko instead. Her parents described their own summer plans with great cheerfulness. They were going to Kedge, of course. Since she was not going to summer school this year, she could have joined them. Well. They were sure that she would be very happy in Algonquin Park, but if she had the time, of course they would love to see her.

Of Doug's parents and from Doug's parents, there was no word.

Canoeing in Algonquin Park with Musko had cemented their relationship. Musko, presumably in his second year, probably a May puppy from the spring before, had excelled in springing from the canoe while pressing on the gunwales, at being car sick on short rides, and at burrowing under the tent. It was impossible to remain angry at Musko, however, panting and grinning through their tirades. Musko taught them patience.

Their second year on the Reserve began without incident. Of course, after sharing a tent and sleeping bag at close quarters, maintaining separate residences seemed strange at first. Julie, however, found that she preferred having her own space. Discreet couplings on the couch on occasional evenings were fine with her; she was focused on her work and did not want the complication of a live-in lover. Besides, the Band had specific expectations of its teaching staff, and these did not include cohabitation of single teachers. *Foul,* cried many on staff. *That is not their decision to make. You have rights. How many of them are shacked up anyway? This is a double standard and you are being forced to live a lie.*

Julie did not see it as living a lie. Their romance was no secret, and was tolerated indulgently, but she had accepted the rules when she accepted her job. The Band was her host; she would follow their house rules. The guest does not dictate to the host. That seemed simple to her.

Musko was happy with the arrangement; he loved having two residences to eat in, to chew in, and to shed in.

By March, however, Doug was tiring of discreet couplings and respecting wishes. Doug was ready for couplehood. Julie was flattered, but felt twinges of alarm. No, Doug reassured her, he was not out to take her independence; marriage was not on the table at this point. No. Doug sketched a picture of Life Together: a small bungalow on the outskirts of North Bay, with a master bedroom and a big yard for Musko. There would be professional conversation over morning coffee before speeding away to work. They would substitute at first, and soon have full-time jobs. They would have careers, with pension plans. They would be a professional couple.

Julie heard doors creak shut, saw a blur of children's hands waving goodbye. This was her career; this was her life. She had carved it in a new land and now, piece by piece, she was moving away from it. However, she really was fond of Doug. Part of being grown-up was *developing the career.* It was time to put aside the bush plane, perhaps. Have a driveway, and drive to the grocery store. Perhaps, in some way, she loved Doug. He was part of her life, anyway. That must count for something. It would be fun. It would be a bigger adventure than Algonquin Park. She was ready, yes she was, to follow Doug into a new future.

Most days, anyway.

Just not while walking along the Reserve roads in the evenings, and not when Simon laughed.

And not when Musko brought home a fresh rabbit. He wouldn't be able to do that in North Bay.

~

The new house was small and not very new at all. Musko did not like his fence, and began excavation maneuvers displeasing to the landlord. Julie had assumed that Doug had done the market research, but he had not. Between them, they were lucky to gather four days of work in a week that fall. Contract work went to the many substitute teachers of long standing. One-and-a-half hours' driving to work was not unusual in this board, which spread out over a large territory. Musko did not like those long days alone, and excavated with increasing determination. The landlord complained with corresponding force. That was a good lawn, he said. He would not, however, kick them out in winter, because the damage was done. But the yard would have to be leveled when the snow melted; it would have to be leveled and raked and top-soiled and reseeded. And then they would have to be on their way.

By mid-winter, Julie was averaging four days a week to outlying areas. Doug was accepting only local calls, and so working once or twice a week at most. His jeep was hard on gas, he explained. Someone had to be there for Musko. Someone had to study the job market. Each had a role in a relationship; fulfilling one's role is what makes it work.

The small SUV Julie had purchased at the beginning of her third contract also burned gas. However, since companionship for Musko and market research were taken, that left her with hours on the road. And meal preparation and light housekeeping, of course. She missed walking with Musko early in the mornings and after school. Some days as she drove, she saw herself heading down the open road, Musko and her treasures packed into the back. She would have adventures out there, always in the copper light of a March evening, snow dissolving into the marshes.

Instead she dashed from far-away school to far-away school, always just in time, always on the edge of the staffroom, never with time for rapport. Musko, meanwhile, settled in with Doug for company, and excavated less. He still burrowed down to the frozen grass occasionally, scratching into fresh patches of lawn in his quest for better digging.

By May, Doug was a fixture before his computer, studying school boards in Alberta, chatting with friends who all agreed that this was the moment for Alberta. They must all go now. Timing was everything.

Just look at all those job postings.

Julie raked the yard and hauled the hundred-pound roller over the surface. Musko's paws twitched in anticipation as he watched, chained on the deck. She wondered, as she shook out the topsoil, if Alberta might not be already crawling with teachers who were snatching up those contracts at this very moment. By the time Doug was packed, the crest of the job wave would be past.

Picture Musko trudging through the grimy slush of southeast Calgary. See the short leash and dull eyes.

The children on the Reserve had an instinct for dropping by just as cookies were leaving the oven. The eyes would widen in laughter; sure, they wouldn't mind a cookie or two. Thanks. Simon would chew a mouthful of cookie, swallow, and then draw the Corn Flakes box near. Quietly and deliberately, he would read each label as Julie listened.

"Do you remember Simon?" she asked.

Doug paused over his laptop, frowning. "What? Oh. Yeah. That weird little kid always reading the damn Corn Flakes box. Yeah. Why?"

Simon at nine had been sullen and hostile. Surely he had a behaviour disorder. This much was obvious. Notice how he turned his face away during the most compassionate and caring and lengthy pleadings for better behaviour from his teachers. Which disorder was the one in which they fought all signs of authority? Wanted their own way?

Oppositional defiant! Yes. Definitely. See? He asserted control by
ignoring his teachers. There must be funding for this. . . .

Sound by sound, word by word, story by story, Simon had learned
to read with Julie. And as he read, he gained the vocabulary to communicate with his teachers. *Shy. See? I told you he was shy.* Simon remained
aloof, but when he spoke, it mattered. Simon would never become a
fast reader, but he became a good reader.

"Simon loved to read," she said.

"Nice. Oh. Look now. See? Eight openings in this school near
Lethbridge. Look at 'em." He twisted the laptop, jiggling the screen.

"I wonder why they all left," she said.

"Left?" Doug exclaimed in amazement. "This is new territory.
Progress! Expansion! Left, she says. Jesus."

As Doug pecked and clicked more furiously at his laptop, Julie
returned to the yard work. She missed the Reserve time. She craved
the enthusiasm of those days—the satisfaction of a good day, exploring
with Musko, laughing over meals prepared together.

She would like for Doug to make love to her on her couch on a
Friday evening, totally absorbed in their intimacy, and then leave.
Awakening in a double bed and then tumbling together had not been
exciting for long. Soon they were working their way through the sex act,
step by step, and then rolling away to sleep.

Couplehood was rather disappointing.

~

She was, however, still surprised when one day in early June she
pulled in the driveway and the jeep was gone, the house was empty,
and the envelope lay on the table. In summary, Doug was on his way
to Edmonton. He felt very strongly about this. He had to think about
himself for a change and start his career while there was still time. Later
there would be time for a partner. Not now. He needed someone who

understood him. She had become cold and unsupportive, but he did not hold this against her because that was just the way she was.

Postscript: He had found a good home for Musko.

Julie stumbled into the yard, so quiet and empty, the latest holes still raw. The perimeter pulsed with the lack of Musko, great-hearted, trusting Musko.

~

Julie filled in the holes and flung grass seed over them. She called the police, animal control, all the vets, and all Doug's friends. She posted flyers. June continued to grind by in Musko-less silence.

The jeep is pulling away, Musko straining and wagging after it. Then he settles on his haunches, eyes fixed on the road.

She does not come.

Perhaps he is chained, day by day. He is tense, watching, but then one day the eyes turn from the road and stare into nothing.

He is somebody's dog now.

~

Doug was part of the rhythm of her day and so she needed him, but Musko was part of the rhythm of her soul and so she was incomplete without him. Baffled and hopeful, head twisting, ears perked, anxious to catch the joke, too.

The grass seed sprouted over the holes by the fence. Julie stopped staring into yards and walking the parks.

She turned east that August. Before the Reserves and before Doug. Before the adventures and before Musko, there was home. Somehow, it was time.

~

Julie scrapes her tin plate into the compost. Tonight she will probably dream of Musko. He will be running on the edge of the bush, but he will not come when she calls. At her voice he will pause, cringing, and then bolt into the undergrowth. She will stumble through the bush after him, and then the branches will be still. The bush will be silent. The dream comes often.

Meanwhile, she is the lady of Meadowbrook Acres, with six bins to show for thirty-two years, and it is time to do something about that lawn.

HERITAGE AND STORMS

The storm has come to Wasaya.

I rise to greet the beautiful sunrise and discover dull grey tones, rain sheeting into the porch, white caps on my tiny cove.

This is not a brush cutting day; it is a bundle up and huddle in a corner of the porch day. I light the lamps at noon, craving a little light for my spirit's sake. I cannot help but think of Nietzsche's madman, but there is no marketplace and I am not looking for God.

I am looking for a way to stitch my scattered universe back together, though, and perhaps that is the same thing. *Re-ligio*: to bind back together.

I light two lamps and worry about running out of fuel. I extinguish one lamp, and am embarrassed. I have caught myself playing pioneer. Like my mother playing farm wife.

I am cozy now, tucked on the sofa in the shadowed main room, the porch being too wet and raw after all today. It is a good place to meditate on all the ways that you have lost your mother.

Great-Grandpa Stephen wanted to build a Great Farm on the small acreage allotted him by his father. Great-Grandma Mary had possibly cut her teeth on Spanish doubloons, remember. Definitely, there was privateer money somewhere. She had also been jilted. Rich and rejected. She was the perfect candidate for Great-Grandfather Stephen.

They had no illusions of romance, and neither did her father. True, he financed the farm, as a thoughtful, wealthy father-in-law might do. However, he was not a fool; he and his money were not soon parted. He made legally sure that his daughter and her new husband were partners, and also that the farm would pass to her. In the event of Grandfather Stephen's death, she would be sole owner until the day she died.

This was unheard of in Meadowbrook at the turn of the twentieth century. The husband owned the farm, and in the event of his death it passed to his eldest son, who was to grant his mother a home under his roof for the rest of her days.

Let us imagine the tension in the typical home after the funeral as the contenders eyed one another. On one side we have the grieving widow, a guest now in the home she had helped build and maintain. She frowns across the bread and pickles at the usurping daughter-in-law, who scowls back, calculating how best to manage the months and, God forbid, years that remain in this arrangement. I am sure that some really did embrace the change with True Charity, but I am equally sure that more often, if one did not return from the outhouse on a stormy night, the other would not rush into the snow wailing her name.

Grandma Mary owned the farm and was not subject to this ending. This was her home and her property; her son and her daughter-in-law were her property managers. To understand why she was so bitter anyway, we must consider that she had been dumped, Grandpa Stephen had an eye on her purse, not her smile, and she could not manage the physical work without her helpers. She was an independent woman, trapped in a dependent body. I would think that she did not have many close friends; they quilted and gasped, no doubt, at the terms of her marriage contract. I wonder, too, if Grandpa Stephen felt less a man in her presence—perhaps the other farmers laughed behind his back or to his face.

I see him in that first Great Barn, fists deep in his pockets, clenching tighter as the stiff little figure emerges from the kitchen and marches to the clothesline. Sheets snap and flare as she jams the pins down. This is you, Stephen, pinned. And this is me, pinned and pinned.

The farm was his dream, but it was her reality.

They both knew it.

I think she locked her heart away.

Anyway, she is a legend in our family. Today she would be medicated. Perhaps certain grandchildren would be taken away by social services. Even by the standards of her day, she was Tyranny Unleashed, if the family's oral tradition has merit.

They had a son, and he married a gentle soul whom he met at a church picnic. Grandma Mary delighted, we are told, in the first two children.

She was, however, not delighted when the children kept coming, and my father had the bad luck to be sixth in a field of seven. She appears to have been least delighted with him. She showed this, for example, by shutting him in his room when he had meningitis instead of wasting away their remaining pennies on a doctor. One night, as he moaned and tossed in his little room, he moaned and tossed too loudly. Grandma Mary stamped into his room, seized his flailing arm, dragged him to the head of the stairs, and flung him so that he twisted and flipped, smacking against all fourteen wooden steps, until he spattered to a halt on the wooden floor below.

His parents stood silent, hunched and staring.

"There's your boy," Grandma Mary announced, and returned to her bed.

You and I would have left, wouldn't we? We would have packed up the seven kids and headed down the road. We would have slept in ditches and under hay wagons while the children whimpered with cold and hunger. We would have been strong.

They, however, kept the seven children fed and under a warm roof. They watched and waited.

You would think that his siblings would have been kinder to my father. He was, however, the odd one, the nervous one, the dreamer; this is not someone you clutch to your bosom and defend in the grand scheme of things. He was the one to build their flower beds, take their chores, and receive their jeers.

There is a moment of redemption. After his funeral, Aunt Iris told me about the time she was wearing her new boots. Grandma Mary was switching my father, and Aunt Iris told how she ran up, kicking and kicking at her grandmother. "Run, Stevie, run," she told him as she swung her little booted toes into her grandmother's shins. Iris's chin quivered, and her eyes brimmed with tears as she told me. I do not know how that story ended.

I am left with an image of a twelve-year-old girl, fists tight at her sides, little foot swinging, smacking against her grandmother's leg, and a switch rising as a hand twists her collar. Moments of redemption are purchased dearly in my ancestral home.

Yet, my father was the one who stayed. His brothers and sisters left and had adventures; he stayed and dreamed adventures. He stayed and stayed, becoming his father's partner and, later, his heir. Meadowbrook Acres passed to this third son, this uninspiring one, and they were amazed.

In those days, my mother came to teach in Meadowbrook. My father, in spite of his past, was a romantic and a dreamer, and the French Catholic daughter of the classics teacher swept him off his feet.

The brothers and sisters froze in mid-adventure and dashed back to save the farm, but it was too late. They settled for frosty acceptance and regular undermining, to ease their outrage.

Grandma Mary might have been a holy terror, but this was simply wrong. They smoked and sipped their rum and muttered on the back verandah. They had always stood together, they reminded each other. For the sake of their parents. For the sake of their heritage. Just look at that barn door. Grandfather would die if he saw it sagging like that. He already had, one in-law observed. It is a shame that you cannot hold your liquor, the others told him.

My parents started out their life together by falling in love at the train station when my mother arrived in Meadowbrook. They should have stopped to consider what the farm meant, but instead they started as two happy children, playing farm couple. I honestly believe that they always stayed in love with the idea of each other, although they grew weary of the day-to-day reality of each other.

My mother was young, laughing, and very sociable when she came to Meadowbrook. She joined book clubs; she sang in the choir; she was busy with civil defense. I have heard those stories.

When I was a little girl there were fun times and gatherings, with days counted down until they happened because they were so rare. There were summer people who came to our house. You could laugh with the summer people, porch lights extravagantly burning and breezes stirring the gauze curtain liners as they sipped coffee and nibbled at cheese and crackers and delicate little maple leaf cookies. The women planned church bazaars and the men planned early hunting and, as the leaves coloured, they packed their cars and migrated south. Porch lights were now off, conserving electricity. Windows were sealed and storm windows snugged into place. The winter people drove by. They knew you, and all your pretenses and failings. They were always there. They were forever. My mother sidled around the winter people.

They would tighten their lips in the parking lot at the grocery store. They would give you their concentrated attention, asking after each of your family members. "We never see you anymore," they would say eventually. "Why don't you come out for . . . ? I bet you would enjoy it," they would say in that knowing way, that we know you won't way, that who do you think you are way, the way that makes children squirm because their family is different.

Meanwhile the aunts and uncles who survived Grandma Mary's Reign of Terror skulked in the shadows like wolves waiting for a lamb to stray. The lamb in this instance would be my mother, but could be my father, as the situation required.

The chin goes a little higher, the eyes a little more aloof. You start to withdraw, and make your own reality, a safer reality.

I think that I began to lose my mother on the day she came to Meadowbrook, and I was still nine years away.

Chapter 4

FLAMES

That afternoon Julie pries open the garage door, which she will later scrape and paint a dazzling white. In the dust and shadows she finds the push mower, which she coaxes into starting with a little gas and a little oil. Soon, the front and side yards are scraggly lawns, not rough patches of hay, although the green is mainly moss. She will lime those lawns in the fall, when the rains come; she will rake them carefully, and then sprinkle lime as a light rain falls. In the spring there will be lush grass.

Now the rider mower beckons. She will roll her way over the fields, reclaiming them, a casual eye surveying her territory, squinting to the sky to evaluate the weather. She applies the last of the oil and the gas, thrilling to the cough and sputter as the engine catches. She churns through the brittle hay around the garden and upper orchard, neat but yellow lawns emerging. She is reclaiming; she is the one for this place. Samuel will be pleased.

The gas gauge is dropping to empty as she parks in the shade of the garage and dismounts. She stretches, chaff-itchy and satisfied. She rubs the dust and chaff from the body of the machine, and splashes in the upstairs tub. Farmers then did not have refreshing showers at the end of a long day in the hayfields; they splashed in a basin and were renewed.

She feels an affinity for all the farm labourers who have gone before her. She dusts off the empty gas cans and sets out for the nearby community. She needs gas, and oil, and pizza. Possibly pizza is not on the farm heritage list, but she must also live in the present.

The gas bar owners are delighted to learn that she is the new tenant at Meadowbrook Acres. That is such a beautiful property, patrons at the coffee bar declare, but they certainly miss that barn. Breaks your heart to see that barn gone. The owners had known Samuel's sister, and direct Julie to her preferred oil, press coffee upon her, and give the nearby pizza shop their recommendation.

The pizza people, too, know Meadowbrook Acres, and while her pizza sizzles in the oven, they recount the virtues of the last tenants, lament that the place went untended, and are so pleased that the old place has someone in it again. It is a shame about that barn, though. Ruins the look of the place.

Julie feels the weight of responsibility. Everyone watches Meadowbrook Acres, it seems. Her mistakes will be seen and documented.

Samuel the landlord is the next topic. Julie learns that Samuel always brought his boys to the Park in the summer, but now they are about grown, so who knows if he will still come. *His wife was never one for the Park, hard to say why*, the proprietress murmurs as she fixes the lid on the box.

Julie ponders her own parents, still resolutely pitching their tent in Kedge, seeing younger images of Julie and her brother, everywhere. They canoe on the lake and on the rivers and meet other lonely parents. Will Samuel come to the Park, too? Will he canoe and meet people and exchange weather talk and gaze at the trails that are empty of his children?

~

Julie returns to the farm and sets the pizza on the sideboard under the west window. She opens her laptop and types the name into the search engine. Doug Simmons, Alberta. The name appears immediately in connection with a school website in the High Prairie area. If the website is current, then Doug is still living his Alberta dream; he has the career and the pension plan, but not Julie. He has moved on, and she has moved back.

Julie had gone back to Waverley and set up a base at her parents' house. She had thought that it was a short visit, while she was getting her bearings, and been side-tracked for nearly a year. She had been through a bad time, her parents said. She needed to rest, they said. They had all that space, and they didn't know what to do with all that space, they said. They were getting older, they said.

And so she had stayed, and been eighteen again within a matter of days. Her travels sounded like another life, lived by another traveller. She found herself in her old room, her new possessions piled on her childhood memorabilia. After all, you can't throw those things away; you never know when they might come in handy and you never know when there might be grandchildren to share those with. You would not want to just pack them away, surely.

So, you go a little deeper into your past.

Now, she goes deepest of all—all the way back to Meadowbrook Acres and the Park Years. Doug is moving forward, and she is moving backward.

Today she has mown hay on Meadowbrook Acres. She has entered her childhood dream and lived it as an adult, and as she pries open the pizza box, she does feel a little foolish.

She fingers a circle of pepperoni from the cheese and then remembers that Musko has a new home.

She slides the box into the fridge and wishes that she smoked. She would sit and smoke on the back verandah, and perhaps deer would come up to the apple trees.

She watches, unsmoking, but no deer come.

She is asleep by ten o'clock, the door by the stairwell pressed snug to the frame against any flickers of heat lightning. She awakens at midnight from her Musko dream, still crying, still stumbling through the silent undergrowth. She slides back into sleep around one, and here is Samuel tiptoeing across the kitchen, working the lock on the attic door. Now he is in the attic, a row of dusty lights overhead illumining the peeling cardboard boxes piled on the antique furniture. He opens the first, his face radiant and child-like as he lifts out the delicate glass ornaments. He holds them to the light, and tears glide over his cheeks as he smiles. Samuel cups an ornament, his fingers tracing its lines, still smiling, the tears slipping down his face. He gazes around the room, and Julie knows that he is seeing his childhood Christmases, caught up in the wonder that is his history.

His childhood memories are happening to him, and he cannot see that he is dreaming.

~

Julie wakens in the darkness, sobbing, the unbearable sweetness of the dream clutching her heart.

She turns to the east window, but the dawn has not come. The window is dark. The north window is dark, too.

The heat lightning was only in the front door panes. It was not in the east window, and not in the north window.

Science does not work so well in the darkness.

When the first logging truck grinds by at 5 a.m., the driver notes the lights on the east side of the house. The new tenant must be an early riser, like the old man was.

~

Thus, Julie is not well-rested and clear thinking on the second morning. She has a breakfast of instant coffee and cold pizza, prints a few resumes and covering letters, and then decides that it is mowing time.

The morning sun beats down as she trundles around the tangled grape vine, which is choking out a scraggly apple tree. She is making progress; she squares her shoulders as the engine throbs, its heat blowing back in her face.

The smell of mowing, of oil and chaff and gas, is thick in her nostrils; it is satisfying, dissipating dark-night fantasies. This is real; this is how she is meant to be.

Laila's car is slowing on the turn; Laila is calling out the window to her, tooting the horn. Abruptly, she speeds up and swings into the driveway.

Julie likes Laila, and appreciates the plant and the card, but right now she is mowing. She does not have time for visits. She is working; this is how you live at Meadowbrook Acres. The smells of mowing waft over her face.

The smell, however, is now thick; the metal, hot. It is now the smell of burning hay and hot oil. The smoke is wafting around her as she shuts down the machine and jumps clear. She stares down the field at the trail of smoke filtering out over the road.

At the edge of her vision, Laila tops up a bucket at the outside tap, seizes the broom from the verandah, and jogs across the lawn.

Laila must be sixty, but here she is, leaping over the peonies, brown hair bouncing, tanned legs firm as she pumps up speed. She releases the lever and the blade drops. With the broom handle she pokes away the wad of smouldering hay from between the body and the blade guard and flings the water over it.

Julie stands by nodding, hands reaching and gripping, miming Laila's movements. She cannot think of what to do.

Laila, it seems, can.

"Now fill this bucket again and we'll get this under control." She stirs the steaming hay, her face taut with suppressed laughter. "Looks like someone warn't checking their blades," she observes.

Three buckets later, the hay fire is out, the ground beneath it soaking. Laila mounts the rider mower and drives in high gear for the tap, parking on the gravel.

"When she's cool, we'll get the hose from the garage and flush her out good," Laila announces. "You really need to keep her clean," she adds.

Resentment, not gratitude, is rising in Julie, and for this she is sorry. However, she was mowing happily, the night far away from the sunny morning, and now it is over and Laila, not Julie, has saved the day and possibly the farm. Soon, every house will buzz with the knowledge that the new tenant has set the prized mower on fire. Heads will shake as hands reach for the phone. This one is surely worse than those bootleggers—remember them? Soon, Samuel will know that he has a very bad tenant, and will be studying the lease for clauses relating to termination of agreement.

Samuel lives out toward Wellington, not so far from Waverley. One day he will stop at the gas bar in Waverley for coffee, and there will be her father, his weathered canoe strapped to the roof rack. Samuel will be drawn to this, coffee in hand, and soon they will be reminiscing about Kedge, and he will mention that he has property out there. *Perhaps you know the place, used to be a barn, for forty head of cattle? You know it? Isn't it a small world? Well, I'm having problems with tenants. Latest one is only there two days, and she's already burnt out my rider mower.*

Her father will shake his head, his lips set in a grim line. *I know what you mean*, he will say.

Laila is watching her face, head tipped to one side. "Now I don't mean to intrude," she murmurs. "If you want, I can move along. You'll see the hose, hanging by the window, and I'm sure you'll be just fine."

Now the gratitude rises in Julie. If Laila had not come along, things would have been decidedly worse. She is resenting Laila because she can put out fires, while Julie stands by helpless.

"Um. Want some coffee? Still instant?"

The left side of Laila's mouth lifts in a smile. Then the smile spreads across her face, and her head straightens. "That'll be just fine," she croons, as she walks to her car. She roots in the backseat and then straightens, holding a bottle in one hand and a plastic container in the other. "Now I've got some real good blueberry juice here, locally made, and some banana bread I made just this morning. If you'd like to try some."

Laila waits, extending her offering, her arms open.

"You're not the first one to set that mower on fire," she says. "You never hurt her none."

Julie relaxes, and meets Laila's smile. "Thank you," she says.

~

The juice is clear, plain, and cleansing. There is no sugar or flavouring, just the vibrant freshness of blueberries washing over her tongue. She swallows, and feels the strength seep into her being.

"A cup of this a day will set you straight," Laila declares. "You been sleeping at all?"

Julie takes another swallow of juice, admiring the rich deep blue through the wine glass. Laila, somehow sensing that Julie possesses two mugs and a set of plastic tumblers, has produced two wine glasses from her car. Since this juice tastes better than any wine, and looks so nice this way, Laila has explained.

"Not much," Julie confirms. "Settling in, feeling a little anxious, I guess."

Laila studies her, wine glass cupped in her hand. "No lights?" she prompts.

Julie sets her wine glass on the verandah floor and slides her hands between her knees to hide the tremors.

"Lights."

"You know," Laila drawls, "flickering in the front window, then on the stairs. That sort of thing."

"Heat lightning," Julie says, but her voice is too high.

Laila studies the orchard for a long moment. "Rachel seen 'em, too, you know," she says at last. "She said it was her great-grandmother Mary, mad about all the changes in the house. She'd laugh about it. Sometimes. Usually."

"Yes, but heat lightning—"

"Don't just show in one window; you'd see it in all the front windows," Laila finishes. "It's just some quirk of nature. Don't let it bother you."

"Oh. It doesn't, really."

"I see." Laila scrutinizes the crab apple tree. "Still a good crop coming there. Makes fine jelly."

Julie does not want to discuss crab apple jelly. "What did the other tenants say about it? The heat lightning, I mean."

Laila shrugs, and holds the shrug. "I don't believe they noticed anything. Not so I heard, anyway. Just Rachel. And I thought, you being by yourself, maybe a lot on your mind. . . . Well, you look a little stressed, is all."

"Who else did you say set the lawn mower on fire?" Now it is time to change topics.

Laila chuckles and leans back in her camp chair. "Oh, that was Nathaniel, Rachel's boy. Well, he was about fifteen, and he was mowing about where you was today, and the grass and chaff was packing in between the guard and the mower and pretty soon Rachel's running with the water and a rake, and didn't she step on a snake. Just a harmless little garter snake, mind, but she was terrified of snakes, and she threw the water on *it* instead of the mower. And the poor snake went rushing at her, and she was screaming and slapping at it with the rake, and the smoke was just pouring off that mower. Anyway, she got it all out, same as we did, no harm done. Not even," she finishes, "to that poor snake."

Julie draws in her feet, close to the verandah. "Snakes," she says.

"Oh, now, not poisonous, just harmless little garter snakes," Laila reassures her. "You leave them alone, and they'll leave you alone. Now I'm OK as long as they don't surprise me."

They always surprise Julie. She suspects one is lingering in the shrubbery, preparing to surprise her if she steps from the verandah. "Where is this Nathaniel now?" she asks.

Julie soon learns that Rachel had Nathaniel when she was in one of her northern communities, and that he spent all his summers here at Meadowbrook until he was about ten. At that time, he began to spend more and more of his summer time up in Labrador with his father, and when he finished college, he moved up there and made it his home. Rachel had tried to let him go gracefully, recalling how much she had wanted to follow her own life, but had found it hard, anyway.

"She had this 'empty nest syndrome' bad," Laila explains. "When you have kids, and they're grown, it's not that you want them to move back in all grown up. It's just that you want those *times* back, and when they're gone, you think so much on those times. And Rachel had no one to move on with. Just her and the dogs. She used to feel guilty, like she was holding him back by missing him. She got enough of that growing up, you see."

~

Julie's father hammers the tent pegs on Julie's favourite site. Her mother places the cooler, the grub box, and the lantern as she has done for all of Julie's summers. The favourite foods are all there. The canoe is lowered from the rack, and they pull two life jackets from the car. When the camping trip is over, these will be placed on hooks in the basement, beside hers and Tim's.

Perhaps her parents are trapped in their role, and are unable to stop the motions of guilt-making. Perhaps they watch from within, wondering how to stop. Perhaps they need, just too much, to relive those times, and the cost does not matter.

She doubts that. They planned it. She knows.

She thinks of Musko, then, but she and Tim and Nathaniel are not like Musko. Musko did not have any ambitions about independence. Musko was content with the routines of his pack.

And what of Nathaniel, struggling to walk free on the low tundra, his gun snug to his back, the mountains dazzling, but somewhere behind them a lonely mother who lived alone with three dogs and was not free upon the low tundra and did not laugh full into an open sky and so how could he? How could he?

"What did Nathaniel think about his mother disappearing?" Julie asks.

"Well, now." Laila hesitates. "We haven't heard from him in almost a year, since we called him that time in September. It was like he knew more than the note said, like it was a clue he understood. It was almost like he kind of expected it. Samuel, now, he just got all in a state, frustrated, like. It was hard for him, I believe."

And how did you feel, Laila? Julie does not ask.

Laila pours more blueberry juice. "You gotta eat right to sleep right," she says. "And I wouldn't worry about those lights if I was you. Everything in nature has its explanation. And don't let those snakes bother you. They're just part of nature, too."

~

Together they connect the garden hose and Laila thoroughly sprays out any remaining chaff from the mower, circling the machine while Julie pays out the hose. Then she snaps the lid down on the banana bread, places it in the fridge, scoops up the wine glasses, and rinses them in the kitchen sink. These disappear into the backseat of Laila's car.

Laila shuts the car door and turns. "You have my number," she states. "You give me a call, whenever you want. I promise I won't keep showing up like this, sticking my nose in all the time."

Now the gratitude and welcome radiate from Julie. Laila *must* come every day; they will drink blueberry juice and plan what to do about Samuel and his sister. Together, they will restore the farm.

"Actually, I'd like it if, you know, you dropped by whenever you want," Julie blurts out.

Laila's eyes narrow and she purses her lips. "When I say 'Drop by anytime,' I mean drop by anytime."

Julie squares her shoulders in a rush of confidence. "Well, so do I," she declares.

The smile begins again at the left corner of Laila's mouth, and spreads across her face. "Then what say we put that mower in the garage, and you and me go to the Park this afternoon. You got all winter to put this place into shape, and I feel Kedge calling to me."

Kedge. She is going a little deeper into the past, but today, Julie does not feel like she is moving backward.

Chapter 5

PARK DAY

Kejimkujik. It is sort of interesting, the way things change and don't change. Parks and watering cans and childhood rooms: these things change and don't change, in same and different ways.

Julie always came to the Park in early August, when the first rush and wonder of summer vacation had passed, but summer was still rich with the promise of freedom without end. When she left in mid-August, the gloom of summer passing was filtering through the campground. The loons called more poignantly; the campfires gave warmth but little cheer. Afternoon showers and cloudy mornings in early August meant adventure with thunderstorms glowering over the tent; they meant a guiltless campfire in the evening. *The woods are so dry. They'll be closing the back country soon. Water that fire pit down good now.*

Mid-August rains were wetter, colder, and darker. They robbed you of the last dazzling bike rides and the last ice creams at the beach.

A lone axe rings hollow and lonely across the campground. Laughter over breakfast hangs in the dark air, intrusive. Grey winds flip the leaves. The boughs swing, damp and distant, and you try to call your summer back but it is gone.

Then the sun is burning down again, but the leaves are no longer dappling. The Park is tired, and you are tired. Soon, you are trundling along the curving road, pool noodles and sleeping bags squashed around you. You ease along the winding coils of road around the hills through ancient hemlock stands, the lake a shimmering flash down the slope as you swing along the turns in Meadow Campground.

You marvel that cars in the wooded sites are disgorging tents and sleeping bags, camp stoves and coolers, hopping children and barking dogs, and parents still smiling. These newcomers do not realize that the summer is passing, that the magic is tired. Recreational vehicles of various types and sizes are hoisting their awnings; elderly couples pipe directions and flap arms as their enormous trailers crawl around picnic tables and fire pits.

Her father purses his lips. *And they tore down the lodge,* he mutters.

In other sites there is the final clack of tent poles folding. The children are pouting; the parents glare at the already packed cars winding toward the exit. The dogs huddle under the nearest trees, wondering what they must do to make their world right again.

It is leaving time in Kejimkujik, and here is Julie, just arriving, fifteen years swept away and the past so near.

~

It is a hot August afternoon, humid and still. The entrance kiosk and the visitors' centre have received some upgrades, but the feeling is the same as it was fifteen years ago. The Blanding's turtles are still endangered, and still nesting in the same locations near the campground turn-off, now with signs announcing their presence. Blanding's turtles are special to this ecosystem, and although they are protected and studied and encouraged, they do not thrive. Perhaps they are not meant to endure and evolve.

Perhaps their time is simply past.

This saddens Julie. She wants to believe that there is a future for this present. She knows that this is mid-August thinking, and so she feels lonely for the turtles and for herself.

"Your parents still come here?"

Julie starts from her reverie and turns to Laila.

Laila shrugs, shifting in the driver's seat. "Well, Samuel did say you used to come here. And your father knew about the lodge."

Yes. Julie's parents do still come here. They come in July now, and stay a week. That gives them plenty of time to gather data on how the Park has changed, lament the rising costs and restrictions, scoff the innovations that encourage reluctant campers but discourage seasoned campers, and miss the Kids.

Tim had two years of solitary camping with them after Julie stopped coming to the Park. Julie speculates that if Tim had family in Labrador, he would have fled there long before Nathaniel did. Tim is a mortgage consultant in a bank in Bedford. Tim keeps a neat apartment and attends the family Christmas dinner. He indulges each year in a resort vacation, where he meets other rising stars of the banking business. Tim does not canoe or camp or fly to remote Reserves. He is not adopted by great black dogs or dumped by visionary partners. He spends two weeks among people that he does not know or need to know or ever see again. Julie suspects that Tim is lonelier than she is.

Julie was busy last winter as an emergency supply teacher in the Metro area. There she met many teachers who explained the Reserves to her. *There was so much alcoholism among Those Natives,* they observed; *work there would be very discouraging, and Halifax students must seem like a break after What She Had to Teach up There. Teaching in Those Places would lead to Erosion in one's Professionalism; teachers would become complacent. Of course, it was the best that some teachers could do, but with substandard teachers teaching substandard students—where would it end?*

And the parents, they added, *did not care.*

Yet they had never taught in an isolated Band-operated school, or visited one, or listened to someone who had. Julie felt her fists beating on soundproof doors as she tried to explain the Simons of her world, the passion for learning and life and love, the wonder at a tiny plant emerging in a Styrofoam cup, for all nature was perfect and these children knew this and their parents were not deadbeats but shy and lonely people whose passion and wonder had been struck down again and again until their eyes could not lift up to the sky and find joy. And finally, Julie was just silent, too, and let these teachers steer her through her days. She was a child to them, playing at their adult game.

In the meantime, she reached out to their Simons.

When others failed, it was the system; when she failed, it was her own doing.

So many lessons to learn.

Each night there was supper with her parents, their faces beaming because she was here to stay. She would look after them in their old age. She would take up their time and their space. She was their salvation and their burden. She was their clever daughter who had seen the world, their poor Julie who couldn't seem to get ahead.

Her mother's voice was hushed on the phone: *"Oh, I'd like that, Martha, you don't know how much. Only—well, Julie? She's going through such a bad time. Yes, I know. But she's still our daughter."*

Her mother's voice called from the kitchen: *"So you are going out? That is fine. We'll be just fine, don't worry about a thing. We'll just watch a little TV; there must be something good on. I think I'll just freeze this chicken; your father and I feel like warmed-over soup this evening."*

It is hard to heal when you are responsible for not only ruining your parents' social life, but robbing them of the will to live.

It is hard to heal when your father insists that you need walking and canoeing and snowshoeing, and then he oversees every step and stroke, and every sentence begins with a yearning, "Oh, I remember once . . ."

Tim set up local walls and she set up distance walls and on the other side were her parents, still trapped in her childhood. Now suddenly there were no distance walls, and yet they stood baffled, unable to understand how they could still be old and alone and she so far away when she was right here.

"You gotta make new patterns, when your kids move on," Laila is saying.

They are walking along the shore of Kejimkujik Lake, above Merrymakedge Beach. Julie has just poured out her reverie to Laila, who has a talent for receiving and respecting confidences without soliciting them. Laila radiates acceptance and openness of spirit. There is no judgment, no looking back, in her. Laila, simply and wisely, has learned to be.

"*You* gotta make new patterns, too," she adds.

They picnic near the playground and cooking shelter off the first parking lot at Merrymakedge Beach. The afternoon is cooling, the clouds building over the lake, grey and heavy. Laila's backseat produces a plastic tablecloth, a thermos of brewed coffee, a plastic cream jug and sugar bowl, potato salad, ham slices, fresh cinnamon buns, a box of blueberries, and camp plates, mugs, and cutlery. Julie provides a plastic bag of sandwiches consisting of store-bought bread spread with margarine and slices of tinned meat, and two diet soft drinks.

Laila scoffs at her apologies. "You're just getting set up. And I had all this stuff at the house anyway."

She heaps the plates with potato salad and selects a sandwich. "Kedge always gives me an appetite."

Up the hill four people are making their way to a table under the trees. Grandmother, mother, and two grandchildren, Julie decides. The wind is beginning to blow.

Their conversation drifts down the hill and Julie soon realizes that it is visiting aunt, single parent, son, and son's friend. The aunt keeps up a cheerful litany of stories of Yellowknife, while mother smacks plates on the table and grunts "Oh?" and "Really?" at intervals. Son and friend play at the swings listlessly, and then meander over to the table.

"I don't eat those kind," son's friend announces.

"Then try these," son's mother counters.

"But I'm allergic," son's friend declares.

Son's mother leans across the table. "Well, you weren't bloody allergic last week, now, were you?" she snaps. "I bet you're not damned well allergic to the cake."

61

Son stands by, rubbing his right running shoe against the back of his left knee as he studies the lake.

Yellowknife aunt stiffens. "I don't believe I'm hungry; you can have mine, Jenna."

Son and son's friend are cramming their mouths with cake. Son's mother clamps her teeth into a sandwich, chewing like it was the last food on earth, plucked from the edge of a nuclear wasteland. You must eat to survive. Yellowknife aunt sips daintily at a fruit juice box, grimacing and clutching her forehead.

"Well. There's worse things than being alone," Laila drawls.

"It's gonna rain." Son's voice drifts down the hill.

The wind is rising, and the first drops are pattering down as Laila expertly sweeps their picnic paraphernalia into containers. Son's mother is clawing boxes and bags into her arms, and Yellowknife aunt is cheered sufficiently by the new adventure to launch into a tale of a rained-out picnic in the Northwest Territories. "'Forest fire?' Gary says. 'You couldn't start a forest fire here with a blowtorch!' Well, it rained for three days, and there we were in the camper; it makes you wonder how anyone survives the Monsoon season."

~

Julie has had enough Park for one day, but Laila would like to wind through all three sections of the campground and see what is going on. The wooded lots in Kejimkujik are close together, yet private, and all the loops and twists in the road give the illusion that you are camped in the forest with others just visible through the trees. In reality, they are just metres away. Some 350 sites dot the hillsides, although you feel like you are out there alone.

Meadow Campground is in mid-August evening-of-rain-commencing mode. A few campfires are starting in defiance, but many campers are still out doing Kedge things. Slapfoot is quieter, and Jim Charles Campground is nearly empty. Julie stares.

"My God. The trees," she says.

Many of the trees in the bottom loop, on the side across from the lake, are gone. Tiny saplings, neatly poled and fenced, sway and droop in the wind.

"Been having some issues with caterpillars." Laila indicates the shedding hemlocks across the road. "You couldn't camp there without a tarp. It was raining caterpillar poop half the summer. They have to try to let nature take its course, this being a park and all. They dasn't spray and they dasn't band the trees or do any cutting, and here you see the result. They had to do some trimming, after all. It's too bad, in a way, but that's the way things go."

This section of the Park is stark and lonely, a glimpse of post-apocalyptic Kejimkujik. The rain falls harder. Once, canoes pulled to the shore, as the People made their way from the interior down to the sea. They journeyed back and forth, back and forth, and there was meaning and reason in each movement, and the hemlocks, the dead and the living, were not lonely.

"That house is different on a stormy evening," Laila says. "If you want, you can stay over with me and Tom."

Laila's husband, Tom, is a quiet, stay-at-home person. He likes Kedge, but not enough to leave his workshop. Julie suspects that while Laila marches through the present, he is still camping with his boys, now grown.

Julie's parents wanted her to come with them, this July. Her father had turned out a paddle, fitted snug to her chin, in his basement workshop. Julie explained that school boards would be calling, interviews were imminent. Her father placed the paddle on the rack, near the life jackets.

No school boards called. The paddle remained on its rack.

Her parents sat at their campsite, and no doubt they saw a ten-year-old on her bicycle. Not too far, Julie. Perhaps they toasted marshmallows, a fork packed for her. You have to keep eating, or you will not survive.

You are not mortal until your children are grown. To stay immortal, you must keep them children. Capture them and hold them, and the present will endure forever.

Julie could have taken the paddle and looked for the portal and the magic with them.

They do not realize that she is as afraid of being consumed by the past as they are of being consumed by the future.

She wants to take the paddle, if only to save them.

She cannot.

Julie needs to go to Meadowbrook Acres and confront the flickering lights, the barn for forty head of cattle, and Great Grandmother the Holy Terror. Then, she can confront, but never take, the paddle, smooth to her chin.

~

The rain is streaming down as they splash along the pitted driveway. Laila is frowning, shifting in her seat.

"I wonder," she says at last, "if this place is really right for you."

She brightens. "Maybe you need a dog."

Chapter 6

DOG, PART 1

Julie does not need a dog; she needs Musko. Later on, she might need a dog, but right now she needs this very specific and special being, who has ghosted her dreams for more than a year.

Musko would sprawl across the den, his contented snores dispelling the gloom of a rainy August evening. Snuffling, tail bobbing, ears pricked, Musko would range along the rough track that winds through the scraggly hay in the fields. He would roam along the Red Pine lot and down to the brook near the edge of the bush, finding and bringing life to Julie's walk.

Julie walks the one-time-truck-road alone as August wears into September. She notes the greens dulling to yellow, emerging patches of red and gold accenting her descent into autumn.

She is well into her second year without Musko. Musko is well into his fifth year, probably mature and dignified, strolling placidly on his leash along a sidewalk in North Bay.

Perhaps, however, he has maintained his essential Musko-ness. He is too much dog for a city. Perhaps his antics are too much. Perhaps his new owners have decided on the Kindest Thing.

For them, but they will not say that.

Julie will not think of these things.

~

Laila might be right about the house, though. As August wilts into September, and school is beginning but not for Julie, and her parents have been redirected away from Meadowbrook yet again but who knows how long she can hold them off, Julie paces the house. She paces the house when she is not mowing and looking continually for snakes. This is real snake weather, and she must discipline herself to walk to the brook early each morning after the schools have not called her. She sports rubber boots and keeps her eyes down, taking mincing steps and making sudden rushes from real and imagined snakes.

She e-mails resumes and checks that Alberta website to find that Doug is still there, but not there for Julie. Lives are beginning and continuing all around her, while she is waiting.

Julie misses Laila's visits. Laila takes care of the children of one of the local teachers, and Julie envies them their childhood of special picnics, outings to Kedge, and hot chocolate on rainy afternoons. Laila will not plant the seeds of future guilt; she will love them and release them with open arms and heart. They will look back upon their childhoods as a snug dream of security and comfort. Laila will be alone again, but living determinedly in the present.

Julie struggles to recall what it was that her parents did or said in those days that chained her and Tim to them, but she can only see their happy, hopeful faces across the picnic table, crumpling and withdrawing as she sneers.

They cannot bless and release the childhood. Perhaps they want to, but they do not.

And in the nights the lights flicker in the stairwell and the floorboards in the great-grandmother's room above her creak in the darkness. The temperature is cooling at night; that is the house settling, in the night, in that room. That is all it is.

Julie listens and watches and does not sleep well.

~

Mid-September is suddenly present, and Julie has had two days of work so far. She does not expect calls so early in the season, but she needs them. Oil bill days loom over a horizon that rushes ever closer, and she must have many days of work to prepare for them. She paces by the phone, and checks the dial tone. It is always working, but she is not.

Both calls come from the local school, and she senses that these are curiosity calls. *Who is that new tenant at Meadowbrook Acres who spends her days mowing lawns and her nights burning electricity? You have that bad cold coming on; you call her and book her for the day. We'll review the situation, and debrief you upon your return.*

The staffroom is vibrant with anticipation that first day. A secretary deposits her there, to leave her jacket and get acquainted. A middle-aged woman with neat copper-dyed curls smiles and indicates a chair beside her. "I knew your landlord's mother," she says by way of introduction. "She retired not long after I started here."

Imagine the same job for all these years, going home to the same house, teaching the children of your first students, perhaps present at their christenings, your life undocumented by bush plane travel, moves, and upheavals. You probably married here and will possibly even die here. You are a force for good in the community; you are not a stranger passing through. Julie visualizes herself in this same staffroom, her own retirement pending, and for a moment she is suffocating. She yearns in this moment for the Reserve days, even though she knows that their moment is past in her life.

This present is about career, and her past in its light should probably be described as experimentation. She smiles back, therefore, a halting but passable professional smile.

A coffee mug materializes at her elbow. A turning-middle-aged man, thick glasses and neat fringe of greying hair accenting his round cheeks, is grinning. "Old Rose was my teacher," he booms. "Not surprising she went a little strange, rattling around alone in that old place."

A hush falls over the staffroom.

"Roger." The older woman scowls while heads lean in and scrutinize Julie.

"Let me show you around." A young woman, crisp and authoritative, yet fresh and relaxed, rises and tilts her head toward the staffroom door. This is the teacher Julie aspires to be but cannot seem to. Julie wriggles out of her chair, beaming at everyone, and follows the neat shoulders into the hallway.

"You know Laila," the woman states as they stride toward the Grade 8 homeroom, Julie's class for the day. At least, her guide, who turns out to be Janice Reid, mother of Laila's children, strides. Julie is still shambling, trying to force her shoulders back and lift her feet and look relaxed, too. "Ooh, look. You gotta love that walk," a high school voice murmurs from the lockers. "That's not a walk; that's a lurk," someone responds. "Like a gravedigger, in some old movie. Give it a shovel." Sophisticated giggles follow. Smile. Smile like a professional teacher, head a little tilted, lips smooth, no teeth. "What's wrong with her head?" Light twitters of appreciation follow. Julie hurries after Janice Reid.

"You can expect people to be curious," Janice explains. "They always are, about the Hardy place."

She launches into a quick listing of bell times, routines, and general expectations. Julie nods and bobs, striving to reduce her flaming cheeks to a professional hue before the kids fully assess her as the weak member of the herd. Gravedigger? That's a new one. Remember your sense of humour. Be open. She feels amusement wash over her. Gravedigger! Not bad. It shows literary talent. Somewhere inside a knot gives way, and then another, and then Julie is remembering that she likes kids, and that is why she became a teacher. The bell rings at 8:35 a.m., and Julie finds her confidence. She is a person who cares about children; she respects them, and wants to discover their learning strengths with them. Gravedigger. Well.

Classroom discipline has always been an issue for Julie. She does not dispense firm and immediate justice; her tactics are based on a gradual building of respect. This served her well in the Reserve schools, where the students were eager to learn once they established that you were a friend to them, but in a one day position there is no time for this. So you build a little today, and hope that there will be another day to build a little more. And that is why in Halifax she was often advised to take a stand and make it stick.

As the students step through the classroom door, Julie feels the last knot slip away, and she is just smiling, hands relaxed in her blazer pockets—a most unprofessional stance but a natural one and part of who she is. They eye her, and ease into their seats. First day moves are made, preliminary probes sent out—not enough to invoke the Office, but enough to gain a general sense of potential weaknesses. They do not speak disrespectfully, or drop things loudly. They ask pointed questions respectfully and with wide-eyed innocence. *You seem like a good person, Ms. Martin. You don't seem like someone who would expect me to sit beside a, well . . . person like. . . .* Student rolls eyes, indicating the student across the aisle. *Hey, she called me. . . . No, I never. I just asked, well, I have a right to ask, don't I?* Julie cuts into the conversation, indicating the text book. This speculation might seem harmless to the first speaker, but it has done harm, and now it is time to start the lesson. *Yes, Ms. Martin. Of course.* And that look you're giving him right now is not helping anyone. *How about this?* Yes, that pout is just fine. Page fifty-two, everyone. No? Then share with the person next to you. Next to you, not your friend in the corner who is waving so eagerly. Thanks.

She wants to be respectful and she wants to be fair, and although she knows that she allows some situations to play out for too long, she also knows that a core group is enjoying her teaching and genuinely wants to learn from her. She is aware, too, of another group, who is preparing a set of strategies that will assist them in classroom domination.

Be fair. Do nothing to harm or damage these children as you guide them through their learning day.

Do not, however, let them manipulate the rules of fairness, for they are adept at this. Perhaps it is a way to make themselves known. Perhaps it is self-expression surfacing. Perhaps it is a way to survive.

Meanness of spirit usually has a reason, if you look deeply enough. Julie believes this, but is not sure that she will continue to believe this.

She is not shambling as she leaves, and is called back for a second day.

She is terrified. They will be ready for her. She relaxes her shoulders, ambles but lifts her feet, and visualizes oil bills. The students walk into the room, and she is ashamed. They are not cash to be exchanged for gallons of oil; they are persons in search of acceptance. Julie accepts each one in their humanness, but does not flinch from consequences today. If she flinches, she will be the sub that teachers and many students dread. *I'm not having that one in my classroom. . . . Mom, I have to come home; she lets people pick on me. . . .* It is all about choices. When you choose to ignore a rule, you are also taking responsibility for the consequence. It does not matter that you thought you could get away with it; you knew the rule and made a decision to ignore it. The responsibility for the "unfairness," then, is yours.

Respect remains, but discipline is maintained. The individual assigned the consequence might continue to mutter, but the others stop developing stomach aches and headaches and other circumstances requiring their swift return home.

Next day, of course, the teacher is better, and ready for the debriefing.

~

Julie attends the parade at the County Exhibition in late September, and wanders the grounds in the heat and dust. She supposes that the parade, the exhibits, the booths, the games, and the rides awaken the excitement of the regular participants, but today she is walking in others' memories, and a little lost on this journey. Several people have stopped to tell her that she has the place in good shape, and that it is good to see lights in the place again, although most conclude that it just isn't the same without that barn. Many knew her landlord and/or his sister, went to school with their older brother, the one in Newfoundland, and were taught by his mother. One bent, elderly man shuffles over to inform her that he used to cut pulpwood with the landlord's father. His back might be stooped, but his eyes are bright as he leans close. "He w'ar a ha'd man tuh wo'k fo-ah, that Stephen Ha'dy. Nevah one tuh think o' one o' them coffee breaks you teachahs seem tuh enjoy so much."

He puffs air past his thin lips and Julie realizes too late that he has been trying to joke with her. Her look of bewilderment gives way to a wooden grin, and she gropes for a satisfactory reply. The old man purses his lips, ducks his head, and shuffles on.

"So you've met Jason."

Julie turns and there stands Laila, two blonde, sturdy children in tow.

"This is Mark; he goes to Primary. And this is Jenna. She'll be in Primary next year, won't you, Jenna?"

Jenna nods, her face grave as she eyes Julie. "We go coasting on the farm," she announces.

"Well," Laila drawls. "Sometimes. On that first big hill. Samuel's been letting us, but now that there's someone in the house and all. . . ."

Julie squats down, addressing Jenna at eye level. "Think I can come?" she asks.

Jenna nods solemnly. Mark places a cautious hand on Laila's sleeve and tugs. "The horses," he urges.

That smile spreads across Laila's face again. "Want to see the horse barns with us?" she asks. "One of Samuel's tenants kept horses there, you know. Now there's something for you to try."

Julie knows that Laila does not really expect her to acquire a horse. She is bantering with her, as friends do, as she and Rachel once did, but Julie will not abandon her as Rachel did, and her step lightens as they walk across the grounds.

"I miss our visits," she says.

"Oh, you'll be getting lots of calls now," Laila declares. "Exhibition and colds just go together."

Julie wants to tell Laila that she needs her for the loneliness that comes whether she is busy or not. She needs her so that she can learn how to be a good friend.

"No more lights," Julie says instead. She does not mention the floorboards.

Laila does not seem surprised. "Rachel only seen them in the summer. Like I said, it's just heat lightning. Something natural. Heat lightning and a big lonely house." She pauses. "No dog yet?"

Laila does not know about Musko.

"No dog," Julie says.

"And no signs of Rachel," Laila says. "Samuel hasn't heard nothing, and Nathaniel's not saying nothing." She sighs. "It's hard."

Sometimes Julie has imagined disappearing, being absorbed into the air without a trace. You would not do that if you had a Samuel. You would not do that if you had a Laila. You would not want to do it because they were there, and you would not want to be where they were not.

And you would not leave them alone.

Laila paddles out to the cabin, searching the woods and shores for a sign. There, by that island, is that blue fibreglass, jutting up by that bush? Is that wood smoke, someone camping, up by the Narrows? Could be Rachel, you know. Samuel paces the attic in his dreams, musing on happy times, weeping with the sweetness of long ago Christmases. Nathaniel walks out onto the low tundra, his eyes on the steep cliffs, wondering at the lost adults of his childhood.

Maybe it is time, after all, to get a dog.

Chapter 7

DOG, PART 2

With the new dog, Julie will no longer walk the Reserve roads or canoe Algonquin Park in memory, yearning for what might have been. She will walk the old logging roads beyond the brook, experiencing each moment in the nuances of this new dog's expression, her new memories overlaid with its enthusiasm and eagerness. The dog will slow and grow old at the right pace, and one day it will lie on the knoll overlooking the stand of red pines, and the days will be sweet as she remembers this dog.

There is no sweetness in the Musko memories.

There is only yearning.

For her parents, the present is empty. They roam the Park, seeking an entry to perfect times past.

For Samuel, too, the present is empty. This house, this property, is his portal to a time when all was good.

She will not be like her parents. She will not be like Samuel.

She had been happy on the Reserves, but that time is over. The spark and anticipation of a future unlived cannot be recaptured. There will only be nostalgia and longing for a past when all was new. She could become her parents, sitting at their picnic table, waiting for their lives to begin again.

That is not how you build a future. That is not how you enjoy the present.

She will release Musko. She will make her stand at Meadowbrook Acres, without a barn for forty head of cattle, rising red and grand above the fields. The dog will range along the fringes of the bush, and she will experience the autumn smells through its eager fascination. She will stand on the fringes of times past, but create times future, and there will be sweet memories to relive on winter evenings, memories of her very own life lived by her.

A great black dog rushes among the tangled brush for an instant, and then is no longer in her line of sight. Her heart twists.

The new dog will find her. That is the way of dogs.

Meanwhile, she buys a bright rug at a garage sale, green with a modest geometric border, cheerful before the fireplace. On either side, she places matching cane chairs from the consignment shop near the Park. Now this room is real. She can afford these things because Laila was right about the work: between illnesses and professional development, the days begin to accumulate. Julie teaches and decorates and waits for the dog.

Julie rakes leaves as Thanksgiving Day approaches, and packs them in bags along the base of the house. She breathes the crisp air and inhales the pungent smells of earth and knows that she controls the oil bills. She scrapes the garage door, rolls thick primer into it, and paints it a dazzling white. Now the red shingles are dull, but that is a task for spring. She buys fresh produce roadside and simmers it into nourishing autumn soups. She bakes carrot muffins and explores beyond the brook as the snakes retreat before the frost. She has sheets and blankets now, and sips real coffee as the deep crimsons and bold yellows of the maples emerge in the morning mist.

In the night the floorboards above her creak, and some nights when the wind stirs the leaves against the window, Julie imagines an old woman, pacing and muttering to herself. She shuts the furnace grate in that room. The room is even colder now and she pads the door with pink batting and closes it tight. The house continues to settle while leaves whisper against the window. The room hangs over her, like a great weight.

People suggest the animal shelter, or direct her to litters of pups just born, but Julie continues to wait for the dog. It might be waiting for you at the shelter, Laila points out. But Julie still continues to wait.

~

Thanksgiving weekend arrives. Dog-less, Julie washes, trims, and salts a turkey, inserts it in the oven in her new aluminum roasting pan, and dices vegetables on Sunday morning. She will join Laila's family on Thanksgiving Day, and has attended a staff potluck on Friday, but Thanksgiving will be acknowledged here at Meadowbrook Acres with the smell of turkey in the house, and with a winter's supply of turkey soups and casseroles ahead. There will be no slamming screen doors and no feet drumming on the verandah and no eager laughter, but there will be the smells of Thanksgiving.

Her parents are disappointed that she will not be joining them and Tim, but understand that meeting people and socializing in the community must be very important in getting work. Perhaps they can sense her empty, turkey-smelling kitchen from Waverley. Julie chops turnip in the sun-filled kitchen, the blade rising and falling, the sound echoing in the emptiness.

The turkey is starting to sizzle in the oven. It is a sultry day, and the back porch door is open. Through the screen door, rich odours of autumn earth waft into the edges of the kitchen that will be her kitchen, but the roasting turkey smell dominates. The knife clacks against the cutting board. Tonight, she will prepare casseroles for the freezer, and then she will boil down the carcass for stock. Tomorrow she will celebrate Thanksgiving with Laila and Tom, who today are with family. This is an excellent Thanksgiving weekend, although not with her family. Everyone else is with family and grateful for family, but Julie is building her future. She is at Meadowbrook, and the kitchen pulses with Thanksgiving smells.

Now a red jeep speeds past the window. Doug. Oh, Doug and his red jeep, bouncing through Algonquin Park. That even looks like Musko snorting at the window. No. Do not think of that. Inhale the aromas, think of your rug and cane chairs framing the fireplace.

But who is calling on her today? A teacher? A lost and lonely teacher also building a future? A lost member of a large family, seeking directions to a wonderful gathering with aunts and uncles and grandparents and grandchildren?

A car door slams and there is a scuffling at the porch door. There is a low but eager "whuff" and then the screen door slams and the kitchen door crashes against the wall. A black shaggy dog, tail flopping in an arc across his back, brown eyes shining with laughter, bursts into the room. Massive paws connect with her collar bones and a wet tongue slops along her neck and chin.

A wiry young man of about thirty or so, with neatly trimmed sandy hair and beard, stands in the doorway.

These are ghosts. She is laying the Hardy ghosts and her own ghosts to rest, or shelving them at the very least, and now here they come, pouring over the doorstep in full flesh, her very own ghosts leading the way. What's next?

"I had a hell of a time finding this damn place," Doug announces.

Musko snuffles with interest around the oven door and then bounds into the dining room. He paces about the empty space, a library in Julie's future, and then gallops across the living room and up the stairs. There is a disgruntled "whuff" from the far end of the hall; Musko has found Grandma Mary's room. He bounces down the stairs and flings himself on the new garage sale rug, panting and sprawling as only Musko can.

The turkey sizzles in the oven; the vegetables soak in their pots. Doug lifts lids and inspects each pot, and pries open the oven door for a quick peak.

"So who's all this for?" he asks.

Julie cannot tell him that she is creating the smells of Thanksgiving so that one day there will be slamming screen doors and feet drumming on the verandah and eager laughter. She cannot say that she is laying the foundations of her future. She is suddenly a lonely and melancholy recluse, cooking for one on Thanksgiving weekend because everyone hopes deep inside that someone will appear to share the day, and it is best to be ready.

"I was going to make casseroles," she says, "and freeze them. And some soup."

"Ah," says Doug. "That's a good idea."

Musko heaves himself to his feet, jogs to the kitchen, and crashes to the floor by the oven. Julie and Doug stand in silence for a moment by the stove, the turkey sizzling and Musko panting in rhythm.

"So you got Musko back."

"Back. Got? Not exactly." Doug frowns, running a finger along his new beard. "Fact of the matter is, he followed me. You know? Jumped in and wanted to come along."

Julie stares. "You said you found a good home for him. You lied to me. You took Musko."

"Ah, but I did find him a good home," Doug counters. "With me. Didn't I, fellah?"

Doug leans down to give Musko's ear a quick rub, but Musko rolls to his feet, plods over to Julie, and flops, tongue lolling, at her feet.

Doug shrugs. "Yeah, we had some adventures out west, Musko and me. It really helped, having him at my side. I would have been all alone out there without him."

Musko's ears perk up and he pushes past Doug, across the dining room and front hall, prodding open the doorway at the foot of the stairs. Doug trails after him. "Not quite the cuddly puppy these days," he observes. "Getting a little more aloof. Maturing."

A low growl issues from the doorway. "Musko! No!" Doug exclaims.

Julie peeks past his shoulder and there is Musko, head held high, great tail whacking her pillow as he grins at her. He is indeed maturing.

"Anyway," Doug continues, strolling back to the kitchen, "the west just wasn't what I was looking for. Not a place to settle down. I kept thinking about us, and the good times we did share back in North Bay, and it finally dawned on me that underemployment was putting a real strain on you, and that's why it was so hard for you to open up, to relax, to take chances—to accept me for who I had to be."

The good times. The strain of underemployment affected Julie, and drove Doug away. Musko fled with him, away from strained and unaccepting Julie. Is this the way it happened?

Doug places a tentative hand on her shoulder and looks deep into her eyes. He always, always does that when he is sorry and wants her back on his side or at his side. Right before he runs away and takes her dog. Julie stiffens. "I want you back," Doug murmurs. "I want us back. I want us to have a second chance."

The turkey grease is spitting against the tinfoil. "You took Musko," Julie says.

Doug waves a frustrated hand. "Yeah, well, what was I supposed to do? He was standing there in the yard, looking all dejected, and I said, 'Car ride, boy?' and he climbed right in. I jotted a P.S. so you wouldn't worry, and then me and Musko headed west on a voyage of discovery. "

Undoubtedly Musko was staring east the entire way.

"You tricked him," Julie declares. "He didn't know you were taking him away."

Doug shrugs and pries open a muffin tin. "Dogs don't really go into all that detail. He just wanted to come along, so he did. And he was my dog, too, you know, and now here he is to see you, good as new. These are good, by the way," he mumbles through a mouthful of muffin.

Here is your dog, almost a year and a half later, and these are good muffins, so let's try again.

"Doug. Just go. Please."

"I think Musko wants us to stay." He indicates her bedroom door with the crumbling remains of his muffin.

"Musko stays. That goes without saying. But not you. No. It's just not....No." Julie is trying hard to sound calm and detached, but the room is tilting and wavering and she is not sure just what is real. The sizzling of turkey is real, surely, because it was real before. Wasn't it? What about the rest?

Doug frowns. "You know what it's like, feeding a dog that size on my budget? And finding a place that will let me have him? You know? I could have just dumped him, but I didn't. He was my companion. My friend. We stuck together."

"But when you left—he should have been there, waiting for me, when I got home from work."

"Home." Doug sneers. "Oh, that was a home, was it? You off doing your thing, me trying to get ahead, Musko waiting by the computer, watching me—he knew."

"He knew I was coming back. That's what he knew."

"Did he? Did I? I did what I had to do. And as I keep saying, I really did find a home for him. I just had to be a little ambiguous, or you would have been tracking me all over Alberta because, frankly, you are a control freak where that dog is concerned, and I did not need any more complications just then."

"Complications."

Doug draws a deep breath. "Yeah. Complications. I had to do this; I had to do this to keep my head together." He relaxes and smiles. "But I can handle it now. I'm ready. I really believe that we can make this work now."

"But I've moved on, Doug." Now she is spouting clichés. "And those are for a dinner I'm going to tomorrow," she adds, as Doug reaches for the muffin tin again.

Doug returns the second muffin to the tin with exaggerated care and snaps the lid shut. "Ooh. Rustic domesticity. Will we have to sacrifice somebody to the corn gods now that it's not an even dozen? Forgive me," he mocks. "I was just hungry, and it's Thanksgiving."

Julie sighs. "You might as well stay for dinner."

"Great." Doug rubs his hands together. "And then me and Musko will report to a nice B and B, and I'm sure they will all be most curious to know why our good friend in the village, who had all this space, turned us out on Thanksgiving. Yep. I'll bet they would like to see me get my second chance."

"Oh, for heaven's sake, you can stay the weekend, then. Put your gear in the bedroom upstairs at the end of the hall, on the right. It's nice and big. Just open the furnace grate to warm it up a little."

The Holy Terror who cut her teeth on Spanish doubloons meets the dog thief. There is an image worth considering.

"Excellent," Doug sighs. "The charity of this house is not lacking after all."

Musko stalks past him and collapses again beside the stove.

~

Musko slurps and gulps through several platters of turkey, dressing, vegetables, and mashed potato swathed in gravy. He would eat more, but Julie will not let him have the bones, and Musko does not care for cranberry sauce. There will not be soups and casseroles.

Over dinner Julie hears story after story of Doug's struggles in Alberta—unfeeling parents, incompetent administration, unprofessional and cutthroat teachers, and spoiled children who tell lies about their teachers. The place, she learns, is a disaster. Would she believe that he was bumped in mid-September to make room for a teacher laid off last spring? Shouldn't the union protect all its members? Oh, don't get him started on the union! Where was the justice in all this mess? He scoops his way through a second helping while Julie picks at her first.

Doug tells her how he had brooded and reflected on his career, his future, and his relationship with Julie. He found himself yearning for the simplicity of the past, for the possibilities that he had left behind. He found himself missing Julie and did she remember canoeing in

Algonquin Park? There was something there that he could just not let go.

Therefore Doug had driven straight back to North Bay, his head ringing with the import of this epiphany. Imagine the bitter shock when he learned that the house had new tenants, all his stuff was gone, and Julie had headed east the year before. Yes, he had left a few things behind, but he had thought that she would look after his books and his furniture and his stereo and a few other things. How was he supposed to take those things in a jeep, for goodness' sake? Now his past, his history, was gone, just like that.

Imagine the frustration of tracking down her family in Waverley, and them standing there all blank and staring. *Oh, it isn't our place to say.* Thank God her brother had some Thanksgiving spirit and common sense and said she was teaching out near "The Park." And thank God for the friendly staff at the gas bar who gave him good directions to this godforsaken lump of a house. They said his dog would love the fields but not to let him chase deer. Apparently, they came out where a barn or something used to be.

Well, here he is, and is she getting lots of work?

He is thrilled to learn that the work has been fairly regular, in the local community and in the towns. Thirty miles is nothing, after all. And there is a maternity contract coming up in special education? She had better be applying for that one; with her background that would be perfect for her, and only three miles away. Couldn't get any better than that. What does she think his chances might be? No, not for supply teaching, not just now. Too close to the trauma. He needs a break from teaching. No, he would not have to go on the sub list to draw EI, because he was not going to draw EI. He was going to stand on his own two feet. He was looking for handyman work—he could do odd jobs for cash, maybe invest in a snow blower and do driveways this winter. Meanwhile, he could rake leaves, harvest crops, and so on. Here's an idea: he could live here, do some repairs and upgrades to the place in lieu of rent, and they could rediscover the trust and commitment that they had once shared. How about it?

Julie suggests that he do the dishes for his first odd job, but is not surprised to see that he is opening his laptop as she and Musko head out for a walk.

Musko waggles up to her, presenting a tattered stick. And now Julie collapses on the autumn grass beside him, burying her face in his thick fur. Musko wriggles around, slurping at her tears as she sobs. Musko will not chase deer. Musko will not go on any more car rides with Doug. Musko will remain with her and help her shape a future. Musko will be with her for years and years and one day he will move a little slower, but they will ease into his old age together. Musko knows what getting in the jeep means now.

The dog has found her, after all.

Julie could have Doug removed. The police could escort him away, wondering, as the whole community undoubtedly will, why their presence is necessary when meek and baffled Doug is not a danger to her or the community. Doug will be bored and gone soon on a new quest, anyway. It is better to let the scene play out.

Musko is charging into the bush, locked on to a rabbit, which will as always escape. Soon he will come bursting out of the bush, leaping and frolicking. The Musko dream has ended, and she has new dreams to make.

~

That night, Laila phones. If Julie would like to be alone with her friend tomorrow, then Laila will understand. If not, then bring him along. There's plenty.

By the way, she hears that he has a mighty fine dog, a big black dog the size of a bear. Better tell her friend to watch him; the season is open now.

It seems that Laila gassed up on her way home from church.

For two weeks, Julie has been disciplining herself to build a future based on a past, but on her own terms. Now, all her pasts have come crashing together at Meadowbrook Acres on this Thanksgiving weekend, and she is once again adrift.

Chapter 8

THANKSGIVING

Samuel picks his way along the old truck road in the misty autumn dawn, pausing by the bend on the second hill. His gaze sweeps over the stand of red pines and down across the yellowed hay. His face warms in a gentle smile as he notes the fiery reds sharp and bold above the low mist. He stares at the place where the barn once stood, and his face drops. His shoulders sag as he turns to the upper trail behind the pines. He is old this morning, saddened by hints of memories unmade, of rich moments missed.

A damp, warm muzzle is nuzzling Julie's face. It is 7 a.m. on Thanksgiving Day, thin rain is dripping down, and Musko tilts his head and watches as she explains about Samuel. Solemnly, he thumps his tail against the mattress.

Musko should meet Samuel.

Doug should not.

Doug has not so much changed as evolved. He has always been an intense and enthusiastic person, whose intensity and enthusiasm have become increasingly self-focused. He is able to justify each action he has made, and is quick to point out how the faults of others have caused his failures. He was always a little like that, but it has become his mode of expression.

She imagines his assessment of Samuel and cringes.

And Laila: He will snicker at her gentle wisdom, he will mock her ways and they must never meet. Julie will not be able to face her friend; she will be ashamed in the knowledge that Doug has parodied and ridiculed her.

Even so, they will meet this afternoon. Meeting new friends is part of his reconciliation plan. He can hardly wait. Julie can.

~

Julie passes Thanksgiving afternoon dreading the aftermath. Laila and Tom had their family dinner yesterday with her parents, her brother and his family, and their grown sons and their families. Today they are just having a quiet get-together to enjoy a simple meal in their own home.

Still, the feast displayed on Laila's table eclipses Julie's modest presentation. There are three types of potato: creamy mashed, broiled, and spiced. There are bowls of steamed squash, of mashed turnip with a hint of vinegar and brown sugar, of diced carrots, of peas and beans heaped high, and of bright sprigs of broccoli. There are platters of white meat and dark meat, a tureen of simmering rich gravy, crystal dishes of cranberry sauce and various pickles, and a basket of crusty rolls. There are brownies, apples squares, pumpkin pie, and Julie's muffins.

Musko has included himself in the invitation and vies for leading position at Tom's knee with his own dog. Both dogs have taken the measure of Laila's quiet and gentle-spirited husband.

"Well, that dog certainly likes you," Laila comments as they stack the dishes and brew tea. "Seems right at home with you."

Julie scrapes a plate with extra force. "He's my dog," she says.

Laila turns from the sink, one hand resting on her hip. Julie clears her throat and launches into the almost truth. "He went with Doug out west when we broke up."

Laila holds her position at the sink. In the living room, Doug is lecturing Tom on the snow blower plan, and Tom is murmuring polite noises at appropriate intervals.

"He took Musko," Julie whispers. "He just disappeared one day, and he took Musko."

Laila still does not move, her face quizzical but revealing little.

"He just disappeared, and now he shows up—just like that."

Laila purses her lips. "Wanting his second chance, I'd wager," she says. She pauses. "You going to be all right, him staying there?"

Julie scrapes a second plate haphazardly into the compost tub, Musko's hopeful eyes following her hands. "I guess," she mutters.

Laila pours boiling water into the teapot and studies the lid before placing it over the steaming tea. "You know, Rachel was always worrying about what people was saying or was going to say. You've got to do what's right for you, and never mind what they're all thinking or saying."

"Oh, he's not dangerous or anything. It's just, well, awkward, I guess. Like he doesn't really fit in there, but it's OK, really, I mean, it's just for a while."

"All the same," Laila sighs. "All the same." She brightens. "That Musko's no fool. He'll see it right."

That is why dogs come to us.

~

And so, after tea, and after brownies and apple squares and pumpkin pie and Julie's muffins, Julie returns to Meadowbrook Acres and braces herself.

"Oh, my, God," Doug begins. "Is this the best you can do? So domestic. So rustic. They're probably plumping you up to sacrifice you at the Winter Solstice."

Julie stiffens. "She enjoys cooking. It makes her happy. She's a good friend."

"Oh! Oh, I doubt that not," Doug declares. "A good and nosy friend, a prier of secrets of the soul. What do you really know about her?"

Laila tells of good things and happy times; she carries your hard things without burdening you with hers. She can laugh, and she can sit without speaking beside you when you cannot laugh.

"She's kind," Julie says.

Doug nods, as if this is precisely what he expected. "Yes. Kind. Kind and controlling. Follow her and you will do well in this place."

"It's not like that."

"Of course. Absolutely. And that husband. Now, there's a piece of work. The whole time I'm trying to spin ideas off him, looking for feedback, some serious assessment of the market, and he just grunts along, and when I'm all done he gets that country drawl rolling and says, like he's talking to the wall for Christ's sake, and 'wal,' he says. Seriously. 'Wa-al.' Then, 'there won't be much call for that here.' And he's staring at the wall; it's really like he's talking to the wall, not me, like I'm not even there. Now what in the hell does he mean: 'There won't be much call for that here.' Doesn't it even snow here?"

Julie tries to explain, without encouraging argument, that there *might* be snow this winter, perhaps even heavy snow, but intermittently. She tries to tell him that many people do their own plowing, and that there are already contractors in place for those who do not. All the time she is picturing Doug as a cheerful eleven-year-old, rake or shovel over his shoulder according to the season, and people surprised and a little amused as they listen to his enthusiastic pitch. She is embarrassed for him, but especially for her, for it will be seen that she has allowed this to happen.

Doug is shaking his head. "I can't see this place working," he announces. "Maybe me and Musko will have to hit the road. Right, boy?"

They are sitting on the back verandah that evening. The thin rain is now a weak drizzle; the air is humid and musty with leaves. Musko studies a corner of the overhang, fascinated by a real or imagined spider.

"Not Musko," Julie says.

Doug rolls his eyes. "Jesus. Here we go again." He leans forward in his chair, his voice low. "I am trying everything here, trying everything to make things work. But you—it always, always has to be on your very own terms. Maybe someday you'll look around and you'll see that you're all alone and everything is gone. Everything you ever dreamed of. Then you'll see. You'll know what it is to be me. Maybe," he whispers, lowering his eyes, "you'll really understand at last."

Julie is not quite sure what Doug is getting at, whether he feels he has already lost everything or whether he just might or she might, but she does suspect that Laila already understands Doug—and Musko— better than she does. What are you thankful for this Thanksgiving? I am thankful for my new friend Laila, because she understands things and doesn't hurt people.

~

Thanksgiving Day concludes with the first oil battle.

Enter Doug. He crosses the dining room, rubbing his arms, and scowls at the thermostat. He taps it, and then twists the gauge.

"That infernal room is cold," he announces. "Cold and damp. I'm turning the heat on."

Deep in the basement the furnace rumbles in response and breathes tantalizingly warm air up through the vents. Julie twists the thermostat back and hands Doug a baggy sweater from the second-hand shop in town. The oil bills for this place, she explains, will be extreme unless careful measures are taken.

Doug rolls his eyes again. "Say no more. Jesus. You got taken in but good. See, that's why they can offer low rent, so you'll be the one keeping the oil companies rich and keeping their precious antique house snug and dry so it won't rot. Let's get an apartment in town instead."

Julie has no intentions of getting an apartment in town, and says so. She does, however, recommend that he get an apartment himself. He counters that he will move into that cozy little blue room at the head of the stairs.

That was Nathaniel's room, Julie has learned from Laila, and Rachel's room before that. It is a room of family history, in which Nathaniel and his friends managed to break Aunt Iris's spool bed during an unsupervised wrestling match. Aunt Iris had painted it white and applied gold flecks. Rachel had named the pattern "hideous dignity," but still repaired the frame and kept the secret from Iris. Before the Big Auction, Aunt Iris had sent a man to collect it, although Rachel had assured her that it would not be in the auction. "You're not getting my bed," Iris had declared. This was after she had left it there for thirty years.

That is also the room across from the bathroom.

Julie has no intentions of traipsing past Doug's door on her way to the bathroom, but does not say so. She would prefer him shivering in Grandma Mary's room. Doug can be in the room above her, but not in her line of sight. She explains that he needs the larger space and that they will close off the other rooms and set the heat low. She hands him a thick comforter, also from the second hand store in town. She pictures Grandma Mary the Holy Terror dragging him away.

Musko is snoring blissfully on her pillow when she goes to bed. Musko understands about Samuel, about Laila and Tom, and about Julie. He also understands Doug.

She is thankful.

Chapter 9

FRAGILE ORNAMENTS

The phone rings early on Wednesday morning. The work is at the high school in town, and Doug is, of course, still there. Julie will make the forty-minute drive home from town, and Doug will be gone. With Musko. She clasps her arms about Musko's shaggy neck as they step onto the verandah following a quick walk to the brook. "Wait for me, Musko," Julie whispers.

Musko's jaws part in a canine grin, and his tail swings from side to side. He trots off behind the house and slinks across the field to the neighbouring orchard, now grown to bush. That Musko is indeed no fool, and Julie is again grateful for Laila.

~

Julie still makes the forty-minute drive in thirty-five that night, all the while checking for deer and tabulating oil bills and reviewing her credentials for that resource position. Images of a jeep-less driveway, a note on the table, and a Musko-less future press their way into her consciousness. Sometimes, the jeep is gone, and a proud Musko sits waiting in the driveway. Other times, the jeep is gone, and the house is silent. Sometimes, there is a note.

The jeep is there, and Doug is there, but Musko is not. Doug is pacing and muttering, signs of an agitated Doug.

"Jesus, the dog's gone," he announces. "I haven't got a thing done. I've been everywhere. I'm standing in the yard like an idiot, beeping the horn and yelling 'car ride!' That always brought him, out west. He always wanted to go on a car ride."

Ah, but Musko has had the car ride he was waiting for, the one to undo that last car ride in North Bay. Julie is sure that Musko only took that one to be sure of Doug, to know where he was going and to see him on his way. He just didn't factor in the return journey.

He has learned. There is an authoritative scratch at the storm door. There sits Musko, shoulders up and proud, panting and grinning. He marches past Julie and heads for her room.

Laila really does understand.

~

Doug has not been idle during his day alone. Besides looking for Musko, whom he probably only missed in the past half hour, he has had a rest (necessary to clear his mind), followed by a thorough inspection of the house. The chipped bathtub upstairs represents a significant health risk, and heads the list of minor repairs to be completed in lieu of rent. The west kitchen windows should be replaced (draining heat into the outdoors), the living room floor insulated (pouring cold air into the room), and the kitchen tiles sanded and refinished (presenting a significant germ trap). If this Samuel would just supply the materials, he would do all the labour, and save him and them a bundle of money. Samuel would save by having committed but low-cost labour, and they would save on rent and heat. Julie asks about tools and experience, but Doug has already moved on. To the attic.

He is, he admits, intrigued by this locked attic. It might need flooring and insulating. Especially, it must have supervision. If they are to be responsible for the security of its contents, then a precise inventory of them will be required, to be monitored and checked regularly, in lieu of rent.

To this end, Doug has located an alternative entrance, through a low door at the back of a closet area between the hallway and upstairs bathroom. True, he has had to remove two layers of vapour barrier with blown-in insulation between them, but he feels it is adequately restored, and most of the mess has been vacuumed. Has she considered upgrading that vacuum cleaner, by the way? The suction is minimal. A place like this requires special suction; a regular vacuum cleaner will burn out in no time. The landlord should be consulted about supplying the necessary machine. Meanwhile, a very rough preliminary survey has been made.

There is antique furniture rotting away in there, cartons of dishes and vases, plus suitcases of memorabilia—probably from the landlord's ancestors. There is a wedding dress, and a First Communion dress (This does not look like a Catholic house, somehow), and a pair of leather riding chaps for God's sake. Catholics and cowboys, Geez. There are cute little love notes from the 1940s, and a teaching contract from 1944. There's even a teacher's day book from the late 1960s—talk about neat and concise writing; no computer could touch this lady for neatness and style. But someone has bent the corner of April 2nd, and would you believe that she had scrawled, I mean, it was her writing, but *scrawled*: 'I'll never go to hell; I've had it here.' Well, that must have been a rough day! And yes, definitely, everything is put back exactly the way it was.

There are all these large, clumsy Christmas lights, the wires twisted together with electrical tape, crammed over some very delicate glass ornaments. Just one touch is enough to crumble them, so a little jolt— well, it goes without saying. And yes, again, everything is carefully repacked, and mice could have broken that one, so Julie does not need to have a nervous breakdown. That landlord probably doesn't have a clue what is in those boxes anyway.

He does, though; he does. He opens the boxes and touches each gentle memory.

He caresses each ornament and revisits its story in Julie's dreams.

Now Samuel will enter his memories with Doug sneering in the shadows.

"So. When do you think you'll be heading out again?" Julie asks, for by now she is not just concerned, she is anxious.

Doug shakes his head, grimacing. "I'm sorry, but I thought we were clear on this. I thought we were going to try again."

"No," Julie replies. "I just said you could stay, you know, until –"

"Precisely. You did. And now, here I am." Doug grins. "I'd say that this is a good start."

~

Musko cannot hold the dreams at bay that night. For here is Julie, turning in to the driveway at Meadowbrook Acres. The years have slipped by. Her hair is still dark, still bobbed short, but her spirit is calm, steadied by the routine of the years. She pauses beside the orchard, which looms crisp and stark in the late afternoon December light. Her gaze turns as always to the marker at the wood's edge, overlooking the meadow and the hills and the red pine. Musko's resting place. Musko had loved Meadowbrook and Samuel and guided her through her first eight years here. Musko, her forever keeper of dreams and secrets, had been claimed by his age as surely as she will be. As surely as Samuel will be.

"I want to be forgiven for who I am, for who I have been, and who I will be," Julie whispers, and is not sure why.

She does know that she has found a career, after all, and it is winding its way to an uneventful closing, as so many careers do.

She never did return to the Reserves, where teaching was ever fresh and new and so creative.

She remembers that she is starting her Christmas break this evening, and that she is no longer the tenant of Meadowbrook Acres. No, she is housekeeper and companion to the aging Samuel, who has come home at last.

So how come you're having Christmas with him? Doug's voice cuts across her dream.

Julie starts, shudders, and then relaxes. She has driven all the snakes from her pathways and trails and can place her feet with confidence as she walks. She has banished Doug.

She and Samuel will decorate the tree this evening. He was almost child-like in his anticipation this morning and she hopes that he has not been climbing the steep attic stairs. Samuel must not be tumbled to the kitchen floor, his bones shattered, his hopes and dreams fading into the ether.

Samuel is in the kitchen, untwisting masses of heavy lights, smiling as he re-tapes the wires. He hauls a cardboard box near, his face eager. "These are treasures," he announces. "Very delicate. You could break one just by touching it wrong."

He eases the cover away, and prods the greying cotton wool aside with one finger. The ornament is brittle shards, and Samuel's face is crumpling.

"Oh," he says.

Now his eyes fix on Julie. She is the one who let in Doug. She is the one who let a snake enter his house, and now here is the betrayal.

Oh.

~

The soft, moist muzzle nudges her into Thursday morning, but the dream clings to her skin. Samuel's eyes gaze on her in reproach. Oh, the voice says. She hauls on jeans and boots and stumbles into her morning walk and it is still blessedly October and she is still young. Samuel is still in Wellington, busy with his family and career. Musko is still here.

Doug, too, is still here.

Julie does not have a career, oil bills are coming, and Doug is established in Grandma Mary's room. He does not hear the house settling. He does not notice the leaves against the window. And yet, they are still there.

Julie walks along the old truck road in the misty autumn dawn, pausing by the bend near the second hill. Her gaze sweeps over the stand of red pines and down across the yellowed hay. Her face relaxes as she sees how the bright reds have darkened and faded and scattered over the land. The season is passing and she is still here and rich moments can still be made. This will be her stand, after all, and Doug is just one moment in this time.

Perhaps she will be Samuel's housekeeper and companion one day. For this day, she will appreciate and guard his memories.

Julie walks deep into the woods this morning, lost in her need to absorb each moment for herself, for Musko, and for Samuel. It is a morning for celebrating old memories and creating new ones to celebrate.

Thus, Julie was not at home when the school board called, the school board that had interviewed her for that resource position last week, and had said that they would be in touch with the successful candidate.

When she returns at mid-morning, Doug is singing along with the radio while perking coffee and frying eggs. "You should phone the school board; they want you to," he calls.

A call to the school board office confirms that Julie is indeed the successful candidate, that she will commence her duties in two weeks' time and continue in the position until the end of June, that she should present herself to sign the contract at her earliest possible convenience today, and that she should immediately consult with the current teacher and shadow her work to ensure a smooth transfer of duties in two weeks' time with minimal stress for the students.

Let winter come and do its worst. There will be cash in the oil bill account.

"You didn't tell me you already had the interview," Doug accuses.

This was to be Doug's orchestration. Now how will he demonstrate that she needs him? Doug remains, to critique her sleeping dreams and her waking ones.

Julie has eight months of work. There will be plowed driveways, and warm floors, and amazing children to meet. There will be coffee in the staffroom. And questions. Musko will have eight months of hiding from Doug each weekday. It is a mixed blessing, as are most blessings in her life so far.

"We have to do something to celebrate," Doug intones. At some level, Doug must be seen to be orchestrating this event.

Doug might yet grow bored and leave. Until then and after then, Julie must guard all the fragile things of Meadowbrook: ornaments and day books and broken hearts.

That is what caretakers do.

FROZEN HANDS

Winters used to be colder in Meadowbrook. Snow arrived well before Christmas and stayed deep through March. Coasting was guaranteed all winter long. My brothers and I were bundled in layers of warm wool, toboggan cords twisted in our mittened hands. "Look after your sister," my brothers were told, and we would trundle off to the First Hill, to coast dutifully until supper time and receive our Fresh Air.

I would wade back at dusk and flop on the snow bank by the back verandah, damp, clammy, and bored. By mid-January, I would hate winter. I would stare at the dense grey sky and see the snow rotting into April with small trout thick in the brook below the bridge.

I was four when my mother went back to teaching. In the house, my mother fluttered about in her flowered apron, hands lifted and tense. Her knitting evaded any gauge; her pickles lacked that final sweet, puckering crispness. She was not solid and calm as she sprinkled flour onto the breadboard and bent over the dough. In the classroom, though, she sped from desk to chalkboard and around the room, quick and enthusiastic. Teaching was work she was born for, work in which she moved with assurance.

Without a doubt, the farm could do with the stimulus of cash. In the past, Grandpa had worked on the roads, bought up small holdings and sold the timber, and juggled daily to keep the farm afloat. Now, my mother worked in the school, so that she and my father could continue the juggling tradition. People with land do not always have money. They have land and they can break their hearts on that land, but that is not the same thing as having money. You cannot go to Florida like the summer people, for example, even if you had the time. You send boxes of boys' clothes to your sister for her twins, and she sends back boxes of girls' clothes for your daughter, for another example.

The kitchen was sunny that winter when my mother went back to teaching, for Susan was there. She lived in the front room, cooked the meals, cleaned the house, and made marvelous cookies. She was mine. My father was working in the woods, my mother and brothers were in school, and I had Susan all to myself. I cannot remember the things we did to fill the days, but I do remember sunlight in the kitchen.

I remember more from the next winter. After all, I was five then. I remember greyness, not sunlight, because Susan had gotten married during the summer, abandoning me so that she could have little girls of her own. I remember tall, thin Marjorie, with her short black curls, who no matter what they said was not going to be just like Susan. Standing beside her, I began to notice that I was a pudgy little girl with long, thin braids. I walked obediently in the yard with Marjorie, and we made snowmen. She read stories to me in a lilting voice, while I sat rigid beside her. Forgive me, Marjorie, for you were kind. We made gingerbread men, we made snowmen, and we did all the wonderful things of childhood memories. But you were not Susan, and so you were always surrounded by grey.

That winter, my father was, as always, cutting pulpwood. My father used a tractor to haul now, since Danny Boy was retired. One evening, my mother and father were talking low in the kitchen while Marjorie stirred kettles and pans on the woodstove. My father was holding up his left hand, and the fingers were solid white down to the first knuckle.

The skin beyond was a milky white. My mother tugged the mitten from his right hand, and her breath slid out in a low hiss.

"My God, Stephen, they are frozen. They are frozen stiff," she murmured.

They must have seen the doctor that night, after my father finished the barn work. You did not delay, avoid, or skip the barn work. Your life revolved around the barn work, because your livelihood depended on the barn work. The sheep must be fed and watered, the milk cow Nellie tended, and Danny Boy, dear retired Danny Boy, brushed and fed. There were stalls to clean, and the pig in the basement needed his mash. When all this was done, then you could go to the doctor.

My father did not return to the woods the next day. He lay on the studio couch in the den, staring at the ceiling sometimes and at his fingertips other times. He seemed to sleep, but it was a light doze, without his usual bubbling snore. My mother, of course, returned to school because she was not a grieving widow and she could still crawl. A husband's frozen hands would not be an excuse; things were different for teachers in those days.

My mother was a teacher who could do a farm wife's housework. She could not, though, step into the farm wife's other role, that of taking on the barn work when the husband was away on farm business or sick unto death. She did not enter the barn. My mother paced and talked long on the phone with the doctor's wife, who was a nurse. Marjorie cooked in the background. My father lay on the studio couch, and then he rose and did his barn work, for that was their way.

The fingertips began to turn black.

I must have been in my room when the aunts arrived the next day. I came down to voices in the kitchen, and saw my father hunched on the bench under the east window, wrapped in a heavy overcoat. His face was flushed, and his glazed eyes were fixed on the floor. My mother must have just arrived from school. She was still in her car coat; she was clutching the handles of an oversized satchel bulging with scribblers.

Aunt Isabel, matriarch of the seven siblings, the favoured one of Grandma Mary, sat in state at the head of the kitchen table while Aunt Iris squared off against my mother. Aunt Iris had trained at the Royal Vic in Montreal, and you could bounce dimes off the sheets when she turned her hospital corners. Aunt Iris could subdue all challengers. It never crossed anyone's mind to challenge Aunt Isabel.

My mother clutched her satchel and started to sink into a chair. At the last moment, she remembered her teacher's training, and tried to straighten. "He needs to be home; he wants to be here," she mumbled.

"Rose," Aunt Iris snapped with one fist on her hip, "he is going to die if you keep him here. Lloyd might still be able to save his hands, if we go now."

"But Samuel—"

"—is a country doctor who knows diddly squat. Rose, don't you want him to get better?"

"I don't want to go to the hospital," my father mumbled.

Aunt Isabel rose. "You're coming to Iris's house," she said. "Your own two sisters are going to look after you, and Lloyd will be treating your hands."

"Well, but Samuel—"

"We're going now." Aunt Isabel nodded to Aunt Iris and they slipped into position on either side of my father, easing him to his feet.

"Wait. Wait, I'm coming." My mother had dropped her satchel and was casting about, clutching at odds and ends—a lipstick, a compact.

Aunt Iris and Aunt Isabel exchanged a glance across my father's stooped shoulders. We have enough on our hands, their eyes said. "No," said Aunt Isabel. "You are not."

Then they were in the car, rolling out the driveway with Uncle Lester (the one who had pointed out the obvious when they said that their grandfather would die) grim at the wheel. My mother stood in the window, hands twisting over the lipstick and the compact. Oh, there is nothing like a well-hated in-law to bring out the strength of sisterly love.

Dr. Samuel would never have let my father die. He would have saved my father and his hands. It was, however, Dr. Lloyd and my aunts who did save my father, and to their credit he received the best of care under their protection. It took time. Probably as much time as Dr. Samuel would have needed.

Aunt Isabel and Aunt Iris were movers and shakers in their world, and my mother was not. She was a worrier and a hesitater, not of their people at all.

That evening my mother squared her petite shoulders, marshaled my two brothers, and vanished into the barn. Marjorie and I waited. Finally, Marjorie fed me, and then we waited some more.

Marjorie was dressing me in my snowsuit for a visit to the barn when they staggered in: Mother taut and clutching her forehead, seven-year-old Sammy thoughtful, and ten-year-old Charles wheezing and scratching.

"My God, that boy is allergic to hay, and I think to sheep, too," my mother declared, collapsing into a chair. "So that explains the eczema," she added with a sigh.

"The hay came down on Charles and he got itchy," Sammy expanded. "And he couldn't milk Nellie, and I petted Danny Boy, and I found the paddle for the pig's mash."

Marjorie passed my mother a mug of instant coffee. "Matthew Winters is coming in the morning," she said.

My mother nodded with lips pressed together, eyes closed.

The next morning, I was up early because I wanted to see Matthew Winters spin down the driveway in his pick-up truck. He would swing down from the cab, fresh from his own barn work, and stride to the barn door. He might squint at the sky; men always did that when they wanted to know the weather. He might spit as he reached for the latch, and then he would disappear into the musty darkness to do our barn work.

There below my window I could see a little bent figure wielding a shovel. She was not rhythmically scooping and flinging, like a farm wife would. No, my mother would scratch up a little pile of snow on her shovel, trot to the driveway's edge gripping the shovel stiff in front of her, and pop her little pile of snow onto the lawn with a sudden jerk. I suppose I was proud of my mother for trying, but mostly I was afraid that Matthew Winters would see. My mother was trying so hard to be a farm wife, but anyone could see that she simply wasn't.

Chapter 10

CABIN DAY, NUMBER ONE

Laila plans a cranberry-picking day by way of celebration. Julie and Musko are waiting in the driveway Saturday morning, with a backpack at their feet containing a thermos of coffee, cookie tin of roast beef and tomato sandwiches on whole wheat bread, and doubled plastic bag of extra socks. Julie packed while Doug was online doing snow blower research, and this morning he is still asleep. This seems easier than explaining why she has not included him.

Laila steers her husband's truck, with a battered canoe strapped in the bed, down the driveway. She looks at the empty spot beside Julie but does not ask where Doug is this morning.

"Perfect morning for exploring," Laila exclaims. "Might even be cranberries left, too."

The described goal is a journey to Rachel's cabin, to enjoy the autumn colours along the lake. Cranberries are incidental. It is more accurately, Julie knows, a pilgrimage for Laila, who has not spoken Rachel's name since Thanksgiving. She needs to walk the shore and see the lake and picture her lost friend skimming over the surface of a lake somewhere far away, where she is having adventures and making peace with herself and then returning, to share her discoveries with her friend Laila. And perhaps one evening they will laugh together again in the cabin porch as the moon rises and the loons call over the water. This is not a pilgrimage for which one requires Doug.

They roll past the Park, and soon swing down one of the logging roads that lead to the lakes.

"My God. She lived here?" Julie gasps, clutching at the glove compartment as Laila swings between the larger rocks and eases through the deeper holes.

"Just in summer," Laila sings out. "And she came out a lot, too, seeing people, all that. She liked to stay out there, though, liked to be out trimming brush or canoeing or other kinds of projects, sometimes just reading the afternoon away and feeling guilty. But now that last summer, she said she was mainly doing what she called 'journaling.' She had some issues, and she said the journaling was helping her."

Laila turns into a small clearing near the lake and sets the brake. "She was always trying to figure things out, always analyzing and looking for advice. Then she'd try to follow everyone's advice and then she'd get upset and say everyone was telling her what to do. She felt guilty if she did as they said, and guilty if she didn't. Had a hard time following her own mind. Doug like the old grandmother's room?"

Julie shrugs as she slides out of the truck. "I guess. He's measuring the bathroom so he can bring it up to standard."

"Got much carpentry and plumbing experience?"

"No."

"Well," Laila drawls, "I doubt he'll stay the winter anyway. Seems kinda the restless sort. Where's his family? They in Ontario?"

Julie knows little, in fact, of pre-Reserve Doug. Somehow, it never came up in the conversation, and she has never thought much about it. They were too busy with future plans. The bottom line is, she was busy brooding over her own family, and Doug did not volunteer any information. Perhaps she did not retain the information. The real bottom line is: she did not ask. "I believe he's an only child," she offers.

Laila is working the clamps loose from the canoe seat. "Well," she says, "it don't sound like you know him too well."

Julie frowns, checking her backpack. "I know him well enough."

"But not about him," Laila explains. "You never talked about his family? Met his family? I'd wager you'd know him a lot better if you knew about him." She pauses, hand on the second clamp. "People that's close usually shares things like that. It's part of understanding each other and all."

Julie casts about for a detail, any detail, or failing that, an impression. "I think his parents live somewhere around Mississauga."

"Somewhere around Mississauga," Laila says. "Good thing we aren't looking for them this afternoon or we'd have a lot of territory to cover and a lot of doors to knock on.

"Sounds like somebody might have been a little too busy with her own past."

Julie stiffens.

"Oh, that's just human nature," Laila says. "People get caught up in their own lives. Rachel was a lot like that. And then she'd notice, and she'd feel guilty again. But lots of people get caught up in their own lives, when they're finding their way."

Laila carries others' burdens. She carries your hard things without burdening you with hers. "Did you find your way, Laila?" Julie asks.

"Oh, I get by," Laila grunts, dragging the canoe from the truck bed.

~

The scratched and faded canoe eases along the shallow lake and they clip several rocks as they maneuver along the shore. Voices are raised as Musko pads from side to side in the canoe and then performs his signature gunwale plunge, tipping the left side nearly flush to the surface of the water. Musko circles the canoe, whining and pawing, because he would like to pad and jump again. Musko is ignored, and alternately swims and romps along the shore.

"Cabin'll be all grown in, I expect," Laila says as they swing into the cove. "Brush won't have been trimmed since the summer before this last one."

Musko is posing on a massive boulder, tail flopping side to side as they lift the canoe over the rocks and up the bank.

Laila purses her lips, hands on her hips as she studies the clearing. "Well, somebody's been here," she announces. "Brush was cut this summer. Shed's been freshly stained, too."

Julie had expected a true bush camp, a small teetering structure built from lumber scraps, not this well-constructed almost cottage. It is neatly stained in a rust shade, with solid shingles on the roof and a screened-in porch. Broad windows face the south. The rusted stove pipe is the only anomaly.

"She was going to do the stove when she started coming down winters," Laila explains, following her gaze.

There should be a deck and boardwalks and a neat floating dock. Instead, someone has built an attractive cabin and dropped it in a roughed-out clearing facing a reedy, untouched cove. There is no sign of a pump, and a weathered outhouse droops in the background beside a meandering trail. The yard is a mass of rocks, roots, hummocks, and dips, exposed among the closely shorn brush. Parts of the site are trim and neat; others, untouched, protrude. Some parts mattered to the owner, it seems, and others did not. There is no underlying connection to unite the site.

"She liked to sit in that porch and listen for loons," Laila says. "And we'd talk."

She reaches under the porch sill and produces a key. "Locks is meant to keep honest people out," she quotes, pulling open the porch door and stepping between wood pile and storage boxes. She unlocks the door and pushes it wide.

A basic second-hand table and chairs are arranged by the south windows, very functional storm windows set in the frames. Matching arm chairs rest at each end of the main room, with a neat couch along the north wall. Wicker end tables rest on either side, one tipped close to the rusted wood stove. There is a painted grey floor with a green, dog-hair-matted rug. The walls, meanwhile, are panelled in rich knotty pine. Another anomaly.

"She bought it like that, and picked it up a bit, but she just liked it, the way it was."

So Rachel liked good panelling, and could sit in her seamy porch, knowing it was there, and the rest didn't matter. Or so it seems.

Laila sniffs the stale air of the cabin, glancing back at the wood stacked in the porch. "Someone's had a fire," she says. "Rachel never trusted that stove, and the trees so close...."

She turns and jogs back through the porch, disappearing behind the cabin. "Those branches are all cut back," she calls. She works her way down to one knee, rubbing ferns and leaves between her fingers. "These was just cut this fall. Someone's sure been here."

"Hunters?" Julie suggests.

"No, no. Usually deer hunters out this way and it's too early. And they wouldn't be wasting their time, doing all this."

"Samuel?"

Laila shakes her head. "Oh, it wouldn't be Samuel. He's got enough to do. He wouldn't be out here, I'd think..."

Julie does not say Rachel, because Rachel should have, would have, kept in touch, and included the friend who sat on the porch and waited for loons while she listened and listened. This is the hardest anomaly.

Julie wanders down to the lake and stares at the islands, patches of faded gold and red clinging amid the emerging grey. A white shape appears at the point, ears pricked, tail pluming across its back. It looks like a white Siberian husky, but it must be a large coyote. A canoe, dark green or blue, edges around the point, pauses, and slips back out of sight. The white shape melts back into the bush. Perhaps it is an early hunter, or a day explorer, photographing the passing into late autumn, his Husky at his side.

Julie wants to paddle out and tell him that she, too, is a canoer of shorelines.

"There's new supplies in here," Laila calls out from the kitchen. "And the note's gone."

It is Rachel, then, Rachel, lost these many months, her canoe a scrap of blue fibreglass as yet unfound, her dogs roaming, starving, and now she ghosts the shores.

Or it is Rachel, hidden these many months, living God knows how, her faithful dogs guarding her secrets as Laila once did.

And when Rachel had filled Laila with all her secrets, she cast her off.

No. That cannot be the way it happened. Rachel is on stress leave somewhere, and the family is ashamed to say so. They are old-fashioned about these things. And the dogs—well, they were old, after all, or perhaps are in care somewhere. There is a photographer with a Husky, and he is a canoer of shorelines, like Julie. A canoer? Isn't it canoeist? But she is not a canoeist. No, she is a canoer. They are different; one is trained and in control and aloof, and the other fumbling along but oh, so close to the teachings of the shore. Rachel would probably be a canoer of shorelines, too.

"Maybe she sold the place," Julie offers. "Or, the estate did, or something."

Do not say these things to Laila. Do not hurt Laila. Rachel should not have hurt Laila.

"She'd'a said," Laila says evenly.

~

They pull camp chairs down from the rafters and picnic dutifully in the weak October sun. Laila makes half-hearted jests about getting in those cranberries and Julie tries to be the listener in the porch, for Laila needs a listener now.

"When Doug left," Julie says, "he just left, like that. Like nothing we shared ever mattered. Like nothing I was ever mattered."

"Rachel is not Doug," Laila mutters. "She'd have to change an awful lot to be like that. Still, Nathaniel didn't seem too concerned. Now, Samuel, he was awful upset, but more of a mad upset, you know?" She sighs. "If Rachel was gone, I mean, really gone, he would have said."

"But did they ever say," Julie persists, "that they didn't know? Or did they just not say? I mean, some people stay in denial, and then there's still the stigma of mental illness."

"Oh, for heaven sake," Laila actually snaps. "We thought of all that. No, it's more likely she did something she decided was foolish, like maybe she decided to buy that farm back and got all that fight going again, and decided to hide out and 'not be a burden' anymore. Always going on about 'I ruined your visit with all my complaining,' like real friends couldn't take all that. She wouldn't be the first one in that family to just disappear."

Laila drops her face into her hands and sighs. "I don't know what's come over me today," she says. "A beautiful fall day and bushes just bristling with cranberries. Too perfect to waste." She rises, scanning the lake. "Just a perfect day for the lake," she declares.

They pass an hour meandering along the shore, plucking a few weathered cranberries rejected by the birds and bears. Laila wanders off along the back trail—looking for signs, or perhaps heading for the outhouse—and Julie returns to the cabin to organize their gear.

The need to explore the cabin is overpowering.

The east end is a panelled bedroom, windows facing the lake. There is a rough bed frame, covered with an air mattress and musty blanket, two sleeping bags rolled and hanging on the wall. A blue plastic bin of towels and blankets rests in the corner, but otherwise it is bare. She treads across the worn rug in the main room and surveys the array of jugs and water buckets in the kitchen area that forms the west end. A set of bunk beds nestles in the north side. The upper bunk has paint-stained jeans and T-shirt, scraps of lumber, and a few tools. The lower bunk has an air mattress, with two plastic bins sandwiched at the foot. The larger is empty; the smaller contains a few clothes: shorts, faded T-shirts, a stretched and faded swimsuit. A plastic bag covers a file folder that is crammed down the side.

Julie is not Doug, but she lifts it free, just the same.

The file folder contains a loose pile of creased and unmatched paper, aged by dampness. Sets of pages are separated by folded sheets of paper, each labeled with a chapter number. The top sheet, enfolding them all, reads: "Sunrise Cove Journal—dedicated to my betrayed brothers, Samuel and Charles; to my golden son Nathaniel; to my beloved Saima and Mikijuk, true friends and bearers of secrets; and to faithful Taggak, loyal companion and guardian. I ask to be forgiven for who I am, for who I have been, and for who I will be."

Julie fumbles the first pages, skimming the words. It is all about snakes and dreams and betrayal and hurting people and being lost. It is raw and elemental and yet self-absorbed. She skims on, for this is the story of Rachel, and it is not so far from the story of Julie.

The porch door creaks open and Julie shuffles the pages into order, poking the file into the plastic bag. She is smoothing it with both hands and opening her day pack as Laila enters.

Laila leans back in the arm chair by the door. "One night we was out here on Rachel's birthday, and we phoned her aunt, all the way to the Yukon on her cellphone. How we got through, I'll never know; that thing hardly worked out here. What you got there?" she finishes.

Julie shrugs, cheeks reddening. One does not tell Laila that she has found Rachel's journal while looking through her personal things, and is entitled to it because it has her very words, from her own dream, and it is almost her story. The words make sense in her mind but not out loud to Laila. One also does not say she is taking it for Samuel, for his closure, for that would be a lie. She begins to cram the folder in its tattered plastic bag into her pack and tries to saunter to the porch.

Laila holds out a hand. Julie places the folder in that hand, because there is no alternative, really.

Laila's eyes skim the first page. Her lips tighten and she nods. "Journals is mighty private things. That's for Samuel, and Charles, and Nathaniel. It's for here. When they're ready."

"But look. Look at what she says on the first page. I know those words."

Laila turns her face away. "That don't matter. It's not for you. Put it back."

"After all she did—"

"Did?" Laila turns her gaze back to Julie. "Did? It's not for you to decide. Or for you to judge. Or me. Put it back now."

It is then that Julie notices the red eyes, and remembers the un-Laila-like bitterness of before. The bitterness is gone now, and Laila looks lonely in a way that no amount of baking or cranberry picking or cheerful living in the present is going to fix.

"There's these little dog bones, up on the rise. Not buried deep enough, I guess. Probably both them smaller dogs. They was getting on." Laila's eyes brim with tears. "She should a' called," she whispers. "She should a' let her friends help her. That's what friends do."

All militant building of a new life once your children and your friends have moved on fails at this moment. Laila is a saddened woman now, one who has built her life step by lonely step, giving and giving, but who gives to Laila, who has given all?

Musko bounds up the steps, splattering mud and water and scrambling his bulk across Laila's lap. His sides heave as his great tongue reaches for her face. Laila sits rocking in the camp chair, her arms about his shaggy neck.

"Oh, Musko. The world needs a lot more Musko," Laila croons.

~

They lock the cabin and canoe back along the shore to the landing where the truck is. Julie, paddling bow, glances back and there is a dark green or blue canoe, sole occupant steering around the point above Rachel's cabin. A white head and shoulders follow the canoe.

"There's that canoe again," Julie says.

"Oh, lots of people go exploring here," Laila replies, scanning the surface for rocks. "Rachel always took her dogs, the little ones hopping in and out of the canoe in their little life jackets, and her big white dog—her mostly Husky, she called him—a-churnin' along behind."

A chill ripples down Julie's back, and she does not tell Laila about the white dog behind the canoe.

Laila is vulnerable now, and does not need chance hopes. It is not Rachel out there, in the flesh or in the spirit, haunting the places that made her own dreams. It is simply a canoer, more likely a canoeist, exploring the autumn beauty with his big white dog.

It is not Rachel; it is not Taggak.

It is not part of Laila's memories.

Samuel and Nathaniel are not being very kind to Laila. Laila deserves kindness and trust and fairness, and Julie will find a way to make it right.

Samuel needs understanding and healing and happy endings to his dreams and then maybe he will be fairer to Laila. Julie will find a way to make this right, too.

Nathaniel lives in the North, learning from his father and following his grandfather. She does not know what he needs, but she suspects that he, too, has many things that need to be made right.

She wishes she could read the journal.

Doug would. She is not Doug.

Julie has the dreams, instead. This is not comforting.

She hugs Musko, her own true friend and bearer of secrets, her faithful companion and guardian. If she is not careful, she will become the Hardys.

It is time to break the pattern and invite her parents for the weekend. They have been hovering in the wings for over two months, paddles clenched, awaiting their cue, so eager.

First, though, she should settle the matter of Samuel and Laila and the journal. Even before that, she must settle the matter of Doug. Then maybe, just maybe, when Doug and Samuel and Laila and the journal are sorted out, there will be a definite place in the world for Julie.

Chapter 11

CARETAKERS AND
HANDYMEN

A ll matters come to a head on Sunday afternoon, while the rain
drizzles down and the cooling earth breathes out the raw odour
of decaying leaves. All matters come to a head, but the resolution, as all
resolutions involving Julie and the Hardys seem to be, is vague at best.

Samuel's aged blue sedan eases past the old well and turns neatly
in front of the garage. Samuel pulls up beside the lawn along the back
verandah and hauls himself out of the car. He is rocking the empty
canoe racks, testing their tightness as he stares down across the orchard.

Julie hurries out the back door, pulling a worn plaid work shirt over
her sweater, and centres herself on the back verandah. She is unprepared tenant greeting unexpected landlord. She is embarrassed hostess,
hoping to hide an embarrassing houseguest.

"Samuel," she says, tugging the work shirt closer over her shoulders.
"Are you coming in?"

The sink is almost clean, the floors are almost swept, if cluttered,
and the rugs are cheerful, if hairier than they were. Doug is sulking in

his room, working on his computer, because he did not know about her damn picnic yesterday until it was over.

Samuel turns. "In. Well. I mean, the notice . . ."

"Never mind, never mind. Come in out of the rain."

Stay in that room, Doug.

Samuel plods across the lawn and stands beside her on the verandah, scrutinizing the crab apple tree beside the garage.

"That blooms on a different side every spring," he says. "Should be the garage side, next year. Much fruit, this fall?"

Julie has been mowing and raking. There is still some mowing and much raking to do; the front yard is again clogged with leaves, the final leaves of fall, the maple leaves and the oak leaves. This year, she has not been harvesting. Next year, she will do all things and do them well. There are just so many of them. She shrugs. "I honestly didn't get around to looking much this year. But next year—"

"Used to be bushels and bushels."

Julie beams and nods. "Really. That must have been something. Going canoeing?"

Samuel's gaze turns to the empty roof rack. "No, I was not going canoeing. I was picking up someone. My nephew is doing some exploring in the back country up past Kedge."

Julie gapes. "Your nephew? Nathaniel? He's here?"

Samuel shrugs. "Nephews do visit their uncles from time to time. I suppose Laila has filled you in. She would know, I'm sure."

Julie tugs the work-shirt sleeves over her arms. "Just a little. Like, he's living up in Labrador, doing a few different things up there. She used to babysit him when he was four. She's fond of him."

"Yeah, well—that's good. But maybe he doesn't feel like being monitored right now. And maybe I don't feel like being monitored right now."

Julie gropes for a way to restore harmony. She can only do this at Laila's expense. "I take it you would rather I did not mention this conversation to Laila," she says.

"Exactly. Right." Samuel's gaze returns to the crab apple tree. "Some things are personal."

Nathaniel is looking for his mother. He is drifting along a shore line, seeking signs of a lost magic that will bind his present and his past back together. He is solitary, so solitary. The fragments of his childhood cut deep into his being.

Recognition dawns. "That was him. I saw him," Julie gasps. "Laila and I went cranberrying up near your sister's cabin. I saw a canoe, and a dog."

"Yeah, a big white dog, swimming behind the canoe. He's getting a little old for that."

"And, Laila said it was OK to go inside. . . ."

"Oh. Sure. She used to go up there every summer. Sometimes check the place in the fall. Not many people went out there, kind of off the beaten track, not a place that you'd just drop in while you were in the area. No, that's not a problem. So. See any snakes?"

"In October?"

"Sure. Especially since it's been warm."

Julie scans the flagstones that line the verandah, peeking down the steps that lead into the hollyhocks. "I thought they were all gone." She has been walking among the snakes all October, then. "I'm not too good around snakes," she admits.

"Neither was my sister," he replies. "I'm not sure what she was trying to prove out there. Or here." He sighs. "Or now."

"She's still teaching? Ontario, was it?"

Samuel is staring at the crab apple tree again. "There was a flowering crab, too. My aunt Iris planted it in memory of my father. Now, when did that disappear?"

"Where?"

"There. In front of the grape vine. Near the peonies. You didn't hit it with the mower, by any chance?"

Julie shakes her head. "There never was a tree, or bush, or anything there. Just grass."

"Well. I wonder when that disappeared. It was kind of special. That's too bad."

There is plain lawn there, no dips or dents or stray shoots. It has been lawn for a long time.

"Samuel, there's a journal out there at the cabin. Well, like a stack of papers, but it looks like something you might want to read or something."

Samuel shrugs his shoulders and straightens his back. "Yeah. Nathaniel said. He said that, too. I suppose we should take it away, but he says she wanted it to stay there. 'It is meant to be read there.'"

"We didn't read it."

"Oh, I'm sure."

"Do you go out there, much?"

Samuel scowls. "As if I didn't have enough to do already." He stares at the door. "Anyway. How's your friend like it here?"

Julie wants to ask about Nathaniel. Has he returned to stay? Is the dog his mother's dog, faithful Taggak? Why does he hide from them, leaving no sign of his passing? Why didn't Samuel go out there with him, and enjoy an autumn afternoon?

However, the reason for this visit is now clear: Who is this Doug and what is he doing here and when is he leaving? Samuel has been talking to Laila—gathering his information but surrendering none of what he knows but perhaps he really does not know—or perhaps he has instead been gassing up in the village. *That new feller seems friendly. Always willing to help out. He'll have to be careful, though, with that big dog and the deer season and all.*

Samuel, what is going on in your family? she thinks. "He's been here for a few days. I'm not sure, exactly, but I think he'll be leaving, fairly soon," she says.

"Oh, no. That's OK," Samuel assures her. "It's just—you know. You're responsible for guests, and all, and well, you know how it goes." Samuel shifts his feet, struggling in the role of firm but kindly landlord.

Doug chooses this moment to sweep through the door, hand extended. "Well, well, well. This has to be our landlord. Good." He pumps Samuel's hand. "Doug Simmons. Now. I need to go over a few things I'd like to get done as soon as possible."

Samuel wipes his fingers on his jeans pocket. "Yeah. I see. But since it isn't a—um—a joint lease, it's Julie here that I'll be talking to. About all that."

Doug closes on the hesitancy. "Sure. Whatever. But I think we're all on the same page here. That tub, you have to admit, is a real sight, and I've drawn up some plans to re-do the whole bathroom. I can get the parts and supplies—you know, ask around, get a deal." Doug nods knowingly as if he frequents used appliance stores on a regular basis. "Now, since I'll be doing the work, we could deduct the whole thing in instalments from the rent, you see."

"No." Samuel swings his head from left to right and back. "I've been down this road before."

"And if you like the results, I could maybe insulate that attic up there." Too late, Doug realizes his mistake. Samuel's eyes are already widening. "It probably does need insulating; it stands to reason, after all. It's old." Doug nods. "Yes. It is old, and that usually means insulation, and maybe floor work," he trails off.

"OK. That's fine." Samuel's voice tightens. "You have plans. Good. And you know what? I don't care. That's my attic. OK? Yeah. I don't need this. You got that? And I don't need you. Or this hassle. You don't like it here? Then go. Just, you know, leave."

He rounds on Julie. "And if you don't like that, then you can just leave, too."

"Under the Tenancy Act," Doug intones.

Julie closes her eyes, cringing for wheeling-and-dealing Doug and for Samuel, who is trying so hard to be the no-nonsense, tough land-lord. Samuel should live here, she tells herself, and love this place and grow old here, steeped in rich memories. Mean, cynical people who scoff at him and tell joking stories about his mother will not be allowed.

She will see to all this, because she will be more than tenant; she will be caretaker.

As the two men stare at her, Julie hears that last word, plain on the air. She hopes that she did not say everything out loud. This is not the dream time. People hear. They remember.

"I see myself as more of a caretaker." She swallows. "You know? No big changes. Maybe curtains or paint. Kind of keeping the house—intact? Um, preserve the character, kind of, maybe?"

Samuel brightens. "Yeah. Yeah. That's all I had in mind. Why is it so hard for everyone to just see that?"

He and Julie both fix their gaze on Doug, who flings up his hands and utters a brief, mirthless laugh. "OK, you guys. So I got carried away. Don't worry. I'll behave. There's plenty of work out there for someone willing to work hard. Elsewhere, though. Elsewhere. Not a problem."

Doug's capitulation restores Julie to her position as favoured tenant. She can stay. Doug, her presumed guest, will be able to stay, too. There will be no return to the gentle rhythm of pre-Thanksgiving. She will have money for oil and paint and quaint curtains and here is Doug to oversee and organize. At least, there is Musko.

"And Musko likes it here," Doug is saying.

"Musko." Samuel's worried gaze fixes on the screen door, and he straightens his shoulders to prepare for more enthusiastic handymen.

A joyful "whuff" issues from the porch, and then a huge shaggy face fills the screen.

"Musko is a Cree word," Doug is saying in his lecturer's voice. "It means 'Black Bear,' and in this case you can see –"

Musko is scrambling at the screen now, and Julie forces the door back and lunges for Musko's collar.

Musko launches himself at Samuel.

"Well. There's a good dog. Yeah. A good old dog. Well. Aren't cha, fellah?"

Musko wriggles against Samuel, his tail pounding against the landlord's leg.

119

"Yeah. Musko. You don't care about bathtubs. No."

Musko slobbers his tongue across Samuel's hand.

"He's housetrained," Julie remarks, because there seems to be nothing else to say in this situation. Samuel continues to croon over Musko, as Doug retreats into the house, muttering about coffee.

"Why don't you and Nathaniel stop by for supper on your way down?" Julie offers. Perhaps then, there will be some real answers to her real questions.

Samuel rubs Musko's ear. "Nathaniel." He straightens and glances at the door through which Doug just exited. "Nathaniel is not really into socializing just now. So, no. Thanks. He's got some things to do, and decisions to make, and I was wondering, well, would you mind?"

"Oh. That's all right. I understand." At some level, she almost does. "I'm the only one who saw him, and I'll just—no problem. Sure."

She will just betray Laila, true friend and companion, who babysat Nathaniel when he was four, and wiped his tears and took him on special picnics. This is the first secret from Laila.

"All right. Good." Samuel gives Musko's ear a final, gentle tug. "Now, your friend. Is he going to be all right here?" He nods toward the door.

"Oh. I'm sure. He's just stopping here for a while. He gets—enthusiastic, but he's OK. Sure."

Samuel's face closes. "Let me know, I guess. Well, Nathaniel will be pretty wet, by now. My father liked canoeing this time of year when he was young, but he never had time later on. Anyway."

He hurries to his car in the raw drizzle, and departs with a feeble toot to the horn.

~

Matters have indeed come to a head, but there has been no resolution. Julie hears echoes of other conversations in the air, of thoughts half formed and hints half given, of abrupt twists in the direction of the words, and nothing ever completed or resolved. She suspects that the

Hardys have regularly engaged in these incomplete moments, in which clarity and focus are absent. In which apology and forgiveness are bypassed. The Hardys muddle on with their lives, but they do not truly live. They analyze, they argue perhaps, and they react to one another. They do not respond. Julie suspects all this, and it is somehow familiar.

November is coming, and with it, her contract. She is still here, and Musko is still here.

Doug is in her kitchen, making coffee in her coffeepot. "A real piece of work, that one," she hears him mutter.

Doug will continue to measure and scheme. He has not given up on the attic. Perhaps it is better to have him here, in sight, than skulking around the perimeter of her life, unseen. Yes. She has done well to arrange this.

She knows that this is a Hardy explanation, as she and Musko head out along the old truck road into the cooling afternoon, the raw odour of leaves stirring at their feet, hinting of unseen snakes.

THE OWL

Meadowbrook Acres was not the right place for me. I lightened it, I brightened it, but it remained shadowed. There were movements and lights in the night, and I was afraid. There were voices and scenes from my childhood in each corner, sweet and gentle, yet suffocating me. I always felt that I was pounding my fists against thick wooden planks and if anyone heard, they were simply annoyed because I was disturbing their own scenes.

I tried to make it mine. I stripped the decaying woodhouse and built a pretty porch. I tore down the barn, and sat amid my flowers on my pretty porch, watching the field roll down to the woods, over the site of the once barn. I planned to move the kitchen into the main house. I would open the kitchen into a workshop, a studio of sorts, and rip out the ceiling to expose the attic. Light would stream through a skylight in the roof, down through the rugged ceiling beams, which I would leave intact. There would be a little loft over the pantry. It would be an artist's studio, and I would invite my brother to paint there, in the artist's studio I had caused to be built.

In one dream, there was a rope over one beam, there, in the east window. A body drooped in the noose, slowly turning. The body could be any body.

The face was mine.

I put Meadowbrook Acres on the market the next day.

I hurt my brother so badly.

~

The changes had bewildered him but now, seeing his birthplace slipping away, he grieved. He bought that place, in the end, although he didn't have the money or time for it, because, otherwise, where would he make his own dreams?

I did not tell him that I was haunted there, because that place was, is, and always will be *his*, whoever lives there. He does not have to wrestle it or compel it, because he belongs there, and it cannot haunt him. Yet he must look forever over the barn-less wastes, and dream of what might have been. That is what I did to him.

Yet I resented him for it.

I face them all now; I call upon them all to come to me here at Wasaya, my last battlefield. Come to me, that I might be delivered.

Perhaps, on the other side, there is a life that is rightly mine.

~

I wanted a place that would be a sanctuary for me and for my son. I saw him canoeing along the shore, growing wise in the midst of nature. I did not see that he was already growing up and away, and had already in his heart found his sanctuary along the distant rocky coast of his father's land.

When I first saw Wasaya, I opened the cabin door and in the gloomy half-light felt a rush of freedom and joy. I was brave there. This was the place. I did not know then that when you are truly haunted, the memories will find and hold you, wherever you go. They will drive out the freedom and the joy.

You travel far, and find you are alone, with no one willing or unwilling to listen to and understand your stories. You become another husk with withered roots, out there in a dusty field.

I need to live the stories down, and so here in Wasaya, with the breeze sweet and the lake shimmering, with the scent of pine resin in my nostrils, I make my stand after all.

I discipline myself here at Wasaya, and I open myself to the memories. Let them come. Here at Wasaya, they will either release me or consume me. I open myself to them.

Now I am pounding and screaming through the thick planks and there are voices on the other side, but they are chatting about something else. My story is important, I am screaming. Listen to it. Their voices are muffled, but I think that they are telling their own stories. Or perhaps they are telling their own story of me, a distorted story, and I am not really in it at all.

They have their story of the owl, as it was for them.

I know the real story, and I need one person to understand it. Then there will not be a dangling body with my face, somewhere in the shadows.

~

I was afraid of my father when he returned to us. When Marjorie and I came back from our walk one day, he was in the dining room, hands in pockets, staring out the west window. He wore town clothes, and he smelled of medicine. He was taller, more broad-shouldered than I remembered. I saw darkness over and around him, and I tiptoed to the kitchen to practise my letters so that I could go to Grade 1 in September. The school was, after all, just out of sight around the bend in the river, and that was too far away for a five-year-old, even with two brothers and a parent in the same building. Meanwhile, the girl who would become my seat mate in Grade 1 got to walk a mile to the bus stop to learn her letters in the classroom. If I had walked a mile each day to learn my letters in the classroom, would I have grown up strong and free, as I have always dreamed of being? Would I still have been afraid of my father that day?

Everyone else was happy to see my father, and to be near him. I kept retreating to another room whenever he came near. I would not hug him, and I would not participate in the bedtime ritual of the good night kiss. "Isn't that the strangest thing," they observed. "Don't you love Daddy?" they reproached me.

Oh, I did, but I could smell the medicine and sickness-just-past thick on his body. The frozen hands sickness was hovering in the darkness that was over and around my father, and if I came near, it would seize me. I would be in the malicious grip of the frozen hands sickness, and then Aunt Iris and Aunt Isabel would drag me off to Liverpool and Dr. Lloyd, not Dr. Samuel, would be the one to save my life. So I did not kiss his dry cheek at bedtime, even to prove that I did love him.

Each night I crept up the stairs, my heart breaking for my father, but even then fearing that I had come too close, and that the sickness and my aunts would come.

Valentine's Day approached and I came up with a plan. Sometimes Marjorie is handing me paper and crayons; other times, it is entirely my plan. With a red crayon I drew pages of clumsy hearts, scouring the interiors red and hacking them out with dull scissors. Each evening I dashed near my father's chair and deposited a curled fistful on the end table. Good-night kisses, I explained. Solemnly, he kissed each one, and tucked them in his shirt pocket, his eyes still sad.

After a week of this, I knew I would have to be brave.

I braced myself, fists clenching and unclenching, and then flung myself across the room, my arms wrapped around his neck. And I kissed him three times on the cheek. I waited, exultant: let the frozen hands sickness come; let the aunts come. I was not afraid of them. Let them do their worst. Let them just try.

My mother settled in her chair, satisfied that the rebellion had been put down and that I had stopped punishing them all. My father said that he had a surprise for me. Cupping his hands, he counted one, two, three, swinging his cupped hands at each count. His hands popped apart and there was a little pin on his palm. It was an owl's face, flat and blue and plastic, with black around its eyes. The eyes flitted to the side, not wise but mischievous, secretive.

I kept that pin in my musical jewelry box, and when I emptied out the house at Meadowbrook Acres, I extracted the pin and tucked it in my small trunk of special memories. First Communion gloves, school certificates and awards, and other childhood treasures are gone, but the owl remains.

I never look at the owl, but it pleases me to know that it is there. I do not think of it as a token from my father, to celebrate the day that his little girl started loving him again. I think of it, rather, as a reminder that once I was brave. I faced the frozen hands sickness and being taken away by aunts to save a heart from breaking. I was powerful that day.

Tell me, I say to my students. I will not be shocked. Tell me your truth, and I will strive to understand.

For I defeated the frozen hands sickness when I was five years old, and everyone thought I was just stubborn.

Chapter 12

PREPARATIONS

The last leaves are bagged or dragged away, the tree limbs reach stark and brittle to the darkening sky, and Julie sinks more deeply into the files that will inform her teaching for the next eight months. There are standard scores, percentile rankings, and grade equivalents. The trick is to absorb the numbers while seeking the child locked behind them. Simon read cereal boxes, slowly and well. Simon could not be explained by these numbers. Simon would emerge low, very low, in these scores, and would have to be referred to the educational psychologist, who would probably find a learning disability. Simon would be defined. But would this definition be Simon?

Take, for example, Tina, a Grade 7 student. In the eighth month of the sixth grade, Tina demonstrated vocabulary recognition equivalent to that of a child in the fourth month of the third grade. Of course, this is just the mid-point in a broader range that Tina could be in. Perhaps Tina was sick that day, her stomach cramping and her attention lagging. Or, possibly, someone had stolen *her* dog that day, and vocabulary recognition was not her main concern. Is Tina's first language English, or perhaps a dialect of English that differs in content and patterns from the standardized test? The tests indicate a pattern of need, but is this pattern Tina?

"Were the Grade 3s in the sample used in comparison perhaps exceptionally verbose," Julie muses, "so that Tina, scoring in their range, is actually at grade level?" She is grinning as she shares this thought with the teacher she is replacing.

The about-to-go-on-maternity-leave teacher's lips close in a thin line. "That is highly unlikely in such a broad sample," she says. "We look to the *range*."

She speaks with authority and with experience and without humour. Her dark eyes flit over Julie and her eyes narrow. Julie speaks without authority; she is inexperienced and untried and a possible threat to the children's progress if she is unwilling to work with the best professional research available. It is the unprofessional sorts who scoff at well-documented results; they go by gut and instinct and the children go nowhere.

"Just speculating," Julie assures her, "about testing overall. Of course, it is our best indicator."

The teacher relaxes, but only slightly. There is a rebel lurking within this new one, suppressed but definitely present. The children's needs must come first—this fact overrides any personal philosophy. This new one should be monitored closely.

Julie feels the measure of those eyes. She feels the haphazardness of her own experience, her passion and impatience with procedure when innovation might serve her better. She knows that passion and impatience with procedure can harm a child. She knows, too, that innovation sometimes can help a child. It is a sacred trust, a delicate balance, an overwhelming responsibility.

She wonders if she was the only candidate available.

"Following directions shows some good scores," she observes, in an effort to redeem herself.

"Visual references," the teacher replies. "All those pictures in that set. She processes visual information. That's the pattern that first suggested that there is a relative strength in visual areas, but a weakness in verbal.

All indicative of a verbally based learning disability. All confirmed, of course, by an educational psychologist." She lowers her eyes.

Julie applies herself to the files, making safe clinical remarks. She wonders to herself if Tina is shy.

~

Janice Reid drops by after the last bell, while Julie is studying work folders.

"I could never handle all the paperwork that goes with resource," she announces.

"Oh, but you have unit plans and all that marking," Julie says.

"Which you also have to study so that you can deliver the best programming to my students. And I'm really just accountable to the students, their parents, and the administration. You, on the other hand, get to be responsible to everyone on the planet. Twice over." She plops into a student chair. "So how's the farm?"

Julie tucks the work folder into its drawer. Does Janice mean the farm-her, the farm-Doug, or the farm-Samuel? "Fine," she says, to cover them all.

Janice grins, her petite nose almost twitching, her brown eyes twinkling. "Laila tells me your partner is a teacher. Will he be subbing here?"

Julie tidies papers into neat stacks and lines up pens. "He's not my partner, not really. I guess he was, once, but, not now. Just visiting. And I think he's looking for a career change."

Janice settles into the stiff vinyl chair as deeply as possible. "I see." She examines the clock. "Not many people move to rural Nova Scotia to find a new career, but you never know. I take it he's the one who extended the invitation. I think that pile is neat enough now," she points out.

Julie selects a pen and starts sketching a horse on the top sheet. She learned to sketch a horse once, step by step, because she likes horses, the way they look and move. It is the one subject that she sketches well, and she hopes that it makes her look relaxed, perhaps a little mysterious. That Julie Martin can draw, you know. She has a hidden talent. She is calm, and aloof, and professional, as she sketches the one thing she can sketch.

"In a way," she mumbles.

Janice leans forward, arms folded on the work table. "Listen. Rachel worked here for a while. She was probably a good teacher, but she didn't really have it together. Classroom management issues, big time."

"What did she teach?"

"She did supply work. Kind of when they were stuck and had the time to watch over her."

"Watch over her?"

"You know. For Rose. She had good ideas, but she just didn't have consistency. Or confidence."

"Ah." Julie pens in a flowing mane, hoping to radiate confidence.

"Anyway," Janice breezes on. "My advice to you is to dump that place. It's quaint and fun for a while, but it's gloomy as hell and your heating bills are going to be beyond your wildest dreams. Rent a little bungalow and spend your diminishing free time walking that big dog of yours—he's yours, right?—instead of picking at cobwebs and mildew.

"I don't think that place was good for Rachel and I don't think it's good for you. It needs a big, cheery family to keep the ghosts at bay."

Doug, in any capacity, does not constitute a big or cheery family.

"I've done a few things, to brighten the place up," Julie says.

"Last ones painted it top to bottom." Janice waves a dismissive hand. "That place was never meant to be cheerful.

"Rose Hardy, if local history is in any way accurate, was a perky young thing when she married Stephen Hardy and moved in. Joined the choir, part of the book club, entertained. Years passed, and she perked less. Very strict about whom the kids mingled with. She and her husband were practically recluses by the time Rachel and her brothers moved out. Came out less and less, more and more aloof. Like visitors, not like residents, when they did come out. She basically shut down, after her husband died. Anyway, she went from being a little strange to full-blown dementia and then she was gone."

"A little strange, how?" Julie is reworking the withers, no longer concentrating on the results.

"Little things. She'd wander into the store, like she hadn't been there for years and years, greeting people like she couldn't believe she was finally seeing them again, then regaling them with every tiny detail of something insignificant, say, how she boiled an egg that morning."

"She sounds lonely." Julie puts down the pen.

"Oh, that she was. People said she needed to get out more, but I don't think she could. That place got to her. It pulled her in—and down. That's my vote."

Julie's mind drifts to the opening pages of the journal: grief and snakes and pleas for forgiveness. The Hardys and Meadowbrook Acres. Samuel's legacy.

"So, there were other children in the family? Rachel and Samuel, and?"

"Charles." Janice runs a hand through her short sandy hair. Janice's hair has body; Julie feels hers, flat to her scalp. "He was before my time. Settled in Newfoundland, I think. He used to come down when Rose was alive, but I don't think he's around much, now. Or maybe he is and I don't know about it. That is possible." She stretches, and bounces to her feet. "Well, I've got to get going. Jenna and Mark adore Laila, but we do have a schedule, after all. Riding lessons at six."

She swings her bulging canvas bag to her shoulder. "We'll have to get together. Doug, too—it is Doug, right?—if you want. It's a long winter."

With another grin and a quick wave, Janice is striding down the corridor.

Doug, too, if you want, and it is a long winter. Doug probably is here for the long winter. Rose Hardy lived there, without even a Doug to occupy her mind, in the long winter. That is something to think about.

~

A Canoe of Shorelines

The evenings at Meadowbrook Acres are long now. Doug mutters over his laptop in the once dining room, a hollow shell in which he has arranged planks and trestles, found in the dusty garage, into the semblance of a rustic table. She hopes that the planks are bug-free. Doug mutters over snow blowers, and Julie applies thick primer to veneer panelling and thinks of journals and heating bills and Doug. And lonely old women who report to the store to describe their breakfast. People listen because what else can you do?

"Doug, why did you leave Alberta?" Julie calls from the kitchen.

Doug snorts, clicking a new site open. "I told you. It wasn't my thing."

"I mean, isn't it unusual to terminate a contract in September?"

"Oh, for Christ's sake." Doug leans back, slapping his palms against the planks. The trestles wobble. "Isn't it bad enough, losing my job, without you analyzing it to death like you really knew what was going on? Just picking away at my life, like I need to go over it again and again. Listen this time: seniority issues. OK? Seniority issues. No contesting it. Clear cut. So I'm here. Oh. Hey now. Look at this. Now *this* is the machine for us—portable, affordable, available. What do you think?"

"I think Tom has the right idea."

Doug's gaze reproaches her. "That's what did us in the last time," he says. "I was always the one on the outside. You never supported me about anything."

Julie is not about to point out that supportiveness involves dialogue, not his monologue punctuated by her agreements at intervals. Doug is enthusiastic about the snow blower. He was also enthusiastic about Alberta. Before that it was North Bay. And before that, it was just teaching. And somewhere, woven through one phase or another, it was Julie.

Right now he is not enthusiastic about Julie, but he is enthusiastic about being here. Julie is a convenient backdrop for the snow blower project.

Julie regrets the affection she wasted, and speculates that Rose Hardy probably staved off strangeness and dementia longer without a Doug.

132

"Doug, why exactly are you here?"

Doug scoops up the laptop and mutters up the stairs to Grandma Mary's room. Musko rolls a lazy head in his direction from the den, grunts, and settles back to sleep.

The dining room and den are separated only by a broad archway, with additional archways opening between the dining room and front hall, and living room and front hall. Samuel has told her that these were once separate rooms. The den and west end of the dining room were bedrooms, but after his father's siblings were gone, his grandfather decided to open the spaces to lighten the place. It must have been extremely dark and grim in the old days.

Today is Friday, and Monday is the first official day of Julie's contract. Julie will be a teacher in her own right, that day. She will establish plans, and set an agenda. She will build rapport with her teaching colleagues and especially with her students, teaching and learning as the days unfold. She will be firm, calm, and professional, but she will not be detached, never clinical.

She will be watched over and measured against her predecessor. Calls will be made in the night; her predecessor will sigh, closing her eyes as she tucks her new infant to her shoulder, muttering into the phone that they were right to call, that she has expected this, but what can she do? She does not know how she will restore order next fall. *We know,* the caller will murmur, *and we did not want to trouble you, or upset you when you're so tired and so busy, but we're just concerned. And we are here for you.*

For a moment Janice's voice intrudes. *What kind of idiot calls a new mother to whine about the teacher and get her upset? You think she cares? She's trying to enjoy her new baby, for heaven's sake.*

Well, you'll never guess what happened this morning. I had a pot of water, and I looked at this egg, and I said to myself. . . .

Julie closes her eyes and draws a deep breath. She pictures herself stepping from her car Monday morning, shoulders back as she strides to the resource room, shoulder bag swinging just a little because she is striding.

She will not hunch her way to the resource room, bag clutched to her chest, grin frozen as the pack circles her. She will not walk like a gravedigger, oh, no.

Given time, she could become Rachel Hardy, trailing from contract to contract, always becoming a teacher but never quite arriving.

Before North Bay, she had vision. She had confidence.

Rachel in her fifties has contributed a torn-down barn and an antique grey house to the family legacy. She has spent her summers journaling in a lonely cabin while she seeks a way to enter the world and her dogs lie beside her, slipping away to age.

What does faithful Taggak feel, his companions gone but not buried deep enough, his leader gone?

Did Nathaniel find him out there? When and where was he left?

Where are the car and the canoe? How did she know that her cabin time was over?

What did she do about faithful Taggak? Did he understand? Did he accept?

Why is Laila left outside?

Musko heaves himself to his feet, stretches long and low, and plods over, nudging the back of her knee. The tail flops over and back, and he grins.

Julie taps the paintbrush until the last drops ooze back into the can. In the old pantry she cleans the brush and presses the can closed while Musko watches, his tail sweeping back and forth.

"You're bored, aren't you?" Julie says.

The tail swings harder.

"You want an adventure, don't you? Just you and me."

Musko begins to pant.

"In the morning," Julie promises. She strips off her painting glove and rubs her fingers through his shaggy ruff. Musko wriggles. "In the morning, we'll have a little adventure of our own."

Chapter 13

CABIN DAY,
NUMBER TWO

This casual promise has become a full-blown obsession by midnight, as Julie tosses and schemes, analyzing and weighing options. *It is meant to be read there.* Perhaps Julie is the reader that Rachel is waiting for. It is not her name on the cover, but those are her words.

Always tell someone where you are going. Never, ever, go off alone. Her father was talking about regular trips, not special quests. This is a special quest; it might be life-altering. Besides, she is taking Musko.

Julie forces away all misgivings about safety and responsibility and privacy, and declares that this will be a day, just this one day, a pure and selfish day. Finally, she drifts into sleep.

~

She arrives at the cabin at nightfall, the waters rippling about the canoe, dark and still. A few copper leaves cling to the birches; the pines loom prominently now. As Julie eases up to the shore, the cabin is gloomy and lonely in the dusk.

A brief light sparks in the porch, and Julie pauses. Now a great white dog, Husky ears flicked forward, tail arched over his back, stalks down to the shore to touch noses with Musko. He lifts his broad head, remaining still as Musko nuzzles around his chin. He rumbles low in his throat, and Musko skips away, crouching. The white dog rushes him, and Musko spins, body low. The white dog stands still, head up, as Musko continues his exploration. The tail begins to swing, and he trots off down the trail, Musko jogging behind him.

The light flicks again in the shadowed porch, and cigarette smoke drifts out to Julie on the damp air. A figure rises in the dusk, a hunched shape with a blanket over the shoulders, a battered hat shielding the face.

"They'll be all right," a woman's voice says.

Julie approaches the porch, pausing in front of the screen.

"It's all right," the woman says, shrugging off the blanket. "Let's get some candles lit."

"I didn't know," says Julie.

The woman stubs the cigarette against a tin can, poking the embers with the filter. "Let's get those candles going. I've been waiting for you."

~

Saturday dawns damp and chilly. Julie stuffs dry clothes in a waterproof bag, fills a plastic jug with drinking water, and selects tins and dry goods for an easy hot lunch. She does not want to spend her time lugging water and washing dishes; she wants to have a Lake Day. She will wrap a blanket around her shoulders and saunter to the porch, folder tucked under her arm. She will gaze at the islands and the hints of coves out there, and then ease into a camp chair, to leaf through the dog-eared pages, communing with Rachel's memories. A few dry leaves will flutter down in the copper light of late autumn.

No, Laila. You are wrong, for this is the way that it is meant to be. The journal calls to Julie with the words of her own dream.

136

She nests her small camp stove in a cooking pot and tucks it into the back between the clothing bag and day pack while Musko pounds around the backseat choosing his window. Julie drapes her life jacket over everything and climbs into the driver's seat. Doug is still sleeping as she turns left onto the road. The copper light is not evident yet.

The hardware store is just opening as Julie arrives, and she hurries to the camping supplies. She had seen the inflatable dinghy in the end of season sale last week, and cannot imagine that anyone would have taken the last one. The box features a smiling couple in cheap swimwear, her sprawled back and laughing into the camera while her partner crouches over the oars and grins. This toy is not a craft for canoers of shorelines, but it will convey her to the cabin, if she is careful. Laila does not need to know. This will be the second secret from Laila, whom she vowed to uphold and never betray. The bewildered clerk asks if she would like a bag, and then wishes her a nice day.

The porch dream replays in Julie's mind as she hunches over the steering wheel, the road dark with moisture; it is not slick but she should be careful, just the same. The dogs were ambling and exploring, and she and Rachel went to light the candles. Then what happened? The stubbing of the cigarette is vivid; she sees the hand, knuckles loose, pressing a stray ember. The play between Musko and the great white dog is sharp and clear. She and Julie went to light the candles, and then it was morning, and she was packing.

She was not meant to look at the journal, then. That would be Laila's ending.

Julie was going to light candles. With candles they could read. . . . That was the invitation, and now she is finishing the dream. That is her ending.

Grey clouds layer in thick masses and a fine mist beads the windshield. This is not really Lake Day weather, but it is her day, her day for self and she will have it.

At the landing, a battered truck is wedged among the rocks and trees. It is caked in old mud, and pine needles clog the windshield wipers. Perhaps it is abandoned.

Julie turns away from the truck and spreads out the dinghy, cramming the smiling summer couple under a piece of tarp in the back of her SUV. She clicks the sections of oar together and lays out her supplies. She is playing at exploring, but playing well. Please do not let the truck owner return.

She hooks up her portable air compressor, and that is when she realizes that the dinghy valves are not compatible with its nozzle. She imagines the truck owner sauntering out of the woods, perplexed or astonished, and leans over the valve. She will remain calm and inflate this dinghy, puff by puff.

It is late morning and a light drizzle is falling by the time Julie has finished inflating the dinghy. She is chilled and annoyed; her idyllic day is wasting past, and she is not in it.

The dinghy bobs and spins on the water's surface, a garish toy against the tangled growth along the shoreline. Julie balances her gear and then eases in, her rubber boots dripping water onto the floor where she will be sitting. The dinghy pitches from side to side as this new weight is added, and she crouches on her knees, facing the bow.

Julie dips one oar in an attempt to paddle, but the dinghy just turns in place, too round to respond to her strokes. She slides the stubby oars into the flimsy oarlocks, and attempts to sweep them in unison while facing forward. The gusting breeze bunts her out on the lake.

Julie needs to get around the point without being seen. *Was down at the landing. You know that new teacher? Well, there she was, just a-bobbing around in one of those pool boats. Yep. On the lake. In the rain. Going on a picnic, she was.*

On shore, Musko cocks his ears and bounds up and down the shore, waiting for Julie to choose their direction.

Julie adjusts the little oars and sweeps one, then the other, and the dinghy jerks forward, zigzagging but angling forward.

The breeze rises to a light wind, and Julie continues her cautious strokes, not daring to change position. Her shoulders already burn from the unfamiliar movement. In a canoe, she would be turning into the cove by now; in the dinghy, she has yet to pass the first point.

The wind continues to rise, but Julie knows that it will probably abate by evening and she will have an easier ride down to the landing. For now, she plans to cling to the shoreline, dipping and sweeping on either or both sides as needed. She remains hunched on her knees facing the bow, her fragile craft not tolerating any more changes.

By the first point, the rain is falling in a steady rhythm and the wind is lashing small whitecaps against the shore. They are just small white-caps, but they smack against the banks with power. She reaches the creek that spills out of the swamp; its tangle of plant life clogs passage along the shore, and she prods the craft out onto the open water. Musko plunges in and churns along beside her. *Now they are getting somewhere,* he is saying. Julie is cramped, her feet and legs chilled, her face burning from the exertion. She pushes out with more force, and the dinghy wobbles forward.

Now Julie has found her rhythm. She reaches and strokes, reaches and strokes, sometimes with one oar, sometimes with both. She is well out on the lake now, and the cabin is in sight around the last point. She drops her hands and pulls back, grips and pushes hard. Grip and push. She feels the discipline in her muscles, the response of the craft, and then one oarlock rips free.

With a sigh, the hard-blown air gusts from the rip and she clamps one hand over it. The dinghy rocks wildly, and then the sides have fin-ished collapsing and water is washing over the bottom. The bottom has a separate chamber, and Julie rolls into the late October water, her numb legs not registering the change, but her upper body and face clenching against the cold that grips them. She treads water, rolling the gear to the centre, clutching the spinning camp stove and tossing it to the middle of the soggy pile. She tosses one oar on, and the deflated outer tube flops in the waves as the second oar scuds out toward the island.

Julie seizes the line and begins to swim, a perplexed Musko swimming along beside her, unsure of this unusual turn of events. People usually stay in the canoe while dogs swim beside the canoe. This is a new way of doing things.

The brush is too thick for walking where Julie comes to shore, and she staggers along in the shallows, stumbling over rocks that her deadened feet barely feel. At the clearing in front of the cabin, she tosses her bundles up onto the shore and drapes the forlorn remains of the dinghy on the wet ground. She scoops up her gear and straggles to the cabin, groping under the step for the key. No one is, of course, waiting. Julie is alone. *Never, ever, go off alone.* Special quests are not an exception.

Rain pelts against the roof as she strips away her clothes and scrubs her numb body with the bedraggled towel hanging from a peg in the kitchen. She pulls on long johns, jeans, thermal socks, T-shirt, and turtleneck sweater—all her spare clothes. Her teeth hammer above the rain as she scrutinizes the ancient stove. She will have to risk a small fire. *Forest fire? You couldn't start a forest fire with a blowtorch.* Without flinching, she strips off her socks and gathers an axe from behind the door.

Barefoot in the rain, a tarp from the rafters shielding her dry clothes from most of the rain, she hacks and splinters fire wood from the porch into kindling. A search of the cupboards reveals matches and candles. She sets her kindling, and snaps a candle into pieces, which she sets among the kindling. The candle pieces begin to burn, licking into the kindling, and the wood catches.

She does not trust the chimney and keeps her blaze low, kneeling before the stove and shivering. It is now 2 p.m., and she should be well into the journal, sipping hot coffee and contemplating a leisurely journey down the lake. Instead, she is wet, cold, unreading, and unfed.

Musko curls near the stove, damp and happy. He is enjoying this adventure.

Julie paces, rubbing her arms. She needs food. Hot food and hot drink. She sets her dripping camp stove aside, and sets the pot on the table. An image of her water jug, resting on the tarp beside the dinghy couple, flashes through her mind. Well, she is not going to be going back for it today. She places the pot on the ground beside the streaming eaves, and rain water splashes into it, dragging along pine needles and specks of asphalt. She dumps the pot, spreads a dish towel over it, and hopes for the best.

Julie selects beans, prying back the flip-top lid and placing the can directly on the stove. Musko's ears lift at the sound, and his eyes mark the can's location. Julie centres the pot of cloudy rain water on the stove and resumes her pacing.

An hour later, they have finished the beans and Julie is on her third cup of instant coffee. Musko has tolerated the beans, but shown a definite preference for the cheese and crackers. The storm appears to have peaked, but refuses to surrender this peak, with no signs of abating. Julie's green anorak has stopped dripping on the stove, but it is several hours at least from drying. Julie keeps the fire low, nursing her soaked rubber boots and considering the icy swim down the lake to the car.

Tonight she must have a good night's sleep before spending one final day in preparation for Monday. She sees herself stumbling into the school on Monday morning, trailing weeds and mud, a child's plastic oar clutched in her numb fingers. *The storm raged for two days.*

It can't. It mustn't. The cabin shudders in the wind. She cannot attempt the lake in this weather. It will have to blow out by morning. If not, then she will have to try. She is here for tonight, with macaroni and cheese and instant coffee, and plenty of time for the journal.

Doug is roaming loose in Meadowbrook, scheming and measuring. She cannot do anything about that. She can, however, do something here.

She snaps open the blue bin, but there is no plastic bag, no file. *That don't matter. It's not for you.* Oh, it does matter, Laila, for those are Julie's words on the cover and she has to know. Need overcomes ethics and Julie lifts mattresses, fingers through drawers and cupboards and boxes, and slides her hands along the rafters.

There is no journal.

Evening is falling and still the rain drums down and whitecaps lash against the shoreline. The cabin darkens too early and Julie feeds the fire small doses of wood. She has a tattered dinghy and one flimsy oar. She has macaroni and instant coffee and a long, freezing swim in the morning to look forward to. She has hours of preparation for school, but will undoubtedly dash in at the last minute Monday, hair stiff with mud and plan book empty. And still there is no journal.

The journal would set her course, and make sense of all that has happened before, during, and since North Bay. It should not be gone. Rachel can be gone, but the journal must not.

Maybe there is more than little dog bones in these woods. This is not a night for these thoughts.

Musko raises his head and whuffs, low in his throat. At least there is Musko.

"Do you remember the Reserve, Musko? You were born there," she says.

Musko utters a low, rumbling growl.

The porch door shudders and buckles in the wind. Musko snaps to his feet, hackles raised.

The main door swings back, and a tall man takes a fumbling step into the room, water trailing from his rain slicker. He extends a cautious hand for Musko to sniff.

"Wal. You got no idea just how glad I was to smell that fire," he declares. "Nevah saw this place open, this time o' year."

Julie sits on the floor, birch log still clasped in both hands. "Nathaniel?" she whispers.

The man straightens, pulling back his hood and running a hand over his rough grey hair. "Nope. Nope. Joe Barnes. Why, Nathaniel, he'd be a young feller, now. You some friend o' Rachel Hardy's?"

"Laila's."

The man nods. "Laila. Ah see." He looks at Musko. "Wal now, you gonna let a feller get near that fire, ol' boy?" To Julie, he explains, "Ah was headin' fo' the landin', cuttin' across open water below the Narrows, thought like a fool Ah'd make it tonight, but no. Rolled 'er over, easy as you please. Need Nathaniel to do one of his kayak rolls. Bad water out there tonight."

"Kayak rolls?"

"Oh, he can do 'em. Goes way off sometimes, sea kayakin', they call it." He glances toward the stove, shrugging in his soaked clothing.

Julie pulls a kitchen chair near the fire. "Want some coffee? Instant?"

Musko's tail begins to swing.

Chapter 14

VIGILS

Joe Barnes had been camped on the next lake for the past few days, doing a little partridge hunting and scouting the area for signs of deer. Mainly, he was enjoying the feeling of the pine needles under his feet as he trudged the shores. He was riding down the storm, looking forward to hot tea and the hockey game and a comfortable fire at home, sure of his skill as he rocked through the waves until that last one slipped in under his guard. He tipped just past the point of recovery and rolled into the water as the canoe went over. He clutched at his tent and grub box as they teetered on the surface for a moment, but then they were sinking, vanishing into the dark water. The boots that trod so lightly on the pine needle above the Narrows dragged at his legs, coaxing him down after them. He treaded water for a moment, fumbling at boot laces and pawing at his rain coat. Finally, he heaved himself across the slippery hull of the canoe, and hitched himself up, still clutching his paddle. His gun and pack were securely strapped in, he knew, so he focused on riding the canoe, the water slapping over his legs, forcing it to shore just above the cabin.

"Wal, you make mighty fine macaroni, Miss Ma'tin," he declares from his seat amid the drying clothes. Dressed in baggy white track pants and white turtleneck found in the bin under the towels, obvious cast-offs from Nathaniel's teen years, he shrugs and grins. "Reckon Ah look like a rap star? Just need a hat. Turn it sideways, maybe."

Julie grins back, ruffling Musko's fur while Musko eyes the bowl in Joe Barnes's hand.

"You lost your canoe?" Joe asks.

"My canoe. No, not exactly," she replies.

Joe stirs the remaining noodles with his fork. "Now, don't take this wrong. But, you wasn't out in that little rubber thing down on the shoah? You was nevah out in that in this weathah?"

"Well. A little before, to be exact. Kind of."

Joe leans back in his chair. "Wal, Ah'll be. Whatever possessed you?"

Julie shrugs. "I'm not sure."

Sometimes, Joe, when your life has turned over and your past has come back, when you have a job at last but you are inadequate and unprepared, and when there is a journal that holds the key to everything, you take a moderately foolish risk.

Joe chuckles. "Don't that beat everything. I guess you must be runnin' from somethin'?"

Julie concentrates on Musko's ear.

"Mebbe someone? We gotta worry about crazed axe murderers hangin' around the cabin, like some movie? No old boyfriends trackin' you through the swamp?" He starts to laugh, and then catches himself as Julie's shoulders slump. "Aw, now, hey, I don't mean that. This here's a good place on a rainy evening." He raises his tin mug in salute. "And here's one wet and weary hunter, mighty grateful."

The rafters creak in the wind and the rain pounds down with new vigour. "We'd be sma't to wait for morning," Joe observes. He sighs. "I sure hope the ol' man is tapin' the game."

Julie's shoulders slump. "I really needed to get back tonight," she says.

"Wal now, they's worse places to be," Joe says. "So yer a friend of Laila's?"

Julie sighs, wandering over to the window. It is dark now, the unseen storm weighing against the glass. "I'm starting a new job on Monday. At the school. I need tomorrow to get ready."

"Are you, now? A teacher, are you? Wal. You musta heard about Rose Ha'dy? She used to be my teacher. Oh, she had a tempah! A real tempah. But, she was fair. Always treated me fair. Used to ask me about my fishin'. Always dressed just so—nail polish and lipstick and hair done up. But liked to fish, too. Now, I was in the same class as her boy, Cha'les. Well, we got through high school and then he was off to college and I was off to Ontario. Lot of us went in those days. I guess a lot still do." He pauses. "Nevah cared for it there, in all the thirty-odd years Ah was there. Wal, I come home. Now I do a little cuttin'. Hunt some, farm some, fish some. Look aftah the ol' man. And I like it just fine."

"Married?" Julie is not about to get caught up in her own life again while she is finding her way. She is going to be a listener.

Joe drums his fingers against his leg. "Had a wife. Back there." He twists his head, nodding west. "She went off, oh—when the boys went, when the boys was grown, kind of. We had all kinds of stuff," he murmurs. "All the boats and four wheelers and every gadget you can imagine. Now, I got peace of mind." He closes his eyes. "I got an old truck that just might go, the pine needles under my feet, and yes, I got peace of mind." He opens his eyes. "How about you, Miss Ma'tin?"

Julie clears her throat. "I was teaching in Ontario," she says, "mostly with the Band councils. That was OK. I was in North Bay, too, for a while, but that didn't really work out, so I came home. To Waverley? Out by Halifax? That was a little too close to home, I guess. I thought I'd try it out here, you know, in the country, out near Kedge. That job I'm starting? It's at the school there, near Meadowbrook; I guess that's your old school. And I'm staying out at the Hardy farm, there in Meadowbrook."

"No! Wal. You're kind of like Rachel Ha'dy then. You're goin' around in the same circle she did. And here you are."

"Kind of," Julie mutters, crossing to the stove and spreading drying clothes to better catch the heat.

"You ever meet her?"

Julie shakes her head.

"I seen her, out on the lake this spring, when I was fishin'. Her and that big white dog. Little ones is gone, I guess. Too bad."

Julie stiffens, clutching a damp sweater. "She still comes here?"

"Ye-es." Joe shifts in his chair. "Not summers and all like before, but I seen her. May month, it was. See signs of Nathaniel this fall some, but he keeps to himself and I let him be."

"But she doesn't call Laila," Julie blurts out. "Laila is worried and nobody tells her what's going on."

Joe shrugs. "I don't know about that pa't. All I know is, Ah seen her May month, up by the Narrows when Ah was fishin'. That's all Ah know."

~

Joe is an immediate and sound sleeper, as well as a loud snorer. Curled on the bunk in the kitchen, Julie listens to the snorts and rumbles from the couch. Joe has claimed that he will tend the fire through the night, but Julie knows that any fire tending will be done by her.

Julie will tend the fire while she holds her vigil for Rachel. She waits, journal-less, for Rachel. She must understand Rachel, for she is becoming Rachel, goin' around in the same circle as Rachel. She might even be living her journal.

There is no journal to prove that, though. Perhaps she has absorbed it. An idea for a horror story, maybe even with crazed ex-boyfriend axe murderers stalking the heroine through the swamp.

"None of that is important," Rachel scolds her from the top bunk. "You are your own journal, and I am mine." She sighs. "It is so good to have people here, out on the lake, even if I'm gone. They used to come, but then they stopped. Now here they are. It's a little sad, but it doesn't matter. And Taggak likes your dog," she adds.

Julie sits up with a start. She has slept, after all. The day is dawning, pale yellow shafts splitting the cloud banks, the wind light. Joe crouches before the stove, stirring out the last coals glowing in the ashes, saying that they'll let it burn down, and get a hot breakfast along the way.

They gather gear in various stages of dryness and bundle it into the canoe. The dinghy remains are hidden in a black garbage bag, and nothing is said about boats or running or Ontario.

At the landing, Joe remembers that the restaurant is closed for the season, but that doesn't matter because they'll both be home soon, and the old man will be worried, anyway. He huddles over the steering wheel of his rusted truck as the engine coughs and sputters, and sits back with a grin and a nod as it catches.

"Ah nevah told no one till now about seein' Rachel," he remarks. "That's kinda the way she wanted it. She's gotta come home her own way. Kinda like you. Remember? Circles." He reaches for the gear shift. "You take care now. And remember—it's the fair ones the kids remember."

Then he is trundling up the hill, eye on the mirror as she weaves through the potholes and rocks. At the road he swings east and is gone before she reaches the flats beyond the turn.

Musko is panting and grinning. He has enjoyed this adventure.

The adventure, however, has been stressful for Doug.

"Oh, Jesus, oh, Jesus, oh, God. *Where* have you been? I checked the gear." Doug draws up his shoulders and nods. "The camp stove was gone. I saw immediately that the camp stove was gone, but not the tent. So. Camping with someone? Another secret mission with Laila? So I called. 'Oh, hi, Laila.'" He grips an imaginary receiver. "'Hey, there, you girls have any weekend plans? No? Oh, nothing. No, I'm just planning a little something for Julie myself, a little surprise. A surprise, for Julie. Yes. Bye.'" He sniffs the air. "You smell like wood smoke," he accuses.

"It's from the fire," Julie explains.

"Which tells me nothing." Doug draws himself up to his full height. "And you left me with the Jehovah's Witnesses," he declares. "Nine o'clock Saturday morning. Ties. Dresses. Tracts! And they pretended to be nice!"

"Maybe they are nice. Did you find the new coffee?"

"Coffee? Julie, you can't let them in the house. You can't feed them. You'll never get rid of them that way."

"You got rid of them? Doug, you had no right."

"Well, where were you while I was entertaining your dear friends? Camping with some other fanatics? In the rain?"

"It just seems kind of mean." She really does think that it is mean, but mainly she does not want Doug to make decisions about Meadowbrook Acres. That is for her to do.

However, there but for Joe Barnes, Julie might have needed Doug to raise a search party. Doug, aided by Laila, would track her to the hardware store. At the mention of pool dinghy, their eyes would meet, and one or the other would nod. It would be obvious to them. Doug and Laila, allies at last, would soon be pounding through the waves to rescue Julie. Doug would need to bring her back to justify his existence at Meadowbrook Acres and to pressure her into giving this second chance that he wanted for who knew what reason.

Laila would be worried about her, but her first task would be to guard the journal. For she is first friends with Rachel.

However, she would still have been rescued. Someone kept a vigil, for whatever reasons. There is that.

"Sorry," she says, dragging her soggy pack into the kitchen. "First-day nerves, I guess. I'll be all right now."

STRAWBERRY CYCLES
AND RAPPIE PIE

The carpenters were planning to jack up the cabin at Wasaya today, and start shingling the roof tomorrow. Rain is forecast for tomorrow, however, and for the weekend. Once you jack up the foundation, the shingles shift, and then you will have leaks. Therefore, they will wait for Monday, and push the job through then.

I acknowledge the good sense of this plan, but suspect that the deluge will hold off until Monday, and I will wait again.

Weather has a tendency to do that to us all.

~

After the frozen hands winter, my father did not work in the woods anymore. He began to winter in the house, because his hands were now delicate. He still did the barn work, but took over the vacuuming, the washing up, and the preparing of meals. The sheep were sold that first fall, because my father realized that he, too, was allergic to their fleece, and that was all his hands needed. There would be no more baby lambs for me to raise on bottles, and no more watching the sheep gather in the hollow as evening drew near.

There would also be no more tattered little creatures, grey-white bodies limp in the crook of my father's arm, their flesh ripped and their eye sockets dripping blood. The pastoral scene hides many levels. Ravens, too, are part of nature.

I was disappointed as I watched the sheep being herded into trucks. At six, I was ready to help herd them, and this was denied me. I wanted there to be more baby lambs to feed and bedeck with ribbons, until they grew and vanished into the herd.

Mischief, the last lamb, never joined the herd. He followed us like a clumsy dog, bleating forlornly when he was not allowed into the house. They had to wrestle him into the truck, and in my heart I cheered him. Fight, Mischief. Fight them and come back to me. I wish to this day that I had cried and begged, at least that I had tried. Mischief would never have missed the other sheep, and he would have been good company for Nellie and Danny Boy. And me. However, I watched them wrestle him into the truck because that is what one did when sheep were being sold.

Our lives were indeed changing: my father was becoming a produce farmer/homemaker, my mother was going to teach at the high school, and my brothers would have a little sister at Meadowbrook Elementary.

We had always had the garden. We had always hoed and weeded, then picked and snipped and canned. Now, we had acres of strawberries and corn. We could bend our backs in the blistering sun all day, now that we had no sheep to herd through green pastures and beside cool waters. I yearned for sheep with all my six-year-old heart as I straggled along the rows in the dust.

Corn will wither if the weather is not just right during planting and growing. Strawberries are finicky: they need dry weather for good, loose soil at planting, because mud will squeeze their tiny roots. If it is too dry, though, the soil will blow away and the tiny roots will shrivel and die. Next, there must be good, regular showers, to invigorate them.

If there is too much rain, you might pack the soil against them. If there is not enough rain, they will wilt and die. Shake straw over the plants before the frost, and hope for a good snow cover to further insulate them. Not too much, though. Pull the straw back after the last frost, but don't wait until frost is no longer possible, or the plants will be pale and weak. Be ready to race to the hill to shake straw over them if a late frost is indicated. Start looking for those regular, gentle showers again, with hot, dry days because you do not want rot.

You are weeding one piece, picking another piece, and working the house garden in between. You look forward to mowing the lawns with the hand mower, because there is shade on the front lawn.

At the end of the day, you are proud.

When my teaching year ends, I can choose to come to Meadowbrook. My mother stumbled from marking exams into Strawberry Season. She was up at dawn answering the phone, organizing the pickers, getting the meals, cleaning the house, and pickling and canning and making jam.

In the midst of it all, she still found time to monitor our salt intake. My mother was a firm believer in replacing fluids and salt. We would drag in from the fields at noon, remembering the sheep that simply adorned the fields and never needed weeding. My mother would greet us with a pitcher of Kool-Aid, generously laced with salt to replace the salt that we sweated out.

That is horrible, people say, as they guzzle their athletic drinks laden with sodium. Those drinks have more salt than our Kool-Aid, but the taste is hidden. Taste is everything, now.

Rainy days would bring respite, but most of my summers were marked by long, calculating glances down the well. The spring would be bailed for the season, and the outhouse opened.

Water was hauled from the river for the crops. Bucket by bucket my father and brothers carried water from the river to the wagon, and bucket by bucket I dumped it into the forty-five-gallon drum. Bucket by bucket I ladled it out to my father and brothers, and scoop by scoop they trickled the water over the drooping plants, hunched over the rows.

I was lucky to be the youngest; I had the best job.

Meanwhile, my mother was handling everything on the home front, and let us not forget that all that pickling and canning and jamming and cooking was done on a wood stove. She escaped only for grocery shopping and Mass. And a visit in the cool of late evening from the summer people.

She always seemed to be strained and bitter in the summer, stressed and exhausted in the winter.

July was the only time of the year that we ate hamburgers and called it a complete meal. I plastered mine with mustard and felt wild and reckless.

In August, the relatives descended. My mother delicately entertained her in-laws, and talked long into the night with her visiting sisters.

In between we had summer catechism, swimming lessons, and two trips to the beach each summer. We had all the fun that the strawberries and corn allowed us.

The very best of all was the annual visit to the French Shore to see Grammie and Grampie. We would pack suitcases, games, books, toys, a cardboard box lined with newspaper for me, a hamper of sandwiches, a thermos of coffee, and a jug of salt-free Kool-Aid (since we were not sweating). By Liverpool, my stomach would start to pulse, and the tension would build behind my eyes. I would swallow, feel the saliva trickle in my throat, feel the pulse and roll deep within. My mother would dole out bits of spearmint gum; when I smell spearmint gum even today I feel the pull behind my eyes, the pulsing in my stomach.

We would inch along the shore as I heaved and vomited into my cardboard box, sitting back as my body settled, crouching forward as it began to roll and pulse anew. When we stopped for lunch, I would feel fine again. I would pack my mouth with sandwiches, suck down Kool-Aid, and then hover on the brink of a sleepy nausea as we pulled along the shore, closer and closer to Grammie and Grampie's house.

There would be patches of fog, and Irish moss drying on the road sides. We stared and stared into this amazing new world, our mother's home.

Then there would be Grammie and Grampie on the porch. Grampie was so straight and a little austere; Grammie was bent, hunched with arthritis, grinning and bobbing her head. Her cousin, Tante Angele, hovered in the background, wiping her hands with her apron. "I got your rappie pie, Stephen, all waiting for you!" My father would beam his appreciation, dignified and shy. My mother would step away from us, just a little, and begin to speak in French, something that she never did with us.

The afternoon would finish with rappie pie, a deceptively simple dish, for there it sits neat and trim in its one pan. Before that one-pan stage, you must first grate some potatoes while you are simmering a chicken. Load the grated potatoes in a length of cheese cloth, and wring the potato water into a bowl. Put the potato pulp into another bowl. Now measure the potato water. When your chicken is done, replace the potato water with the same amount of chicken broth, and stir it into the potato pulp. You also need to debone the chicken, and lay the meat on a platter. In a loaf pan, place layers of potato and layers of chicken. Top the last layer of potato with little pork cubes, and bake. At this time, you can start washing your pots, bowls, grater, utensils, and platter, and rinse out the cheese cloth.

Grammie always put a jug of molasses on the table near my plate, and I suspect that she knew this is why I loved her rappie pie. Grammie and Tante Angele always made firm loaves. Often, rappie pie is loose and runny. I do not know if Grammie and Tante Angele did it the right way, but for me, it was the best way, the way of my childhood.

Many people use rabbit or clams instead of chicken. My mother would never touch rabbit, though, even though she was from the Acadian district. Grampie was very much français de France: his own father came straight from Le Havre. We never even knew that his mother was Acadian. And we never thought of Grammie or Mother as

Acadian. Grammie kept her Acadian heart tucked deep inside, and my mother was français de France, because she knew it pleased her father.

The French—standard French, not Acadian in Grampie's house—would fly around the kitchen, but the moment my father entered the room they would click into English. If he stepped outside, they slid back into French, all without missing a beat. The United Nations could have learned something in that kitchen.

That night I would lie in the little bed by the window in the girls' room, the bed that had been my mother's when this was her home. I would watch the headlights appear from the fog on the far side of the river, way down past the great church of my mother's childhood. They would emerge, silent, from the fog, and then vanish as they swung past the church. There they would be again, piercing the fog as they started across the causeway, sliding by, the engine muffled in the night. I would wait for another car, and imagine that I was my mother growing up in this room, my five sisters around me.

My mother always seemed to flutter on the surface of this, her old home; she was a watcher, smiling from the sidelines, not really entering. Yet at Meadowbrook Acres, we were constantly lectured on the Wonderful Childhood, rich in love, laughter, and wisdom. Even Grammie's meningitis, which nearly killed her, was a good memory. Most of the children were sent away, but my mother and her sister were older and so they stayed. They could be quiet. They could help. They were there when the priest came. The priest intoned the *rite of extreme unction*, which does sound more terminal than *anointing of the sick*, the term we use today as we mince around the truth of our mortality. The priest completed the rite, rocked back on his knees, and addressed God: God could certainly take this woman, as was His right, but He should bear in mind that she had all these children and a husband to care for, and so much work that had to be done.

That night, Grammie started to get better, and soon she rose from her bed and was scrubbing clothes and floors like nothing had happened.

It is my belief that she, not God, was most affected by that prayer. She felt too guilty to die.

My aunt Claudette, of the ashtrays and flowered skirts, was a baby at this time. When Grammie became sick, she was taken by relatives to Boston, just until my grandmother got better. It seems it took Grampie five years to convince them to return his daughter, that help was no longer needed. My aunt Claudette had been an only child, speaking English and living in a great city, with her own dog, since she was an infant. Here she stood, five years old, with only English and no dog, in rural Acadie, sharing a room with five French-speaking girls. It must have been strange for her, strange for them.

Another aunt stayed with family down the shore. When the uncle touched you, I heard from another aunt, you shivered. You wanted to wash that arm or cheek he touched.

There are untold stories that these aunts could have told. In those times, untold stories were kept untold.

So my mother would flutter through the visit, cheerful and anxious. Perhaps she was discovering that she had lost her happy childhood, and wanted everyone to know that it was all right after all. Then again, perhaps she had created that childhood, and now everyone would see that she had.

I remember this as her time with her family, and that loved and welcomed as we were, no one seemed to wish that we were closer.

The day after we arrived, after more rappie pie and kisses, we wove off along the coast, and that was all for another year.

Twenty-six hours each year: For me, it was a summer ritual, faces behind the Christmas presents.

I never knew what it was for my mother until I stood on the spot where the house had stood, and it was now a pasture. I wanted my son to be with me, so that I could say: "See? That was the porch. Grammie waved to us here. That is the ditch where we picked blueberries. I would lie awake at night and watch the car lights in the fog. Yes, it was always foggy along the river at night. We came here every summer, and we had rappie pie."

My son was not there, of course; he was on a northern coast, learning with his father's people. He had so little time with them, growing up. It called to him.

So I told the dogs, who stared at the pasture, panted, and wagged their tails. I showed them the Great Church, and the cemetery, and they stared, panted, and wagged as my voice rose and fell.

Maybe that is what my mother saw when she tried to tell us.

I stood in that pasture that had been her home, and it was silent.

When we returned to Meadowbrook, I would hug the house, spreading my arms and resting my cheek on the clapboards. I would have a sore throat from the fog and be so happy to be home after my adventure.

My father would head for the barn, and my mother would unpack. There was corn coming, after all, and then apples, and in between more pickling and canning and jamming.

The relatives would continue to pour through during this break. We would count the days in anticipation of each visit, and embrace old routines with a sigh of relief the moment they left.

My mother had been given her annual vacation trip, and so nothing was owed her. I wonder if coffee and a sandwich in the staffroom in September seemed more like a vacation to her.

Chapter 15

NEW BEGINNINGS, OLD PATTERNS

On Monday, Julie is reasonably prepared. Plans have been revisited and revised. She senses loose ends dangling, medical details forgotten, and scheduling details overlooked. She has taken enough time for rest, although images of fluttering dinghies and visiting hunters crowd her mind and she is not rested. The cold of the storm is still deep in her bones. Still, she is there, smiling and mimicking confidence, dry and clean, as she walks through the door.

The journal, the lights in the summer window, Christmas in the attic, and the oil bills are pushed into the background as she opens her day book. This is what she was meant to do. Here, she will shine, and then she will go home—yes, home—to paint, write cheques to the oil company, and listen to Doug grouse about the cold in Grandma Mary's room. Soon, he will move on. And then, she can invite her parents for a weekend. She will settle into the rhythm of her new life.

The first week develops its own rhythm. Julie walks the wet fields with Musko each morning, the sodden hay squelching under her boots. She is at her desk by eight o'clock, teaching and testing by eight-forty.

At lunch time she nibbles a sandwich in the staff room, listening and answering as required. It is important to develop rapport with one's colleagues. It also prevents them from speculating about her. After school she works on case notes and plans until five, slips any remaining work into her shoulder bag, and returns to Meadowbrook. After a walk with Musko, she prepares supper, although Doug would prefer supper at five. A schedule of regular meals, he explains, is important. Then there is more schoolwork, perhaps a little painting, and then it is bedtime. The rhythm is disciplined, but she can cope.

At lunchtime on Wednesday, the copper-curled teacher knits while droning about her approaching pension. Retirement, she explains to Julie, is two years away, and she will claim a full, immediate pension. She would like to retire this year, but she knows that she can handle two more years. When she retires, she will sub on the days that she chooses to sub, for the classes she chooses to work with. She will try some other subjects; she has been teaching home ec for so long that she could teach it in her sleep. Probably has. She waits for appropriate laughter, and Julie manages a conspiratorial grin. Of course, she won't just be working, she continues, or there would be no point in retiring. She and her husband will travel, too. She would like to go to Florida. Do they still have all that antique furniture down at the Hardy place?

The teachers scattered around the table lean in as one, except Janice, who continues marking.

"I think it's in storage," Julie says at last, for this sounds both safe and knowledgeable.

"Mildewing in the attic," Roger sings out, and several smirks are exchanged.

Margaret of the copper curls frowns. "Gossiping is not professional," she says, doing a quick row count. "I hear that Helen is doing very well—any day now."

Heads nod around the table, and for a few minutes updates on the new baby-to-be are exchanged.

"Janice," Roger says abruptly, "we appreciate your work and all, but don't you ever take a break?"

"Mark's riding lesson's tonight," Janice says without looking up. Her eyes continue to scan the pages; neat, quick comments are penned.

"So busy," Margaret sighs. "I won't miss all this when I retire."

"Oh, but you will," Roger declares, rolling back in his chair. "You'll be old Rose, hanging on and all thrilled to be here."

"She was a good teacher in her day," Margaret says, needles now flashing.

"Not after her day," Roger quips. "She stayed on well past her best-before date."

Margaret scowls. A few smug looks are exchanged around the table. Janice scoops up her notebooks and crams them into her shoulder bag. "They'll be talking this way about you and me someday, Roger," she announces over her shoulder as she opens the staffroom door.

Margaret glances over her pattern. "We were thinking of a nice trailer. We could camp in the States on our way to Florida. We wouldn't invest, not yet anyway. Just a month or two in Florida, and then back here, and maybe I'd do a little subbing to keep my hand in, and of course we'd want to head up to Ontario sometimes, to see the kids. They'd like that. We could help with the grandchildren, give the parents a little break. Just go at our own pace."

Julie continues to nod and smile, washing down dry bites with sips of coffee. If she leaves, she will be right up there on the block with Rose Hardy and all the Hardys. Isolating oneself is not wise. She nods and eats and anticipates her afternoon classes.

~

The first week brings Tina, who does not speak. Tina can speak, but she chooses not to. Her condition is described as selectively mute. She is also described as having a learning disability; her verbal skills are weak. If she does not speak to the tester, then how do they know what her verbal skills are? The teacher that Julie is replacing has explained that the low verbal skills result in lack of confidence, and so Tina does not speak. Julie thought of chickens and eggs and did not ask how the muteness can then be "selective."

Tina is now almost thirteen and in Grade 7. A slight figure, she hunches over the page, her long dark hair tumbling nearly to her waist, and her bangs draped over her face.

"Can you see the page, Tina?"

The hair moves in a small nod.

"Will you read it to me?"

Tina tips back her head, giving her hair a brief shake. She gazes toward the window through her fringe of hair.

"Will you read it with me?"

Tina gives a small shrug. One finger slides across the page, tapping hard on one word.

"You don't know that word?"

Another slight nod.

"But you know the others?"

The nod is emphatic this time.

"Then what if you read the rest, and I could read that part, or we could practise that one together? OK? See the beginning sound; that's 'puh.' Now slide in the 'ah'—pa. Move into the middle sound, those Ts. Patt. Focus on the end sound now; the 'e' sound is a little funny—urn, not ern. Like a 'u.' P-a-tt-urn—pattern. Now you."

Tina's face contorts. "I miss my cat," she wails.

"Your cat? Oh. Oh, what happened?" Julie slides the tissue box toward Tina.

"She's gone," she whimpers. "I let her out, and she's gone."

"Cats like to explore," Julie reassures her. "They explore, and then they come home. You let her out this morning?"

"Christmas," Tina whispers. "Last Christmas. And I dreamed about her last night. I let her go." The sobs are rising now; Tina's shoulders heave and her breath comes in heavy gasps.

Julie rests an arm on the back of Tina's chair. "Sometimes, these things happen. They happen, and we don't know why. It's hardest when we don't know the ending to the story."

Julie wants to tell the story of Musko, and that happy ending, but that is not Tina's story. This is not the time.

"It will be harder now, with Christmas coming," she continues. "Everything will make you think about her. It will get easier; it will. But not just yet." Julie stands. "And you did not 'let her go.' It just happened. It wasn't you. Understand?"

A quick rap sounds on the door frame. A young teacher with light hair that brushes her straight shoulders leans in the doorway. "Excuse me. Hi. New schedule and all, I guess. Anyway, you were supposed to get Eric and Daniel five minutes ago? And, well, you are going to follow the schedule? That's the plan, right?"

Julie smiles back, teeth showing. "Of course. Definitely. I guess I lost track of time."

"I see." The teacher indicates Tina with a quick nod. "You get her to talk?"

Tina withdraws into her hair, nose hovering over the text.

"Actually," Julie drawls, "I was so busy talking that she couldn't get a word in edgewise."

The teacher rolls her eyes. "I'm sending Eric and Daniel in. They have math pages you need to help them with."

"Of course. I'll look those over, definitely. And we'll work on the concept of patterning, to make sure that they have the background to do more on their own. As scheduled."

"Whatever. I need those pages in. They're behind." She gestures Eric and Daniel into the room as Tina slips through the door.

Eric and Daniel are a different challenge. Eric crawls under the table and stretches out, insisting that this is his usual place. Daniel's head lolls on his folded arms, and he proclaims that he can't do math and that Ms. Martin is very unfair to expect him to do patterning, the very hardest thing there is. Also, Eric is poking him under the table, and she is not even doing anything to stop him.

Julie directs him to a small table at the side of the room, where she lays out patterning blocks. Daniel slumps into a chair, protesting that he is not dumb, and blocks are for Primary, not Grade 8.

"These are manipulatives," Julie says. "You'll be using them in senior high, too. Now: What comes next in this pattern?"

Daniel grunts that this is a trick question. It could be a triangle, because the triangles went up one in each group, so now you'd need four triangles. On the other hand, you had three blue, then three red, so you were due for a blue one now. To be safe, you'd need a blue triangle, but there isn't one, and that is simply not fair. He will have to use a blue square.

"Exactly, if you are extending the pattern by shape, then it's a triangle. But if you're extending the pattern by colour, then it's a blue anything. You're right both times."

Daniel pushes the pattern blocks aside. "You're giving me baby stuff because I have a learning disability. You think I'm dumb."

"No, if you have a learning disability, then you can't be 'dumb.' It just means you have your own way of learning things. This is beginning work, not 'baby' work, to fill in any ideas you might have missed along the way."

Eric hauls himself out from under the table and slumps down beside Daniel. "Gimme a hard one," he demands.

By the end of the session, the boys have moved to describing pattern rules and extending tables of values. They work competitively to describe pattern rules, using the common difference to identify more complex ones. The grade-level questions are still challenging, but they solve the initial questions with the level of enthusiasm they used to resist learning at the beginning of class.

"We'll get 'er tomorrow," Daniel declares as they saunter out of the room.

Julie writes up brief case notes and draws up a rough schedule for a reduced workload, based on the teacher's unit plan. This will take performance pressure off the boys and their teacher, while fundamental skills are strengthened.

~

"We can do this?" the teacher demands, marching into the resource room with the schedule in hand.

"Sure. We should go over it with their parents first, make sure that they understand that this is just to support them while they're catching up—not a permanent measure or anything."

"I don't want them to get slack. They're capable."

"Oh, they are. It won't take them long to get their strategies in place."

"So, meanwhile they get a little holiday. That's what they'll think. So they'll slack off, so they get even less work."

"How much math have they done so far this term?"

The teacher sighs, holding up the worksheet. "About this much."

"So, if they're working harder than they were, then you're not slack, and they're not slack, right?" Julie leans forward. "The way I see it," she continues, "we're a team. You have the skills and the learning goals set out, and I'm here to support you with the Erics and Daniels. I bet they take up a lot of your energy in the classroom. If I help you with that pressure, then you can invest more energy in the lesson overall. Hopefully, they'll be more onside as we work together."

"Yeah." The teacher is nodding, tapping the schedule with one finger. "I think this will do. OK. Let's go ahead with this."

Maybe, just maybe, Julie reflects, we are all mimicking confidence here.

~

There are larger reading groups and math groups, there are organizational coaching groups, and there are tutorials. There are transition meetings, testing sessions, and assistive technology support.

There are evenings of paperwork and professional reading. There is discussion of oil bills and furnace settings and, of course, the snow blower. Doug has developed a folder on the topic.

Halloween spins by in a blur, barely noted. No children come to Meadowbrook Acres.

There are walks with Musko in the damp evenings, around the near fields as deer hunting season swings into full force.

~

One Sunday afternoon, Joe Barnes appears, offering a glistening venison haunch in a plastic grocery bag.

"Bagged 'er up above our lake," he says, extending the sack.

"Stay for supper?" Julie blurts, staring doubtfully at the mass of raw meat. Musko's nose quivers.

Joe grins. "You got a good five hours o' waitin' for that feller," he chuckles. "You got some onions? Lots o' pepper?"

Julie nods, and Joe settles on the edge of the verandah, pulling the bag near. He draws a heavy hunting knife. "Now you fetch me a cuttin' boa'd and a plate, if you will." Musko settles nearby, eyes fixed on the process.

Doug is scrutinizing Joe from the kitchen window as Julie enters the kitchen. "Jesus, will you look at him?" he hisses, as she rummages in the pantry. "Is this your camping buddy? How did you hook up with this character? I mean, just look at him—the boots, the hat. The knife. My God, the knife."

He maintains his vigil in the kitchen while Joe cuts thick slices from the roast and lays them neatly on the plate. He wraps the plastic bag around the remaining meat and pushes himself to his feet. "Now, if you'll put this in the freezah, Ah'll look after the rest. You got a cast iron skillet?"

His smile drops when Julie admits that she does not. "Wal, we'll just make do," he says, following her into the kitchen, Musko crowding at his heels.

He falters at the sight of Doug, hands on hips, frowning at the platter of fresh meat. His shoulders slump, and he balances his offering as he crouches, plucking at his bootlaces.

"It's all right. Don't worry about your boots," Julie urges, reaching for the plate. Doug continues to stare, and Joe continues to fumble with his bootlaces. "And this is. . . ." She hesitates.

"I'm Doug." He extends a hand. "Julie's friend."

Joe rises, wiping his blood-smeared fingers on his trouser leg and eyeing Doug's clean hand. Doug smirks, lowering his hand. Joe's eyes drop, and he mutters about time getting on. Julie rushes about, collecting her larger frying pan, and onions, pepper, carrots, and potatoes. Musko settles near the stove, tongue lolling.

"Joe's staying for supper," Julie tells Doug. "He's going to show me how to cook deer meat."

Doug purses his lips and gives a vague shrug. "Oh. That's good. Really fine. Well, I have *work* to do." He stalks off in the direction of Grandma Mary's room.

"Ah should be goin'," Joe mutters, but Julie is steering him to the low counter under the west window.

"No. Stay. He really does have work to do."

"What's he do?"

"Oh, he's—looking for a job, sort of," Julie replies. "He's staying here for a while."

"Wal, I thought—he never came with you, to the cabin." Joe eyes the kitchen door, sees the traces of mud left by his work boots. "Ah don't want to interfere," he mumbles.

Julie slaps the frying pan on the burner. "You're not. Now show me what you have in mind."

Joe rubs the back of his neck. "You just fry 'er," he says. "A little onion, lots of pepper. Then stew 'em up with them carrots and potatoes, nice and tender. You really don't need me," he mumbles.

"You get started, and I'll make some bannock," Julie replies. It is important that Joe stay. He is her visitor, her guest. Having visitors and guests is part of the reclaiming process. *A friend dropped by on Sunday afternoon, brought a fine piece of deer meat, and we cooked up a regular feast.* "Please don't let Doug scare you off."

"Scare? Wal. It just feels kinda funny. I mean, he wasn't out there with you, you see. Figured he woulda been, if he was still . . . he know about our set-to out there?" Joe hovers before the sideboard, waiting. "Ah mean, Ah don't want t' make trouble fo' you, with your boyfriend. He might take the wrong slant o' things."

People will be driving by, observing the truck. They, too, will take the wrong slant o' things. *Was up above Kedge, late on a Sunday morning, it was. Joe Barnes was coming out of the lake country, that new teacher driving along behind him. Now, this Sunday afternoon he's parked there at her house. Yes, the boyfriend's car was there, too. Wonder what they're up to, now?*

Julie starts peeling potatoes. She will reclaim this place, with friends dropping in on Sunday afternoons, and relaxing meals being prepared in the kitchen, which will become bright and cheerful. "Remember I said things didn't work out in Ontario?" she begins. "Well, he's part of what didn't work out. He disappeared. He stole my dog." She gestures with her paring knife. "Then, he just showed up here a few weeks ago, and he doesn't seem to want to go anywhere."

Julie freezes. She has just unloaded her North Bay history, recklessly and succinctly, to a near stranger, with whom she spent a night in an isolated cabin in a storm. Everyone knows what that means. *They were alone out there.* Meaningful nods all around. *She and the boyfriend don't seem to have much to do with each other. Too bad; he seems like a nice fellow.* Heads shake in bewilderment.

Now, she is sharing secrets. She hopes that Joe keeps secrets.

Joe gives his shoulders a small shake and scoops a wedge of shortening into the pan. "I see," he says. "Samuel know about that feller?"

"Yes. No. He knows he's here, I mean." Julie scrutinizes the potato, picking at miniscule spots.

The first slice sizzles as it hits the pan. "Come t' win you back. Lookin' for a second chance."

Julie's face burns and she hacks at her already thoroughly peeled potato. "I am a little tired of hearing that," she says.

Suddenly, Joe grins, and he is again the Joe of Sunrise Cove, with peace of mind and a truck that just might go. "Mah older boy's near your age," he offers. "Mechanic, out in Alberta. Mebbe Ah should fix you up, show him yer not in the market for second chances," he teases.

Julie selects a carrot and starts scraping. "Save some carrot for the pan," Joe remarks.

Joe's son. Not Joe. Why not Joe? Why is she even thinking this way? This is not how one thinks of friends who drop by on a Sunday afternoon, and with whom one prepares a regular feast.

Joe works the meat around in the pan. "Now me, I got peace o' mind. I got the pine needles under my feet, an old truck that just might go, and I got my peace o' mind. Ah like people fine, but I like my peace o' mind. You need friends, mebbe, not all these here relationships that everybody's talkin' about. Good friends, people like Laila and Tom, folks like that, people you can depend on. Keeps the loneliness at bay, and the peace o' mind close."

"Do you see much of your sons?" Julie asks.

Joe slices onion into the pan, taking his time. "Wal, Russ—he's the mechanic—might be home next summah," he says at last. "He's settled out in High Prairie. A long ways."

"Really? What a small world. That's where Doug was teaching. Near there."

"That so?" Joe drawls, squinting as steam rises from the pan. He shakes pepper over the browning venison. "He got a last name?"

"Simmons."

"Simmons. Wal. Ah'll ask."

Julie pauses over the cutting board. "Ask?" she prompts.

"Oh. Rumahs. Always a scandal somewhere. It's just, ya see, Russ was sayin' somethin' about a teacher out there? Got involved with one of his students, seems like. She was seventeen, but still—he was her teacher, and all. Parents was real upset. Then he up and disappeared before the investigation took off."

Julie's mouth goes dry. "When?" she whispers.

"Oh, long about Septembah." Joe concentrates on the pan. "Things got kinda obvious once school sta'ted. Heap o' difference between a deserted beach and a science lab. Anyway, that's the story they're tellin'. That teacher did take off, though."

Julie has not enjoyed Doug's company at Meadowbrook Acres, but she has grown accustomed to it. His planning and complaining hover around the perimeter of her life here, giving it shape and contrast. She pictures him gone, hauled away by grim-faced police officers, broken and humiliated. Poor Doug. She sees a pretty, wide-eyed science student clutching him close as she stares into his face. Was she temptress or fool? Or was she a dreamer of elaborate dreams? Poor science student. There on the edge is Julie, protector of the seducer. Oh, poor Julie.

Perhaps it is all rumours. Perhaps he just had the urge to come east, and the story grew to suit the gossips. He had the urge to move east, and find Julie, and do casual work, only for cash. It might still be rumours.

Yet, Doug might be leaving. She has grown used to his planning and complaining, but now she will step free into her real future. She and Laila and Musko will have sledding parties for Janice's kids and their friends. There will be bonfires and hot chocolate and laughter in the night.

There will be friends dropping by, and they will cook and laugh together.

And somewhere there just might be a seventeen-year-old science student, temptress or fool.

No. Somewhere there is a seventeen-year-old science student, eyes red and back hunched, creeping through the school while others jeer. She will not be a temptress or a fool; she will be a broken human being, broken by Doug.

Her shadow accuses Julie as it falls over her plans. Her own liberation comes at the price of this girl's breaking.

"Think Samuel might want a little cuttin' done this winter?" Joe asks, working carrot and potato chunks into the mixture.

Chapter 16

STAYING POWER

"I can't believe how fucking small the world is," Doug moans, burying his face in his hands.

Julie sits in the rocking chair by the kitchen window, absentmindedly rubbing Musko's ear.

Doug Simmons has not come east because he was a victim of cutbacks. He has not come east because he remembered the good times and wanted a second chance. Or, perhaps he did remember the good times, and saw a chance of escape.

For Doug Simmons is under investigation for misuse of his professional position. Doug has been written up in the dark pages of the profession's journal. His contract has been terminated. His license is under review. The parents are pressing charges. The girl is no help whatsoever.

All that is needed is a word from Joe Barnes to Russ Barnes. Father and son: heroes of virtue.

They are only doing what Julie should do, but she cannot, because staying on her feet takes all her concentration just now.

Who is this child who claimed the man who had claimed Julie? *Let us have a relationship. Let us be lovers and conquer the world. Or at least get a job with seniority and a pension plan. Let me find a good home for your dog.*

"She was kind of quiet," Doug is saying. "Mousy hair, shoulders always a little hunched. She wasn't really toned, not like an athlete, but she was no slob. Kind of trim. And shy. Shy about her braces, shy about her glasses. She was in my environmental science class in Grade 11. One of the few who came regularly for tutoring after school." Doug rests his chin on his folded arms, staring at the place mat. "I ran into her when she was waitressing last summer. I hardly recognized her. Contacts. Braces off. Blonde highlights. Make-up, too. And not mumbling and shy anymore. Oh, no. Plain as day she said she needs a ride home after her shift, which is, surprise of surprises, just ending."

"I thought they had to provide transportation after a certain hour," Julie says.

Doug raises his head and scowls. "Well, apparently this was before the certain hour, then, wasn't it? I mean, three o'clock in the afternoon? Are you going to let me tell this?"

Julie transfers her attention to Musko's other ear.

"So, she sat down at my table, and we talked about environmental science, and I drove her out to her road, and she said she could walk the rest of the way, it was just around the bend. Well, that was the first of many drives to her road, and soon we were just going for drives—so many range roads to explore and she wanted me to see the country. Before I knew it, she was coming onto me like—well, Jesus, if you'd been like that I wouldn't be in this mess."

"Where was Musko all this time?"

Doug pushes back the chair. "Oh, Jesus. My career is in shambles. My life is ruined. And you're worried about the fucking dog? That figures. That tells you something, doesn't it?"

Doug hauls himself to his feet and drifts over to the sideboard. He leans over it, studying the window, his back to Julie. "Anyway, it was summer and I was free and she was company. We had a good time. It wasn't hard keeping things quiet, because we just went off, the two of us. It was summer, you know, a summer thing we had. Now, when school started, the story changed. She had no sense of discretion and she could not seem to understand that summer things had to be kept under wraps. Oh, no. There she is, leaning across my desk and oh, so obvious. I'm cringing and backing off and conducting myself professionally, and she's crawling across my desk like this is the most natural thing in the world, and you can bet this gets noticed and, guess what? I, it seems, have turned her into this little wanton to satisfy my carnal desires. I have trained her up and brainwashed her and she is shocked and ashamed. Like she is waking up from a bad dream, for Christ's sake. Yes. Can you believe it? Well, the board decided, in their infinite wisdom, that the best solution was to fire Doug—quietly, of course— and shake their heads in dismay. They want Doug's license? We'll do an investigation, and take that license. Never fear, parents of the school, your board will look after this. Never mind Doug, who was in fact the victim here." He sighs, his head drooping. "I worked so hard for everything. Now it's all going to be taken away. Everything."

Running does not resolve a situation. If you run far enough, you will come to earth in the centre of all your unresolved issues. Julie knows. Now Doug knows. Does Rachel know?

"You didn't have to, Doug," Julie says.

Doug stares over his shoulder at her. "I was lonely," he says.

Julie closes her eyes, and canoes along a lakeshore where only she and Musko have ever been.

~

In the night, Julie pictures Doug's removal. The scene plays out with increasingly bizarre detail. At least, Julie hopes that it is bizarre. The constables grimly intone his rights as one presses a hand to Doug's head, guiding him into the car, its lights pulsing. (Why do they always put a hand on the head in the movies? Is the arrested one likely to bump his head, and then sue them? Julie broods over this, because it is better than remembering that somewhere out there a seventeen-year-old science student has learned a bitter lesson.) By chance, Samuel will pull into the driveway. He will stare, dumbfounded by this latest outrage on his ancestral home. Laila stands by the well, clutching a wilted welcome plant, while Joe shuffles in the background, a bloody shopping bag tucked behind his back. Janice walks down the driveway and puts an arm around Laila's shoulders, declaring that she knew this place was not good for Julie. Julie's father paces the barn site, scuffing the stony soil with his work boot as her mother wrings her hands. Last of all, the principal pulls up, demanding to know Julie's role in this sordid cover-up.

"Joe was supposed to make the call," Julie explains.

Laila stares, understanding dawning. "She knew," whispers Janice. "She knew and she didn't say. This is her third secret, isn't it?"

"He didn't belong here," Rachel announces from the top bunk, and then Julie knows that some of this, at least, is a dream. Rachel sighs. "Poor Doug. He did the best he could with what he had."

"How could you?" asks the trim but soft young woman with blonde highlights.

Her eyes are on Julie.

~

When the police come, it is a November morning and there are papers to be read and signed and then Doug is in his jeep and on his way to Alberta. Forwarding addresses are important, they tell him; he would have saved them all time and aggravation by simply remembering to provide a forwarding address.

It is not an American police show, at all.

He is a brief entry buried deep in the local newspaper, and then passes smoothly from Meadowbrook.

Julie's transition is less smooth. All eyes and questions focus on her. She has harboured a child molester. Laila campaigns on her behalf: Julie did not know.

But later she did know, and still she did nothing, many reply.

That is because Joe's boy was already looking after it.

Did she know that for a fact? Was she really sure?

Well, probably. It stands to reason.

If it'd been me, I'd of turfed him out first thing, they declare.

"You got any more pervert boyfriends hiding in your attic?" Marla, a Grade 11 student in her organizational coaching group, sums up public opinion. "I was wondering, do you get off on it?"

Honesty is hopefully still the best policy. "I don't, actually. I find it kind of upsetting," Julie replies.

"Yeah. Right. He got caught this time. Before he tried it here."

The situation calls for more than honesty. It calls for a stand. "He's gone now; that's the main thing." She cannot add "Good riddance." She knows that if she does, all will be forgiven, but she cannot say those words.

Why would she give away Doug's name, location, and position, if she were hiding him? She was always open about him, Laila declares. She just didn't know.

Perhaps she thought he wouldn't get found out, many speculate in return. It's a long way to Alberta. And she did have something on her mind. Remember the way she took off all of a sudden? With Joe?

They speculate further. Perhaps Joe wanted the new teacher for himself. So he blew the whistle on the boyfriend. Maybe he has his eye on Meadowbrook Acres.

For goodness' sake, that doesn't make any sense at all, Laila counters. She's renting.

Rachel wasn't, they remind her, and they pause to contemplate a number of interesting and possibly irrelevant connections. They settle back to look for signs of a simple romance between Joe and the new teacher.

Someone else will be harvesting Samuel's timber this winter, they predict.

Nervous grins replace open smiles at the gas bar, where the staff struggle to keep all factions apart. Staff at the hardware store stammer friendly greetings. Who, after all, buys a pool dinghy at the beginning of hunting season, unless they are trying to escape something? They should have known, and now they are at the crux of this awkward mess.

Bland smiles greet Julie in the staffroom, and Margaret steers the conversation toward her retirement plans. Roger asks about heating costs in Old Rose's house, and suggests that she consider a wood stove. Yet they all know. They are all waiting. Julie chokes down her sandwich and hurries off to gather resources. She feels the shift as they turn to one another, even as she closes the door.

Julie walks and works through the days, waiting for the storm to pass. Musko sprawls in the kitchen now, while Julie is at work.

~

Late November brings the first snow, and Laila shows up Saturday morning with fresh muffins, a thermos of coffee, and cross-country skis.

"Got to enjoy it while it lasts," she proclaims, as they head across the fields. "Might help if you got active in the church or something," she adds.

Musko burrows in the drifts, rooting for mice, as they survey the farmhouse, now a Christmas calendar page of snow-dense limbs and frosted windows dazzling in the morning light. The woods are silent, snow plopping from the pine branches, muffled against the drifts below as Laila and Julie push out a trail.

Finally, Laila sidesteps onto a narrow trail, where a rotting lean-to frame looms over the remains of a plank table. "Used to be a bough shack here," she puffs, working at her ski bindings. "Rachel's dad would cover that frame with fresh spruce boughs, and there was a fire pit, and they'd sit and toast bread and make tea. Her and her father and mother. Rachel kept it up for a while when Nathaniel was small. Well, people change."

Julie props her skis beside Rachel's. "I guess Doug changed," she says.

"Oh, I guess he kept his secrets. Seems to be a lot of that going around," Laila observes, brushing snow from the rocks that once formed a perfect ring. "I guess we won't be seeing that snow blower, after all," she adds.

"He's going to lose his teaching license."

"I thought he didn't want to teach no more," Laila says. "Had other dreams."

"I think he was just running." Julie crouches beside Laila, brushing at the rocks.

"A lot of that going around, too," Laila mutters, laying spruce boughs on the snow in the fire pit. "What about you? You gonna take off or face 'er down?"

"I've really got nowhere to go," Julie admits, snapping candle pieces to go with the bark and kindling that Laila is laying on the spruce boughs.

"So where did you go in that little boat of yours?" She leans back as the kindling catches.

Julie selects a muffin, nibbling around the top. Musko tenses beside her, eyes on her lips. "Boat?"

"Out to the cabin, was you?"

Julie takes a swig of coffee.

"Good place to hide. Good place to think." Laila offers Musko a taste of muffin.

"I just felt . . ." Julie hesitates.

"Got that journal on your mind, have you?" Laila pours coffee into her own mug.

"I only wanted to understand," Julie blurts.

"It's Rachel's business, not ours." Laila shrugs. "You can't go trying to figure her out that way. You have to find your own way."

"You are your own journal," Julie mutters.

"Exactly," Laila replies, biting into her muffin. "Now, if Rachel found out about Doug, she'd of kept quiet, too," she mumbles through the crumbs. "But when everything happened like it did, she'd of took off. You've stayed. You've got staying power."

"Which is mainly because I've really got nowhere to go," Julie reminds her.

"Oh, there's always places, if you look hard enough," says Laila. "Rachel's gone to one of those places, but she'll be back. Oh, the Hardys. The Hardys always come back."

Laila gestures toward the fir trees that dominate the open hillside nearby. "This was a Christmas tree lot one time. This was one more thing that Rachel was always going on about. Going on about it but doing nothing."

Laila's voice is flat as she prods the small fire. This is not an amusing tale of Rachel and the burning lawnmower, nor a wistful recollection of evenings on the lake. Rachel had a secret, and Laila was found wanting. The Hardys have closed ranks, and the friend is left outside.

"If you could have seen me, when that dinghy collapsed," Julie begins, and then all is right between Julie and Laila again.

All is not yet right between Laila and Rachel.

~

The snow retreats, and Samuel again walks his fields, slogging along the old road. His gaze sweeps from the emptiness where the barn would be to the stand of red pine that he and his father planted. Hour after backbreaking hour they dug and stomped until 5,000 tiny seedlings squatted in neat rows in the old hay. Now, they tower above him, the ground beneath them a carpet of needles to soothe his feet. He turns back along the track to the house. He plods up the attic steps, and there the Christmas lights glow about him. He reverently caresses the shattered glass ornament, tears spilling down his cheeks as the Christmases of his childhood slide by in his vision. There is love in his eyes, and there is loneliness and bewilderment, too.

Musko is nudging her cheek with his soft jowl, and it is Samuel the landlord who is tapping at the door this first Saturday morning of December.

Samuel is hoping that he has not disturbed her. He just thought that since he was going for his Christmas tree that she might want one, too. Not a sheared tree, you understand, but a natural tree. A little thin, a little uneven. An honest tree.

Julie flings food in Musko's dish, dresses, and crams an energy bar into her pocket.

The house has been larger and quieter since Doug left on that November morning. At first, Julie walked free in the house, painting when she wanted, walking when she wanted, working where she wanted. There was freedom, but so much of it. Sometimes, the silence and the space pressed against her temples, but still she did not ask her parents to come and still they mentioned seeing more of her when she was in Ontario. They do not want to intrude, but she knows that they are waiting, one hand on the suitcase, puzzled and ready. They have waited while Julie works through the traces of Doug that have lingered after his departure. An honest tree is what Julie needs to draw the goodness back into her life.

Every branch and every stalk is stark and clear in the opaque light of early December. The air is raw, the odour of leaves muted now. They trudge across the fields, Samuel babbling to Musko and Musko capering at his feet. He does not have a dog of his own, he explains to Julie, who is surprised.

As they wind through the old Christmas tree lot, Samuel asks how Doug is doing. He is not here anymore, Julie explains. Samuel is aware of that; he meant about the charges. Oh, yes. He has heard. That is how things work. No, he is not upset. After Grandma Mary, who, according to tradition cut her teeth on Spanish doubloons, nothing can be a shock in this house. He really means that he hopes that she, Julie, is all right. That is, is she staying?

In spite of all the stresses of November, Samuel still believes that Julie is good for this place. He smiles when she says that she is going to stay.

Samuel has only seen the broken glass ornament when Julie dreams.

"Just what the old place needs," Samuel declares, trimming the lower boughs from the first tree. "Someone with staying power."

Julie sees Doug, twisting in a slow circle, clutching at drifting balloons as he falls. The balloons burst into images: there is Doug teaching, Julie laughing in the canoe, the first day in North Bay, the mountains in the distance as Doug drives through Alberta, a wide-eyed young waitress smiling, a snow blower growling through the drifts. Each slips from his hands and Doug continues to fall. He will come to earth eventually, because it is, after all, such a small world.

The Wasaya Journal of Rachel Hardy: Part 6

ACADIAN AUNTS

When visitors come to Wasaya, the clouds lower, the wind rises, and fog and rain roll across the lake. Today, though, would be a perfect day for guests. The sun glitters on the water, and a gentle breeze fans the mosquitoes away. No one is coming, however, and I sit alone with my cottage treats in my porch overlooking the cove.

I have just returned from a weekend visit with my friend Laura. Our mothers had been colleagues and friends, and now we are friends. I have swum in her pool, sipped her wine, and enjoyed an excellent barbecue prepared by her husband. So many tastes, so subtle, no tins and boxes. I have luxuriated in electricity and running water. We have talked of parents passing, of estate settlements, of children leaving home, of health, retirement, and our futures.

As I drove back to Wasaya, I made brief stops to greet several people. I do not know them well, but they are part of the fabric of memory and therefore special. I want to remember each of them, and be remembered by them. They cannot drive past me at Wasaya, toot the horn, and wave, so I must seek them out. Distance. Isn't that what I wanted? Yet I stare at the empty lake each day, and picture crowds of people paddling to my cabin. I picture afternoon picnics out at the island, swimming in the cool, deep water, children's laughter ringing.

The children have grown, however, and have slipped to the edges of our lives. I think that we all hear the laughter, and grieve for it in the silence. We do not want our restless, grown children back under our roofs, but we do want those years back, to live them better and cherish them better.

There lies the problem: If we knew we were living them again, we would dread their passing instead of enjoying their presence. If we did not know, then we would again sigh over fighting, whining youngsters, and wonder why we came.

I would hug the house when I returned to Meadowbrook Acres, pressing my arms and cheek tight to the chipped paint. My mother would unpack, silent, her chin set just a little. Perhaps the memories hovered too closely for her, too, even though she also was in the place she had chosen.

When the car was empty, the supper ready, the dog greeted, and the news on, perhaps little hauntings would ease in through the cracks. I know that my mother was always silent her first night back, her eyes fixed on a point beyond us.

I know that when I return to Wasaya, the memories of Meadowbrook are strongest and harshest.

My mother told us repeatedly that she came from a Very Happy Home. Her father was a Very Intelligent Man. She told and told the stories, but she sneered as she told them. I felt ashamed and guilty: this home, our home, could not, then, be a Very Happy Home, and we could not be, then, Very Intelligent. My mother treated her present as her own personal Fall; she was, in her own way, roaming the earth trying to find her way back to Paradise. The Angel of Time, though, was barring that gate with a flaming sword.

~

I want to go back to Paradise, too. I want to stay here yet access Paradise at will. I understand that much of you now, Mother.

~

The Hardy aunts were strong, regular presences in our lives. When they spoke, it was done. The Acadian aunts were delicate presences, shifting along the borders of our lives.

Aunt Juliette came to live with us for a while when I was two. I do not remember her, but I have the stories. Aunt Juliette lived with us until her cancer advanced and she went to the hospital to die. One day while she was still living with us, she did up her hair and put on her best bed jacket and waited at the kitchen table for her husband's visit. As it was, when he rolled into the yard, he was too drunk to walk to the door. My mother stood straight and firm on the verandah, frowning and pointing down the driveway until he and his driver finally left. Now, my uncle could not face his wife's impending death sober, so perhaps she should have let him in. However, that would be a violation of the Very Happy Childhood: your husband does not visit you drunk when you are dying. At any rate, my aunt continued to sit at the kitchen table, with her hair brushed and coiled and her best bed jacket over her shoulders, while my mother told and retold the story of my uncle's departure.

They say that my aunt was crazy when she died, that she stumbled screaming from the hospital and had to be restrained. She was screaming for her little girl.

I did not think she was crazy. She was a dying mother wolf, flinging herself with her last strength between her pup and the world that threatened her.

I felt her courage. Her courage and her rage.

~

Every summer, just before school started, we would visit my serene, gentle Aunt Cecile for the day. She presided over her table with grace, and you became a humbler, better person in her presence. We would stare across the bread and pickles at our Real Acadian cousins, who spoke English to us because we were Anglophones and they were already bilingual. Even estranged members of the family communicated with Aunt Cecile. She had that effect on people. She was like Laila. She was not typical in our family.

We heard the stories of Aunt Rejean, who joined the Air Force and went north and had wonderful adventures. She married and stayed in the North and raised her family. When I met her I was nearly twenty, and she was young and vibrant and played guitar. She was always laughing, always ready with a joke. More aunts should be like her.

Aunt Cecile and Aunt Rejean could have taught us so much about self-discipline, each in their own way. We did not see the struggle of poverty; we did not see the shadows behind the laughing eyes.

I slide ahead to an image of my mother, long after I had gone to university. She was standing at the back of the church, her palms braced on either side of the guest book, staring at Aunt Claudette's name. She was the one of the shorts and the Immaculate Mary and the five years in Boston, remember. She had visited every summer, at least until I was sixteen; that was my last summer with her daughter, my close summer cousin, who was growing up and away and working. So, she had come once again, and she had been here, but she had not phoned. Was there a message in the name and date? It might have been: *I came, but they kept me from you. Please read this, and come for me.* It could be, however: *Yes, I came, and where I go and what I do is my business.*

My mother brushed her forehead with holy water, genuflected, and crossed herself on cue, her rosary beads clicking. Perhaps she thought of the story of Aunt Claudette and the mouse. That was a good story. It seems that my mother and Aunt Claudette were at Mass in the Great Church by Grammie's house when they were girls. Aunt Claudette had the bad luck to glance up at the sanctuary lamp, and there on the chain was a little mouse. It would shuffle down the chain from the ceiling, extend a cautious paw to the hot lamp, and then scurry back up. Somehow it had gotten on the chain, but could not find a way off the chain, and alternately shuffled down and streaked back up the chain.

Aunt Claudette unwisely nudged my mother and pointed, and they stifled giggles for the rest of the Mass while the Sisters frowned.

I do not know why Aunt Claudette, who laughed and hid cigarettes and hauled skirts over shorts when the Sisters came, who giggled while the mouse danced with the sanctuary lamp, wrote her name in the book and did not call. It is something you put behind you, and draw up memories of the Very Happy Childhood to soothe your bruised heart.

There was another aunt, Aunt Janine, who visited us often when we were young. She was the one who stayed with the uncle with the unclean hands. She had her second child while visiting us, and my mother hired a driver to take them home to the city afterward. My mother and the driver took her to her new apartment to wait for her husband. Now my mother said that although her sister had never seen that apartment, it was all set up, and obviously by a woman's hand. She did not think that her husband had hired a decorator. They left Aunt Janine with her little girl and her new baby, staring at the walls of her new apartment, the one that a woman who was not a decorator had prepared.

Years later, after her divorce, she wrote to each member of the family and politely informed them that she no longer wished to be a member of the family, and did not want to be contacted in any way. Did they know that she shivered at her uncle's house when she was a little girl and was sent away? Did they wonder if she still shivered?

My mother was dumbfounded, but she coped. She continued her new life, her Happy Childhood refrain now bitter and defiant. She seized her Very Happy Childhood and the Very Intelligent Man in her fists and she shook them in our faces, daring us to defy her truth.

I felt more and more like an intruder, who had taken the Happy Childhood away. Surely I could not be related to the Very Intelligent Man, for I was so unlike him.

And then one night my aunt Claudette, she of the sanctuary lamp and the guest book, she of the five years in Boston with her own dog, went home from work with a headache. A few days later she was found comatose in her apartment, while her husband, who survived gassing in the war, cried in a corner of the room. She died not long afterward in the hospital of a brain tumour.

My mother developed high blood pressure that day, and it never was low again. She stopped coping that day, and never coped well again.

I want there to be laughter on the verandah at Meadowbrook Acres. I want to hear feet drumming on the boards and screen doors slamming. I want to spread salads and fresh rolls across the table, and steaming platters of corn. They will crowd the kitchen there and here, at Wasaya, and I will laugh and greet them all as I weave through the crowd.

I came here to be alone. I am afraid of crowds. I am tormented by very happy childhoods, real and imagined.

Chapter 17

PASSAGES

Tina offers the creased sheet of loose leaf to Julie. "I write things, sometimes," she whispers, eyes on the window.

Julie unfolds the paper on the table, smoothing it with her palm, and reads.

> Warm toes knead in and out,
> Pressing into my pillow.
> Her eyes are wide, watching me.
> I am her world, and she is mine.
> She purrs against the shadows
> And I stop dreaming.
> I stop dreaming that I am falling
> While dark arms lock me tight.
> I smile.
> Do you want to see the snow? I say.
> She purrs.
> Her face rubs mine.
> I am her world, and she is mine.
> I opened the door and I broke the pattern.
> Now the dark dreams hold me.

I am alone, falling in darkness.
Arms press me. I cannot breathe.
My pattern is gone.
My world is gone.
I am alone.

By Tina

"You are very talented," Julie begins. Tina lowers her head, her long bangs trailing over her face.

"But what are these dark arms?" Julie continues.

Tina shrugs, hair still spilling over her face, eyes again on the window.

"Tina. Is someone hurting you?"

Tina moans, rocking, arms folded tight, eyes squeezed shut. "Please, no," she whispers.

Julie leans forward. "Tina, please. I have to do something. I can't let someone hurt you."

Tina sobs. "It's just dreams," she says. "Dreams because I lost my cat."

"But you say here you were dreaming before." Julie feels perspiration gathering on her skin. She hates doing this. What if it is just a child's poem? But, oh, what if it is not?

"No, no. no," Tina says, her hair whipping back and forth as she shakes her head. "I always had dreams, bad dreams. Now they're worse. They never happened. Not for real. It's just dreams. You dream."

"I dream?" Tina has spoken with such conviction that for a moment Julie sees Tina perched on the attic window ledge while Samuel walks through Julie's dreams.

"When you dream, it doesn't mean it happened. Just maybe it might happen. But maybe, not at all. That's how I dream." Tina places one palm over the poem. Her body spasms as she crushes the words into her fist. "I made a poem for you, about my cat. You made it ugly."

Tina slides from her chair and wanders into the hall, the paper squeezed in her clenched fingers.

Julie will have to report this. She should have taken her time, built some trust, and gathered more data. Instead, she has charged in, alienated Tina by pressuring her, and doesn't even have the poem for analysis. Nevertheless, the report must be made. A social worker will interview Tina, talk to her parents, and investigate her home. Everyone will be in turmoil, and it just might be a child's way of saying that she misses her cat.

After all, Julie dreams, and the Hardys are not really gathering in the night.

But what if the dark arms are real? What if they really do lock her in the night?

Oh, Tina. I cannot take that chance. Yet you have finally, finally trusted me, and will you ever trust me again?

~

Julie calls her parents that night, for they have waited, puzzled and ready, far too long. She has had time for Laila and for the Hardys and for the cabin and even for Doug. She has not found time for her own history.

Then again, perhaps Laila and the Hardys and the cabin and even Doug are now woven into her history, part of her past, her present, and her future.

Her parents will not simply pack an overnight bag. There will be an agenda of preparations, no doubt, involving memorabilia and rituals, that will fill in the hours between now and Saturday morning. They suggest that Julie try to get all her school work "out of the way" Friday night, so that they will have Saturday and Sunday "for family."

Julie knows that Tina is not someone to be gotten "out of the way." There are questions, so many questions by so many people. And maybe, just maybe, the problem is right there, in Tina's family. Julie needs her own family to keep these thoughts away. Her family will purge the last traces of Doug and of dark arms.

Do Tina and the science student have someone to do this for them?

She could have faced her parents sooner. Perhaps she should have. However, she has not.

~

Her mother glides her hand over the red maple table in the kitchen and gives a blissful sigh. Her father frowns at the ancient fridge and stove, hands on his hips. "Those safe?" he says.

"So open," her mother murmurs, taking in the dining room, den, and living room area.

Her father eases himself into one of the cane chairs in the living room. "We've got some things in the basement," he begins. His attention drifts to the stairwell, takes in the plain bannister and newel post. He purses his lips, considering them.

"I like it fine just the way it is," her mother breaks in. "No clutter."

Her mother is gracious about the double air mattresses in their room, across from Grandma Mary's lair. "It'll be like Kedge," she declares.

"I could get some lumber and throw together a frame this afternoon," her father says.

"Theo." Her mother raises a cautioning hand.

"I just want to help out," her father mutters.

"You're not," she murmurs. She beams at Julie. "We know how busy you are. We packed everything for lunch, so we can just enjoy our time together."

We will smile and beam at one another and wallow in our lost memories all afternoon.

Julie hides her salad preparations deep in the fridge and slides the lasagna into the freezer, her hands trembling. She shuts the door a little too firmly, but she manages to exclaim in delight over the roast chicken, homemade rolls, potato salad, and spice cake. They have even brought paper plates, so that they can enjoy their time together. They have thought of everything to make her happy. She wishes that she could tell them that she had lunch all prepared. She had made a good lunch, one that would make them proud of her. She recognizes that this is childish, but she feels it just the same.

Musko sidles up to Alice Martin as she arranges the chicken. "Such a friendly dog," she says. "Wasn't Doug nice to bring him back to you?"

"He shouldn't have taken him in the first place," Julie replies. She pictures Musko, pacing a dingy apartment while Doug drove free on the range roads through rolling fields, a laughing young woman with blonde highlights at his side.

"Well, he's here now," Alice says, slipping Musko a piece of dark meat.

"That's a fine dog," Theo remarks. "How's he behave in a canoe?"

Julie pictures a perplexed Musko, squashed in the centre of a sixteen-foot canoe, while her parents point out Tim and Julie's favourite haunts, and suppresses a smile. "Oh, he likes to jump out once in a while," she says.

Theo considers this. "You could train him out of that, with a little time and patience."

That would not be Musko, Julie thinks. "This all looks so delicious," she exclaims instead, for this is their day, in her kitchen, and they will be happy and welcome. She will not say that this is better than the lasagna she prepared, or would they like leftover salad for lunch tomorrow. "How about a walk in the woods, after?" she does say.

Her father's face lights up. The mystery Hardy house has turned out to be hollow, just a plain shell with a little workmanship along the door casings. The woods should reveal a better reality.

"I've got the fixings for a venison stew for tonight," Julie continues, "and then maybe we could bring in my little tree and decorate it."

Her mother produces a flat, rectangular box, which she waves playfully. "Guess what we brought?" she sings.

~

All in all, the visit is a qualified success. The patchwork of woodlots and overgrown pastures beyond the stand of red pines has been investigated and its potential—if not its management—approved. The tree has been decorated with cross-stitched and beaded ornaments crafted by Alice all through Julie's childhood. The history of each has been duly recalled. The Park has been visited on Sunday morning, and a picnic consumed at the favourite campsite. The departure of Doug has been avoided. After all, Doug is not really part of family history; he is not part of Kedge times. The parents depart late Sunday afternoon, hardly able to believe that Christmas is only two weeks away. Two weeks is nothing. Soon, they will all be together again.

In the evenings, Julie sits cross-legged in front of the tree, fingering the little gold trumpet stitched with a red bow inside a tiny brass circle. It is so delicate, so detailed. Her mother worked it, stitch by intricate stitch, when Julie was four. Into the pattern she worked her hopes and her love for her daughter. Did she mean to bind Julie to her four-year-old self? Julie wonders who will dream her, tucked away in a closet or an attic, weeping over her lost Christmases.

When you dream, it doesn't mean it happened. Just maybe it might happen. But maybe, not at all.

For Tina, it turns out, it did happen. Days before the Christmas holidays begin, it is learned that twelve-year-old Tina has indeed been falling, crushed by dark arms in the night.

Tina's uncle no longer lives with the family.

Tina's father is outraged, although whether on behalf of Tina or the uncle is not always clear.

Tina's mother, typically quiet, withdraws a little more. The head ducks a little more and the shoulders cringe a little more when she ventures to the store or post office.

Many watch the parents, pitying both because this is the worst thing. There is also relief, because it is not them, not their child. There is a hint of reproach, too; they should have known.

The uncle, all agree, was always a strange one. You could sense it. But the poor man, he needed help.

Tina is watched and pitied because, oh, she was so young. But she, too, is reproached: why didn't she speak up right away? This could have been nipped in the bud.

While they watch, they look for signs. People who have been through Tina's experience are changed, remember. They act differently now. They might even act out, doing things. They might do angry things. They might do unto others as was done unto them, but Tina doesn't babysit anyway so it is probably not a problem. Yet. They might also act in. These are the silent signs. Remember, Christmas is a dangerous time for this sort of thing.

Her classmates watch and wait and wonder. What will Tina do? What did Tina do? What *does* Tina do?

And through it all wanders Tina, victim child on trial. Her eyes accuse Julie, but she is silent.

Julie sits by her tree and it occurs to her that she had a stable upbringing and here she is, lost, weeping at childhood portals but not willing to let the past in. Tina has not had a stable upbringing. She weeps for her cat, but she is truly weeping for a childhood that never was.

Twenty years from now, will Tina be coming home for Christmas? Will she hug her burly father, a little gruffer, a little greyer? Will she wrap her mother's shoulders in a shawl that she saw at the bazaar and knew would be perfect for her? Or will she sit in a bare apartment while her balding husband belches and complains about the game? Will she dare to slip out, just for a minute, to see the stars? Will he let her have a cat? Will he be kind to Tina and her cat?

Julie sits by her tree and wishes she were free. And she wishes her four-year-old fingers could grasp the little trumpet and hold Christmas snug and safe forever.

Julie cocoons herself by her tree, and although she feels concern for Tina, her grief is again mostly for Julie.

Julie rises and strips the remaining signs of Doug from Grandma Mary's room. She peels away the floral wall paper in the evenings, and paints the walls a soft cream. Light blue curtains are chosen, and they grace the tall windows.

When winter's damp is past, this will be her room. She will cheer this room and that will push back all the shadows. The floor will stop settling; the leaves will not whisper against the windows in the night. They did not whisper for Doug, only for Julie. She will send them away with new curtains. She will look at her garden from this window and that will help to reclaim this house. Future memories will be made. She will not miss being four, and she will not resent her parents for wanting her to be four. This room will be a sign for her future.

Musko paces in the doorway, whuffing occasionally as she works.

Chapter 18

FIRST STEPS

Tina's bangs drag over her cheekbones as she hunches before the test panel. Thirty seconds have passed.

"Try this one," Julie murmurs, tapping the next entry on the word-recognition test.

Tina's mouth twists and she turns away. She tips back her head, her eyes fixed on the window, her hair still spilling over her face.

"Come on, Tina. Please?"

Tina leans forward again, shoulders stiff, arms rigid. Fists clench beneath the table. She begins to rock.

What should one say to Tina to put her at ease? You are among friends, Tina. How was your Christmas, Tina? What did you do over the holidays? Are you glad to be back in school?

Do you want to hear about my Christmas, Tina? You might find it very interesting. Well, I passed four days at my parents' house in Waverley, where I was immersed in rituals and traditions? Each moment was heart-warming and tender and threatening to pull me back into my childhood and trap me forever. Did you know, Tina, that there was sweetness and yearning and restlessness and a sense of doors swinging shut on well-oiled hinges, so that I would not notice until it was too late? Do you know what I mean, Tina?

How did they do this, you ask? Well, my mother stirred and baked serenely through the days while my father turned out fine ash axe handles in his workshop. You see, Tina, he stopped making paddles after I rebuffed the one he made for me. He hung it on the wall beside my life jacket. It was hard for me. My parents were a little greyer this Christmas, a little sadder, even for them. They seemed bewildered, Tina, that their children were grown, and they were still growing.

I have a brother, Tim. Did you know that, Tina? He came for Christmas Day and Boxing Day. He was very hearty, Tina, in a clinical way, if you can imagine that. When he was a little boy, Tina, he would go charging through the campground at Kedge, his bicycle weaving and wobbling. Then he grew into a banker. But do you know something, Tina? The Martins and the Hardys do not really grow with change; they fade.

Tina, I used to be enthusiastic and looking forward. Now I am teetering and wobbling, Tina, like a child on a bike one size too large. I might find my rhythm, but then again I might collapse. See my parents hovering on the sidelines, Tina, clutching bandages? Do you know the feeling?

~

Before her sits Tina, who is about to turn thirteen. Her almost-thirteen-year-old body has been squeezed and prodded and bent and rammed, and because this is now known, she is an outcast. What place does Julie's heart-tugging Christmas have in this context?

"Let's try something else," Julie says instead. "I'm going to ask you to do some math."

Tina's eyes skim the first page, and then she turns away. "You told," she says.

Julie tucks the workbook away and folds the test panel back into its binder. "Maybe we could do this another time," she says.

"You told. I didn't want you to," Tina insists.

"I had to," Julie explains. "It's the law."

"You told."

"Like I said—"

"And he's got court—"

"But he was hurting you—"

"It's like I'm dirty. Everybody knows. They're ashamed of me."

"You're not dirty, Tina. No one should be ashamed of you."

"In the store. I heard. They said I liked the things, so that's why I never told."

"Oh, Tina. Whoever said that is wrong."

"They all think it. They look at me, and they think it. I wish you never told."

"I bet Christmas was kind of hard."

"It's worse now. In school."

"It will pass. Give it time."

"It won't. I can't."

"Are you seeing the counsellor?"

"Are your dreams always sad?"

Now where did this come from? "My dreams?"

"That's the dream house." Tina gives a little shake. Julie waits, shivers running goose flesh over her arms. "My friend? Amy? They had that place a while. Amy says it made her mother cry so much they didn't stay. It was the dreams. She got a depression."

"Do you know what she dreamed about?" Julie knows that she should be redirecting the conversation back to Tina's pain, yet here she is, invading the privacy of Amy's mother instead.

Tina shrugs. "She would just wake up, sad. And she'd cry. She cried a lot."

"Well, my dreams are fine," Julie assures her.

Tina huddles in her chair, her face again hidden in her bangs. "I don't like it when you lie," she says.

Musko had been happy to return to Meadowbrook Acres, to leash-free roaming of the fields and sprawling on beds. Musko has nudged her awake when the post-Christmas dreams have become unbearable. For Rachel has been smashing the frail glass baubles from Samuel's honest tree with her paddle, but all Samuel can see is a rosy-cheeked child in ringlets, shaking wondrous presents that she clutches from under the tree. A soft muzzle nuzzles Julie's face into wakefulness just as Samuel's face begins to contort in shock, his eyes wide as he sees the paddle.

"Well," Julie admits, as if it had just occurred to her, "sometimes I get sad dreams, but I suppose it is natural, in January, I mean. It's so gloomy out."

Tina considers this. "Miss Hardy taught my mom once. My mom said she confused everybody."

"Well, substitutes sometimes do."

"She was worse, my mom said."

"Well, that's all in the past now, Tina."

Tina leans forward, still rocking a little. "It's still happening, there."

Julie frowns. "What do you mean, Tina? Why do you say that?"

Tina finally pushes the bangs back, revealing dark eyes that are deep and blank all at once. "I don't know," she says. "Maybe I should do my test?"

"Tomorrow," Julie decides. "I'll test someone else today, I think. You need a little time."

"But I could," Tina insists. "I could do the test now, I think."

Julie sighs. "Actually, Tina, I think I'm the one who needs that little time."

Tina pushes herself to her feet. "I still wish you never told." She pauses. "I got a new cat now. A kitten, like."

"Oh!" Julie exclaims. "Is she nice?"

Tina swings her head. "She's just a cat."

"Maybe now."

"Yeah. Maybe." Tina fades into the hallway.

There was a time in history when Tina would have been marked to become the wise woman of her village. In more recent history, she would have been burned as a witch. In this day, she is an abused poet child becoming an awkward, lonely presence, an embarrassment, a stranger with no place in the world.

~

Julie receives an e-mail from Doug. Teaching licenses in Alberta and Ontario are now revoked, based on the board's investigation. He is still waiting for his court date. He is drawing employment insurance, and will go on the rigs when the dust settles. He will not teach again, even when his name is cleared. He has had it with the profession, and he cannot understand how she can continue in it, after what it has done to him. He has had it with deceitful boards, parents, and students. They get you when you're lonely and they come after you when they can't control you. All of them.

~

Russ Barnes, Laila informs her, has a different slant on the story. The science girl has dropped out of school. She never leaves her house out on the range road. She admits that she had a crush on her science teacher. She admits that she flirted with him, and could hardly believe it when he returned her interest. She had never thought that what they shared was an affair; she had thought of it as a step to marriage—not now, but maybe when she got to college. Why would he sleep with her, how was it possible to sleep with her like that, if he didn't care for her?

It is said that she is no longer trim and neat. The highlights have dulled. The brace-less teeth never show in a smile. The contact-shielded eyes are red-rimmed. There is talk that the family will move soon, once things are settled.

"Well," Laila says, rinsing her mug in Julie's sink and stretching, "it just goes to show. Everything you do is gonna do something some-where. People get hurt that way."

Julie offers Musko a piece of cheese from their snack tray. "Is Russ Barnes credible?"

"Oh, I would imagine. And I would bet Joe toned it down some, before he passed it on. He can be awfully shy. You know about his wife?"

Julie casts back over the cabin conversation. There had been a wife. Yes. "She left him, didn't she, after their kids were grown up?"

Laila leans back against the sideboard, arms folded, head tilted to one side. "You could say that. They had two sons, you see."

"Right. I remember. There's Russ, in High Prairie. Drilling?" She did focus on someone besides herself that Sunday afternoon, Laila. She did listen to another's story, not just tell her own.

"Mechanic."

"Right." Julie sifts through her memory. "Boys. He said boys. So there's at least one more son. But he just talked about Russ."

"That would be Jacob. He's named after his grandfather. You met him. At the exhibition?"

"*That's* Joe's father?" Joe's father worked fo-ah that ha'd man, that Stephen Ha'dy?

Laila nods, as if this were obvious. "Well, young Jacob went off to Alberta, too, after he finished high school. Only he wanted to go on the rigs, instead of university right away, like his mother wanted. She was happy enough with Russ going to community college, but Jacob was university material. Oh, he could've gone straight through university, no problem.

"Now Joe thought it was just fine, him going off to Alberta. Man's gotta find his own way and all that. That's the way Joe had lived his life, and he was doing fine—regular work at the assembly plant, family provided for, weekends at the camp to make it worthwhile.

"But there's accidents on the rigs. Bad ones. He was only out there six months. Oh, they took it hard."

Julie's chest tightens. Joe walks on the pine needles, doing a little hunting and fishing, a little cutting. And at the back of his mind always, always, there is Jacob, spinning in space as he falls, or lying crushed or burnt, or all of these. Joe raises his Winchester to his cheek and the dawn is still and Jacob will never do this, will never know this, and the leaves flame along the island but not for Jacob. Oh, Jacob. Oh, Joe.

"Those things," Laila is saying, "will either make or break a couple. This time it broke. Joe took to drinking heavy when it happened. His wife left, not long after it happened. Said she couldn't bear to be around all those memories, and I suspect, too, facing Joe was hard. He encouraged young Jacob to go—while his mother was fighting to get him to go to university. Hard for both to face that, I imagine. Well, they went their separate ways, and Joe was in hard shape for a while. He came home, then, and he got sobered up. That's been a few years now—oh, more than that." She frowns, muttering over her fingers.

"And his wife?"

Laila pauses in her calculations. "She's with her own people. They say she gets through the days. But you don't get over something like that. Now Russ, bless him, tried to keep on good terms with them both. He's the one who lost a brother, and he's the one got his parents through it, as much as they did. Joe seems all relaxed and content, says he was never meant for big industry, just for doing a little cutting, but he's one lonely human being."

Julie leans her elbows on the table, and pokes crumbs together. She ponders what to say in response. "I wonder what the real story is. About Doug," she says at last.

Laila straightens her back and sighs. "Well, Joe told me what's said, but that don't make it so. Only Doug and that girl know what happened and why, and I wouldn't wager they know for sure. It's like that mess with Tina Anderson."

"Tina?"

"Oh, you know what I'm talking about, I'm sure. Little Tina? Maybe thirteen? You must see her at school."

"Oh, yes." Julie catches herself. Is it a fourth secret if she does not tell Laila that she is responsible for exposing the first mess and creating the second? After all, the report is confidential, even though the details certainly were not held in confidence. "I know who you mean."

"Well, it turns out her dad's brother, he lived with them, and he was at her—oh, for a while now. She finally told, which she has every right to do, and now she looks sadder than ever." Laila shakes her head.

"But the abuse must have been worse," Julie insists.

"Oh, I don't doubt." Laila focuses on the floor. "The point is: it's never over. Stopping the problem is just the first step. You still got all the mess afterward to get through. And she's just a child now; she needs a lot of help."

"She will get counseling," Julie points out, and the words resonate, detached and cold in her ears.

"Friends," Laila declares, shrugging into her down jacket. "They all need friends. Friends from all ages and walks of life to see them strong."

Friends for Joe and his lost wife. Friends for Doug and the science student. Friends for Tina, especially Tina, so fragile and alone: her pain is exposed in all its rawness.

Friends for Doug. She is ready to hope that he finds friends, but she is not ready to be one.

She can, perhaps, manage Tina. Maybe she can see her strong.

"She's gotta know someone believes in her," Laila calls over her shoulder as she tugs on her boots. "You're in a good position to help, here."

The idea is hovering on the edges of her mind. Julie presses away images of the many ways she could do this wrong. She seizes the idea, and it spills open, warm and snug. There will be a sledding party, a great sledding party, out on Samuel's hills. Janice will bring Mark and Jenna and their friends, and there will be hot chocolate and marshmallows and soft, melting cookies and maybe even a bonfire. There will be laughter and wet mittens and glowing cheeks. There will be too many children, so they will need helpers. Janice can select these from her Grade 7 students. She can select Tina.

It will be a training of sorts, an afternoon of fun. Joe and his lost wife and Doug and the science student and Tina: there is all the mess to go through afterward for all of them.

She has the strength for one. She has the strength to see Tina strong. She only hopes that Tina is ready for the dream house.

Chapter 19

BLACK ICE

January brings black ice on the roads. Black ice means school closures: no buses, no cars, no walkers will attempt the school on black ice days. The trick of black ice is its subtlety; there are no grey patches, no frosted edges of warning. You are gliding along the open, clear road, and suddenly your vehicle is soaring over the road out of control, perhaps swinging into the other lane or hurtling toward the ditch.

As your hands and feet work the steering wheel and pedals, you see that there are no banks to cushion you and you are now helpless, although the skies are clear and the light is dazzling.

Black ice is a deadly secret in the midst of this calm.

The schools close on black ice days.

Julie and Musko walk the stubbled fields on black ice days, crunching footprints into the patches of crust. Julie gazes back at the house, its snug leaf bags tucked around the sills, and sees the heat pulsing from the furnace through the high-ceilinged rooms and out of cracks and seams into the frosty air. On January evenings, she shuffles about in heavy socks and extra sweaters and imagines twisting the thermostat all the way up to 18° and soaking in a steaming tub of water.

Laila anticipates a great snowstorm with drifts piled high and a brush of crust and children toppling down the gentle first hill at

Meadowbrook Acres. There will be shrieks of excitement and rosy cheeks and hot chocolate. Laila becomes like a child herself as she studies weather forecasts and hopes. She and Janice have a sliding party emergency crew ready for the event: Mark and Jenna, their four cousins, and helpers Amy and Tina. All are waiting for the great snowstorm, for as soon as it is over, the phones will ring and all will rush to the hill.

Tina's mother has had some reservations about the event, but Janice has managed to override these. Yes, there were going to be six children. Well, you're right; they did say that, that people with Tina's trouble might "do things." Never mind them; you have to go on living. Janice herself will be watching over Tina, after all, and Tina gets along well with Ms. Martin. And Laila—well, Laila is like a mother to everyone. Amy has an active imagination; the house is just a house, and will not give Tina a depression. At any rate, they will be coasting outside. And, yes, that fellow from the West is definitely gone now. This will be good for Tina.

The long-awaited snowstorm sweeps down on a Wednesday evening in late January, packing the fields, the woods, the trails, and the roads in dense whiteness. School is closed on Thursday as the plows wallow against the drifts. On Friday, the snow is falling lightly. The temperature holds. Saturday, Laila decrees, will be perfect.

Saturday afternoon is, however, not perfect. The sky is dull and overcast, the air raw with the promise of more snow. It is, though, sufficient to bring joy to six children for an hour or so. There will be soggy mittens and damp socks, sharp exclamations of frustration and boredom as fingers and toes chill, but then there will be hot chocolate and piles of cookies in a warm kitchen. Julie bakes on Saturday morning, anticipating squeals of delight and sighs of satisfaction as little teeth sink into the soft dough. She braces, too, for tears and wailing. There will, after all, be six children on that hill.

Laila arrives promptly at one-thirty, her car disgorging Mark, Jenna, and an aloof Amy, who promptly needs the washroom. Laila lugs in homemade doughnuts while Mark and Jenna trundle about the kitchen trailing open jackets and unsnapped snow pants, in the manner of all children caught between outdoors and in.

"My mom's room looks nice," Amy announces as she strides back from the washroom.

"You shouldn't go snooping like that, Amy," Laila tells her, arranging the tray of doughnuts on the counter. "It's not right."

Amy rearranges her long wispy ponytail. "I wasn't snooping. Besides, it was right down the hall. I like the blue curtains and stuff." She turns to Julie, her face grave. "Mom never got around to fixing it up. She got sick. Very sick," she whispers. She waits for anticipated murmurs of sympathy and understanding.

"Oh," Julie says, and arranges the Styrofoam cups.

Amy frowns and leans on the table. "Those," she declares, "are bad for the environment. You should use real ones and wash them."

"Are you offering?" Julie asks.

"If I have time—with the kids and all." Amy squats down and grins at Jenna. Jenna regards her with a solemn expression.

Janice swings her minivan around Laila's car and parks beside Julie's SUV. The door slides open and two freckle-faced Grade 1 boys clamour out, stiff in their snowsuits. Arms rigid at their sides, they survey the hill. Janice leans in, fumbling with belts, and emerges with a four-year-old in her arms, arguing or encouraging until a Grade 2 girl slumps out and picks her way over to join the boys.

"The twins," Laila explains. "They'd be her husband's brother's boys, and that girl is his sister's. She's too old for coasting with kids," Laila adds gravely.

The bundle in Janice's arms begins to thrash. Little legs kick and churn; short arms flap up and down. Janice releases her and she clomps up to the verandah to grip Jenna by the hand. Mark stands apart, rubbing Musko's ribs.

Janice is at the front passenger door now, leaning in and coaxing Tina, hunched down in her seat. Finally, Tina leans forward, teeters in the doorway for a moment, and then drops to the driveway. Forlorn in a quilted jacket and unlikely tasseled toque, Tina jams her hands into her pockets and stares at the roof.

Amy pelts down the roughly shoveled path, arms spread wide. "Welcome!" she cries. She locks her arms around Tina's shoulders and hauls her toward the house. "Welcome to the dream house," she continues in a hoarse whisper.

Tina shrugs her away. "Don't," she says.

Musko has been waiting and observing, tail swinging as Mark's hands move over his ribs. Now he trots from the verandah and stops in front of Tina. She stands rigid, her eyes wide. Musko whuffs, his tail waving. Tina holds out a cautious hand. Musko's tail flops rapidly over his back and he brushes Tina's fingers with his tongue. She withdraws the hand, but does not return it to her pocket.

"Let's get his harness on," Julie calls.

Soon the pilgrimage is organized. Musko plods in the lead, his head turning frequently to ensure that the two little girls are secure on the toboggan behind him. Julie jogs at his side. Mark is towed by Laila, and the twins by their auntie Janice. The Grade 2 cousin, Samantha, pulls her own toboggan and chatters away at Amy, who strolls along, staring at the pines. Tina drifts at the rear of the pack, her hands once again deep in her pockets.

The coasting part of the sledding party goes as any experienced parent might expect. There are wails of disappointment as the toboggans inch their way from the top of the hill, soon bogging down in the dense snow. The twins declare that the second hill, the steep one that sweeps down into the marsh in the flats below, would be "way funner." Grade 2 Samantha smiles indulgently as she minces about in the deep snow, while Amy and Tina stand in the background, scuffing their boots in the snow. Musko romps about, barking encouragement to all.

Julie realizes now that she should have been up at dawn, figuring out a way to make a track—a broad, slick track with interesting bumps. Instead, she is tugging at the cords, willing the toboggans forward while the sledding party grinds to a standstill. Laila and Janice stand together, chatting about coasting victories past, relaxing and not seeing the grim spectacle that is today's party.

Julie wades up to them. "Do something," she pants.

Laila regards her, a smile easing from the corner of her mouth and spreading across her face. "Somethin'? Well," she drawls. She seizes Samantha's toboggan and flops down on it in one of the pitiful tracks. Janice pumps along behind her, pushing her shoulders and whooping. Then Janice is face down in the snow and Laila plummeting down the hill to screams of delight.

Janice follows with Jenna and little Rayanne, and the twins fall in behind them. Julie races behind Mark, springing on at the last instant in the second track, and they meander all the way to the bottom.

The tracks are set, and the sledding party takes off. The helpers creep forward, and are soon pushing and running, at times even tugging a loaded sled back up the hill. Soon they can fly down the hill, slowing only as they reach the flats.

Samantha sets aside her maturity as Amy jumps on behind her and they scream down the hill. Tina's cheeks are wind-flushed and her eyes bright as she runs behind the squealing four-year-olds, laughing as they leave her behind.

The thrill continues for half an hour, and then crusted, soggy mittens are flapped off and red fingers presented for scrutiny. The twins plead for the second hill, and Samantha wanders in the background, chattering to Amy and Tina, who look away. Mark sits in the snow beside Musko, fingering his harness and murmuring to him. Even Julie feels the chill sinking into her feet and hands.

"Just one more," Laila intones, and immediately there are wails of protest. There are three *one mores*, and then one final, crashing run, with rolls and whoops and sprawling children demanding hot chocolate.

This time Mark rides behind Musko, straight and proud on the toboggan, a lone musher crossing the trackless waste with his great black dog. Julie and the helpers divide up the remaining children; even

Samantha wants to be pulled now. Laila and Janice saunter in the rear, reviewing moments of this and other sledding adventures.

Hot chocolate, sugar-dusted doughnuts, and chewy chocolate chip cookies are sipped, nibbled, and strewn as suits, mitts, and boots are shaken and spread out along the upstairs railing.

Amy sighs over the Styrofoam cups that are shortening her future, but Tina is nowhere to be seen. Julie finds her staring into Grandma Mary's room. Julie steps up beside her, watching the girl hug herself as she eyes the creamy wallpaper and light blue curtains.

"I was checking the jackets," Tina says.

Julie waits.

"It's not so bad," Tina continues. "It's a sad room, kind of an angry room, but not too bad." She turns to face Julie. "It's only a dream room if you let it."

Shivers run down Julie's arms and she shakes her head. "It's just a room, Tina."

"I know. It's just sad. And angry. Kind of."

"I think it's a pretty room, Tina," Julie declares.

Tina inspects a damp jacket. "I still don't like it when you lie," she says.

Julie sighs. "Tina. What is it that you want from me?"

Tina shakes the jacket and smooths it along the railing. "I have dreams," she begins.

"You will. That will pass," Julie murmurs.

"I dream you old," Tina continues. "And you're still here. You're all alone. And you're sad. Like now. Only more."

"Like now." Julie considers this. "Well, I'm not really sad now."

"No." Tina clenches her fists and shakes back her hair. "No. You're sad here." She looks around the hallway. "And you're sad here." She pokes a finger toward Julie's chest. "It doesn't get better here. Not for you."

~

The sledding party has departed. Julie is wiping down the counter and table while Musko snuffles for stray crumbs. The house has been so still since the last car door slammed. Here, Rose Hardy waited for the sounds of grandchildren, day by day by day. Here, Rachel Hardy came, and here, she fought her guilt and her anxieties and finally she fled. And then Nathaniel drifted free, seeking a history in which there was a place for him.

Here, Samuel holds his memories and casts her as caretaker. *A sledding party. Now that's just what this old place needs. Lots of hot chocolate. Have a bonfire next time.*

It was less quiet before the children came. Now, the emptiness vibrates.

It's only a dream room if you let it. Ms. Martin, you don't stop it. You let and you let it and you let it. You paint and make it pretty, but still you let the dreams in. You make it a dream room.

Maybe you have to be Grandma Mary to face down the dreams. A Holy Terror who cut her teeth on Spanish doubloons.

Then again, perhaps Grandma Mary was the first dreamer.

You do not see black ice, even when it is beneath your tires. Black ice creeps in, without a trace. Suddenly, it is there, and you are sliding out of control.

That is the trick of black ice.

Chapter 20

WINTER SNAKES

The winter slides past, with black ice days, snowstorm days, and long days of grey rain and brown fields. The sledding party is a shining memory that is reviewed and retold but not repeated. The snow sparkles in the sunlight only on weekdays, and winter is passing. They plan, they anticipate, and they wait. Weather and scheduling conspire against them.

Julie pictures the cabin on Sunrise Cove, nestled among birch trees, the water high on the shore. The cabin is waiting for its moment, for carefree canoes to beach in the cove, for coolers and laughter on the trail. It is waiting for a time when people will gather to hear its story, but it waits alone.

The house closes around Julie, and she is tempted to drive to Waverley whenever Friday approaches, but sees herself collapsing in tears on Sunday evening and begging to stay. Her father will be clearing the bed of the truck to bring her things home, while her mother dashes to the kitchen to prepare a suitable meal for the occasion. They will be making up her bed and suddenly she will realize that she cannot stay. She will leave, then, and the silence will vibrate in their house.

So she does not go to Waverley.

Her parents risk a weekend in late February. They arrive on a Saturday morning when the fields are bare and the clouds are heavy with snow. They grin and joke about getting snowed in at the old farm, and Julie hopes that they will be stuck here, crowding in around her until the silence is welcome again.

They leave Sunday afternoon in light flurries, and the silence vibrates in the house in Meadowbrook.

~

Julie dreams Tina that night. Tina hovers in the doorway of Grandma Mary's room, clutching a brindled kitten in her arms. She stoops and releases the kitten, and it hisses and slithers, a snake now, across the room and into the closet. Its tail disappears very slowly; it is a long snake.

"It's just a harmless garter snake," Tina says.

Julie dashes for the stairs, then halts, weaving at the top. She must go back for Tina, but her legs are leaden; they will not turn and lift, up and down, until she can seize Tina's hand and drag her to safety.

"Ms. Martin." Tina is sauntering down the hall behind her, crooning to the snake, which is now cradled in her arms. "Think of it as a kitten. It's only a snake if you let it."

Julie flings herself into her SUV, the key jabbing at the ignition. She skids out onto the road and forces the gas pedal down. Musko races along the field, barking.

~

Now Julie is awake, and Musko is rushing back and forth at the foot of her bed, barking. Julie pushes away her sweat-damp sheets and curls her toes against the cold floor. Musko bolts for the den, and Julie forces her legs to move after him. Musko rears against the east window, toes splaying against the sill.

Julie leans against the window. It is still night, but clear now, and the moon washes the snow-dusted field. Three deer stand under the McIntosh tree near the road, browsing in the stubble for frozen apples. One head swings up in a swift, graceful movement, and the ears swivel forward as the deer stares at the window.

Oh, she should have dreamed this for Samuel, not Tina, cuddling the kitten that was a snake if you let it.

She should have dreamed Samuel, pacing across the moon-drenched hill, his face shining as the deer caper and prance in the lower field. She should have dreamed a cool, sweet dream, not the fevered miasma of the harmless garter snake oozing into Grandma Mary's closet, which became Doug's closet and will be her closet.

Perhaps there is a snake for each of them.

Julie concentrates on the deer, seeking the details of winter-thin flanks and rough coats, the delicate arch of the neck as the leader watches.

The leader tenses suddenly, and the other heads swing up. Now all three are soaring for the woods, white tails lost against the snow patches and moonlight.

It is four o'clock on Monday morning, and the silence no longer grips the house. It no longer vibrates and hovers against the walls. Julie dresses, pulls on warm boots and parka, and paces the fields with Musko beside her. She walks until the horizon lightens and the snake dream disperses. She walks until she is one with the silence, and she is ready for the staffroom and the last meaningful looks that linger there.

~

The dreams are growing, mutating into horror. The bittersweet dreams that pull at the heart are giving way to darker dreams, nightmares that cling to the skin when you awaken.

The pattern is broken.

Much as sad, lost Tina broke her heart, she prefers that Tina to the calm one, crooning to the hissing snake that she cradled in her arms.

Julie's project on Monday evening is to strip the odds and ends that are still in that closet. Wire hangers and shoe boxes are discarded. She examines every crack and seam and applies crack filler. Finally, she paints the interior, even the floor, a stark white. On one level, she realizes that she is structuring her life around a nightmare, but on another level, she is past caring. She does not want to see Tina stroking the snake's head, singing to it as if it were her kitten.

She wants to dream winter fields, where deer frolic and feed, and Samuel watches entranced from the hillside near the pines.

Julie sits in the den that night and sips hot chocolate crammed with marshmallows. This is the food of moonlit dreams, not snake dreams.

Julie does dream Monday night, and at first it is a moonlit dream. She dreams her way into the attic, but Samuel is not there. She works her way around the furniture and boxes to the fly-crusted window, and there he is. He watches from the second hill, near the pines, leaning on his walking stick while three deer caper on the flats below. Samuel is smiling, and Julie's heart lifts.

A low tapping begins in the background.

The deer continue to prance and play, and Samuel continues to smile. Julie shivers in the window, and the tapping grows urgent, drawing her to the tattered cardboard box on the dusty sofa. Julie eases the cover open, lifts the twisted mass of lights, and reaches for the little case. "Fragile" is neatly penned in faded ink.

She removes the lid and places it beside the lights. The case itself is divided into twelve tiny compartments, each swathed in cotton batting. The tapping is almost jubilant now as she sets aside the batting in the first compartment and cups the dainty glass ornament in her hand. It begins to vibrate.

"It could be a kitten if you want," says Tina's voice.

Julie's hand squeezes shut and the fine glass crumbles in her palm, evergreen and silver bells and red bows fragmenting. A blunt little nose, cool and smooth, nudges at her fingers and now it is sliding out between them, and Julie drives her fist through the window pane, evergreen and bells and bows scattering on the wind and the snake tumbling and hissing into the snowy darkness.

Julie crams the lid onto the case, her blood smearing over the neatly penned "Fragile." She stuffs the case into the cardboard box and heaps the lights over it. She hauls the flaps of the cardboard box together and crams it under the sofa. A sad little mew rises from the snow below.

"What are you doing out here in the cold?" says Samuel, cradling the shivering kitten against his chest.

There are no nightmares for Samuel here, just dreams that pull at the heart.

~

Julie is amazed when her hand is unmarked on Tuesday morning. She feels the bite of the glass, but her hand does not bleed. She walks early and long with Musko, until the pain is gone and she no longer sees the snake, tumbling down into the darkness.

March is here; the snow is scattered dull patches in the sodden fields. Soon the earth will quicken and green, and the non-dream snakes will slither in the long grass.

Soon the oil bills will lower.

Soon the contract will end.

Julie wavers through her teaching day, walks with Musko, drinks strong coffee, and does online crosswords late into Tuesday night. She wraps herself in a blanket in the kitchen rocking chair and waits for morning.

"I think you need to get away," says Rachel from the top bunk.

Where can Julie go? There is no place left in her past or her future. Coasting parties do not help. Family weekends do not help. Painting does not help. The cabin might have helped Rachel, but it does not help Julie. And if it helped Rachel, then where is Rachel?

Musko snores in front of the refrigerator. He has love, good food, and room to stretch out. He will live out his days just appreciating these facts.

Perhaps Musko has the right idea.

BREAKING

Oh, to return to the past when all was perfect. To drive again down over the Canadian Shield, sweeping down the highway and all the way to Meadowbrook, to a summer of swimming lessons and Park days and driving over the fields with the rider mower. Visitors and laughter.

The car was hot and stuffy, I was exhausted and irritable, and Nathaniel buried himself in a book and waited for the journey to end. We dashed in and out of restaurants, one eye on the dogs leaning from the open car windows in the heat. We arrived at 5 a.m. from the ferry, and my son's friends were soon in the yard, eager for summer. I scrambled to swimming lessons, cursing the schedule and the repairs that controlled my summer.

I dreaded returning to work. I clutched at the days, trying to force them to my will.

I yearn and yearn for Meadowbrook Acres, for if I had kept Meadowbrook Acres, my son would still be young and home and I would know my future and this time I would be happy.

I was happy once at Wasaya, and now I grip my own past and shake it, to sift out the truth, and offer it on the wind.

~

My mother did not really cope well, but the Happy Childhood dies hard.

It dies hard when your sister runs screaming from the hospital as she is dying, and people talk about the time that she went crazy.

It dies hard when your sister, who still shivers from the time of meningitis, turns her heart from you. It does not matter that perhaps it was your heart that started it; your heart is hers now and she must, must come back.

It dies hard when you find your sister's name in your own church's guest book, and you are alone.

It dies hardest when it is your sister, who was lost to Boston for five years but grew up to giggle in church and hide cigarettes from the Sisters with you, who left her name in your church guest book but did not call, who lies dying on her apartment floor with a tumour festering in her brain.

This is not the way that Very Happy Childhoods end. You are faced with that reality, and so you grow quiet.

Over the years, the Happy Childhood had come between my parents more and more. My father had been the winter housekeeper for more than ten years, and he had found time to brood. It started with him sitting on the stool by the stove, staring at the floor as he smoked his pipe. It continued with winter afternoons tapping his feet and staring past the floor, the pipe long finished. Brooding time became addictive, but I like to think that he brooded his way into his youth, canoeing in moose season on a distant lake, the silence sweet and the pine needles soft as he stepped onto the shore.

My mother would come home from the high school and collapse into the rocking chair by the east window, head back and fingers pressed delicately to one temple. My father would serve the supper that he had prepared after his brooding time. My mother would sigh, flinch, stir her food, and nibble through several tiny bites, while my father grimly shoveled and chewed.

The work came between them, the meals came between them, and Charles came between them.

We were not kind to Charles, who had nightmares that screamed us into his terror. He was awkward with farm work. He brooded over world events and sin. We did not learn from Grandma Mary. We teased him, my mother sighed over him, and my father muttered frequently about French blood coming out in them. My mother would wince, and avert her face. She would sigh more heavily over supper and observe that she had not been raised to eat such heavy, greasy food. My father would glower and fork it down.

Charles grew tall and strong, though, and moved with confidence through university. My father found room in his heart to become proud of his son, although he was still not the son he had dreamed of. He was the son with the university education, the one who became a journalist and broadcaster. The son of his heart, though, would love the forests, tame the land, hunt deer, and fly fish, as he had. He would recreate his youth, and be a legacy. That role fell to Samuel, his last hope; there was no escape for Samuel.

In those days, Grampie came to Meadowbrook. He came between them most of all.

~

We no longer had family trips down the shore after Grammie's health began to fail, and Mother went down on the bus from Liverpool, shoulders straight and a sleek suitcase in her hand. Grammie died when I was sixteen, and shortly afterward, Aunt Janine left the family. Grampie stayed alone in his little house, with the twisting staircase leading to the two bedrooms upstairs, now empty, with the little bedroom off the kitchen where there was one side of the bed, now empty. His shoulders were rounded now, and his frame was not so stiff. His little wire-framed glasses perched forlornly on his nose, and he wandered the house, muttering, no longer very français de France with a grandfather dying in the Franco-Prussian War.

His house became dirty, the neighbours told my mother. He forgot to light the fire, or else stoked it up hot, so the piles of newspapers on the kitchen floor were almost smouldering. He was eating out of tins, if he ate at all. He was not washing. The neighbours did what they could, and waited for my mother to do something, her duty as eldest and most financially secure. She was a teacher, after all, and they had all that land. There were two brothers with the Armed Forces, and a sister in the distant North whose smiles, it turned out, hid some dark shadows. There was a sister who had dropped contact with the family, and one who had issues, as they say now, in the areas of health and marriage. One was dead. The gentle one, the peacemaker, was in the hospital again, with a long-term condition. My mother was the perfect choice. She had the space, the time, and the money.

Perhaps by now my father should have accepted the fact that his in-laws came for prolonged visits when they were dying or expecting babies, or unable to cope any more. Families do this.

But he would be the one on duty during the waking hours, since winter was coming and my father did the housework in winter, since he had frozen his hands.

My father respected his father-in-law at a distance, and willingly tolerated him each year for twenty-six hours. He really was not comfortable with him, though, and would rather not have him living under his roof. Even just for the winter. However, Grampie would come here, because that is what one did. Grampie could not go on forgetting the stove and all the rest.

Glowering, my father brought his father-in-law into his house, and trembling, my mother brought her father home. *I just wish your father would make him more welcome,* she would sigh, flinching when my father entered the room. He would scowl and mutter off to the woodhouse; she would clutch her forehead and flinch again.

My grandfather was shaky on his feet, wandering in his mind, and not quite continent. He was old in ways that my father would never be. In a soft, disgusted tone, he would report the faults and shortcomings of the day to my mother; her mouth would draw down and she would tremble. If my mother's car did not arrive at the exact moment Grampie had selected as the right one, he would loudly chime off his rosary, in the kitchen, in French. In between he would stoke the stove so high that we could not bake in it unless we left the oven door wide open. At Christmas, he sang hymns in French. During the homily at Mass. At home, he would hop along the hallway, crouching, as he hurried to the washroom. *"J'ai peur,"* he would moan. *"Oh, comme j`ai peur."* He is *afraid of your father,* my mother would declare.

Grampie was shaky on his feet, but he was not always wandering in his mind. In March, he announced that he wanted to return to his own home. My father had already broached the subject with my mother, and in her telling of family history it became the Time That She Chose Her Husband over Her Family. My father stood grim and tried to straighten; my mother shrank and pressed a finger to her temple. They did not talk things out; they did not lighten up. They each stood on their own shore and stared. Grampie stepped in and saved everyone's dignity, whether they deserved it or not, by claiming the decision as his own. Perhaps he was still a français de France, whose grandfather died in the Franco-Prussian War.

My mother still became the daughter who turned her father out while it was still winter.

Yet even after the Very Intelligent Man came to live with us, it was possible for her to believe.

My mother still brandished the stories of the Very Intelligent Man and the Very Happy Home. There had been laughter and joy, and during the Great Depression when there was no work, he had translated Homer just to keep his spirits up. He could not thrive in *this* environment; he was not used to living like this. My father now muttered about goddamn French blood. He brooded on the stool in the corner on March afternoons, without the rosary and hot stove, and at four o'clock, he would bring potatoes and carrots from the cellar. He would scrape and peel and place them in water. He would fry meat with onion and bacon fat, but less bacon fat now, to make up for the silent, cooler kitchen he had forced upon them.

My father should have drawn solace from the knowledge that Grandma Mary must have been spinning like a lathe in her grave knowing that she had a French Catholic fearless rosary chanter Homer translator in her very own kitchen. He should have laughed and chortled and sung along with the hymns.

And my mother should have giggled and grinned and done her hair high and run for cover when the nuns came to call.

Instead, she became the one who watched as the child flipped down the stairs, and he became the one who threw him.

Hauntings overtake us all. But then my aunt Claudette died, and my mother did not mention happy childhoods again. And my father stopped muttering about French blood.

~

I grow weary, recreating the past. Let us see it, bless it, and release it. Let it become ashes on the wind.

Chapter 21

RETURNS

Julie sleeps on the kitchen floor, on an air mattress near the refrigerator. She disciplines herself to feel contentment, to draw solace from the little moments that shape the day. Pull the March air deep into your lungs. Listen for the low rumble of the river below the bend. Savour the aroma of fresh coffee after your walk. Look for the little successes: Catherine, in Grade 11, uses colour coding to organize her binder with some effectiveness today. Ah, that is good. The resource room is such a peaceful place to eat your sandwich; it is soothing there, and then you drop by the staffroom. They are looking, aren't they, but that is all right because soon you will be walking in the field and it will not matter. They suspect something, but they do not know. Whatever would they do if they knew? You sleep on an air mattress and listen to the refrigerator hum and gurgle, to the furnace grumble as it breathes the heat up through the vents. These are comforting sounds; all is well. The dreams hover on the edges of your mind, but they cannot reach you here, not here in the kitchen, where you stretch in front of the refrigerator like a contented dog.

Laila describes her March Break plans and describes them again. She keeps saying that she hopes that Julie will find something fun to do. She wonders why Julie does not go at least to Waverley. It is important to take a real break, after all. She watches Julie while she talks; she suspects something but she, too, does not know. Laila tucks carefully foiled casseroles and diverse salads and desserts into coolers, arranges the coolers in the back of the car, and heaps warm blankets and duffle bags over them. She and Tom are on their way to a friend's cottage in LaHave for a few days. Julie is to feel free to use their house.

Julie has quite enough with this house, thank you, but she does not say that.

Janice and her family are visiting relatives in the Annapolis Valley. There will probably be a great snowstorm but no coasting party. However, who really wants a coasting party in mid-March, when the sun is beating on the snow and green things are imminent?

Julie will spend her March Break drawing solace from the little moments that shape the day. She will be like Musko. However, unlike Musko, she will be ever vigilant for snake dreams.

She will not do more reclaiming activities, for she painted the dream room and then the snake came. She will not create a delightful plan to brighten the living room, for the snakes might crawl over it in the night, and that will be worse. No, she will walk and watch and appreciate the little moments. She will doze by the refrigerator, but if she does not sleep, then that will be all right, because she does not need to be fresh and alert for school. Not for a whole week.

And when school opens again, the snake dreams will be deep in the past.

Julie considers her options for fun. There is late winter camping. She could go to Kedge and camp, for some sites remain open in winter. She would have to call her parents, though, so they would not call and call and wonder where their daughter was. And after she called them, they would descend on her site, brandishing paddles and favourite foods, for the prodigal has returned to Kedge times.

Perhaps she could camp by the brook instead.

Was out checking on the brook, back of Samuel's place. Not long and there'll be trout below the bridge. Good spot, yes. Well, I saw that new teacher.

Had a little tent up on the ridge, a little fire pit, and a chair. Camping, she was. All alone, yes, boiling her little pot of tea.

Perhaps the Yukon should be her next final destination. Far away where the gossip cannot touch her. Unless she stays.

~

She is lugging her air mattress and bedding from the kitchen to her room on Saturday morning when her landlord's car rolls past the kitchen window. She tosses the sleeping bag on the den sofa and tips the mattress against the TV stand. Pulling on a light jacket, she rushes to the verandah, running her fingers over her hair and massaging the skin around her eyes. She must appear relaxed, vacationing, not dishevelled and pursued by snakes. Samuel must see only his confident caretaker tenant.

Samuel does not notice anything. He is pacing beside his car, scrutinizing the crab apple tree. "Well. You made it through the winter," he begins. "You're through the worst of it with the oil."

He studies the bags of leaves that Julie stacked around the base of the house last October, when she was Building a Future. They insulated the base while she was Bringing the House to Life, and are shrinking now as she is Living Out Her Life in Contentment and Finding Solace in the Little Moments.

"Those will rot the sills, remember," he reminds her.

She reminds him, in return, that she plans on removing them in April. He brightens for a moment. "Hear anything from your friend?" he asks. Julie stiffens, not because he called Doug her friend, but because suddenly she can barely remember November. It is so far away now, in the long daylight of March. Samuel paces anew, head down, shoulders hunched, hands in pockets. "Yeah. Yeah. I know. It's none of my business. Just making conversation. Sorry. Don't know what I'm thinking," he trails off.

Julie relaxes her own shoulders. "It's OK. Really. No, not much. He's out of teaching, though. Looking for work on the oil rigs." The snow blower was only five months ago, and yet a life time has slipped past. She has painted and decorated and made cookies, but now there are snakes in the night. Perhaps if she had Doug to focus her anxieties and resentment on, it would be easier. Instead, her anxieties and resentment are diffusing into the air at Meadowbrook Acres, and the snakes are slipping through the gaps in between.

At least she can still ask and answer questions and make sense. She does not say to Samuel, for example, that there are snakes in his attic but they appear to him as kittens, because he does not let them be snakes. No, that would not do. She must continue to ask and answer questions and make sense.

"Oil rigs," Samuel mutters. "Sometimes I think I'll just let all of this go, and head for the oil rigs myself." He raises his eyes to the red pine stand on the far hill. "It took three days to plant those. Long days. That was pasture before."

"Well," Julie says. "Coming in for coffee?"

Samuel winces. "Coffee. No. That's fine. Well. The thing is, I've been thinking."

Julie waits, tugging her jacket closer against the morning chill. "Oh?"

"The thing is—it's complicated. I've got a mortgage," he rushes on, "and this place is nothing but trouble, and sometimes my sister wants it back and sometimes she doesn't, but it doesn't matter because she can't get a mortgage. And if she did get it back, then we'd all be doing this again in a few years. I'm tired of it. You know? Tired. I'm going to have to sell the place," he blurts.

"But it's your home," Julie exclaims. *If you sell it, whose attic will you explore in my dreams? Whose fields will you walk in the night while the deer play on the flats below? Who will dream you into your attic and your fields?*

Sometimes his sister wants it back. "Is your sister back, then?" Julie asks.

Samuel sighs, running his hand along his fringe of hair. "Back. Now there's something. Back and forth. She's never really here."

"But last spring she was here," Julie insists. "In May. Up at the Narrows above her cabin. Joe said—"

"Joe? Oh, you mean Joe Barnes? What the hell does Joe Barnes know? She wasn't out here, that's for certain."

"But he saw her—her and her dog."

"Oh, That dog. The big white one. He's getting some old now. She does say she wants to bring him home. She wants them to be home, for his last years or months, or whatever. Oh, she talks about it."

"But the dog was there last fall, with Nathaniel, and he was swimming."

"Swimming? That's Nathaniel's dog. Another big white Husky swimming behind the canoe. Oh, that one's only about four years old. Maybe five, this spring. He was down with Nathaniel most of last fall."

"I thought you said he was old. 'He's getting a little old for this,' you said."

Samuel stares. "Why would I say that? I didn't say anything like that."

"But I'm sure you did," Julie insists.

"Well, you can believe whatever you want." Samuel sighs. "Nathaniel has all the adventures. I wonder when he'll settle down and be stuck with a place like this."

"So you are going to sell then."

"Yes. Yes. Oh, I don't know." Samuel resumes pacing. "I can't bear to see all the changes. And what if they tear it down, or cut the trees? I won't be able to stop it. Rachel wouldn't take responsibility for the place. I had to take it. I just don't know how much more I can take. There are so many things to do, and I just can't keep up. There's the shingles, and the new bridge, and the mowing, and it will be painting time again soon."

Julie steers Samuel into the kitchen where Musko bounds up to welcome him, bumping chairs askew, his tail thrashing against Samuel's leg.

Samuel rubs his hand along the big dog's ruff. "Yeah. Old Musko. Good place for a dog. Right, fella?"

As he sips at his coffee, Samuel asks Julie when she plans to remove the bags of leaves from around the house. They will rot the sills. She tells him again that she plans to remove them in late April. She does not remind him that they just had this conversation, because Samuel is so pleased to hear that she is removing them in April. She is doing a good job, he tells her, and he hopes that she will remain a long time.

"But if you're selling," Julie begins.

Samuel lowers his coffee mug and covers his face with his hands. "Oh, I don't know, I just don't know," he mutters. "I just can't decide. I love this place; I grew up here. There's so much here. But," he continues, clutching the coffee mug in both hands and staring at the crab apple tree, "there is just so much baggage here. And so much work. But if I sell, it's gone forever. It's over. Are you staying on, come August?"

"If you're not selling, you mean?"

"No." Samuel closes his eyes and swings his head back and forth. "I was simply wondering if you were planning on taking the place again next winter. I was hoping you would."

"So you're not selling."

"No, I have to think about something like this first."

In spite of the warm sweaters and heavy socks, the winter has been expensive. Julie is not saving money here. She is not getting ahead in the world. And she might not have a contract next winter.

"I don't seem to rest all that well here," she says.

Samuel straightens. "Dreams? Rachel always said that our ancestors haunted this place—creepy lights, bad dreams. But she was, well, you know, kind of that way anyway."

"That way?"

"Weird imagination. Always looking for signs. Some people are like that; they don't accept that they have the responsibility, that it's their choice, not some dream thing. She got kind of carried away with it all, in the end."

Musko thumps his tail, his eyes on the platter of muffins.

"I do like it here," Julie says, "but I do find it a little oppressive at night." *I sleep by the refrigerator, Samuel, because then I lie content listening to night sounds like Musko, and I do not see little blunt snake noses poking out between my fingers.*

"Try some music," Samuel suggests. "Plant a garden."

"Could I use that piece down by the orchard?" Julie asks.

Samuel's head bobs up and down. "Sure. Now that's the thing to do. That's just what this place needs. Perfect."

"But if you decide to sell. . . ."

"Oh, no. Don't worry about that. I think this is just fine." Samuel is sweeping muffin crumbs onto his palm, Musko's muzzle hovering close. "No. I won't be showing the place. You just carry on."

"Samuel, is your sister here now?"

Samuel is tugging on his work boots. "Here? No. She knows the place is rented."

"I mean, around here?"

Samuel straightens. "Well, it's complicated, but family always seems to be. Our family, anyway. Let me know if you need help cultivating that garden plot."

As Julie waves him down the driveway, the first plan of March Break clears before her.

~

One hour later, she eases onto the gravel road that meanders out behind the community above Meadowbrook. The grey brush clings along the crumbling edges of the road, screening dull snow patches that linger in the woods. Watery potholes shimmer in the late morning light. The clouds above are parting to reveal a deep blue March sky. Musko plasters his nose against the crack in the window, inhaling woods smells, eyes half shut and ears back. By the time she turns in at the cluttered dooryard, the air is light with hints of spring.

The rolling door hangs open on one of the outbuildings, and Joe Barnes is leaning over the engine of a low, grease-caked tractor. He glances up, his mouth opens, and then he is frowning into the machine, reaching for a wrench. Musko wanders into the field, head down, seeking mice, while Julie steps up to the doorway.

"Wal. Miss Ma'tin. You got a holiday, I reckon. Nice weathah fo' it." He wipes the surface with a greasy rag, intent on the engine.

"I haven't seen you since last November, Joe. I really enjoyed that deer meat." She holds out a tin container. "I felt like going for a drive, and I was thinking you and your father might enjoy some muffins."

Joe glances up for a moment and then ducks his head into the engine again. "Did you now? Mighty thoughtful. The ol' man will sho'a appreciate that." Joe reaches a hand deep into the engine, and his lips press together as he turns the wrench.

Jacob Barnes shuffles out onto the porch of the small house set back near the trees. "Got tea made," he declares, "an' stew's a-warmin'. You come in now."

Joe grimaces, laying the wrench on the worktable. "You like rabbit, Miss Ma'tin?" he addresses the tractor.

Julie shifts in the doorway, clutching the muffin tin. "I wasn't think-ing. It's lunchtime, I could come back later, maybe. I should have called."

"You come in now," Jacob Barnes insists. "Got plenty, just a-waitin'. Muffins, you say?"

Joe slouches toward the doorway, swinging his arm to indicate the house. "Now's fine," he mumbles.

They walk in silence toward the porch, Musko trailing behind them. Jacob hurries inside. He is cheerfully scrubbing the faded red checked oil cloth on the table as she enters. "Always got enough for company," he says, hauling bowls and mugs from the listing cupboard. "You get back t' the lake much?"

Joe wilts over the sink, lathering soap over his grease-dark hands.

"No," says Julie. "I've been busy." *I have been having dreams, dreams to chill the blood in your veins.*

She places the muffin tin on the table's edge. "Homemade," Jacob cackles. "How's th' ol' Ha'dy place? Samuel get out much?"

"Oh. A little. He's busy. He dropped by this morning."

"Good, good." Jacob is piling rabbit and potatoes into the bowls as Joe fumbles with the cutlery. Julie plucks paper towels, and begins folding them into napkins.

Jacob's face closes. "Napkins," he mutters, glancing about the cluttered little kitchen. "Got napkins right here." He tugs at a drawer, rummages briefly, and comes up with a fistful of yellowed paper napkins edged in violets. "Napkins," he announces, peeling one from the bundle.

Joe shovels stew in silence while Jacob tells story after story about Ol' Man Ha'dy and his staunch work ethic. "So there we was, wet snow pilin' up around us, an' Stephen Ha'dy bringin' the team around and that big bay geldin'—Danny Boy, if you can believe that—a-starts in pawin' the air, and them logs go tippin' and rollin' and down they come ovah Stephen Ha'dy an' he caught one fair on th' side o' his head. Well, he's a-staggerin' and he jest sta'ts staggerin' off fo' home and he tells his wife, he says, 'Ah fractured my skull,' he says, an' he walks up the staihs and lies down. Down fo' seven days with some fevah, an' then he's up an' gone again. Ha'd man." Julie takes small bites and says "oh" and "really" in the infrequent pauses. Finally, Jacob takes a deep swallow of milky tea and sits back. "Too bad about yo'ah friend," he says.

Joe seizes the bowls and begins to stack them. Musko rises, alert and hopeful, from beside the stove.

"Oh," says Julie. "He was, well, you know."

"Yep. Nevah know what a fellah's gonna do," Jacob agrees.

"No," says Julie.

"And people will talk. They's still some says Joe heah's got his eye on you—or the Ha'dy place. Or both. Ah say he's got mo'ah sense." He bites deep into a muffin, his eyes closing in satisfaction. "Mighty good," he sighs. His eyes pop open. "'Bout the Ha'dy place, th' sense pa't, I mean," he adds.

Joe moves for the door, muttering about engine blocks.

"No, now sit," Jacob snaps, sitting up. "Ya tell her now."

Joe sighs, leaning back against the sink, his eyes on the floor. "Ah'm sorry fo' ruinin' things fo' you, Miss Ma'tin, but some things gotta be done. Now people's been talkin' about you, an' talkin' about us and the place. Like mah dad says, an' Ah just feel bad about it all."

His father nods. "He do. But he done right. No cause fo' ha'd feelings."

Julie sips at her tea. She sips and calculates how long it would take to sprint to her vehicle, start the engine, and spin out onto the road. "I'm just glad that it's over, and turned out as well as it did," she says at last. "He came here to hide, I guess, and it caught up with him. There was an inquiry, and he lost his license, so he won't be teaching any more. The parents filed some sort of lawsuit, and he's working in the oil fields or something."

Oh, the oil fields. Oh, Jacob.

"A ha'd place, that," Jacob whispers. Joe lowers his head, studying the cracked linoleum.

"I'm sorry," Julie says. "I'm sorry for letting him stay, and for you worrying about me, and for, well, that. It's been hard for you. For a long time."

"Ye-es. It is that." Jacob places his muffin on a saucer. "It is that." He looks up at Joe. "But we get through." He nods.

"Rachel Hardy," says Julie. "Was she really there? At the lake? Last spring?"

"Rachel Ha'dy's been gone a'most two yeahs," Jacob declares. "Nevah quite knew what she wanted, that one."

"I don't know where she is, or what she's doin', or why," Joe breaks in, "but she were at the lake last May. Up by th' Narrows, in that ol' canoe, workin' along with that big white dog runnin' the shore beside her. 'This is a secret, Joe,' she says. 'I'm not supposed to be here.'"

"And then?" Julie prompts.

"Ah was workin' around the rocks. 'Sho'ah,' Ah said. When Ah looked up, she were gone. Around the bend there."

"Weren't her," Jacob declares. "Laila'd know."

"I know what I saw," Joe insists. "Were a bright and perfect May mornin', and there she is all bright and smilin' and that big white dog runnin' along the sho'ah."

"You never saw Rachel Ha'dy," Jacob says. "She's been gone a'most two years. No one's seen her. Not Laila, not Samuel, no one. Not even the young feller, there, Nathaniel."

"Ah saw her. So mebbe it's only me that's seen her."

"Only you. Hah."

Oh, Joe. You hunt and you fish along the Narrows to see her there. Laila picks cranberries and listens for the loons to see her there. Nathaniel canoes the shorelines for a glimpse of her.

She is dead, isn't she? And it hurts too much to admit it.

Or she is lost in her mind, and cannot return and it hurts too much to admit it.

Or she has abandoned all she held dear, and this hurts the most of all.

"She was there. Ah'd swear it. She were right there."

"I really was, you know," Rachel whispers from the top bunk. "I always am here. I never left."

Chapter 22

NEW JOURNEYS

A t the end of Saturday, Julie does not know any more about the whereabouts and wherefore of Rachel Hardy than at the beginning. Rachel Hardy appears to be here and not here, physically or mentally or both. Julie should lie down in Grandma Mary's room and dream her way to an unsettling answer, or hike off to Sunrise Cove and wait for Rachel to light up a cigarette and say something enlightening.

Perhaps a new final destination is in order after all. The Yukon, for example, does not sound conducive to dream rooms and snakes infesting Christmas ornaments. When you begin to wait for the next dream to learn what happened to Rachel, or when you begin to wonder if your dreams are placed in your mind by Grandma Mary to warn you or inform you or drive you mad, and when all these things begin to make sense, then perhaps you are truly mad, although you were never like this before.

Perhaps the house has chosen you. There is a low chuckle from the top bunk. You're starting to get it, Rachel says.

You let it, you let it, Tina whispers, leaning over the stairwell.

Amy's mother cried all the time; she 'got a depression.' Julie will learn to sleep and find contentment in the little moments and she will not go the way of Amy's mother. She will walk down the frayed nerves; she will walk down the last snake. She has Musko; Amy's mother didn't.

~

On Sunday afternoon, Julie has just returned from the brook when her parents pull in to the driveway. They are calm and cheerful. They smile and say that they were wondering if she could make her lasagna. Could Mother help with the salad? Oh, there's that big, beautiful dog.

Musko races back and forth between the car and the verandah, licking hands and panting. He knocks against Julie but weaves around her parents. He spins in circles into the field, barking and crouching.

A walk? Oh, he would like another walk? Now there's an idea, what a smart dog. A walk is just what they need after that long drive. Exercise is so important, you know. It is vital if you are going to stay healthy. Health is everything. Smart dog, Musko.

The March afternoon is raw and still. Julie and her parents slog along the old truck road. The grey, white-edged house perches grim in the light mist, brooding over the barn-less wastes rolling away to the woods below. The orchards are particularly unkempt and gnarled today.

Julie's father has a few days' vacation time and they thought that they would start by visiting their daughter, maybe giving her a hand with the place. Perhaps Julie's father could help with a little pruning? He brought a few tools along. Oh! Here's an idea! How about a day trip to Kedge? Pack along a picnic lunch, and see how the Park looks in the late winter? Just a little family time. What else will they do this week? Well, now. They seriously have not thought beyond the moment; this is, after all, vacation.

At the brook, Musko wallows in the shallows above the bridge, stomping down patches of rotting ice, ears cocked as bubbles escape to the surface. At the brook, Julie's mother remarks to her husband that she is tired, and he slides an arm about her shoulders. They rest there, at the bridge, and as a light drizzle begins, turn toward the house. Julie follows.

In the kitchen, Alice Martin arranges her salad while Julie thaws ground beef and starts the sauce. Theo Martin plods about the orchard plotting his task as Musko digs for mice in the sodden hay.

The kitchen is bright that evening, although the mist outside thickens and the drizzle condenses to light rain. Julie tells them of dyslexia and learning disabilities and her parents nod and widen their eyes sometimes while they push their lasagna around on their plates and stab at their salads.

She is tired, Julie's mother says, but perhaps a little coffee and maybe some TV and an early night?

Julie does not, of course, sleep on the kitchen floor tonight. She lies rigid on her bed in the room where the minister led prayers, where the dead were laid out, and where Samuel's grandfather breathed his last. Upstairs she hears her mother's soft weeping, and her father's gentle rumblings as he soothes her. Julie slips into sleep, and there are no Christmas ornaments and playful deer for Samuel this night, no kittens and no snakes.

The next afternoon, while a weak sun struggles to warm the landscape, they huddle at their old camping site above the lake. There, over chicken and potato salad and thermoses of scalding tea and slices of pound cake, Julie learns why there were no dreams.

Julie's mother has absorbed them all, even as she approached the dream house.

Julie's mother carries all the dreams.

Gentle, timid Alice Martin, whose great joy has been attaining motherhood and whose life's work has been maintaining motherhood, carries all dreams and faces all dreams and they are nothing to her.

For Julie's controlling, sentimental mother is going for surgery on Wednesday, and then there will be treatment and perhaps treatment again.

Afterward there will be waiting, and if Alice is among the fortunate, there will just be waiting.

"They can do so much for breast cancer today," Alice Martin observes, offering Musko a piece of chicken.

~

On Tuesday morning Julie and her mother sip coffee in the kitchen while Theo Martin, who has vacation time, finishes sawing and pruning in the Gravenstein trees.

"Your father likes to be active," Alice Martin says, leaning over the table to better see him through the window. "It's harder for him, you see."

Julie yearns to sink into her mother's arms. There she will tell her about North Bay, all the loneliness and the hurt and the mistake that it was. She will tell her about Meadowbrook Acres, all the memories and nostalgia that drew her here, and the way it now looms over her, both uplifting and crippling her.

She yearns to cry in her mother's arms, because she has loved and she has given and has been emptied out. She yearns to cry for Tina, now thirteen, because Tina is pitied for what happened to her, scorned for what she did, and feared for what she might do. She yearns to cry because Tina creeps through the school day, and even Amy's loyalty is wavering.

She would cry for Samuel, for the loneliness that he finds in his home, for the place that is both his burden and his portal to innocence.

"The past always seems happier," Alice Martin says. "I always thought that if we could just keep doing the same things, then those times would never be over. I thought that we would always be there, in them."

Julie's eyes burn with tears, and now she does indeed collapse into her mother's arms, sobbing but not telling, but it does not matter because Alice Martin already knows it all.

"You're still a mother when your children are grown," she murmurs. "You want, oh, you want to let them go, but you can't. And it hurts. Oh, it hurts them."

Julie cries until she is limp and empty, until she is weak and sleepy, while Alice holds her, eyes closed.

Perhaps Rachel needed to weep in her mother's arms. Perhaps Samuel did, too.

Alice Martin holds out her empty arms and lifts up the Simons and the Tinas and the Samuels and even the Dougs for blessing. She lifts up and blesses the Julies, and eases the snakes from their dreams. She blesses them all and releases them for she is wise now. Timid, controlling Alice Martin is now a wise woman emerging. She is a Laila, embracing her Laila-ness.

Theo Martin climbs into the first McIntosh tree, and begins to saw methodically at a dead limb.

The Wasaya Journal of Rachel Hardy: Part 8

REDEMPTION

My third summer at Wasaya is speeding by all too quickly.
Wasaya has been the dream that has kept me sane all winter long; I have sat on my deck watching the snow whip across my driveway, feeling the raw wind sweep in from the river, and I have closed my eyes to dip the paddle low and to hear the loons speak.

There would be afternoons exploring my special places, with packets of bannock and life jackets for the dogs, my companions. There would be afternoons of coffee and reminiscences with friends while the sun beat down. There would be canoes sweeping around the point, cards and laughter in the evenings, lamps burning late while the loons called across the water.

Friends, however, have their own duties and responsibilities, and the loons call just for me these nights.

Wasaya is a one-time adventure for many.

~

Today was the day of our annual restaurant lunch, the day on which we share and laugh and then return to our own worlds. I had shopping to do in the village, and I crept around the edges of my childhood, greeting and being greeted, ever aware that each greeting brought me nearer to my August departure.

I want to be alone. Yet I want to grow old here, among my own people, and wrestle my story into theirs.

I drove on to the Park, where first my son and I stayed when I sold Meadowbrook Acres. Oh, the dogs knew where they were, crowding to the windows, anticipating campfires and wiener roasts. Dogs exact their joy from what they are given. If not a campfire, then the sight of a squirrel will fill their moment. They do not look at it longingly and say, *That is like the squirrels we used to chase when we stayed here. But we cannot chase them as we could in those times.* No, they pant and wag and rejoice, because each moment is possibility and not to be wasted.

There is no place more desolate on a windy, grey Friday evening than a campground with all too few campers. There were too few campfires, too few families. There were just quiet, isolated pockets; the beaches were empty and the trails silent. I would have welcomed the crowds of bicycles that had careened down the trails before; I would have guided the dogs to the side of the trail with joy, and blessed all those cyclists rolling by with smiles of gratitude. Instead, I shadowed the dogs along the trail, and even the squirrels were still in the gathering weather.

I think that the Park was lonely, too, dreaming of the time when it was all in all for so many. It, too, was yearning for a surge of people to celebrate it.

The mist rolls across the lake at Wasaya this evening; the wind gusts in the maples and pines. Tonight I shall gather rain water, and set a lamp in the window. I like to think that if anyone is out in the storm, then I will be the one to save them. They will see my light, a beacon guiding them to warmth and safety.

Tomorrow, I will explore the lake with my dogs again, and I know that as I paddle, the loneliness will slip away, and I will be content. When I come back to Wasaya, or when friends leave, those moments are the hard ones.

I picture myself at Meadowbrook Acres, where my son is still twelve years old and exploring the woods with his friends. In the evening we watch a movie in the den, and we read. We walk in the fields. We plan.

I was glad to get away from Meadowbrook Acres, but now I believe that it holds the key to retrieving my past.

A heron rises from a rock at the foot of the Narrows, and I almost miss it, because I am in the grip of Meadowbrook Acres these days.

Meadowbrook Acres is a big, lonely place, and it binds you. You do not find joy in the little waves lapping the shore in the cove. The sun sparkles on the water, and you pace the shore, seeing only Meadowbrook.

It robs you of the moment, and you let yourself be robbed. That is its trick.

~

The day came in my parents' lives that my brothers and I were grown, and although our rooms were kept intact from childhood, we were visitors now. The relatives who once sat in judgment on the verandah had either passed on or mellowed with the years. There was tolerance now, and fond recollection of all the happy times shared. The great summer visits were past now, and my parents were alone.

They stopped muttering about French blood. They stopped flinching at the greasy food.

They had fished together before, but now they became fishing companions, and started going for hikes in the woods.

They built a little bough shack, far back on the old logging trails, with a little table and a fire pit where they brewed tea and toasted sandwiches. They became regulars at the old eel weir in the Park, with thermoses of coffee and tins of sandwiches, and my father bought my mother a pair of waders and a fly rod.

These became their new rituals, and we were pulled along as observers on our visits home, but it was their passion, not ours. They were so glad to be there, and we were not.

Perhaps my dogs and I are developing our own rituals, and I just do not realize it.

I had expected my parents to turn on one another when my mother retired and they were alone together, but somewhere along the way, between my wandering in and out of home, between my suffocating there and being consumed by homesickness elsewhere, my parents found their niche. I do not think that they forgot the days of Aunt Isabel or the Very Happy Childhood or the damn French blood, but they let those days slip away, and shopped for good hiking boots together.

And so the years moved on, without the grim silences and tremblings. Instead, there was growing together in a lonely big house, where they recalled the strawberry days with a fond smile. I suspect, too, that they remembered the times when they were all in all to so many, and that sometimes the winds were grey and cold on their trails. Like the Park, they would be gloomy sometimes, but like the Park, they endured.

My memory slides back to a grey, mosquito-filled afternoon at the eel weir. I sit on the bridge, forcing through a paper on comparative religion for my correspondence course. My father has rigged his rod and my mother's, and is knee-deep in the river, his casts strong and deliberate. My mother minces along the shore in her waders, her dark curls carefully shrouded in a clear plastic rain bonnet, the beak protruding over her pale forehead. A once dressy scarf is knotted at her throat. She wears a faded red pantsuit, and over it all a stiff, square-cut fleece jacket, a variation on the car coat theme. My mother is resplendent in her worn-out dress clothes and hand-me-downs from American summer people; she can afford but does not need authentic sportswear. She squats on a rock, right arm extended for balance, left holding fly rod aloft, and swings her right foot and then her left, until she faces the river. She stands and plods through the marsh grass to the riverbank. She shakes out her line and snaps an amateur, but very smooth, cast. Again the line flicks across the water, and her tightly compressed lips relax a little, twisting into a small smile.

There are three photographs of my mother that I placed in the parlour at Meadowbrook Acres. The first is of my mother as a young teacher, radiant and so ready to dance and laugh into her future. In the second, she peers grinning through the folds of a Spanish mantilla, mischievous and mysterious, a little embarrassed. My son's father took the third; he had an eye for the incongruities that define the story. My mother perches on a log, framed by spruce and birch. Her dark hair is coiled high on her head. She sports a worn plaid pantsuit, and new hiking boots. Well-manicured hands curve gracefully around cup and thermos, and her smile is serene as she pours.

She is frivolous, yet dignified, in that photo. She is not the farm wife who couldn't be, not the exhausted, but persevering teacher, not the guardian of the Very Happy Childhood. She is Woman, Learning to Be.

There was a setback.

In my third year of teaching on the Labrador coast, my father had his heart attack and we all flocked home. Aunt Iris rose from the shadows and she was young once more: my mother did not cook the right foods; she did not look or act as the wife of her brother should. Clothes were provided, and advice dispensed. Hearty meals were prepared. It was like old times.

At first, Aunt Iris provided common ground for expressing frustration. It was, alas, too much like old times, and my mother slipped again into the role of resentful martyr. *You are as strong as what you eat,* Aunt Iris would proclaim, clapping a heaping platter, dripping in gravy, before my mother. Mother would daintily press her fingertips to her forehead, pry her lips apart, force the fork between her teeth, grimace, swallow, and shudder while Iris lectured the table at large on the virtues and many sources of potassium. Aunt Iris herself did not eat much, for she was the conductor of this orchestra and had cast my mother in the role of soloist who must be brought into line.

And so my mother dragged through her days with an air of grim finality again. She flinched and trembled, and my father started glowering again.

He mended, and Aunt Iris returned to her lair. My parents planned a new bough shack, a closer bough shack, with a plank table and benches that could be taken down and neatly stowed. Off they would go across the fields, past the red pines, my father plodding along with a small backpack bobbing on his back, my mother marching behind, swinging her walking stick. It was almost old new-times, but not quite, for my mother watched constantly for Signs, and declared that she must now be with him at All Times.

Yet sometimes the sun shone through, and at one such time, my son's father captured her in that black-and-white portrait: she shines in all the beauty that my father recognized in that moment at the train station in 1945.

My son's father saw that, and captured that forever. In that act of insight, she shines, and I am grateful.

~

The loons are calling across Wasaya now, and my dogs sprawl near the doorstep. I am lonely here, but here the loneliness can be kind and sweet, if I let it. In the loneliness I can find all the kind and sweet moments, and ease my heart with them. From here, I can see my mother perched on a log, in a faded plaid pantsuit and new hiking boots, polished nails displayed across the thermos. My father stands outside the photo, but she smiles because his eyes are on her.

It is a moment of lifting up and blessing, and I am ready to canoe to the Narrows.

Chapter 23

CARETAKER

That afternoon, Julie packs for herself and Musko, closes up the house, and follows her parents' car back to Waverley. She waits with her father the next day while her mother is prepped for surgery and wheeled into the operating room. She and her father sit side by side in the waiting room during the surgery; they stare at the floor, eyes sometimes flitting to the wall or the door or another part of the floor, but never meeting.

"That could be a mighty fine place, with a little work," her father says. "Too bad about that barn."

"Laila was telling me that Rachel said the foundation was tipping," Julie replies.

"Hmm. Well. How much, I wonder."

"Oh, I don't know, something like twenty degrees, I think it was."

"Oh. Well. Still. It's a shame."

"It was good, at the Park."

"I guess."

"We were together. Like Kedge days."

"Not much like Kedge days." He sighs.

"Well, a little colder. No leaves. But being together like that."

"That summer you went to Algonquin Park," he breaks in, "she missed you. And then, all that time in North Bay. She was some glad when you finally came home. And then you left."

"Well, I was thirty, that summer in Algonquin Park."

"And she was thirty years your mother. She feels things."

"Did you live with your parents, when you were thirty?"

Theo Martin stretches, tapping his feet with slow deliberation against the tiles. "I was married. It was different. Besides."

"Besides?"

"I had a job. I had you. And Tim. Tim's coming over tonight."

This is not the time to argue that she had a job, that fateful summer when she broke the pattern. "Is Tim happy, do you think?"

He sighs again. "Maybe. Some. It's hard to say. I don't think either of my children is too happy." In spite of Kedge days, in spite of paddles turned out flush to the chin for wandering daughters.

"I don't think I'm trying to be happy. I guess I'm just trying, trying to find a way. I'm just not sure, sometimes. Now Musko, he just *is*, you know. He just enjoys each thing as it comes along. I'd like to be like that."

"Yeah. Good dog, that one. You like your job, out there?"

"Oh, it's good. But it's nearly over. Wait and see, I guess."

"Tim now, he's in banking. For the long haul. It's a good job to have, today."

"Teaching's a good job."

Theo Martin taps his feet against the tiles and settles back in his chair. "Sure. It's good. But you're always going, like. Never getting anywhere."

Julie sighs. Meadowbrook is so far away.

"I'm just trying," her father blurts out. "Trying everything, to understand, what it's all for and where it's all gone."

Now Julie rubs her father's back as he sobs into his hands. "All we wanted, always, was to make you and Tim happy. And you're not. And we're not. And I can't for the life of me figure out why."

Happiness is not made. It is recognized and embraced. That is why Musko is always happy. He knows how to recognize and embrace it.

"You've been wonderful parents," Julie says instead. In April, she will remove the banking from around the sills. There will be a garden, and then lawns to mow, and she and her parents will watch the orchard for deer on Saturday evenings, as her mother grows strong and well. There will be Kedge afternoons as the days grow warm and sultry.

Julie has said all these things aloud, for her father is nodding and seeing them. "Maybe. Maybe," he says. "We've got to be near the hospital for a while now. Maybe."

Until April there will be weekends here, while she makes nourishing soups for her mother, who will grow strong nestled among her plants and her memories, knowing they are real.

Now the doctor is approaching and his lips are moving, forming words, and the words are that Alice Martin came through the surgery well and she is resting and there will be chemotherapy but it looks very good. It looks promising.

Julie will be a good daughter always, she vows. She will guide her parents through this time and she will guide them into adult parenthood.

That is what caretakers do.

~

Her mother is resting among her plants and memories when Julie returns to Meadowbrook Sunday night. March Break is over, and there has been no camping.

There has been Rachel, who may or may not be physically or mentally present or both, who seems to be spiritually somewhere, who may or may not have been seen by Joe Barnes, who may or may not have needed to see her. There has been Nathaniel with the great white Husky that is not Taggak, dropping in and out of his past.

There has been Samuel who cannot find happiness and Musko who recognizes and embraces it in the little moments of his life.

Especially, there have been her parents, who have embraced and offered up their need to be one with their past, perhaps just enough to start being one with their present, to savour it in the long days ahead.

And now there are lessons to prepare, because the spare moments in Waverley have slipped by, but school will start in the morning, just the same.

And in the night Julie dreams a happy ending for Rachel and Samuel. They are walking along the old truck road, along the second hill. They are in their late fifties, his hair a greyish fringe, hers a thick shock of brown and grey, but their eyes are ten years old and bright in the April sun. They each clutch a fishing rod and they are laughing. He swings the knapsack that holds their lunch.

Julie knows that inside the knapsack are cheese and sliced ham sandwiches with a little lettuce, apples and chocolate cupcakes, and juice boxes to wash it all down. She knows because the lunch has been prepared by Julie, who unbanks the house at the right time, and who grows strawberries over the foundation of the old barn while her father forks mulch around the crab apple tree and her mother rocks on the porch, wrapped in a blanket, smiling as Tina pirouettes beside the well. Laila is serene as she drives away, her tasks all accomplished, her hurts lifted, and her presence blessed.

All the children of Julie the caretaker are at peace.

Musko snoozes at Alice's feet, his paws twitching as he pursues his rabbits.

Chapter 24

PROTECTOR

"You look better," Janice declares at recess Monday morning. "Rested."

Julie is not sure why she should look better. *My mother has cancer,* she would like to shout from the school roof. *She has cancer, and she is not afraid, and I, finally, am unafraid.* Yet, she is not in the staffroom, is she? She is not there to hear smug Roger chortling over Old Rose stories. Not there to listen to copper-curled Margaret, knitting retirement dreams. Not there to face down the chorus as they lean in to support the main act.

No, Julie slouches over coffee in the resource room, and Janice props her feet on the desk. They are unprofessionally sequestered apart from their colleagues this day, and unrepentant.

"Spring is coming," Julie says with a shrug. This is a safe remark, whereas explaining that you have wept out your dark dreams and fears on your mother's cancer-ravaged breast is not. Janice lives in structure, whereas Julie is just starting to realize that she never will. She is, after all, a canoer of shorelines, and if she were a dog, she would sprawl under the desk and not dream past the next rabbit.

It is all very simple, but not easy to explain, nevertheless.

"You have Tina next," Janice says.

"How is she doing?" Julie asks.

"Oh, a little quieter, a little more withdrawn, if you can imagine that."

"Oh." Julie can imagine it, only too well. And yet, she can also see Tina, pirouetting before the well while her mother smiles.

~

Tina hunches over the table, fingers tracing over the faint scratches in the Formica veneer.

"How was March Break, Tina?"

Tina tugs the reading lying open in front of her a little closer and chimes each word, lulling through the paragraphs musically but without particular emphasis. The words spin from her mouth in a rush, and then they stop.

"That was beautiful, Tina."

"I'm not stupid," Tina whispers. "I know what is beautiful, and what's not."

"But you did read well, Tina."

"And I know things. Other things. And I'm not what they say I am."

"No. Of course not." Julie pauses, considering. "What things do you mean?"

Tina signs, reaching for a pencil. She grips it, and it hovers for a moment over the loose leaf. Then it is scratching, slashing, stabbing, and the words spill out on the page, raw and unedited. She shoves the page in front of Julie.

> In one dream room
> I am the dark one.
> I am marked. I am hated.
> I am their puzzle and the pieces do not fit.
> But in my dream room
> I cradle my kitten.
> I dance beside the old well and she smiles at me and

I am light.
In your dream room
You dream other lives—
Dark lives, bright lives,
But not your life.
In my dream room
I am myself.
Outside my dream room
No one understands my puzzle.
They cannot see
The pieces all lock into place
And I am a Good Life.

"Tina, you have talent."

Tina's lip curls. "My mother wrote poems," she says. "My mother learned things in school. I don't. But I know things. I'm not stupid. And I'm not bad."

"You are different, Tina. Different is good."

Tina slides the paper away from Julie. She studies it for a moment, and then she tears it, a jagged wound ripping through the words. She folds the pieces and tears again, and again. Finally, she scatters the pieces over the table.

"Different," she says, "is like that. It hurts like that."

She scoops up the pieces and crumples them in to a ball. "Sometimes they find one piece, and they hurt that. Sometimes they hurt all the pieces at once. It all hurts. It always hurts." She squeezes the pieces tight in her fist. "Different hurts," she repeats.

"Tina," Julie urges. "You can read. You can write. You can say such incredible things. You can go far, Tina. You just have to believe in yourself."

Tina shuts her eyes. "Why do people say that? 'You have to believe in yourself.' I do believe in myself. I'm real. I'm really here. It's like I'm a ghost or something if I don't believe enough.

"It's easy to believe in yourself. But they'll still keep hurting you. It will keep hurting and hurting. I just want to *be* myself and be one whole piece. Not like this." She twists the pieces of paper in her hands.

"Tina. Your uncle? Others? Are they still hurting you?"

Tina shakes her head, her long hair whipping across her face. "You don't understand. For you, it has to be some *one*. But you have to see that it's every *thing*. That's what happens when you're different. Different isn't good. It's like you, by yourself, and everything else keeps hitting you."

"Math time!" roars Eric. Oh, the schedule. The schedule has escaped Julie's control yet again.

"Hey, Tina, Tina, Daddy's little darlin'!" exclaims Daniel, plunking down in the chair beside her. "Daddy got a smile on his face this mornin'?"

"Daniel!" Julie's voice vibrates off the windows.

"What?" Daniel's eyes are wide and his shoulders up. "I just asked her a question."

"A friendly question," Eric adds, nodding his support. "No need to get all cranky with him."

Tina scatters the pieces of paper into the wastepaper can, wiping her palms together.

"Aw, aw. Love letters," exclaims Eric, snatching for fragments and lining them up on the table.

Tina sweeps the pieces away and spits into the wastepaper can. Eric is chortling and Daniel shaking his head as Tina rushes from the room without looking back.

Chortling and head shaking give way to hurt expressions. What did they do? They were just trying to cheer that little girl up; they didn't mean any harm. Detention? Now that is just harsh, Ms. Martin. What did they do to earn a detention? Detention for being friendly? What? Interrupting the lesson? That just isn't possible. It was their time. Check the schedule. They had every right. Well, of course they would knock next time. If they had thought Ms. Martin would be so uptight—no, no, they didn't mean that in a bad way. Just trying a little joke to smooth things over. An apology? To that little sl—snob? Why should they apologize? She was the one spitting. Very unhealthy habit. Extra math for time wasted? But who was wasting the time? Of course, they were very understanding when it came to Tina. But there were things Ms. Martin didn't know about this place yet. Now, naturally, they were going to follow all of her rules next time, but someone should explain to her about how some people just weren't right. No, not right and wrong—"right." Up there. Look, we're sorry. We'll do extra math drills at lunch time, and could we please do our lesson now? The time being wasted, Geez.

There will be Erics and Daniels everywhere in this world.

But there will be Lailas and Joes, as well.

Not to mention Rachels and Samuels.

Probably Julies, too.

And woven through them all, there will be Tinas, pirouetting beside the well, bringing smiles to wise women emerging.

~

Laila swings into the driveway on Monday evening after her day with Mark and Jenna. Laila is still exuberant from her March Break in LaHave, where her friends had purchased a cottage on the river after their own children were grown. They had decorated it with durable antique furniture gleaned from yard sales, and with touches of native art and sculpture selected in Lunenburg. They had decorated it without cherished toys and teddy bears, without childhood photos and precious family moments. It was a retirement cottage, where one day grandchildren might visit for the day, or perhaps even sleep over in the bunk-bed room, but for now it was a retreat for parents of adult children. Together they committed themselves to laughter over cards late into the night, to carefree treks along the river, and to all the food—far too much of it, but it was all so good. Laila revels in her recollections of these carefully constructed new memories.

"And your parents came," she pronounces. "Orchard looks good."

Now Julie recollects her own March Break, beginning from the arrival of her parents, but hazing over Saturday with Samuel and Joe and Jacob, for these are a separate story, a story for dreams and journals. She speaks of the walk to the brook and the visit to Kedge and the pruning of the orchard, but not of the tears and the knowledge that came with them. These are her own story. She tells of the surgery and the waiting room and the homecoming, but not of her father's bewilderment that he cannot make his children happy. This is his personal story, glimpsed by Julie but not to be touched or held by Julie. She talks of the weekend ahead, and the many weekends ahead, but not of spring evenings at Meadowbrook Acres, in which each, Laila included, experiences a happy ending. She tells the shell of the story of her mother's illness, and drops it into Laila's hands.

Laila studies the west window for a long time. "A positive attitude," she begins, "can go a mighty long way."

Laila brushes through her own story then, and that is when Julie learns that Laila has faced cancer twice, but right now she is more interested in going skiing later this week. She thought for sure she had mentioned her experience, but it might have slipped her mind. A person does get busy. Anyway, snow is coming, probably Wednesday, and they need to get in a little more skiing before the winter slips away from them. And because those weekends are going to be mighty important, Julie needs to be at her best.

Laila writes out her friend's recipe for a broccoli casserole—so easy but you would never believe the taste—while Julie gropes for appropriate questions about how long ago, and how difficult it must have been or maybe still was, and Laila replies with vague answers and suggestions that Musko stay with her and Tom on some of those weekends. Kind of free Julie up a little.

Julie's mother needs Musko there, Julie explains, and Laila stares long at the west window again.

Tina, Laila reflects, is not so different from her mother. Tina's mother had been kind of different in school, too, a good person, but kind of on the dreamy side, a little in her own world. That might not be exactly what Tina needs, given her troubles right now, but then a person never knew. Tina's more shy than anything else, when you come right down to it; she hides inside her head more than she should. She needs someone besides her mother to turn to, and it looks like Julie is gaining her trust. We all need someone we can trust.

So Julie does trust Laila with her father's bewilderment, and comes very close to trusting her with her own grief. She holds this for now, but senses that Laila, like her mother, already knows.

Rachel had Laila, and she turned to her and turned to her and when she had used up her need for her, she turned away. Rachel is surely ashamed because she has pulled Laila out when she felt like playing; she has opened the box and dusted her off, restoring a once-cherished doll to first chair, and then tucked her away again.

Rachel is wandering the world, or lost in her world, and when she thinks of Laila she tells herself that it is too late to return. On some days, Rachel plans to restore the farm and all that was, but cringes over the wasted opportunities, the wasted time, the wasted trust. Julie wants to tell Rachel that Laila will wait and then listen, understand, and forgive, and walk beside her for as long as it takes because that is what Laila does. She wants to tell her that Laila is more hurt by being spared than by being used. She needs to return and walk side by side with her.

So Julie does tell Laila how she cried for her mother and for herself and all her wasted times, and that her mother already knew.

Laila already knew, too.

~

That night, Julie dreams of Laila and her mother, skiing side by side among the red pines. Julie jogs behind, urging them to turn back because more snow is coming, but they continue to glide over the crust, exclaiming at the beauty of the snow-laden branches. Now the broad flakes are tumbling from the sky, and Julie peels off her jacket and flaps them away with it. Not one of those flakes must fall on them, for even one flake is lethal. Still Laila and her mother swish over the snow, laughing and free in their own joy, and Julie wallows in the deepening drifts, madly flapping her jacket as the sweat drips from her forehead and her eyes well with tears and the flakes reel and tease around their shoulders and they cannot see or will not.

She has just found them, and she will not lose them.

There is more than one Samuel to protect now.

Stumbling through the deadly snow, driving off the flakes that would burn the flesh from their bones. That is what protectors do.

Chapter 25

UNBANKING

Today is the day of unbanking the house. It is the last weekend of April, and the snow has melted away everywhere; even the shaded woodland floor is raw and exposed, craving just a little more sun to quicken and renew. Now, though, rotten limbs lie slick and fat among the dreary remains of last year's renewal. Here and there a string of dead grass drapes over the sodden branches pressing into the earth. Soon, the pale new green will push through, shrouding the limbs, eclipsing the murky yellows and browns of old leaves.

The sky is grey and still on Unbanking Day; the air warming, but damp. Julie backs the rider mower from the garage and into the dull morning. Oh, she is wiser now, no longer a newcomer. She is a canoer of shorelines, a survivor of snake dreams, and the creator of healing dreams. She sleeps in Grandfather's death room, no longer on the floor beside the refrigerator. She grows stronger in the night; the killer snow does not touch her mother or Laila, her father spades the compost at the base of the apple trees while Samuel and Rachel laugh carefree on their way to the brook and her mother sleeps serenely with Musko at her feet.

She does not admit that she awakens anxious, desperate to dream again, while Musko crowds against her and licks her cheek. She longs to touch her mother's blanket, to arrange the chair to better catch the heat of the sun, perhaps to bring hot water for the tea, to better drive off the cancer. Musko wants to walk, but she wants to dream again, her mother smiling, serene on the verandah, her daughter watching and protecting. Julie likes to pull herself into that dream, although Musko resists her.

On Unbanking Day, however, Julie is alone at Meadowbrook Acres. No mother graces the verandah, no father mulches the crab apple tree. Samuel and Rachel have faded into their fishing brook world, a world into which they do not bring Julie. There are no voices from the top bunk these days, no Christmases are held in the attic, and no urgent little snakes tap within glass ornaments. The floors above have finished settling; the light in the stair well has not returned. On Unbanking Day, there is the starkness of late April and a caretaker performing her spring rites, while a great black dog hunts mice in the orchard.

On Unbanking Day, Julie spreads a tarp behind the rider mower, ties it to the seat with nylon cord found in the garage, and drives up beside the front lawn on the east side of the house. She bunches the bags of leaves into her arms; they are flattened now, bulging at the bottom and loose above. They have settled.

Julie smiles. She has settled, too. She has settled and this evening her parents will settle here, too. It will be too cool for her mother to recline in a rocking chair on the verandah, but Julie will dream that, and when it does happen, it will be right.

Julie piles the bags on the tarp, and then folds it into a loose pocket. She mounts the rider mower and eases forward. She realizes then that the orchard is to her right and behind her, and she cannot turn on the steep side lawn. She should have turned first but she has not and she does not want to undo her work and start again. She stops and surveys her yard—yes, her yard today—and sets her course. She will drive across the front lawn, around the back of the house, and down to the orchard. Ah, the solution is so simple when you take your time and consider your options. Again, she eases forward.

The puffy tires press deep into the old lawn, grinding back the moss. The tarp scrapes along the ash tree and bags of leaves tumble sideways onto the lawn, the weathered plastic tearing and spilling their contents. There is a smugness to the scattering leaves that sets the calmest of caretakers brooding.

Julie strides around the pile, picturing her parents coming down the driveway, her father's lips tight as he surveys the mess and plots his solution and her mother frail and forgotten in the Unbanking Day struggle. She flings the bags back onto the tarp, clawing handfuls of leaves over them, and draws the tarp tight. She rips into the moss again, brown gashes bursting open in the old lawn, the load jerking and swaying. She rolls down the west side of the house, across the once barnyard, and down to the orchard.

She turns to find the load teetering to one side, bits of plastic and frayed cord trailing, a few bags fluttering defiantly in the barnyard. She scoops armfuls of loose leaves around the Gravenstein trees, splits and empties the bags because she no longer cares about preserving them, and pulls the leaves back from the bark. The orchard looks good; it will not do to rot the bark.

She turns the rider mower before gathering the next loads. Unbanking Day is now an event to be overcome, not enjoyed, and Julie slogs her way through the task. By eleven o'clock, the house is unbanked, the now ragged tarp draped over the well, the tattered bags bundled away to be processed at some later date. The foundation is bare and slick in the weak sun that presses through the grey. The sills are safe now.

Julie grows calm again as she rakes down the front lawn. She reaches and pulls, dragging into the moss, which peels back and leaves brown patches. She sprinkles lime and is the caretaker again, restoring the lawn, year by year, until it is lush and verdant and Samuel comes home to stay. There will be contract after contract for Julie, and one day, when Samuel comes home to stay, she will be his caretaker and companion and he will not be lonely again.

Musko roams the orchard, sniffing out mice. Lime stings the pads of his feet, and his dreams are of squirrels and rabbits.

Now here are her parents, her mother reclining in the passenger seat. The treatments are grueling, but then the sickness lifts. The sickness lifts, but there is such weakness; the body sinks deep into itself, seeking its healing. There is weakness, but still these are called the good days, and the good days will continue until next week, when the treatment begins again. Today, Alice Martin comes to her daughter.

Her father surveys the front yard, purses his lips, and shrugs. He does not mention the brown patches, or comment on the tire marks, or tell Julie that she should have waited for wet weather to lime the lawn. The Next Treatment is coming, and today must be perfect.

Musko frolics in front of Alice, spinning and crouching but never touching, dancing out his ecstasy while Alice laughs and makes patting motions in the direction of his head. In the kitchen, he hunkers down near her feet, bouncing up with ears at attention whenever she changes position. Musko guards Alice Martin in the present, because he does not have dreams of the future to dream for her.

"I wonder," says her father as he stares into the bowl in front of him at lunchtime, "I wonder if Samuel would sell a little piece of land."

Julie ladles soup into her mother's bowl, considering. "What did you have in mind?" she says. They are talking, simply talking as one adult to another. Julie squares her shoulders and feels her maturity. She is almost thirty-three, and excited to be responsible and mature. All you have to do is accept that you will always be their little girl, and then you are free. A paradox. But that is the way it works.

"Theo wants to build a cottage," Alice explains. "Down past Samuel's orchard. He'll be retiring in a few years, you know."

"But why there?" says Julie. "Why not on a river or a lake or somewhere less . . ."

"Boring?" her mother finishes. "Something that's not just a field?"

"I like it here," Theo says. "I always have. I'd clean up those trees in the front yard, paint the house up white, take care of the place, like."

Oh, oh. That is Julie's job. Julie is the caretaker and although she is not a handyman she has the heart for this, and it is her right.

"But it's kind of far from the hospital," Julie says instead.

"I won't be sick forever," her mother says.

Julie's adult relationship with her parents falters and she resents them with all the fervour of a frustrated seventeen-year-old. She would plant strawberries on the barn site. She sees her father nailing the clapboards of the new barn in place, oh, so satisfied. Oh, it would probably be of forty-head-of-cattle proportions. And then he would strap her and Tim into the backseat, helpless amid the pool noodles and sleeping bags, and he would drive up the road proclaiming what a great farm this was and is again.

Her anger rushes in her forehead and Julie closes her eyes. Her mother has cancer; she must get along. Let him talk, let him talk; Samuel wouldn't let him paint the bathtub let alone build a barn. A cottage, a cottage; he doesn't really want to build a barn. Your mother has cancer; say something productive and wise.

Just because you have everything sorted out yet again, and the pieces have all fallen into place again, just because you have found your place and your reason, that does not mean that your parents can no longer slide your dream out from under you. But never mind that: your mother has cancer; be calm and wise.

Julie pushes back her chair. "Well, I'm not altogether sure that Samuel would sell," she says, rising to prepare the tea.

~

All in all, it was still a good weekend. Alice rested and Theo started spading over the garden piece while Julie worked on her lessons. They prepared meals together and ate parts of them; they walked almost to the second hill. Julie and her father continued working the garden piece while her mother read.

Best of all, Samuel did not stop by to see how the place was doing. Julie was spared the sight of her father's hopeful face as he laid out his proposal for the farm. She was spared the sight of Samuel's face lighting up as the plans took shape before his eyes, and then collapsing in nervous frustration because these are his plans, too, and he cannot bring them to be. Both men with a vision, both men disappointed and hurt.

On Sunday evening, after the car is packed and her parents gone, the image tugs at her heart and draws tears to her eyes. Samuel and her father, side by side, looking down over the orchard and neither can have his dream because it belongs also to the other.

She does not want to share the part that is her dream, either.

Meadowbrook Acres is so large; it should be able to handle all their dreams. But it can only handle one.

Oh, it was a good weekend, but still the image pulls Julie, and therefore that Sunday night, Samuel creeps across the kitchen and up the attic stairs. He cups the glass ornament in his palm, but the Christmases do not come. He stands long with his forehead pressed to the coarse window casing, but the deer do not play for him this night. The tears slide down his cheeks as he sways, back and forth, in the silence of the attic.

Ah, the snake dreams cannot be far behind.

The Wasaya Journal of Rachel Hardy: Part 9

PARTING

I will be leaving Wasaya in two weeks, and I am anxious. I analyze each moment, each movement. Have I relaxed enough while making my morning coffee? Have I really appreciated that sunrise? Have I been analyzing too much? Should I read in the porch, or trim back some brush, do a little painting, clear the shed? Should I be canoeing more? Should I be content to be alone here, or should I make the place more amenable to company?

Am I spoiling my last two weeks? Probably.

I sweep the floor, and trim the brush and saplings by the big rock. Now I am doing something; I am participating. The canoe calls to me, and I tuck away saw and bush nippers and reach for my paddle.

The three dogs scramble to their feet, their eyes on the paddle. They are like children to me, but they are aging children. The little ones are old now, and the great white Husky mix is growing stiff. We must swim and explore now. Do they miss the Park? Should I take them to the Park, so people can pet them and ask about them? Is this our last summer of good health? Am I letting them down, too?

They bound to me as I produce their life jackets. We are wearing life jackets! That means a long exploration—probably with snacks. There will be geese and ducks along the shore, and squirrels in the woods at the Narrows. That is perfect. That is all we need.

Saima taps the gunwale with one creamy paw as she springs into the canoe. Mikijuk, her daughter, scrambles into the bow, tail swinging. Taggak watches from the shore, waiting to see where we are going. Then he lopes along the shore for a while before churning out to follow the canoe. Mikijuk curls at my feet, but Saima always stands. Eyes half-shut, she studies one shore, turns, and studies the other shore. She is the watcher.

We skirt the islands, and the little ones bound over the side to frolic in the shallows with Taggak. They run the shores together, finally swimming out and presenting their lifejacket handles for lifting. Saima continues to scan the shores, and Mikijuk sits before me, eyes on my paddle. Taggak puffs along in the water beside me, grinning.

They are content. Should I be content? Am I doing it right? Will this memory sustain or undo me this winter? Will I be disappointed because I analyzed too much? Is there something strange, perhaps, about a solitary woman in her fifties out there canoeing around the islands with three happy dogs in lifejackets? Will this be a good memory, or a disappointment?

Sometimes I want so much to be surrounded by people out here. I yearn for them, and when they come, I imagine the return to the natural flow of my life when they are gone. And when they go, the emptiness grips and grips and I cannot rest. I feel foolish out here.

The paddle dips; the water ripples and gurgles against the canoe. Saima is alert; there are loons near the long island. We coast in silence.

My mind goes still.

I remember when I was five. I was afraid to eat the toast that was put before me, because it might not be mine. "Is this mine?" I asked. "Is this mine?" "Yes," they replied, kindly at first and then with increasing exasperation as I persisted. I would not eat the toast, in the end. If they were angry about the toast, then perhaps it was not mine.

I filed from the church to the hall with the other children one rainy afternoon. They rushed into the hall, eager for games. I waited outside, because no one told me personally to go in, and I might not be included. I waited outside in the rain, and no one came looking for me. I must have been right. When I got home, soaking wet, I was told that if I caught my death of cold, then that would make a lot of extra work for my mother. After all, she had almost died giving me birth, and had been unconscious for three days. She couldn't have any more children. She neglected to mention that this all took place in a record hot August; I knew all the details, in order.

Mikijuk clambers over the side with a great splash and surfaces, tipping one ear. I laugh and dip the paddle again. I relax now, and my five-year-old self fades. I am fifty-two, and not shaped by my past in this moment. This splash, this tipping ear: this is important.

Now I produce car keys, and the dogs are ecstatic. A car ride! A perfect end to a perfect canoe ride.

I come again to the Park, and this day the Park is sunny and windy. Most sites are full, toddlers squeal and play catch with parents, and everyone wants to pet my dogs. Is the big one the mother? Are those the puppies? Taggak stares past them, but grins as little ones twist their fingers into his thick white fur. The dogs curl under a tree at my brother's campsite, filled with treats and adored by all passersby. Is this where they belong? Am I wrong to hold them at Wasaya?

I descend again into Wasaya that evening, cold and damp. The beaver splashes at the entrance to the cove, and the dogs spring from the canoe to swim and frolic along the shore. The loons are active this evening, and the ducklings venture out from the creek.

They belong. I belong. I left the Park because the social atmosphere wears thin with time. It, too, is artifice. I remember this now. I think that the Park is still lonely, crowded with happy visitors who do not know her. She spreads her hemlock boughs over them all. Is it benediction or mourning? I cannot tell.

Taggak wriggles and grunts on his back. Mikijuk stalks a squirrel. Saima stands smiling on the shore. I sip my instant coffee and I smile.

~

My mother was in her sixties when my father developed congestive heart failure. Now she never left his side. She never let him out of her sight. She did not dare. She descended into martyrdom again, and this time she did not return.

I do not think she meant to. I believe that she had found her peace, and now it was about to be taken from her. She had found him, and now he was going away. She watched and analyzed and feared, gobbling down each moment and dreading the next for it might be the last. She would tumble and tumble, down into darkness. She would be there alone.

By now I had a son and a not particularly happy marriage. "Never let him take music out of your life," my mother said. She was the third portrait, that day, Woman Learning to Be.

I arrived, freshly separated, to help out for a month. My father had been in and out of hospital, but was home the day I arrived. He stood there, on the verandah, and he was old: his shoulders stooped, his big frame poking through his jacket, his glasses huge on his gaunt face. My mother stood beside him, frail and frightened.

They no longer walked to the far bough shack or the near bough shack or the brook or even the maple tree in the field. Mother's hiking boots stood in the corner of the porch, stiff and dusty. Her eyes were on his face, watching his every breath.

I look back from Wasaya and I see how that can be.

I have pictures in my soul from that summer: Mother, cautiously guiding the Raider up and down the driveway with her grandson laughing beside her, my father and my son seated on the verandah and gazing out together over the orchard with the family dog beside them, my mother chopping bananas over vanilla ice cream and sprinkling it with brown sugar while my son watches. Her smile is relaxed in this last picture; it is wide and honest.

Aunt Iris loomed on the horizon, and there were hospital moments and medical appointments and all the moments of dying slowly by congestive heart failure. There was an early birthday party for Nathaniel, and he refused to remove his new Smurf sneakers our first night on the road. I could feel my mother's tears as I told her.

They were alone now, facing down the Last Happy Moments Together while Aunt Iris directed from the wings. They could not enjoy these precious moments any more than I can enjoy the precious moments of Wasaya.

~

I do not think that I understood Aunt Iris until the next summer, the last summer, the summer my father died.

It is my belief that in those last summers, Aunt Iris was struggling in her own way to create good moments, to outrace the darkness of their childhood together.

Then, when he passed from this life, my father would remember only these times, for those other times would be gone.

I see her at the picnic table outside the hospital doors. She sits, the remains of a perfect picnic supper strewn before her on the table. The nurse is leading my father, who totters on his feet. My mother follows, fingers to forehead, mouth twisted, chin tucked. "I thought it would be good for him," Iris says. "A nice picnic supper, outdoors. He always liked to be outdoors. I thought it would be good," she repeats, and tears trickle over her seamed cheeks. She has remembered all the things that he liked; she has offered this up to him. Yet, he is tottering away. She is too late. "I know," I say.

When the call comes, it is Iris who takes it, Iris who breaks down and sobs for her last brother, the ill-favoured of Grandma Mary. "I kicked her," she whispers as I rock her. "She was beating him once. And

I kicked her as hard as I could with my new boots. 'Run away, Stephen,' I said. 'Run as hard as you can. I got her.'"

"I know," I say again.

She hovers on the brink of memory, imploring forgiveness. I reach out, here from my cove in Wasaya, and I bless her. I lift her. I love her.

A breeze fans the trees and the waters, and I know that here, at Wasaya, my plea is heard.

As for my mother, her death began that second summer. I must rest, before I tell more of that second summer.

Chapter 26

CASTING

Joe rummages in his tackle box and draws out a small tobacco tin. He pops it open with his thumb and plucks the top cotton batting layer away with his fingertips. Six neatly wound flies are nestled in the layer below.

"Now, Mrs. Hardy was the most prim, proper lady you ever laid eyes on," he says. "Make-up just so, nails all perfect, hair coiled up high and neat. But she surprised us all in the end. Took to fly fishing, she did, after Charles and me was well grown, round about the time I was headin' for Ontario."

He nods toward the boulders protruding from the river above the bridge. "They call this the eel weir," he says. "Native people set those boulders like that. They had nets and baskets catchin' the eels as they was comin' through the gap, every fall and spring. Kind of a history feel to the place, ain't it?"

Julie breathes in the May air, feeling it fanning her face as the buds quiver in the early morning air. Musko splashes in the eddy below the bridge. The black flies are sleepy, but already digging into her neck as the air warms.

Joe selects a fly with a body of red wool wound with gold thread, the wings a tuft of deer hair. "You'd see her and old Mr. Hardy down along the shore below the bridge, him casting slow and calm, her flittin' that fly here and there, happy as a kid."

He slips the leader through the eye of the hook and weaves a figure eight, drawing it tight.

"They come more and more, after Rachel and the boys was grown. Kids never liked it much, but it got to be kind of special to Mrs. Hardy and him. Regulars, they was."

Julie laces a figure eight. It slips through the hook, and she begins again.

"When Rachel was in Grade 7, she went to her first dance at the high school. Charles was right proud of his little sister, dancing away with her and her kind of shufflin' and lookin' around, no one to dance with but big brother." Joe shakes his line out and presses the hook into the corking at the base of the rod. "So, I asked her to dance. Now she's lookin' all excited, lookin' around and grinnin', to see who's noticin' her dancin' with one o' the seniors. There she is weavin' and turnin' with the music, all happy. Now, Mrs. Hardy was a chaperone and the next one was a slow one, and I knew better than to hang around there, so Ah said my thank-yous and give her a little bow, and off she goes, sittin' and grinnin' with her friends, lookin' all around. She'd had a *dance*."

Joe Barnes asked Rachel Hardy to dance, and perhaps for a minute she dreamed that she was sophisticated and popular and dancing into her future. It would all be easy. Step would follow step into a rich and fulfilling life.

"Kinda shy, she was. Mebbe a little awkward. Never fit in, like some do. You know, it's natural for some. She tried, but, well . . ."

Some are canoeists. Others are canoers of shorelines.

They are stepping among the rocks and weeds at the river's edge.

"She did come back there, last May. Ah wasn't dreamin' it."

He flicks his wrist and the line coils back and back, hovering behind him and then floating and rolling out over the water before him, the fly easing down to skim the surface. "She liked it up there, on the lake," he says. "Always come back summers, found the Ha'dy place too much, but then she found that place. A little strange, I guess, out there alone with all her dogs, but it seemed to suit her.

"Then one day I guess it didn't, and she was gone."

"Laila says she left a note," Julie says.

"Prob'ly. Nathaniel would figure it out. He comes there, from time to time."

"But the canoe and everything was gone."

"Buried it under spruce boughs, back in the woods, far down from the landing, she said." The fly flits over the surface at Joe's touch on the line. "Sometimes Ah think she's been there all along, hidin' out, comin' in sometimes."

"But Laila—"

"Laila's a good friend. Mebbe our Miss Ha'dy will figure that out some day, and stop pushin' everyone away. It's like she can't believe that people really care about what happens to her, and get mighty hurt when she pushes them away like that."

"Joe, why is she like that?" If she understands Rachel, then maybe she will understand herself.

Joe guides his line to the ripple above the rocks. "Oh, we all got our story, somewheres. We all got something we got to get our mind around."

Every day, every moment, Joe has to get his mind around his son Jacob. Every day, every moment, Jacob moves a little closer to the right, or leans down to tie his boot, and the cable fans past him. He lets out his breath in a great rush. Sometimes, he laughs. He pulls away his hard hat for a moment, pushing back his thick hair while the rest of the crew gather close, clapping his back, needing to touch him because he has come so close but he is fine. And yet, every day, every moment, Joe kneels beside Jacob's coffin and it is closed because the cable did not fan past that time, the real time.

"Yer mother comin' along OK?"

Julie flicks back her line and the hook snags below the rocks. She tugs gently, feels it give a little, and tugs again. "She's feeling better again, one more treatment and then we'll see."

"She'll make it," Joe declares. "She's got spirit."

"And you know that how?" Julie yanks the line tight, holds it tense, feeling the hook give a little. She gives a steady pull, and the line drifts free, the broken leader trailing in the water.

"She's got a daughter that pulls hard," Joe says. "And I gotta teach you to tie them flies yourself, the way you seem set to go through them."

~

By mid-morning, Joe has two small speckled trout, and Julie has lost two flies. The black flies are dense around them. Joe slides his knife along the belly of the first fish, scoops the guts out, and tosses them into the water while Musko's ears droop.

"Not for you, young feller," Joe tells him. "Make a fine mess on your grandmother's carpet, that would." He opens the second fish. "Now these here would make a nice little pan fry for your folks," he says.

"Oh, but your father—"

"Will say: 'Why didn't ya give 'em to those Ma'tins? Be a nice little taste o' home for 'em.' Wrap 'em up now, your dad'll like a taste of Kedge. And it'll give your mother her appetite back, I expect."

~

That afternoon in Waverley, her father rolls them in just a little corn-meal and crisps them up in a little butter. "When we retire," he says, "we'll be catching our own trout at Kedge."

Theo talks often of their future, weaving Alice into his plans as he recites them, for if she is in the plans, she must be in the future.

272

"There's a new hospital in Bridgewater," he says. "About as close as the one in Halifax is to us now."

The new hospital in Bridgewater is at least twenty years old, but it is fresh and powerful in his mind's eye.

"I could have a workshop, up there in that old garage. I could make some furniture, maybe do a little carpentry. Keep my hand in."

"He'll be busier than ever," Alice murmurs, shifting in her chair. "The road is so noisy here now, so busy. The country might be nice."

"And we'd come around Waverley, perhaps once a month, and your mother can visit with all her friends, have tea and all that, and I could stock up."

"Overhead, dear." Her mother closes her eyes. "You'll overstock your business and go bankrupt."

"A bannister that does that front justice," Theo declares. "That's what it needs."

"And I imagine I'll do a little gardening," Alice prompts.

"Well, sure. A little rock garden, some nice flowers. You don't want to overdo it," he says.

Alice moves her piece of trout with her fork, nibbles at it, pronounces it delicious, and sips at her water.

"Fresh air will give you an appetite," Theo says. "We can go for walks in the evening, and the Park is close for camping."

"Yes, Theo," Alice says. "It will be like it was when we were first married."

Theo brightens. This is the way. They will live in the country with the workshop humming, flowers blooming, and family all around. He will retire today, capture Alice in his dream, and they will live forever like that, exploring along the shore at evening always. Alice will paddle bow, smiling over her shoulder, Jeremy Bay calm in the summer evening. At the far end of the bay, a loon will call.

On winter evenings there will be coffee and quiet conversation beside a woodstove. He will glance over and there will be Alice, curled in her chair, eyes glowing with contentment.

~

"I just want to be home," Alice whispers, as Julie eases her into the tub that night. "Home with him." Her eyes brim with tears. "Anywhere he is. That's all."

"Does he really think he can build a cottage out at Meadowbrook?"

Her mother squeezes her eyes shut. "Oh, just let him have this, Julie. It's only words, and it makes him so happy. It takes his mind off things."

Her parents would be so right at Meadowbrook Acres. They would know how to greet Samuel, and would ask for the story of each ornament. If they saw flickering lights, they would pronounce it heat lightning and it would be so. There would be no snake dreams, because there would be no one who would receive them.

They would swap recipes and stories with Laila on the verandah on summer evenings, while they waited for Samuel and Rachel to come back from fishing. Her father would crisp up the trout in a little butter and Samuel would exclaim that that is what they always did.

Maybe Charles would come home again.

And Nathaniel would find his way.

But where is the caretaker? Where is Julie?

She is adrift somewhere, trying to find the turning point in her life yet again, trying to piece together her life into a whole before all her years are used up. Her line floats at first, but always, always, it snags in the rocks and is broken.

Chapter 27

BANNISTER

You can't let the snakes keep coming around the house and the garage, her father has explained to Julie. They'll nest there, and you'll be overrun with them. Before you know it, they'll work their way in through the cracks and find their way into your house.

How do you stop them? Julie asks.

I use a shovel, he replies.

But they're part of nature, just trying to find their way. Laila's horrified voice echoes in Julie's mind.

Julie dons knee-high rubber boots and marches to the garage, clutching a shovel. She swings it high and slaps it against the spindly hay growing in clutches behind the garage. She too is part of nature. Nevertheless, she will not share this moment with Laila. The shovel bounces against the earth and she gives it an extra, defiant smack. She stomps her rubber boots as she works her way along the garage wall. She slaps and smacks at the hay, poised to run. A solitary toad evades the shovel with a sudden leap. Julie springs back, flailing the air with the shovel. The toad eyes her for a moment, and then wriggles its way back into the hay. There are no snakes.

Snakes wait until you are ambling along in sandals, looking at the trees. They sprawl across your path so that you stumble over them, and then they writhe in protest, with much pretense of panic as they thrash against insteps and ankles. Snakes know when you are vulnerable. Snakes play to win.

Julie hefts her shovel and strides back to the house. She has faced them, even though they are not there. She has made a stand. She is pro-active. She wonders what people driving by think.

When your mother has cancer, your own life comes into focus. You do not obsess over family relationships, yours or the Hardys. You take charge. You do not sleep on the kitchen floor beside the refrigerator and wonder how you ever let things go this far. You are, ultimately, ready to be an adult and finally understand that you blamed your parents for holding you back when you were in fact too afraid to go forward. You do your job, you look after the farm, and you look after them.

You seem to keep dreaming, however. You dream your mother well. You dream the happy ending. Sometimes, you dream Samuel alone in the attic, but you know that this is just a dream. Only the healing dreams count.

~

May is testing month for Julie, with tests and reports and interviews and teachers with strained patience asserting that they really do understand that she cannot take groups this month.

Julie had started the test with Tina last winter, but set it aside, hoping to continue it with the others in May, when Tina's life might be going more smoothly. She was going to start the Grade 7s this week, and specifically start with Tina. Julie, however, will not be testing Tina this May.

Tina's mother has gone to Truro to look after her sister, who is ill. Tina has been brought along to help out. Her mother has collected a substantial homework package from Tina's teachers, and has been unusually alert and focused as she reviews the assignments and nods in agreement with their requests. She will make sure that Tina does everything, she says. Education comes first, even at a time like this, she affirms.

Today, however, a school in Truro has requested Tina's transcript.

Tina's aunt must be very ill.

No, Tina's mother has just come to her senses. When she becomes very sincere about the homework package, then that is code for "She is moving out." She does this once in a while, the others explain to Julie.

Julie decides to prepare detailed notes to ensure consistency in the delivery of reading and communications support.

There are other things that need consistency even more, Janice reminds her.

Doug vanishing was acceptable, even preferable. Tina, though, should not vanish. Tina knows dreams. Tina understands dream houses. Julie disciplines herself to remember that she is not governed by dreams now. She does her job, she looks after the farm, and she looks after her parents. She is becoming the caretaker that she was meant to be.

She is her own journal, and the author of all her dreams.

She would still like to read the journal of Rachel Hardy, but perhaps later, when she returns. *But I've never really left.* That is just her winter imagination at work. Rachel does not talk to her.

But sometimes Samuel really is so lonely.

Musko sprawls in the May sun, snorting away the flies that probe at his nose. Musko likes to wallow in the brook, and then root in the spreading greenery for mice. Sometimes, he seems far away from Julie. She walks and he walks, but each in a separate world, each with separate thoughts. He lies by Alice Martin and watches over her healing. He connects with Alice, but not with Julie.

Alice's latest treatment has gone well. Everyone agrees that she did very well, and that everything went very well. Does this mean that she is very well? We must remember that she still has cancer. We have to wait and see. Time will tell.

Julie misses Tina. Tina is not in school, not in Grandma Mary's bedroom doorway stroking the kitten-snake, not by the well caught by the sun as she dances. Tina is gone.

~

A brief e-mail from Doug arrives in May: The rigs are deadening. Money-grubbing consumerism prevails. The drive is killing him. Now here is a thought! They could open an outfitting shop to serve that Park place. Nothing fancy. Geared to the clientele—skis, canoes, camping gear rentals. Maybe do some guiding. Think about it. They never really got to explore that second chance. Meanwhile, that family is driving him crazy. They are insisting on child support, but blocking all visiting rights. He wishes that they would just get over it. They will drive that poor kid crazy. Now, here's another thought that deserves serious consideration: What if *they* were raising the kid? Seriously. Their own outfitting shop, his son growing up close to nature, growing into the business. At least think about it. It doesn't always have to be about Julie.

Julie sends a reply: She never agreed to a second chance. Park visitors are typically self-sufficient, and what services they do need are already in place. Doug has a stable job, and he should keep it. Sounds like he will need the income on a regular basis. Also, Doug is on his own in this, and every other, situation.

Doug's ten-line reply, in capital letters, could be summarized as: Julie is unsupportive.

Julie blocks Doug's name and e-mail address at the server, and hopes that he does not start inventing new addresses under pseudonyms. Or, worse yet, show up like last time. You cannot evict someone from a property by pressing "delete."

He did bring Musko, oh, dear Musko. And now Julie walks beside him but does not talk to him. Perhaps Musko has come for Alice.

~

Julie plucks the weeds that crowd around the infant carrots, beans, peas, squash, and potatoes. The mosquitoes crowd the blackflies as they press close to find her blood. A few blossoms unfold in the apple trees. The crab apple tree does blossom on the garage side, but it is a scattering of polka dots, not the clouds of Samuel's childhood.

~

On the long weekend, Julie leaves for Waverley early Saturday morning. Her mother is feeling well, oh, so remarkably well, considering, but she is so tired. They will have a quiet weekend at home. Tim will take time to come out on Sunday afternoon; he is so busy.

Julie's father has purchased eight sacks of sheep manure on sale, which he will stuff into and strap onto Julie's SUV. You have to get some mulch around those trees, and this is a start.

In his basement workshop, Theo Martin has started The Bannister. He has found just the right mould, the proper antique mould, and made a thick strong rail with deep grooves on either side. The bannister is oak. He will turn out spindles on his lathe, with simple curves, nothing fussy or ornate, and a fine newel post—sturdy, no curlicues. It will be statuesque. It will be just what you expect when you see that front door.

Incidentally, he could replace those panes around the front door; the frames are worn and rattling. It needs good, solid frames, the same size. Then, you open the door and that staircase is simply there. There is power in a good staircase with a proper bannister.

Julie runs her palm along the railing. Meadowbrook Acres will be frail, dwarfed by this massive bannister. No amount of reframing of panes will provide balance here. She pictures a massive oak newel post stained dark and carved in brutally raw pineapples, the stairway rising and curving away into a sprawling second, and then third, storey. It will burst out of Meadowbrook Acres, ludicrous in its muscular prowess.

A Canoer of Shorelines

Samuel will cover his face in his hands and disappear into the attic. He does not want a better, more powerful Meadowbrook; he wants his Meadowbrook, with "Fragile" neatly penned on little boxes of glass ornaments.

Julie watches as her father grooves and sands.

"The trick to any project," he says, "is to take your time. You have to think it through. Plan what you need and take it one step at a time. Like my uncle used to say, you can't just barrel your way through the Pearly Gate. " He chuckles, then catches himself, in horror at his own words. Pearly Gate, yes, but not now, not soon, in a long time. Jests about death summon death. He will not again, he promises.

Julie sits on the basement step, groping for words to fill the vacuum and make his world right again. Finally, she says, "I wonder what Samuel will say."

Her father shakes his head. "Oh, it doesn't matter," he says. "He probably won't even see it. It's for the house, you see, the one in here." He gives his temple a shy tap.

Julie's brow furrows. "Then why make it at all?"

Her father sighs. "It's the making that matters to me. It's like, bringing a little piece of my dream to life, making it real." He sorts through sheets of sandpaper, considering the grain. "I know it's probably not going to happen."

"It's your vision, Dad. It's important."

"Yeah." He sits down by the tool bench. "To an old man."

"Oh, Dad."

"I just want—every minute—it's precious to me, precious, and it's all running out and away. You, Tim—now Alice." His voice breaks, and he leans forward, hands clasped and elbows pressed to his knees.

Julie crouches beside him. "I'm here now. Really here now. I'm not going anywhere. I'm staying, this time. And I won't go."

Theo leans a little more, swaying back and forth now. "I dreamed," he whispers, pausing to clear his throat. "I dreamed your mother and I were up in Kedge, canoeing along Jeremy Bay, just enjoying the

280

morning. It was calm, and peaceful, and she was dipping her paddle so easy, singing, like she always did. 'What's the name of that song?' I say. She looks back over her shoulder; she's got her paddle up, ready to swing. She stops just like that and she smiles at me. And then, she kind of, looks serious, sad almost, and her hand lifts away from the paddle and she gives a little wave. The sun catches my eye, just for a second, and then the bow is trailing off, and it's empty. And I'm just sitting there, trying to hear the singing. It's almost there, but it just—isn't."

"Dad. It's just a dream. It's what you're afraid will happen."

"Yeah?" He stares at his daughter. "Well, what if it's a premonition, like? Those things happen, they say."

~

"Healing is hard work," her mother observes. "It takes away your appetite."

Her mother's wisps of hair are tucked back under the flowered head scarf. Her eyes are sunken above her sagging cheeks. She chews, swallows, and smiles. "Delicious, dear. That extra garlic does give it a nice flavour. I think I'll rest now."

"Mom, you should try to get a little more in."

Her mother's jaw tightens. "I am not a processing plant," she whispers. "I am just tired."

She presses her palms to the tabletop, thin fingers splayed, the ring she never removes loose on her left hand. Soon she will raise that hand, the May sun will catch the stone in a flash of brilliance, and the hand will wave.

The chair will be empty.

"Perhaps some ice cream," suggests Theo.

"Some custard," says Julie.

"Lovely," her mother affirms, pushing herself to her feet. "Right after I take a little nap."

She sways, catches herself, and then teeters to the couch in the den, Theo hovering beside her, hands reaching but not quite touching. He spreads a thick comforter over her, tugs and frets at the pillow, and stands over her, hands working at his sides.

Musko spreads his length along the base of the couch, head up and alert. He will watch so that she can rest.

After she stacks the dishes, Julie creeps down the stairs to the basement workshop. She reaches past the lifejackets and grips the paddle. Her paddle. The portal to Kedge days with bicycles wheeling out of control, marshmallows and campfires, and her mother, just a little plump now, with her thick hair swept up in a ponytail, presiding over it all.

She flexes, sweeps the paddle experimentally, and forces a smile for her father, who now stands on the basement steps. "The balance is good," she declares. "We'll give it a try this summer, won't we?"

"I was under the impression," he says, "that school boards could call at any time, and a person had to wait by the phone."

She shrugs. "Well, they'll just have to call back. All of them. And they will."

Her father drifts over to the rough bannister, sliding one had over the surface. "It's a little heavy, yet," he says, examining the mould. "It just needs to be a shade lighter. Maybe just a little tool work," he mutters, reaching for a narrow chisel.

Julie perches on a stool and grips the paddle with both hands while her father works.

"I think Samuel might let that little piece below the orchard go," Theo says. "I could run a driveway up along that place just down from the old grape vine there. He might let me use his garage, maybe. Good place for a workshop."

"Sounds good." Julie nods for emphasis. "He'd probably like that. Seeing a little cottage there, the old garage put to good use. It would make the place brighter, somehow."

"And your mother's got a good hand with gardening. She'd brighten the place up in no time."

Julie does not point out that she was going to grow strawberries on the old barn site. Julie does not mind today. There is room for more than one caretaker at Meadowbrook Acres today, and perhaps there, all their dreams can merge. Her mother will rock on the verandah while Julie tends the budding strawberry plants. Her father's table saw whirs merrily in the garage. Samuel and Rachel sort through cardboard boxes in the attic, exclaiming as they uncover treasures. Now here comes Charles; he is Joe's age, but a little rounder, a little balder, grinning like a happy child. And this must be Nathaniel, tall, lean, brooding. There are children laughing. Who are they? And now it is Christmas, and Samuel presides over a great table, his tree glittering with ancient glass ornaments.

There is laughter, and feet drum on the stairs. Now Nathaniel is handing his mother a neat wooden carving of a kayaker, Inuit face tipped back to catch the sun or the spray. "But I am also a canoer of shorelines," he tells her. Rachel cradles the carving and smiles.

Samuel's sons sit on either side of their father. And now here is Samuel's wife, and his eyes light in wonder as he touches her hands. They are all here, all here to celebrate with Samuel, but tomorrow they will all go home, for this is not their dream. For this one day they will dream with Samuel.

Meadowbrook is big enough to hold all their dreams.

She, Julie, spins all their dreams into one as she clutches the paddle, and the dreams weave out from the paddle, filling the workshop.

The snakes draw back and slither into the forest to find rotting logs and rock piles to claim.

Julie clutches the paddle and draws all the dreamers into the farmhouse, where all good things come to pass. There is a couple walking up the orchard from the little cottage on the meadow. They carry a steaming pudding, wrapped against the cold. They will not stay, no, this is family time, but they wanted to wish a Merry Christmas to their good friends. The caretaker wipes her hands on a towel, ensures that the platters are filled and the stove off, and walks back down the orchard with them.

The dreams are massive, but the house can hold them. They are not too big.

Musko sprawls on the floor beside Alice Martin's couch. While Julie dreams the future, Musko guards the present. Alice Martin must first rest, and then awaken strong. And then, they will see.

Chapter 28

FUTURES

Laila paces along Julie's little garden, down by the orchard. The June air is dense and muggy, and she brushes at the flies that gather along her neck.

"Slugs always seem to get the lettuce," she observes. "You'll be thinning those carrots soon."

Julie rests against her hoe, digging into her hair where the blackflies nestle. Her nails come away smeared in blood. "The squash are looking good."

"Ye-es. Gonna be climbing the apple trees soon, I expect. No more fires in the mower?"

Way back across the ten months there is a smoking mower shuddering by the grapevine, two new friends sipping blueberry juice and exchanging stories on the verandah. There is Musko about-to-be, there is Doug who walks again on the perimeter of her life for two short months but not short then, there is Samuel and the Christmas dreams, there is Tina who revealed the snakes, there is one incredible sledding party, and there is her mother. Her mother has cancer, but the treatments went well. She is waiting and seeing, but she will be well.

The ten months hold the accusing eyes and the legends of the barn, the Hardys with Joe shy on the edges of their lives, Rachel not returning, faithful Taggak still gone, and the little bones still scattered in the bush. Ten months of bundling sweaters and tweaking thermostats and now the heat is unbearable, Thank God, but still her mother has cancer and it is watching and waiting time.

The dreams have become sweet again, flowing from the paddle that she clutches in her mind because what would her father do if she took the paddle from its place and left with it? He made the paddle for her-with-them, not for her-alone. So she carries it in her mind, and the dreams flow and weave, blissful images of family spread out on the old verandah, sampling the first strawberries, gathered around a great table in the house. Samuel is there, and Rachel, for Julie is generous in her dreams and carries a happy ending for each of them.

Yet the dreams are a little sad, as they yearn to cling to each moment, to squeeze every drop of the dream present into their lives. Julie awakens weeping sometimes, her heart straining with the need to bring the dream present into the waking present, so that it flows and weaves through them all and always. So much time has been wasted between the first memories and the now memories; she longs to fill the long, sad gap with the dream present and make all their lives whole.

"You seem preoccupied these days," Laila comments, watching Julie lean on the hoe with her eyes closed. "House not getting to you again?"

Julie opens her eyes and slaps at a mosquito on her arm. The spot blooms red. Laila understands her so well, but even Laila could not possibly understand that Julie is even now weaving dreams of health and future happiness into Meadowbrook Acres. She chips away the tight layer of soil around the hill of squash. "Just another two weeks to go. I'm filing my EI claim."

Laila frowns. "Are you looking?"

"Some." Julie shrugs. "I'm working on my resume. I'll have more time when school is out."

When school is out, there will still be no Tina. Julie wonders what she is doing now. It will be a year since Doug started driving the science student out on the range road. There is a baby, but not for Doug, although he plans to bring the baby to her, so they can raise it with an outfitting company for a legacy. When school is out, Julie will be free to wander and plant and mow and dream. Musko ranges along the edge of the woods, but he will come home to sleep. He is more independent now.

"He's looking for something," Laila remarks, and Julie looks down. Musko is pushing at her thigh with his broad muzzle, whuffing low in his throat. "He seems to do that a lot, these days."

Julie gives the hair between his ears a brief pull. "He's starting to roam. Not far, but he's not around much."

Laila shakes her head. "No, Julie," she says. "That dog is always following you. It's like he misses you."

"But I'm always around. He shouldn't run off then."

Laila sighs. "Anyway. You should be looking. Have you tried the Park? Might be something, you never know."

"My French is pretty bad."

"Still. You never know. And there's the pharmacy, and the hardware store, and the grocery store. Lots of people work there."

Julie does not want to sell pool dinghies. She especially does not want to be available to the public. Julie wants to hide. And dream. "I might do a little work on those fields. Get at some of the bushes before they take over."

"Well." Laila opens her arms wide and stretches. "Oil bills'll be higher than ever next winter, and you never know what's gonna happen when you're subbing day by day. You might want to save that claim."

"Margaret's retiring after all. The Grade 8 teacher is switching to home ec. So I've applied for Grade 8 next year."

Margaret knitted her way into her retirement dream so deeply that she decided not to wait for two more years. Margaret is going to seize the moment now, while they still have their health, and in the grand scheme of things the monthly difference is not so great. Some things are more important. They are looking at travel trailers on the weekend. And the teacher of Eric and Daniel has been commuting to Bridgewater for an extension class in home economics, plotting this takeover since January. She is prepared. She has struck while the iron was hot.

Julie has read the Grade 8 curriculum documents and relates well to the Grade 7s. She would be perfect for them in Grade 8. The board will see that. She will teach each day and swing into the driveway and perhaps her parents will already be there, relaxing on the verandah and waving. Samuel will see the garden and lawn flourishing, the fresh paint on the walls, and then he will flourish, too.

"I said, 'That's good.'" Laila has raised her voice and her eyes are troubled. "But there could be a lot of people wanting that one. You've got to be prepared."

Prepared did not prevent Doug. It did not prevent North Bay or the Dream House. It did not save Tina. She was tested and identified and profiled but still she was raped.

Prepared did not prevent cancer.

"You'd be Tina's teacher, then. That would be good for both of you."

Julie straightens. "Tina's coming back?"

"Oh. Probably. You never know. Last time, her mother only lasted a month or so."

"So she has done this before."

"Sometimes. Her husband's kind of a hard man. But she has a real hard time on her own. The sister? Well, she's not exactly what you'd call supportive. Kind of the type who points out non-stop how good she is to take them in, and complains about every mouthful they eat, but gets a lot of free babysitting and housework out of them. Tina's mom held out real good this time. I was kind of hoping she'd make it."

"She'd take her back into that house? Doesn't the uncle still visit, someone was telling me?"

"And the father dropping hints when he's mad that it was all Tina's fault anyway?" Laila finishes. "Yes. She would. She don't have too many options."

"But social services—"

"Too bad the world's not perfect," Laila says. "Anyways, I expect we'll see them back this fall."

Perhaps the missing piece of the dream will come home. There will be a girl to pirouette beside the well while Alice Martin smiles. But will it be a good dream for Tina?

Julie suspects that Tina will dream horrors day by day, but day by day she will also go to her own dream room, where she is a Good Life.

The cottage window catches the afternoon sun, and Julie smiles.

"What are you looking at?" Laila asks, following her gaze down past the orchard.

Laila is silent as they walk up to the verandah, now shaded and almost cooler as the sun rolls its way west. At the step, she turns. "You sure you want to teach Grade 8?" she says. "That's a hard age. And you've got to be, well, you know, on top of things."

"I've taught Grade 8 before," Julie replies, crossing to the rocking chair, the one where her mother will sit.

"Oh, well, you'd be fine and all. It's just that, well. You know."

"I know what?" Julie almost snaps, almost alert now.

"Well." Laila hesitates. "You're just so, tired like. Thinking of some-thing else sometimes, maybe."

Julie begins to rock, back forth, back forth. "My mother has been very sick. Dangerously sick. So, yes. I do think about that. A lot."

"Oh, I know. Of course you do. It's natural. But you've got other things. This house. Maybe if you just got out of this house," Laila says in a rush.

"You just think I'm not up for it." Julie rocks harder.

"I didn't say that. You know that's not what I meant." Laila sighs.

~

Get yourself into an online course right away, Janice advises. Show them you're serious; let them feel your commitment.

When Julie opens her computer, though, she checks her e-mail and sometimes plays cards. It is relaxing. When she relaxes, she sleeps better. When she sleeps better, she dreams better.

~

Julie tugs at her blazer and straightens her skirt. She is professional chic in second hand spring line. She has been skimming the Grade 8 curriculum online, with all the expectations spilling into each other and couched in language that radiates power and enthusiasm, understanding and rapport. They will reach these students who will rise to these expectations with joy if they know what is good for them. They will not dare to be unenthusiastic. The words themselves vibrate with professionalism.

Think now only of the curriculum and the students who serve it. Do not think of oil bills or ornaments or new bannisters. But do not say "students who serve it." Then they will know that you think the students are enslaved to the curriculum, not privileged and graced by its presence.

Simon liked to read cereal boxes. Simon was a good reader, a slow reader, but a clear and strong reader. *Simon will demonstrate awareness of the text features of the cereal box, reading with fluency and with appropriate expression.* Just be, Simon. Be happy. Grow and find joy.

~

"I believe that students learn best when they are happy learning," Julie therefore tells the panel, and their faces light up in recognition. Everyone knows this, but everyone loves to hear it. It is only important to coach the words in the appropriate tones of amazement, as if one's soul has just been touched by the ministry's teachings, moved to repent and begin anew.

"After all, the curriculum expectations are just so many words—meaningless to them." The faces drop. Where is Ms. Martin going with this? Will she deny that the curriculum documents are sacred text, revealed to the initiated? That they will take fire in the blood, and teachers and students will be caught up in a whirlwind of ecstatic learning? There must be a "but" or an "until" coming.

Julie stretches to save herself. "I mean, if they're not ready to learn. But if they like what they're doing, if they're happy with what they're learning, if you start where they *are*, then, well—they can soar."

The dubious looks remain. "But it follows that if the curriculum is well-delivered, then they will be ready and therefore *will* be happy," one member observes.

"Exactly," confirms Julie, and hopes that what she said somehow meant what he said. "That is your starting point. A good delivery."

"Tell us how you would accomplish that," another member directs her.

Julie launches into a patchwork overview that somehow involves individualized learning, differentiated instruction, and personal culture.

At "personal culture," the panel begins to shift in its seats. Personal culture is a phrase that can be tossed on the table and mean anything if the definition is not laid down clearly, and in the wrong hands can do hurtful things. Personal culture is a fertile field, seeded in landmines. What references on personal culture would she recommend? Oh. Then in what way is she familiar with personal culture? Through observation based on personal experience? I see. Well, maybe Ms. Martin could publish. Automatic laughter ripples around the table and then fades.

Now, Ms. Martin has been working in the resource program. Why is her contract not being renewed? Oh, of course, yes, that's Ms. Henry's position. Did she like working in the resource program? She would again? Good to hear that she has had a positive experience. Yes. Now, is she prepared for the workload involved in a classroom assignment? Not that the resource program isn't busy. Automatic laughter ripples about the table again. Would she describe herself as a—ah, a—focused individual? Really. That's good. Provide us with an example of a time when this worked well for you. He read cereal boxes. I see.

"You're staying at the old Hardy place," a member says as they are shaking hands and making rumblings about only the successful candidate being contacted. "Must keep you busy."

"Old Rose Hardy was my teacher in Grade 8," says another.

"She had dementia, didn't she?" says a third.

"Not when I was in Grade 8. At least, no worse than any other Grade 8 teacher has."

Dutiful laughter fills the room and Julie, a grin stiff on her face, tugs the pockets of her blazer straight.

~

The job goes, she learns, to a vigorous recent graduate from the Liverpool area. He has enthusiasm, has in-depth knowledge of the curriculum and current policy, is a consultant in internet technologies, and did part of his practicum in Grade 8. He also plays the guitar and is an athlete. He is an excellent match.

Julie is a canoer of shorelines, with big oil bills ahead. In her heart she is an excellent match, but as she plods along the old truck road, she knows that she really is not. Musko ranges down across the field, and she does not call to him. He looks up, and waits, but she does not call and he ranges across the marsh below the second hill.

Tina will drift in from Truro, pirouetting into a world of sharp edges, and Julie will not be there to blunt them for her.

She wonders, though, just how she would do that.

Chapter 29

A DREAM FOR THEO

In July, Theo and Alice plan a camping trip to Kedge. Alice is doing so well this July, and although undoubtedly she will do even better in August, they do not want to wait for August. July has become their time, after all; they come to the Park for a week in July, not two weeks in August, because the kids are grown and a week in July is what suits them, as a couple.

Alice is pale, and her eyes are shadowed, but she is unquestionably on the mend. The cancer has been aggressive, but Alice Martin is so strong. She is not strong in body, not yet, because her appetite has not returned, although it will. However, she is strong inside, strong where it counts. Although it will probably get worse before it gets better, there is no doubt now that it will get better. Kedge is a good place to celebrate.

Julie will be with them, because even though they can cope quite nicely on their own as parents of adult children, it will be good for her. Besides, she mentioned that she wanted to try out that paddle her father made last summer. It would not do to disappoint her; not getting that job was hard on her.

This will be a peaceful family time, with no heart-tugging remembrances. Tim is going to join them on Saturday afternoon. He has found a gap in his schedule. He will come out on Saturday for lunch, and spend the afternoon. The entire Martin family will be gathered around the site. Imagine that.

After Alice's illness, it will be nice to have a pleasant family afternoon. Just what they all need to put this business behind them.

~

Julie and her father pitch the tent on Friday, a clear July afternoon when the wind is light and the leaves of Meadow Campground ripple and dapple. Alice presides from a lounge chair, a plaid blanket draped over her untanned legs. Is the ice holding? She wonders. She worries about the potato salad while Theo tugs the lines to centre the tarp overhead, and because she worries about the ice and the potato salad she sees him slow and fidgeting with the tarp. A mild resentment rises in her bones; she wants him quick and efficient, the meal on the table and the rituals enacted and then, at last, sleep. She would sleep now and, oh, how she needs to, but then cherished times would be unfolding without her, and it is the ritual participation that makes them cherished.

She wants them to unfold and be cherished quickly, and then she will sleep against the grinding exhaustion, ever present in her body.

The pain invades her body, sucking her resistance, and with her remaining strength she pushes it back. But it continues to seep into her flesh, into her muscles, into the core of her bones. But Theo is so clumsy today, fumbling and slow. Alice snaps her mind closed, draws a smile over her face, and announces that this is just perfect.

Theo and Julie jerk coolers and grub boxes from the bed of the truck, the broad grins on their faces not yet peeling. Yes, it is, they agree.

Musko does not smile or lie to bring pleasure to the memory. Musko huddles forlorn at the feet of Alice Martin, his muzzle tight to her instep.

Now the tarp is centred, the tent is taut and straight, and the chicken and potato salad are displayed. The stage is ready, but the actors are unsure of their roles, it seems; there are smiles and nods but little dialogue to move the plot along. They are not entering their characters effectively, and thus the presentation lacks authenticity. It is, in a word, wooden.

Alice slips a morsel of chicken to Musko and pokes at her potato salad. Julie comments on the perfection of the weather several times. Not too hot, she elaborates at one time. Nice breeze, she observes another time. No bugs, she points out yet another time. Each time she speaks, all three heads nod. The Martins are in agreement. The weather is perfect in every way.

Theo eyes the lake hopefully. It is sparkling and bright, with tiny waves lapping along the shore of Jeremy Bay. Alice shivers in the not-too-hot sunlight. She suggests that they wait for dawn, because this afternoon the wind will surely rise, and they should canoe with the loons as they always have.

At dawn there will be tone in her muscles and power in her bones, not water and ashes. She will rise at dawn and she will cast out the pain. Her body will quicken and her legs will carry her to the lake and her spirit will rise and spread out, out over the water and all the loons will call with joy because Alice Martin has come. They will greet her and celebrate with her. Dawn will be the time.

Alice naps that afternoon in her chair while Julie and her father play cards. Ten-year-old bicyclists crash past shouting, and Theo sneaks glances at the canoe and the lake.

Musko hunkers down beside Alice, his nose flat to the pine needles.

The afternoon trickles away to silence. Alice reads and naps, and Musko's nose stays flat to the pine needles. Julie prepares hamburgers too early and organizes the table too early. Now the clean sweep of Theo's axe snaps the maple into even splits. But it is too early, and the sound hangs lonesome over the summer afternoon. Others are out hiking and biking and swimming and canoeing and touring. Theo will have a neat wood pile long before others return from their Kedge adventures. Theirs will be the first wood smoke curling among the trees. *Those people must be anxious to play at camping*, others will say.

A Canoer of Shorelines

It is a simple evening of eating too early, watching the campfire too early, and entering the tent too early. Others' magic pulses through the campground, but their fire pit is bare and lonely. *They're missing the best part of camping,* others will say. *Not much spirit at that site.*

~

Alice arises to mist and half-light on Saturday morning, and feels a fragile power pulsing in her legs and back. She touches Theo's shoulder. "I want to go out on the lake," she says. Theo rolls from his sleeping bag and springs for the canoe.

And so she balances on the bow seat on this still July morning, and there are loons calling far down Jeremy Bay. They are the first on the bay, and Theo works his paddle, proud in the stern.

"Hear the loons," Alice says, and as they glide down Jeremy Bay her voice warbles softly into song.

Theo clutches his paddle, his eyes fixed on his wife. When the sun catches his eye, in that moment when he loses sight of her for just an instant, she will shimmer into the mist and be lost to him forever.

"Don't go," he says, the words wrenched from his heart.

Alice shifts on the seat and twists around so that she faces him, her paddle resting on her knees. She is the one facing east, not him, and she shades her eyes with her hand. The sun shines on her face, not his, and she is lit up from without and from within.

Far down the bay a loon emits a short, authoritative summons. Alice smiles. "They want us to go to them," she says.

Theo dips his paddle, drawing the water in gentle ripples along the canoe. "It's our time, this is," he says. "This is us, all we've been. Always."

"Always," she agrees.

They paddle west, and talk of Kedge times past, but neither speaks of what will be. There is no cottage, no workshop in the garage, no garden this morning. This is a morning to let memories rise and be cherished.

And then you bless them, and release them to come to you again when you need their strength.

Theo struggles to absorb every breath, every sound, every ripple on the water on this, the last Kedge time.

And then he lets go, feels the water ripple around his paddle, and hears his wife's soft voice rise and fall, and he knows that this is where he will always be, and this is where he will always find her.

The loon raises one last ecstatic call from far down Jeremy Bay. It rises, breaks, and catches. Then it falls silent.

~

Tim arrives at precisely noon and tosses his cellphone onto the driver's seat. "My commitment to you," he declares.

Musko grunts, flopping by Alice's chair.

"We heard the loons this morning," Alice says.

"Great," he enthuses, accepting the coffee mug Julie passes to him. "Well, this brings back memories."

"You didn't drink coffee then," Alice reminds him.

"I was talking about the atmosphere," he says.

Alice, wise woman arriving, closes her eyes and smiles. "This is a new memory," she says.

And thus the afternoon begins. Alice drowses, Julie paces, Tim alternately enthuses and falls silent, and Theo twitches, his eyes on the lake. He longs to be on the lake, for there he will see her. She will shine, and she will be singing.

The silences in the campsite grow, and finally they simply *are*— feeling the moment, savouring it, not looking back, not looking ahead. It is not a return to Kedge times, it is the arrival of something new, perhaps unexpected. Something surprising and necessary.

~

On Sunday, however, they agree that they would do better to move closer to the hospital. It doesn't do to tempt fate, and their trip so far has been a real success. Besides, it is going to rain on Monday.

~

They can do so much for breast cancer these days, but not for Alice Martin. Nature is stronger than man, and can be more aggressive. Alice Martin had cancer, and it was very determined.

It turned out, though, that she was more determined. When Alice felt her life slipping from her body, she knew that it could draw Theo with it. Now Alice Martin, wise woman arriving, knew Theo's dream and she took that dream and she blessed it and turned it so that Theo would always find her on a summer dawn on Jeremy Bay when the loons were calling, and he would not be lost.

Theo clutches his paddle, and he and Alice drift along Jeremy Bay, her voice mingling with the loon's call. They are smiling and somewhere there are Julie and Tim who will find their way but not here because this is the place and time of Alice and Theo. This is their very own present, their very own moment, flowing from the paddle.

The others have to find their own way. That is the way things are.

Alice Martin died that August, but first she made sure that Theo Martin would live for her.

SEPARATION

A grey and shining morning has come to Wasaya. The lake is still, reflecting back mottled clouds with a glossy lustre. Glimpses of light break through the grey. It might rain today, or be humid and sunny by noon. It is so still.

The one that I will always think of as the puppy will be ten years old tomorrow. She was born at the veterinary hospital in town, and I brought her, her mother, and her siblings home to Meadowbrook Acres the next morning. She was born on my son's tenth birthday, and he came back from turning ten among his father's people to a dying grandmother and six tumbling, whimpering puppies. He would sit in the evenings on a little camp chair in the woodhouse, his face filled with wonder as he watched his puppies.

This was the puppy we kept, a sign of life and joy in the summer of my mother's death.

Mikijuk has spent all her birthdays with me, and she is my loyal confidante. She will not grow up and away as Nathaniel has, for this is natural for a boy but not for a puppy. She will grow old before long, and die, still trusting and a little baffled, for this is Mikijuk's way.

Her mother watches me now, observant and a little aloof. She is my guardian and my guide. She is Saima, as Saima has always been. She grows old, and her heart is weakening, but her spirit remains great. She is Saima, always.

I am terrified of life without my dogs. I dread burying them, far apart and away and alone. I want a place where I will always be, and our graves together in a little row.

I want to live in one place. I want to make a home.

I think that my mother was trying to do that, the summer of my father's death and all the summers that she waited for hers.

~

I return now, to the second summer, to the time before the phone call, when Aunt Iris was still a nagging voice, when my father was still alive.

My father was much weaker that summer when I arrived; my mother frailer and more withdrawn. My father shuffled between the couch in the den and the kitchen table. My mother tottered behind, watching every step, her mouth trembling. Somewhere was the step, somewhere was the moment, that would carry them to the bough shack, to the eel weir, to the first meeting at the train station.

I had resented my father in his strength, in both his stubbornness and his warmth. In his weakness, I could accept him again, as I had in my childhood.

I did not accept my mother, not yet, in her tottering and trembling.

The summer passed with hospital times and daily visits, with times at home and watching. It was a wearying summer filled with waiting but no resolution. He would become strong enough to leave the hospital; he was not strong enough to stay out of the hospital. Still, I did not think of him as dying; I saw him continuing in weakness with good days through the years to come.

I stayed into August. I cut the deadwood from the mock orange and snowball bushes; I cleared the moss from the flagstones on the front walk. I weeded the garden. "The garden that killed me," my father called it. He had decided to plant it one clear spring day, and Samuel tried so hard to get there on time, but he couldn't. My father had never waited for anyone before, and so he had planted the garden at the moment he had chosen, but his heart was strained and he went to the hospital. And he called it the garden that killed him.

I wish that he had waited for Samuel. I wish that he had thought of Samuel, and let him share the moment. Here, from Wasaya, I turn back that moment, and my father sets his tools aside, nods, and says, "I believe I'll wait for Sam. He'd like that." And Samuel pulls into the yard as the evening cools, and they talk of many things and together they plant the last garden.

I offer that memory for Samuel, here in Wasaya.

With a wave of my hand, I brush away the moment when Samuel hears the plan, dashes through his morning with his infant son, speeds out from the city, flings himself from his car, and there my father stands, pale and shaking, that cursed garden planted and accusing behind him.

I know that my father had to take on his own mortality that day and prove himself to death as his heart muscle stretched a little more.

Poor Samuel. Take the memory that I offer you, not this one. Hold it and be blessed.

~

In the background of that summer Aunt Iris grumbled and glowered, but since the picnic, when the tears slid down her face, her grumbling and glowering sweetened to me. My mother flitted to the post office, or the store, or the church. She banged pots and stirred. She fled to the hairdresser. The hairdresser? When her husband was at death's door?

Oh, how he had always loved her shiny dark curls.

During the hospital stay before the last, I zipped to the hospital alone one evening for a quick visit. My father sat in a chair at the end of the hall, watching the breeze fan the trees bordering the hospital lawn. He turned to me, his eyes soft and filled with wonder. "Whoever planned this world," he declared, "did things just about right." He gestured toward the trees. "You see, all the moisture in the air, it keeps those leaves fresh, everything so cool and alive."

I had not seen my father happy and child-like in this way before, and I was alarmed. And so I talked in cheerful hospital tones about what everyone in the family was doing. My father watched the leaves rippling in the breeze and smiled.

As I drove home, I saw my father on a hot summer afternoon, treading along the sidewalk in town, the concrete stiff and unbending beneath the soles of his town shoes. "Oh, to feel the pine needles under my feet," he crooned. I saw him sitting on the verandah, gazing down over the orchard as he smoked his pipe in the cool of evening. I knew that he only farmed because it kept him close to a world in which he had hunted and fished and felt the pine needles under his feet. He had been a bitter farmer, but he had loved the earth that he farmed.

I knew that he was being gathered from us, and he had received a psalmist's voice to celebrate his wonder.

I pulled to the side of the road, and wept at his passing.

~

My father came home, but he coughed long and often. I delayed my departure, again and again. I weeded the garden. My son dragged rocks and weeds and branches in his little wagon, to his grandfather's delight. My uncle Alphonse, my mother's younger brother, came to be with us.

And there came a night when my father was resting on the couch, and he decided that he was of a mind to smoke his pipe. My mother called me and I lifted him to his chair. Yes, I know that he should not have been smoking, for he had congestive heart failure and emphysema, and perhaps that last pipe did shorten his time, but his time was short anyway, and my father wanted his pipe.

I am glad that he had that last pipe, for he and his Rosita, the young teacher he had met at the train station, held hands and talked long into the night. When I returned to lift him to his couch, they sat shy and sweet, a young couple in love with their whole future before them, when nothing mattered but their love.

In the morning, my father coughed and choked, and Uncle Alphonse cleared his breathing. His military bearing clicked into action as he directed the phone call to the hospital, cleared the fish peddler from the driveway, and loaded my father in the Raider.

I was a little sorry for the fish peddler, so happy with his fine, fresh mackerel, and Uncle Alphonse ordering him from the yard as he marched through the door, my father in his arms.

I should have known something when my father told me I could drive a little faster if I wanted to. Even when the doctor said that my father could go at any time, I thought he meant in the next few months, not that day at all.

Therefore, when my father told us that we should go have coffee with Aunt Iris, because he wanted to rest, we took him at his word. We sat in Aunt Iris's living room, drinking her coffee, while he died.

"But I wanted to be with him," my mother cried. "I was supposed to be there."

Here at Wasaya, I rock my mother. "I know," I say. "I know now."

She had lowered her guard for one instant and he had slipped away from her.

It was as though she had come home from the store and he had gone to the eel weir or the bough shack and had not waited for her.

He would stalk along the wagon road, backpack bobbing, and she would trot along behind him, her walking stick swinging.

After he died, she would deliberately don her little hiking boots, grasp her walking stick, and march off to the brook. Soon it was the maple tree, then the second gate, and soon the first gate, and then she would just hike a few laps around the outside of the house.

He was not on any of these walks, and soon she stopped walking at all.

I think that he did not want her to see his fear that last day. And he did not want her to follow him that day, for she would never be left behind.

He held hands with her that last night, and they were young and sweet with love.

The next day, he had to sneak away, and leave behind his beautiful Rosita, with the long curling hair.

From Wasaya I lift up that last night and the young lovers, innocent and filled with wonder. I bless them and release them on the breeze.

Chapter 30

ICE CREAM WAFERS

The late August sun soaks into Julie's bare arms as she and Laila walk along the lake shore near the picnic site of last summer.

"You should cover up." Laila offers a loose cotton shirt from her canvas tote bag. Laila is, as always, prepared: legs and arms tucked away beneath loose cotton slacks and shirt, a floppy hat shielding her face and neck.

Without speaking, Julie shrugs into the shirt, folding her arms across her chest. Musko wallows in the water, then wanders to the shore. He nuzzles Laila and she pats him. His tail swings once and he flops down by a scraggly birch tree that leans over the beach.

"He's grieving, too," Laila observes.

Julie shrugs. "He hardly seems here anymore."

Laila crouches by Musko, hugging his shaggy neck. "He's here. He's waiting for somebody, aren't you, Musko?"

Musko's tail gives a little quiver and his tongue brushes Laila's cheek.

"How's your father doing?" Laila asks.

Julie sighs. "He's spending a lot of time in his workshop. The first week, he just sat there. Now he's working on his bannister thing."

"Bannister," Laila prompts.

"For the farm," Julie explains. "He's got it in his head that the front stairs need a new bannister. He keeps picking at it, says it's not quite right yet. And you know? Now it looks just like the old one. Exactly. And the newel post. Paint them white, and you'd never know the difference. But he keeps picking at it. Planing and sanding. And it's just the same."

"Maybe he just needs to," Laila says. "Maybe he thinks better when he's working at it."

Julie hunches down on a rock and wraps her arms tight around her knees. The sun pounds against the cotton, heating the skin beneath. July sun scorches the skin; August sun probes deep, burning the flesh, seeking the bone. August fights its way into her body, and she is motherless and unemployed and oil bills are looming.

Laila, the listener, casts about for the words that might address this moment.

"Well," she says finally.

"We came here when I was five," Julie begins. "Lots of other times, too, but when I was five, we came to this place for a corn boil. Dad was up in the shelter, stove going in the heat and the pot taking forever to boil, and I was bored, fussing, and my mother got rummaging in the cooler and she brought out these pretty little pink sticks—you know the kind I mean? Like ice cream cones, flat, and with icing in between?"

"Ice cream wafers."

"That's the name. Anyway. I bit into one, and it was just so light and cool. Fresh. I crunched it down, and then I took another one. This time, I nibbled off the top layer and licked out the icing. I took the other piece and I sucked it against the roof of my mouth until it was melting and then I let it slide down my throat. 'Those won't ruin your appetite,' my mother told me."

"Tooth tracks," Laila says. "You can make some awesome tooth tracks in the icing. Little swirls and little dents. Think the canteen has some?"

But Julie is crying now, crying like she could not at the funeral beside the coffin and her father, like she could not in the workshop while he stared at the floor and tapped his feet and said how quiet the house was. Then he started sanding the bannister, because a new bannister would spruce that old place right up.

In August, they always go to Kedge, and Meadowbrook Acres rises on the bend: house freshly painted, orchard trim and laden with fruit. A tractor is pulling out of the great red barn.

"We should retire here," Alice says. "You could have your workshop in the barn, and I'll have a garden, and we'll take our grandchildren to Kedge on Sunday afternoons."

"Our grandchildren?"

"Our grandchildren," she laughs.

Tim and Julie scowl and pout in the backseat.

"Think they'd sell it?" he asks.

"Would you?"

"I can't imagine what it would be worth," he sighs, casting an appreciative eye along the buildings and back to the hills that roll away behind them.

"I can pretend, can't I?" says Alice. "We're on vacation."

~

Now Julie remembers this and other little moments, and sobs out her stories to Laila. Oh, her parents never planned to buy it, they never really meant to, but they pretended and dreamed because it was summer, and Kedge was opening before them and they could be reckless and imaginative in their dreams.

Then Julie came to Meadowbrook Acres and shut it into a little dream for herself, and did not want them to build even a little cottage there.

"Oh, Samuel would never have gone for that anyway," Laila reasons. "And you weren't really preventing them, just maybe wanting some space to yourself for a while. You've got to let those things go, stop judging yourself all the time."

Julie continues to cry, for she dreamed her mother well, and she died anyway. She dreamed Samuel happy and this will not happen either.

Laila is looking at the point across the bay, at the sky, at the beach. Her eyes settle on Musko. "He watches you all the time," she says. "He follows you everywhere. And it's like you don't even see him anymore."

Julie sways on her rock, arms clasped around her knees. "The snake dreams are the worst. I started one again, but I woke up."

Laila leans forward, eyes intent on Julie's face. "Now listen. You've been through a shock. But you'll get over it. You can't go on letting your dreams get to you like that. Dreams is just that—dreams. Not warnings, not premonitions, not any of that stuff. You're letting it take over. Now, don't take this the wrong way." She hesitates, and then plunges in. "But maybe, just maybe, if you was a little less fixated on dreams and a little busier, say, active in the church or library committee or coaching a team or anything, well, you just might have gotten that job."

Julie rests her forehead on her clasped arms. "Laila. I don't have time for all that." I am the caretaker, she does not add. Speaking the dreams was mistake enough. "I just want to see Samuel happy. Happy and coming home to Meadowbrook."

"Oh!" Laila exclaims. "Well, the odds of either of them things happening is mighty small. Now look." She settles on the pebbles beside Julie's rock. "That place is too big and too lonesome for you. What you and your dad need is a nice little place, a cottage like, maybe up by Kedge. You live there and do your subbing; he comes down weekends and such and goes to Kedge or whatever. You both need to find something new. You both need to move on with your lives. And pet that dog; he misses you."

Julie gives Musko's head a quick rub. She pulls herself to her feet and steps away. "Laila, my mother died two weeks ago. Why am I supposed to move on? Why do I not get a little time to just miss her?"

Laila shakes her head, sighing. "No. You're misunderstanding me. I'm talking about the way the place weighs on you, moving on from that. And all these dreams. You put way too much stock in all that. You got your imagination working way harder than it should. It's like it's eating you up. You get away from that for a while and you'll see. And all these dreams tangle up and take your energy so you can't just grieve for her like you need to."

Julie has a sudden urge to tell Laila about little snake noses pushing out of glass ornaments and between fingers and then tumbling to the snow below. She wants to shock Laila and horrify her. "You've let Rachel Hardy put your life on hold, haven't you?" she snaps. "Waiting and watching and nobody telling you anything. She was here, you know? Last spring. Joe saw her."

Laila lowers her eyes. "Joe would see her," she murmurs. "And I know that Nathaniel's been coming around, checking up on the cabin, trying to figure things out. And I know that Samuel knows but doesn't want to say. It's too hard for me, too, sometimes." She stands and walks to the shore, probing the water's edge with her sandal. "We all play in our dreams, but I've said it before and I'll say it again. The Hardys always come back. She'll find her way when she's strong enough."

Julie waits. Laila knows, too?

"You think about getting away from that place for a time, spending some time with your Musko. You need each other more than ever now," Laila says instead.

"But I like it there," Julie says. "I like my garden, and all the painting I did, and remember our coasting party?"

"You need to do more of that stuff," Laila says.

"I need some time alone there, first." Another year, perhaps, to consolidate all she has done and learned, waking and sleeping. Maybe then, she will be ready to be Active in the Community.

~

Julie stayed with her father for two weeks after the funeral, sorting and tidying her mother's things. Theo agreed that some things must go, but they could go later, he insisted. First, Theo must touch them enough, walk past them enough, hold and stare at them long into the night. After two weeks of Julie's sorting and tidying, he told her that he was worried about Meadowbrook Acres. Perhaps she should go out and catch up on the mowing and weeding. He would be out later.

Theo needs this time to hold his paddle and feel the rising sun touch his neck, while Alice faces him and loons call far off in the mist. This is the time for Theo's memories to flow from the paddle and weave around his aching heart. This is Theo's time to be alone in the house of Theo and Alice.

It is Julie's time to be alone at Meadowbrook Acres, tracking her way deeper into the past.

Ultimately, she will arrive at the moment of her birth, and there is no lonelier moment.

Except, perhaps, the moment of her death.

Alice Martin would know.

Alice turns, her face quickens in a brief smile, and her hand lifts in a quick wave as she fades into the morning.

Chapter 31

A GARDEN FOR SAMUEL

The farm kitchen is grey that evening, although the sun streams through the west window. It is bare and soundless; there is no sense of Alice Martin approaching, no hampers of favourite foods emerging, no cross-stitched ornaments gracing the moment, no anticipated rocking on the verandah.

Musko pads about the perimeter of the kitchen, surveys the pantry while his tail swings, and settles beside the kitchen rocker with a sigh.

"She's not coming," Julie tells him. "Not ever again."

Musko grunts.

"Wanna look at some stuff, Musko?"

Musko's ears twitch, and he tips his head to one side.

Julie retrieves the box of Christmas ornaments from the bookcase in the parlour-bedroom and sits cross-legged on the kitchen floor beside Musko. She eases the cover open, and lifts away the tissue paper layer that holds the ornaments in place. She selects one, and dangles it in front of Musko. Musko lies still, head up and attentive.

"This one," she says, "is my favourite. See the little trumpet? My mother made that. Yes. She stitched it by hand, see? Isn't it pretty? I always put that one on the tree myself. Ever since I can remember. Wanna look, Musko?"

Musko snuffles around the brass rim briefly, then lowers his head between his paws.

"C'mon, Musko. Let's look together? Please?"

Musko shifts away and closes his eyes.

Julie returns the little trumpet to its place and retrieves a second ornament, a tiny blue-and-red-stitched soldier with gold trim. "Never mind, then. I'll do this myself." She holds up the tiny soldier ornament, chanting its history to the silent kitchen. A small green tree, with delicate French-knot ornaments, is next. Her voice rises to the empty ceiling as the fridge hums and the sun's rays slant into sunset. Julie summons up her mother as each history is told and her tears stream down her cheeks and onto her throat, soaking her collar. Her voice breaks and keens and still the stories tumble out until the box is empty and her eyes are empty and the room is shadowed. Musko lies still, eyes closed.

The attic door creaks open and here is Samuel, his face lit with boyish wonder. "Do you want to see some really neat stuff?" he asks, holding out a flimsy cardboard box.

Julie glances at the slumbering Musko, who does not bounce to greet Samuel. Perhaps Musko is splashing in the brook while Alice Martin laughs on the bridge. His paws twitch and he whuffs deep in his sleep. "Of course," she says, but it is an automatic response to be kind; she wants to be with her Christmases, not his.

It is enough for Samuel, who squats on the floor beside her, pulling the flaps of the box open. "Now these," he explains, "were always on the dining room table. My mother would spend hours getting the silence cloth and the drop cloth and the table cloth just right. Then hours more with the centrepiece—candles and pine cones and sprigs of pine and ornaments. Then at each of *our* places, she put one of these mugs."

It is a cheap plastic Santa Claus mug with a merry face and eyes that roll left to right. It is a silly mug, a tawdry souvenir, but in Samuel's eight-year-old hand it is rolling and laughing, delighted to find Christmas once again.

"See the tape on the bottom?" He indicates the strip of stained adhesive, peeling and grey, a name scratched in pencil sprawling across it. "This one is Rachel's. She only liked milk when it was in her Santa mug. One year Mom kept hers out till Easter."

"Now this." Samuel draws out a flaking, white sleigh about a foot long, packed with holly and pine and red bows. Two Styrofoam reindeer cut-outs with tiny bows pinned to their throats caper across the top. "My aunt made this. Not the sleigh, but the decorations. I think it still plays."

He fumbles with the stiff key at the back of the sleigh. The motor snaps and grinds as he turns the key, and then there is a sharp click. He releases the key, and the motor whirs and hums as the key unwinds. A fragmented "Jingle Bells" rasps from its gut.

"Not very well, I guess." Samuel sets the sleigh aside, selects a crumpling paper bag, and gives it a shake. "Streamers. Not very interesting. Ah!" He retrieves a light box, with "Fragile" neatly penned in faded ink, and slides the lid away. "How these have lasted all this time I'll never know."

He prods aside the cotton batting with his forefinger, revealing wafer-thin glass painted a delicate silver, its centre red and gold. "From my grandmother's day to this," he declares, plucking the rest of the batting aside. His face darkens. "When did this happen?" he demands.

An ornament lies in fine silver and gold flakes in the bottom of one compartment. There are red flecks that may be glass, but Julie is not sure.

"My father loved these," Samuel says. "He'd walk into the living room there and just stand there, studying the tree. He had a big chair in the dining room and he'd watch TV there, but he'd have one eye on the tree. He was Christmas to me, he was everything to me, and—he wanted to plant this garden, see? And I was going to help him, and he just had to wait a few hours till I took my own son to swimming lessons and then drove clear out here, but I arrive and it's all planted and he's so proud of himself, but he wasn't supposed to because of his heart, and it strained his heart and it just got worse. And Rachel comes sailing out of some corner of the north all divorced and free, and she tends the garden and prunes the shrubs, and I'm the one who didn't help him plant the garden. The garden that killed him.

"But I can't be everywhere at once, and I can't be all things to all people, and still I want to be here and stay here, but when I do I just can't. I can't."

Samuel is rocking, his hands covering his face, and Julie replaces the cotton batting and tucks the box away. She places her own ornaments, layer by layer, back in their own little box, the golden trumpet on top. "They need the memories more than they should," she says. "They tie us to their past, and we let ourselves be held to them.

"We should," she continues, "enjoy the good parts of the memories but not let ourselves be bound to them. We need to be happy remembering. And happy living, too."

"Yeah. Well, this is the dream house," Samuel observes, rising and walking toward the attic. "And another winter coming."

Now Samuel is gone and the kitchen is dark, and Julie's neck is twisted from leaning against the old red maple table. Musko's tail thumps against the mat and his tongue slurps over his lips. He paces to his empty dish and pushes it with his nose. It grates against the floor. Slowly, the tail begins to swing and Musko grins.

"I wish you wouldn't go off like that," Julie says. "I worry about you."

Julie packs away her Christmas treasures, really and truly this time. She piles kibble into Musko's dish, and prepares a cheese sandwich and glass of water for herself. She turns on the porch light and sweeps the verandah while Musko checks the perimeter of the yard. Julie does not venture into the cooling yard because you do not see snakes as they slither in the shadows.

So she sweeps around the rocker that would have been her mother's rocker and glances at the spot by the well where Tina would have danced for her. Her mother is not coming back and Tina is not coming back. Wherever they go, either here or there, they will not be with Julie again.

You do not dream your own life, Ms. Martin, just other lives—dark lives and bright lives. I am a good life, Ms. Martin. You could be one, too.

Because it's only a dream room if you let it.

The next step snaps into position. When all the dreams are merging and twisting, it is time for the dream room. After all, another winter is coming.

Chapter 32

A DREAM FOR JULIE

Julie dozes in the parlour-bedroom that night, and rises early, for it is Preparation Day for the Dream Room. She dismantles the bed, proud of her work with screwdrivers and hammers, and hauls it up the stairs, piece by piece. She fits the frame back together, and although it does not go back together as easily as it came apart, it is finally solid and ready. She slides the box spring up the stairs on its edge; that is, she plans to slide it, but it gouges at the paint on the steps, and in the end she tugs and wrestles. The mattress is floppy and no easier, but it can be done and it is done.

Musko moans, low in his throat, and retreats to the pantry.

Julie snaps the blue flowered comforter and it floats down over the bed, offsetting the cream walls and the blue curtains to perfection. She opens the curtains wide and retracts the blind to the casing, but in spite of all the light streaming across the floor and the blue and the cream, the room is stark and tense.

Julie sets a vase of hollyhock on the bookcase. It is translucent, colourless against the pale wall.

Musko paces in the hallway, but does not enter the room.

~

Julie attacks the garden with hoe and fingers in the afternoon heat, as Samuel's father would have done, working until spots dance in front of her eyes, and her head is reeling with dizziness.

She weaves her way back to the verandah and collapses on the step, fighting nausea. She sits with her head between her knees until she feels the sweat chill on her forehead and her stomach ease to pulsing waves. Her mouth is dry, her tongue grating on the roof of her mouth.

She yearns for the innocence of last August, for Laila and the fresh burst of blueberry juice cleansing her mouth, for mowers not quite on fire, even for mincing through the fields and scuttling away from the occasional snake. She enters the school for the first time, smells the polish and chalk dust, feels the eyes that follow her, and gives herself over to the bliss of not quite knowing what is and what will be. She spreads her first bright little mat in front of the fireplace in the days when Rachel Hardy is just a puzzling enigma, and Samuel a well-intentioned and sweetly sad landlord. Doug is a baffling but not impossible encounter, and her parents are still dear but irritating presences pacing on the boundaries of her independence.

Thanksgiving and the snow blower are tender moments, and Joe Barnes is a wet and weary hunter, mighty grateful, the pine needles soft under his feet. The dinghy flaps comically on the shore.

A great black dog leaps from a red jeep and ranges in front of her. Musko. Musko returned to her.

All the possibilities flowed around her in those days. There are walls now, tight and fast. The dreams have woven around her, binding her to Meadowbrook. Meadowbrook Acres holds her now, for better or for worse.

"You ought to get out in the community; mingle more," Laila's voice says.

"This place is like a great weight," Rachel comments from the top bunk. "I brightened it, I lightened it, but nothing ever changed. Here is a better place to dream."

A warm muzzle is rooting at her hands; a gruff bark is summoning her.

Julie's head snaps up. The dreams come to her waking now. Soon she will be living in them, everywhere.

She walks to the kitchen on rubbery legs, the floor rising and pitching beneath her feet. Musko whuffs at the door. Let's walk, please. Let's walk to the brook and wallow in the shady pool above the bridge. There are frogs to hunt and rich smells. Please, let's go. Then we will stretch out in front of the fridge, and simply be. We will dream of frogs and rabbits and good things.

Julie drives the rider mower along the wagon road, cutting out the trail, Musko jogging ahead. It is cool beneath the pine tree that hangs over the brook, and Musko plunges and burbles, hunting frogs. She wants to be like that again.

First, though, there is one more dream, the dream that will bind her life together and make sense of the hints that may or may not be real.

~

Julie bathes in the old tub, and then she and Musko share a sandwich of tinned meat and margarine with a leaf of lettuce for vegetable. It is like last year, when all was simple and new. She rubs Musko's ear and he trembles, licking her hand. When did he start trembling? she wonders.

Julie lies on the flowered comforter in Grandma Mary's room and waits. Musko paces in the doorway, and then sprawls across its threshold, head up.

Light gives way to shadows, and then darkness. Sleep does not come. The dream does not come. Julie turns on the lamp and opens a novel. She reads the words one by one and has no idea what the plot might be. She dozes and reads, dozes and reads the same passage, but there is no sense to the words. The night passes and Julie waits for the dreams. She longs to see Samuel on his hillside, watching the deer, or Samuel and Rachel sauntering along the wagon road, fishing poles in hand. She wishes that Samuel would enter his attic, only this time she would reach out to him, talk to him and soothe him, and listen to his

Christmas dreams. She goes through each moment of Tina and the snake dream, and finds that this one, too, has become precious. It is part of her now.

"Young lady, you are a fool," snaps a voice by the window.

Julie turns. The dawn light is soft, greyish. The old woman in the rocking chair (what rocking chair?) is in shadow, but her hawk-like features and severe hair are clear even so.

"Best time of the day," she grunts. "Cool. Quiet. No bawling and fussing. Peaceful. Lord, she had so many babies. So, so many." She sighs, rocking back and forth.

The old woman shifts, smoothing her apron. "I expect," she says, "that you heard I cut my teeth on Spanish doubloons."

Julie shrugs.

"Of course you did. That's what they all say, so it must be so." Her mouth twists in a brief grin. "Fact is, my grandfather was in privateering. Patriotic and legal. Sanctioned by the crown, no less. He got his land grant as a reward. Good service to the government. And he did well. Oh yes, he did." The old woman nods, rocking again. "Anyway," she continues, "you could learn all this in the family museum, back at my old home. That would be what you'd do if you had any ambition. But you, instead, seem to think that everything is owed to you in dreams. You just lie back, and let the family history fill you up. Along with all your fantasies about what this family may or may not be up to. When you could be doing something with your own life. You really are a fool, you know."

"I need to dream," whispers Julie.

"No, you don't. At least not all this snooping and meddling. You are a tenant, not family. You have no right."

"But I'm the caretaker," Julie insists.

"That's just plain foolishness. Samuel is the caretaker. His sister wasn't much good at it. You are just the tenant, sucking ridiculous dreams out of that girl's gibberish."

"I didn't read it," Julie says.

"I want to tell you about my own dreams," the old woman says. She stops rocking and leans forward, eyes bright in her lined face. "I had dreams, too. Oh, dreams of love and dreams of happiness. I put them all in my hope chest. I expect you don't even have a hope chest." Julie shakes her head. "I didn't think so. Of course not. Well, we all had them in my day. You filled your hope chest with all the special things that you would need to start your own household. Embroidered pillowcases and nice linens, crocheted doilies and all the pretty things that were going to make your marriage special and perfect. You see, you and the women of your family made each and every thing with hope. Hope that you would be the one, finally, who was not disappointed. That you would be the one who would rise above and keep rising and look back on your life with a smile on your face. Every little handkerchief, stitched with *hope*. A chest of dreams." She sighs, shutting her eyes.

The eyes snap open. "I was courted all right. I got engaged. Oh, they always love the ones who come from property and they make you think they would love you in rags. Then along comes someone from a little better property. That's when they say they cannot lie to you; they have found someone they truly love, and it would not be fair to you, and you deserve better, and then they're gone." She shrugs. "The way of our world. So, then my husband came along. He was a practical sort. Told my father that he wanted to build this place. It would belong to him and me both. Partners. Now, for that, he would need my father to put up the capital. So we got married. Just like the kings and queens of old. The real ones.

"When he passed on, the place became mine. My father had that clause put in the agreement. The usual way was, the oldest son got it. And he and his wife had to put you up and put up with you until the day you died. My father made sure he got the best for his investment. No, there was not much romance in the marriage of Mary Hardy, but Mary Hardy owned a farm, in the end.

"There I was. I owned Meadowbrook Acres after a lifetime breaking my back and crippling my hands with my husband, who was also breaking his back but did not have the strong heart of my people. I ruled from this room while my son and his wife and their brood filled up my house. And I was still breaking my back and crippling my hands and this room getting smaller and tighter and if you think you can't hate your own grandchildren, you're wrong."

The old woman rocks harder. "Rose was a fool. And that Rachel. Something like you. All about dreams and signs and wonders. All of them talk about me and the past, and they laugh about the cantankerous old woman who cut her teeth on Spanish doubloons. And they shake their heads about the mean old woman who was nasty to her own grandchildren. What they do not know is what it is to live each day trapped, each day another door slamming shut, and each day a little further from all your hopes.

"Then one day you realize that you will never reach them. And yet the women of this house keep spinning in smaller circles, serving this house until it drives them mad or away or both.

"You and that great beast of a dog of yours do not belong here. He knows that. He only came here and he only stays here for you. Go find a place, your place, and let this place go. Forty head of cattle in that barn. It's the only thing that Rachel did that made sense. Why keep an old barn just to walk around in?"

"But the heritage—"

"Oh, stop. It's not your heritage or your business. Get a nice little cottage near that new Park place, and let this place rot. The house should be made for you, not you for the house."

"Why do I dream then?" Julie asks.

"Because you are a fool," the old woman snaps. "These are just your wild imaginings, fueled by that journal you almost read. You put far too much stock in dreams, like that Laila woman says. (Now there is a woman with sense.) None of it is real; none of it is sent to you. It is just your wild ravings. You spin away all these ridiculous dreams by reading a few words, and you are not a prophet although you seem to think you are. No, you are merely a fool."

"I want them to be happy," Julie says.

"They will or they won't. It's no business of yours either way. And now I am tired. Talking to you gives me a headache. And this, by the way, is just a dream, too. You have not been chatting with the notorious Grandma Mary. This is just you, coming to your senses. But you knew that all along, didn't you?" She addresses this last part to Musko, who thumps his tail.

Musko bounds across the room and Julie awakens to his rough tongue dragging across her nose. The dawn is grey in the east window.

~

Julie and Musko rent a canoe at the Park that morning and spend the day exploring the islands between the river mouth and Minard's Bay. The waves are rough in the afternoon, and Julie sings as she plies her way back.

CONCILIATION

On a bright and sunny October afternoon, my cousin took her three young children to the field to watch the plane. Her husband, a mechanic, was giving a final test run to an ultralight that he had been working on. He was soaring up the Bay of Fundy, and the toddler laughed, clutching at the sky. It was a light day, a gentle Sunday afternoon, with the children capering in the field while the engine droned out over the bay.

Then there was silence.

She cast about. There was no reason, nothing that had absorbed the sound of her husband's engine. There was just silence, and a little plane, quivering above the bay. And three still children, staring wide-eyed at the sky.

A crosswind buffeted across the Bay of Fundy. Like a giant's hand, it scooped the little plane up. It rolled it and flipped it and then flung it down on the water and rocks near the shore.

There were three small children, drooping and starting to whimper under the empty sky, and my cousin in the waves, clawing and screaming against the metal and the rocks, and there were neighbours, dragging her back to shore.

When I came at last and reached for her, her eyes were wild and far out on the shore, where a little plane eternally stalled and flipped and crashed.

It was then that I saw that the soul can be dragged out through the eyes, and still the body endures, for the soul to be dragged and dragged again.

~

She sits in the porch, here at Wasaya, and watches for loons. We are older now, she and I, but the living of her life has come at a far greater cost than mine has. I have looked over my shoulder, agonized and analyzed until I was weary. She, though, has had to grip each moment with all her strength and drag herself forward, stumbling and tugging her children by the hand forward. She staggers, reeling on the precipice, then steadies her feet and takes a step. I am humbled, now, in her presence.

Here at Wasaya I lift her up. I lift her up for healing and for blessing while I stare in awe at the light that shines through her.

~

My mother, unlike my cousin, had had time to prepare for the death of her husband. You are never, though, truly prepared for the rupture of your soul. The two shall be as one, my cousin reminded me. And now, you are not even one anymore, as once you were. You are something now that you never were. You are emptied, and there is nothing to fill you again.

My mother's soul had ruptured, and she simply lost the will to see to its mending.

She did try at first, in little ways. She drove herself to the lawyer's office, and returned a little confident, a little excited. She seemed surprised that she could do these things, and she even pushed the lawn-mower for two cuts.

I see my mother, seventy years old, both hands gripping the bar, a shy little smile in place, a child-like wonder. *Look at me. I am mowing the lawn. I can do things, things that you never knew. I can scratch up a little pile of snow on my shovel. I can trot to the driveway's edge gripping the shovel stiff, and pop the little pile of snow onto the lawn with a sudden jerk. I am a farmwife, doing my chores.*

She drove less, she mowed less, and she walked less. The little hiking boots grew stiff and dry again in the corner of the porch; she no longer oiled and buffed them while a little smile played around her lips.

We could all approve and applaud while she did these things, but we were not the audience she needed.

She had done these things for him, and all that remained for her was the waiting: the vigil over his house and his barn and his land, until her hours were complete and time released her.

She craved companionship and conversation, but could not relax to these when she had them. She would look into our faces and she did not find the one face that she sought. She flung her loneliness in my face, the winter I lived with her. She chanted her abandonment and brandished her Stark Aloneness, shaking it in my face as she had the Very Happy Childhood. She was bitter and pained, pitiful but hard to pity. She fought her healing, because if she healed then she would have to find a new path, and she had struggled too hard in all her old paths.

My three-year-old son was sweet and kind to her. With him, she could act out being a grandmother to her grandson; accepting his comfort was not a betrayal. She took him to the parade that September, and he watched nestled at her side in the Raider. "Clap for the parade," she would exclaim, as each float rolled past. And together they would gravely applaud each passing float.

The fire department ambulance eased by, lights pulsing, streamers waving. "Oh, clap for the parade," she whispered, tears streaming down her cheeks and hands held high as she patted them together in tribute to the good men who had come so many times, so willingly, bearing oxygen and open hearts on those nights when my father could not breathe and she was afraid.

They never judged her. The community, as the years rolled down, also did not judge her. They puzzled, perhaps, as her grief went down the years unchanging, but they accepted her.

They watched over her.

I judged her. She was not an easy woman to be a companion to. She had an instinct for manipulating guilt, and I was, as always, the ideal candidate.

I should have laughed more, had more picnics and play days, but in family tradition, I flinched and trembled, and flaunted my burden.

I think now that she was so afraid of being left alone that she drove people away, so that the dread of their departure would be over.

Uncle Alphonse came to visit one summer and stayed two years. Everyone said what a good thing it was for both of them. He was retired now, and had a smile for everyone. He left suddenly after two years, and everyone was surprised. He had seemed so content, and it was so good for them both. I do not know the story, but I do know that I stayed one year, not two.

She wanted to be alone, I told myself. I should not have left her alone, I tell myself.

Here is what I would do if I had those times back: I would shrug off the comments and take her for a drive. I would take her on a trip and visit churches and museums all along the coast. We would go to restaurants, and invite friends to join us. We would rent a cottage far away, and when we got home, I would put on music and laugh and we would dance. That is what I would do.

Instead, I went to Baffin Island and left her to be haunted. Grandma Mary and the privateer stock, cutting their teeth on Spanish doubloons, oozed out of the shadows where they had hovered and needled her for years, and filled the living spaces of her mind and her house that was their house.

I am not talking about cold zones, shifting furniture, and all the flash of cheap superstition. I am talking about the grim, brooding mood that gripped that house. I had seen it in my father, staring past the floor as the winters wound on, and he was not in them. I saw it in my mother, in the eyes that were never quite resting, never quite on you, always a little elsewhere.

That place needed air, light, and the voices of many people lifted in laughter to press back the mood. It needed a continual child's birthday party, bursting with sugar and colour and still the haunting would be merely driven back, not gone.

One lonely, bitter woman was no match for that house.

Let it go, Samuel. Let it go.

She shuffled about the house, staring at china cabinets, bookcases, and albums. She would stare, but not touch, not open. Remember. Remember the times that these things witnessed.

She could stand in her kitchen, complete with fridge, freezer, electric stove, and microwave (*Like an appliance shop,* Aunt Iris growled), see the old woodstove and the canning kettles belting out steam, and hear the crank phone rasping all through the strawberry season. There was the door; he would come through that door, dusty and dragging his feet. He would sit in that chair, and at Christmas, he was at the head of that table, smiling over his family, his eyes on her.

She could sit in her chair and watch TV, there by the dining room table, but all the other chairs were empty and there was no festive Christmas table, faces poking around each other, trying to get in the snapshot. And him in the centre, at the head of that table, his eyes on her.

She could wander into the children's rooms, and the old books and pictures would still be there, dusty and silent. You can hear the air in the furnace pipes, the hum of the refrigerator from the kitchen, the occasional snap as the house settles. You feel far away, and these sounds are happening somewhere else, for someone else. The silence presses against your temples.

She could see that the guns and fishing rods needed oiling, as she walked past. The silence crushes against your shoulders and weighs on your heart.

Aunt Iris would call her, and they would talk. Aunt Iris would talk and my mother would talk, two parallel monologues, but they tried, didn't they? Did I? Can I?

When no one is left to judge you, you judge yourself and you imagine the judgement of others. That might not be right, but it is what happens.

You stare at all their possessions and yours perched on top and around, and you say that you have no right to move these. You have lived here for fifty years, and have made a home here, but it is not your home. Not really. Grandma Mary built this place, not you. You could, like I did later, clear out everything and place a few choice items in a memory room and your own baubles all around, but the memory room will be a silent reproach.

You leave everything alone. You lift each item to dust, and return it to its rightful place. You scatter mats over holes in rugs that must not be moved. You shuffle from room to room imagining light, bright renovations, but you see the fake panelling you and he installed in the seventies when it was so clean and uncluttered, and your new renovations will be clumsy blunders marring the work that you and he did.

You reach out to touch the hand that is resting beside yours, but it is not there. He is not resting on the couch, or gone to the bough shack without you. He is dead. He has passed on, and you are left behind. Your times will never be again.

The rooms vibrate with images, the lawns pound with the feet of children, the memories rise in a swirling mass but you cannot touch his hand and he will not smile and share this with you. It would be sweet, bittersweet, but gentle in the sharing.

The images and the sounds consume you. Your legs cramp and you wander in the night. You put on music and dance by yourself in the night while the dog watches in mild alarm.

You surface and go to the store. A familiar face smiles and asks you how you are. The words spill from your mouth and you cannot stop them and you see the smile grow fixed on the woman's face as she nods and nods, her eyes darting to the check-out. You have, however, taken the time to cook a full breakfast today, and want to celebrate and share the details of its preparation. You want to tell, and you cannot stop the rush of the telling, even as your cheeks flush and you know that she is restless. And you know that you have done it before and will do it again but right now, oh, right now, you have to tell.

You surface in the night and the porch light is on. You did not put it on, but there it is, and you summon help, pressing your special button. Help arrives, and there are no intruders and no tracks and perhaps you brushed against the switch, they say, but you did not and you are afraid. You surface completely and they are looking at you and you are looking at the light switch, and you are afraid. You are not afraid of intruders now; you are afraid of yourself.

You surface and it is Christmas. You look around and know that you are not ready, have not really begun. "My family is coming home," you say to the woman in front of you. Why has she brought a child to work? "We have a lot to do," you tell her. The woman glances at the child, a boy of about nine years. "Yes. We're here," she replies. You pause. What kind of an answer is that? "This is Nathaniel," the woman says, not patiently. You stare. Nathaniel is a round-cheeked little boy, who plays horse with the dog, not this thin-faced almost adolescent leaning against the counter. But if this really is Nathaniel, then this is your daughter, her eyes flat and sullen. Yes. Those are her eyes. "They are *all* coming," you amend, "and I need all the help you can give me." You say this brightly, conspiratorially, and maybe, just maybe, she did not notice that you were away for a moment or so.

You preside over your Christmas table, but is it your table? Is this your house? Your life? Your daughter has steamed wild rice to go with the turkey, and prepared a tossed salad. Where is the mashed turnip? The dressing? The fried parsnips and all the steamed puddings and little cakes? But that is your centrepiece, with pine cones and boughs and fragile glass ornaments tucked among the greenery. You place a wobbly-eyed Santa mug in front of Nathaniel, who smiles and returns his attention to the food. The centrepiece and the mugs and the cutlery and plates and the table and chairs are yours. Yours and his. But whose table is this? Who presides? Who smiles at the centre of the photo?

Nathaniel covers your hand with his and smiles at you. He should be laughing over the verandah and the lawn and the hills with all his friends, always. Then, this could be your house.

Bitterness oozes from the fake panelling, drips from the drapes you selected. *Fifty years is a long time to live in someone else's house,* the voice whispers. *It is not your house; it is ours, hers and mine,* he would say to that voice if he were here. He would banish that voice. And he would smile down the table, his eyes on her.

You awaken one day, and for a moment you cannot remember the day or recognize the den, where you are napping. It is only for a moment, and just this once, but you agree to go to a manor for a little rest. You swing your legs over the side of the bed and you stare. This is not the river, packed in mist, the great cathedral looming beyond. And it is not the other place, with the strawberries and the verandah and the great red barn, where you and he grew apart and then together, and he bought you waders and a rod and hiking boots. Before he sent you away to Iris's house for coffee, and sneaked away and now you are stark alone.

"Help," you scream.

You surface in a hospital bed with hospital window and hospital walls and everyone wants you to eat, just a little. If you eat, then you will go home, they say.

You surface a little in a hospital bed beside a three-panel window, with little panes of glass. Across the yard is a great red barn, tilting a little, the white doors shut. *I had a barn like that,* you tell the attendant. You shift a little, and study the cabinet opposite the window. *My husband had guns like those,* you say.

That is your barn, the woman says, *and that is your gun cabinet. You are home, Mother.*

Your daughter is a teacher, not a nurse. But you say nothing, in case you say the wrong thing. Instead, you look at the barn roof. You look knowingly, appraisingly. You do not ask where the fence is, however.

The attendant wheels you to the front porch to find some relief from the stifling heat. She wheels you past the living room where the curtains are open in the west window and the afternoon sun beats down on your rug. *My rug,* you wail. *Why are you fading my rug?* She turns your chair away.

You surface a little, and a whiff of pipe smoke brushes your nostrils. You shuffle and you turn your head, but you cannot find him. You twist your leg over the bed rail, and that is the day they slide a strap through the soft pink belt of your housecoat, and attach it to the mattress. It doesn't matter; it doesn't matter. When he comes, he will fix everything.

You look out the window and see the summer haze and you shiver with the cold.

You surface completely, and you know that you are in the house that you lived in with him for forty-three years and waited for him for seven. You see that the guns are dusty and the barn is tilting, just a little. But that does not matter to him. You know that it is August, and you are so cold. Colder than the deep earth.

And you know.

You demand make-up and a hairdresser. You have yourself dressed in a fresh pantsuit, and a little red beret perched on your freshly styled curls.

Mother is getting better, you hear them say.

You sit up, shoulders straight, and announce, "I want to be with my husband."

The one who says she is your daughter replies, "Do you know where he is? What it means?"

You nod.

"You know that he is not here? He is passed on? He is dead, not here?" she continues.

You nod again. "Yes," you say. "I know where he is. And," you add, "he understands."

You close your eyes to rest them, and you open them in the bed by the window, and someone with a watch is counting your breaths.

You are breathing less often now. You do not need to breathe so often now. *It is like that,* he says. *Soon, you will not have to breathe at all.*

Three children kneel by the bed, chanting the rosary with you. The sweetness of a Catholic childhood. No. Those are three adults. They are mumbling the rosary, standing, their arms about each other.

See? he says. *They'll be all right. It's all right now.*

But, oh, it is not all right. You are terrified now. What if you cannot find your way? What if you lose sight of him, along the way, and are alone again?

His hand folds around yours, and he gives a gentle tug. You are hiking beside him now, his pack bobbing just a little, your walking stick swinging, your hiking boots beading with the dew, and you vanish beyond the red pines with him at the breaking of the dawn.

~

I weep here, at Wasaya, for the mending that was offered to me but I couldn't make.

I offer up this vision of those last days, as it comes to me here at Wasaya, and I offer it on the wind. For their blessing and my healing.

I took the role that my mother could or would not take; I faced the past and stripped it down. I tore down the barn; I stripped the house. I painted and plastered and changed.

I tried to pound the props into submission, but when it was all done, when I had broken my heart and all my changes hung empty, and I had seen the figure rotating from the beam, the unknown figure with my face, and still the bitterness oozed from the seams as it always had, and the presence of ancestors still vibrated in the air and accused, I fled.

I fled to Wasaya, my last battlefield.

Poor Samuel. I sold him the shambles of Meadowbrook Acres to have and to heal.

For Samuel, to see the place and walk on its fields is enough. He rents it, repairs it, and at times resents it, but he does not need to tear it into submission. It is the portal to memory, and not a haunting.

It is natural to him.

I have sat here at Wasaya, and not enjoyed the water or the sunset, angry because he belongs to Meadowbrook Acres, and I do not.

~

The lake is still and grey this day, and I cannot wait to be gone. Yet I will yearn for Wasaya all winter, and it will sustain me.

In the week remaining, the dogs and I will explore the shorelines, sit and listen to the loons, read by lamplight, and be together. Saima is weary with her years, but her eyes are young as they survey her cove.

I have wrestled with my past for too long; it is time to wander in the present. Time to be. I have one week, or a lifetime, and it will be as I choose.

The time for change is at hand, but for now, it is time to relax to Wasaya.

I shall stroll in the evening, the breeze sweet on my face.

Let us canoe now, my three friends and I. I shall caress the water with my hand, and it will be warm and still.

Chapter 33

SURFACING

The miasma of the dream world is fading, but as in all illnesses, a sense of weakness pervades. Relapse is a constant fear.

Perhaps it is the dream house, a conduit of sorts for sometimes dark and sometimes poignant dreams, dreams that slip into the cracks of your consciousness until they become a part of you. You do not notice how odd you have become, how unusual your way of relating to the world.

You become a little too much like the Hardys, caught up in longings and insecurities.

You lose job opportunities because you are not alert and aware. Once you were, but now you are not.

You think of Joe Barnes and his father, and how you must invite them over or drop by, but then the dreams creep in and you drift.

You wonder where your dog is when he is at your side, waiting.

You wonder how your father is coping, but then you slip into your dreams.

You do not notice that Laila is worried; you no longer think of the hurt she has endured in being friends to the Hardys. You drift from her, but she does not drift from you.

But then you have that one last, consuming dream. After you canoe to Minard's Bay for the day and explore the islands, this is the beginning of your return.

~

Laila drops by one afternoon before school starts. The lawns are freshly mowed and wilting in the sun; the garden is clean of weeds and ready for watering when the evening cools. Julie sprawls on the verandah beside Musko, revising her resume and discussing the changes with him. Is she skilled or highly skilled with assistive technology? Highly skilled suggests an aggressive blazer with square shoulders and flaring lapels. She looks misplaced in a blazer. In a vest, she looks like Julie. She looks skilled. She is skilled. She makes the entry.

"I suppose you don't have time for a Kedge afternoon?" Laila asks, her eyes taking in the neat lawns and garden.

"Oh, I think Musko hears Kedge calling," Julie laughs, saving her resume and shutting down the computer. "And I've done enough to make me feel like a responsible person. I'll just pull a few things together."

"I've got plenty," Laila says, studying the floorboards. "All you need is you and Musko. Maybe something for walking," she suggests.

~

"You seem different, somehow," Laila observes as they rearrange the backseat to make room for Musko. "Like you're coming out of things, a little."

"Not so dreamy?" Julie smiles at her own attempt at humour.

"Like you're set on doing things and being happy," Laila amends.

"I got kind of sidetracked, when Mom got sick."

"Ye-es. More so then, but a little before. Not sure of yourself. All those things going on would get to anyone."

"And I let them."

"And you let them."

"You hear about Joe?" Laila's voice is grave.

Julie tenses. "Joe? No. What?"

"Oh, nothing much. Gone to Ontario to see his wife. They do that once in a while. She's married again, but he wants to be friends. Feels bad that he wasn't supportive when they lost Jacob. She lost her son, after all. She's the mother. So, he tries to visit and talk and listen, and then he'll be back and spend a long time hunting somewhere."

"We've all got things to live down."

"Yes. Live through and live down. Hard way to live your life, but there you are."

They drive on to the Park, turning well before the truck road that leads down to the lake and Sunrise Cove. The road leads on, but they turn, for this is a Kedge day. They should go to Sunrise Cove again, and pick some cranberries, they decide. Julie asks if Nathaniel is still around, and Laila shrugs. "Hard to say," is her only comment.

The Park has not really changed from August to August. The hemlocks are brittle and dusty in the heat, no better but no worse. They are maintaining, perhaps healing from within and it does not show yet. The campgrounds are somnolent in the afternoon heat, as families without dying mothers track down their favourite Kedge moments. Or perhaps that couple reclining in their camp chairs overlooking the long slope down to the lake are here for their last Kedge time. Perhaps she clutches his hand and laughs so that he cannot leave, or so that he can hold her to the moment. Then again, perhaps they are already missing the little girl who waves and calls from the swings nearby. Or maybe there is already an empty swing beside her. On the other hand, they might just be a contented family, relaxing in the August afternoon. "Don't stare so hard," Laila says.

They park above their picnic place and Musko bounds ahead, eager for the cool water. Now at the table that overlooks the shore Julie sees a lone woman. She is thin, her greying hair sticking out under a battered canvas hat. Her elbows rest on the table, and her hand strays to brush along the back of the ancient white Husky that lies at her feet. His ears are up, and he pulls himself to his feet. He shuffles toward Musko, who pauses in his rush for the lake, tail up and stiff. The Husky paces about him, sniffing, while Musko stands still. Then Musko ducks, brushing his muzzle against the great white dog's jaw. Both tails swing briefly, and Musko follows the Husky down to the lake shore.

"They seem to get along well," says the woman, her eyes fixed on the lake. "I'm glad you came, Laila."

"Oh, when you said Kedge, I couldn't resist, you know that." Laila's voice rings out, forced cheerfulness. It is the voice one reserves for the ill to lift their spirits or for the unforgiven to let them know that you are a good sport.

So this is Rachel Hardy, who is ill or unforgiven. Laila always forgives, so she must be ill.

"I am doing so much better," Rachel Hardy says, rummaging in a day pack.

"Well, the pressure gets to us all, in different ways," Laila replies. "This is Julie, by the way, and that's her Musko. He and Taggak seem to get along real well."

"Taggak is feeling his years, but he'll always be Taggak. You're the one at the farm, then?" She turns to Julie, studying her face, fingering the cigarette pack she has drawn out.

Julie nods.

"I bet you've heard about me," Rachel continues. "I'm the one who took down the barn and set the place on the path to ruin."

"Rachel, I don't think anyone took it like that," Laila interjects.

"Pretty close." Rachel studies their faces for a moment, and then sticks a cigarette between her lips. She snaps her lighter and draws a quick breath, expelling it away from them. "Hope you don't mind."

"You going to stay with Samuel for a while?" Laila asks.

Rachel closes her eyes. "For a while. He's been really good about it. Actually," she says, turning to Julie, "I would like to move out to the farm. But you're staying, I hear."

"Why, you could both live there," Laila exclaims. "It would help with all the expenses, and the dogs get along so well."

"But Samuel would never go for it," Rachel adds.

"Well. Maybe not. But you never know." Laila shrugs.

Julie sits outside the conversation, which is really about her future, and wonders if her recovered confidence is going to survive this day.

"I've put Samuel through too much already, anyway," Rachel says. "I can't see him taking a chance on terminating the lease, and he'd be afraid something might happen if we both stayed there."

"That place was hard on you, Rachel. You left there for a reason, remember."

"And it didn't help, did it? That place follows me, wherever I go. I wonder how many people in this world can state that their childhood home can still haunt them, 2,000 miles away. Maybe I just need to face it down. So, I hear you found my journal." She seems to have just remembered that Julie is present in this private conversation about her.

"I didn't read it," Julie insists.

"Only because Nathaniel hid it for me," Rachel says. "And if you stay long enough in that house, the whole journal will come to you, anyway. That place haunts you."

"Me?"

"Anybody. Anybody with sensitivity and a little imagination." She takes a furtive pull on her cigarette. "I really got over things staying up there at Sunrise Cove. I felt at peace, finally, but not at first. Then, it all came apart for a while."

"Where were you, if you don't mind my asking?"

Rachel turns her head and blows out the smoke in a quick breath. "If I don't tell, you'll ask someone who doesn't mind, so I might as well. I was up there, up in the lake system for a while, just drifting along, camping with Taggak. Samuel and Nathaniel brought me out, maybe in October that first year. I had already put the car and my gear in storage, and then Taggak and I came back down. Know what a taxi costs from Annapolis? And paying to have my packing done when I quit my job in Ontario? Not cheap, but it was good out here, living up in the lakes above my lake, avoiding the last tourists, and gone before the hunters and trappers moved in. Taggak and I did some contract work in the Yukon that winter. I came back in May, thought I'd go out to the cabin for a while, but I couldn't seem to be there. You know? You plan and plan, and you can't seem to get there."

"Didn't you go there in May, though?" Julie asks. "Didn't Joe Barnes see you?"

"Joe." Rachel shrugs. "He might have. I saw my cove again and again that winter. I thought I could just be out there again. I felt myself there. But it wasn't the same when I got there. It was empty, in the places where Saima and Mikijuk should be."

"Things change. We have to change to keep going," Laila says.

"And so I went back North, on another contract. Having adventures like I used to. But Taggak and I were lonely. There used to be five of us on our adventures; now there were just the two of us to share them. Arrive in a new place and it is just us, at the end of the day. It seemed so empty. And then driving back, just us, Taggak sleeping on the seat. He's tired of it all, you know."

"Because you are. You have to find a place to put your feet down."

"And so I called you. Finally. I felt like I had abandoned you."

"You had."

"But you were just glad to hear from me."

"That's what friends are for."

"I would have resented me."

"I did."

"But you didn't seem to."

"Well, I was your friend, wasn't I? And you needed your friends."

"So, you've known since spring?" Julie interjects.

"Oh, before that I had a pretty good idea," Laila says. "You hear things. You sense things."

"You get seen in malls," Rachel says.

"You do," Laila agrees. "I had to keep pretending," Laila says to Julie, and this is supposed to explain everything.

"Covering for me," Rachel clarifies. "I think my time at Sunrise Cove is over," she adds.

"You never know," says Laila.

"Would you live out there again?" Julie asks.

Rachel considers her for a moment. "I already said that it wasn't the same."

"But does it have to be?" Julie counters.

Rachel lights another cigarette and blows smoke toward the lake. "That's the question, isn't it? What I'd really like to do, is try the home place again."

Laila purses her lips and stares at the lake.

"You must have had dreams," Rachel says to Julie.

Of course Julie had dreams. She has been the caretaker of Meadowbrook Acres. She has been a canoer of shorelines. She has been building a future in which all her dreamers are healed. Oh. Rachel probably means the other dreams. "I sometimes dreamed about Christmas ornaments in the attic," she admits.

Rachel draws a quick puff and forces the smoke away. "Christmas ornaments in the attic. I see."

"They're delicate blown glass, silver with red and gold trim."

"They're cheap foil daubed with paint."

"But they're delicate, and beautiful, and they bring the past back to Samuel."

Rachel is trembling now. Julie does not mention the deer. Or the fishing day. She fumbles for an idea. "Sometimes I dreamed about snakes," she offers.

To her surprise, Rachel's countenance brightens. "Snakes. You do."

"It's a kitten first, and then it turns into a snake and crawls into the closet."

"Sometimes it's a dog at first, and then it turns into a snake and crawls into your house and under the sofa. Snake dreams are about betrayal, you know."

Julie does not feel betrayed by anyone, so she shrugs.

"Betrayals go way back in that house," Rachel continues. "All the way to the time they built it."

"But I don't dream anymore," Julie tells her. "Not since the last dream."

"I wouldn't bet on it," Rachel says, turning to Laila. "I really did hurt him, and he's been so good about it all."

"Because he does value you more than the place, more than these ornaments or whatever." Laila slips back into the conversation with a gentle smile. "And now, I say we eat something. It's a perfect day for a Kedge picnic."

There is no potato salad, no chicken, no fresh little wafers. There is new food, for the new time, the time when Julie can meet Rachel Hardy and not sink into the dream house. This is a turning point, yet again. There is coleslaw, and sliced meats, and sweet little pickles. There are slices of cheese and tomato. There are crisp rolls to split and brush with margarine and then stuff with good things. There is juice and a thermos of coffee and carrot cake to change your taste. Julie is sitting down with her friend Laila and Laila's friend Rachel and there is no farm and no cabin and no dark or poignant dreams that can touch her anymore. Rachel might snap her fingers and the lease will be terminated but that does not matter because the farm has permeated her consciousness and will find her wherever she goes, as it finds Rachel.

Hopefully, it will not find her as it does Rachel. Rachel is now trembling again. "I put him through so much," she tells Laila, and Julie knows that this is about the fragile ornaments.

Laila pours a little hot coffee from the thermos. "Like I said, he values you more than the place. You have to stop worrying about every little thing."

Taggak shambles up to Rachel and roots under her elbow until her arm rests over his neck. He grins, baring yellowed stubs of teeth. Rachel gives him a quick hug and offers him a sliver of roast beef. "On one level I know that, and on another level I can't do anything about it."

"Like I couldn't seem to do anything about Doug," Julie says.

Rachel leans down, rubbing her forehead against Taggak's head, but Julie continues anyway. "He just disappeared. He took my dog and he disappeared." Rachel lifts her head, and Julie continues, encouraged. "And he showed up here, well, at the place, actually, and insisted on staying, and then he had to go back to Alberta, because he was involved with a student, and there was a lawsuit." Rachel shifts her gaze to the lake, but still the words tumble out. "And he's working in oil now, and I guess there's a baby. Anyway, I have Musko back," she finishes, her cheeks red because Rachel is in crisis and Julie is still talking about Doug.

"That's good," Rachel says. She turns to Laila. "So I'm camping out in Meadow for a few days. There's this man camping all by himself a few sites down. Well, technically, I'm by myself, but I have Taggak, which counts as far as I'm concerned. He's got an old canoe that's seen better days, and he's been coming back each morning from up Jeremy Bay, so he must leave around sunrise. He goes out and he comes back smiling, but he looks so sad at the same time. The rest of the time, he just seems to sit around the site. I'd like to go over; he seems so lonely. But, he'd probably think I was after him or something."

"Send Taggak," Laila suggests, and then her face tightens and she looks at Julie. Julie is rigid on the bench.

"What site did you say?" Julie whispers. Her father has driven past Meadowbrook Acres, past his daughter, who is grieving too, to be alone on the bay with Alice Martin. Jeremy Bay is his Meadowbrook now.

"It's on the bend, above the lake, there in Meadow. Anyway, he must have gone on a day trip or something; he and the canoe are still gone. It's probably good for him. What?" she asks Laila, who is snapping lids and folding tin foil.

"I expect we're going to visit your campsite now," says Laila, rising to yet another occasion in her long affiliation with Meadowbrook Acres and its inhabitants. "You got your canoe here?"

Chapter 34

RIPPLES IN THE WATER

Julie gives up trying to calculate the date on which Laila started to keep the secret of Rachel. *The Hardys always come back.* Come back from the Yukon? Come back from the asylum? Perhaps the Hardys come back from the dead. *You have not been chatting with the notorious Grandma Mary. This is just you, coming to your senses.* However, to accept that advice is to accept that she does communicate with you.

In the clouded August night, when stars and moon are hidden, the lone figure slinks through the shadows, the heavy can gurgling and swishing. Muted and just discernible. Ominous. In the sticky air a lone match flares. The flames rip through the structure, open palms arched against the heavens and the vapours releasing with a sigh. Snakes ooze from the rock foundation, arching and twisting onto the lawn, bellies scraping the gravel as they burrow into the fields.

Julie snaps her attention to the road. They are nearing the campground kiosk. "I dreamed about snakes, too," Rachel is saying. "Once one bit me in the neck, and I could feel the pain there when I woke up."

"Perhaps you should wait with the dogs," Laila is saying. "That canoe is small, and Julie and I could go up the bay and have a look around."

"Taggak likes to tip the canoe, anyway," Rachel agrees.

Conversation this afternoon has been, at best, a series of parallel monologues and disconnected observations. Yet each phrase seems relevant to all the other phrases. "It's like being trapped in a French existentialist play," Rachel says, and so Julie must have said this out loud.

"The age of prophecy closed before the time of the Maccabees," she continues. "So all your dreams are just that. Dreams. Imaginings. You can't dream the future into reality."

But perhaps Rachel is telling her this in a dream. Julie's jaws are aching, and she unclenches them, muscle by muscle. Her father is out on the lake now, and she is hiding in the dream days. This must be a defence mechanism. She is relieved that it is not Rachel who says this.

They park in Rachel's campsite; her car is still at the picnic place and so they are not breaking any Park laws. The dogs spill from the car, Taggak landing stiff and dignified, Musko capering around him, tail wagging. Laila marches down the hill, paddle in hand, Julie and Rachel meandering behind her. Suddenly, Rachel rushes back up the hill and steps and slides back down, holding out a paddle for Julie. "Life jackets," snaps Laila, and Julie jogs back to her father's campsite. In the back of the truck, under the tarp, is her life jacket. Her life jacket is in the truck, because Julie does not canoe with her father. Alice's life jacket, though, will be placed on the bow seat. That is where she sings with the loons.

Rachel has a life jacket for Laila. Laila steadies the stern in the shallows as Julie climbs into the bow. Musko gives a whuff and splashes into the water. "I think he'd better go with you. He'll be fine," Rachel says. "Musko," she mutters. "They always call the black dogs Musko."

"It's a fine name," Laila declares, her paddle biting into the water. "Now we'll just go for a little ride, and we'll just happen to run into your father along the way. He'll be fine," she says.

Musko sits rigid, nose to the breeze, seeking. Julie scans the horizon, seeking the flicker of green that will be her father's canoe. Now the dreams and the twisted conversation fall away and she is free again. Free to soar over the water. Free to build a little cottage, below Samuel's orchard, for her and her father. Free to bundle totes and packs into the

SUV and park near the airstrip and fly over the muskeg and teach as she was meant to teach again. Free to bundle her father into the SUV and carry him to her world. Free to leave him in his.

They are both canoers of shorelines, now. Alice Martin, on the water's edge, points to the wonders that are there to be discovered on the shoreline. She is a wise woman, now, and teaches them.

Laila's gaze swings from shoreline to shoreline in rhythm with her strokes. She is the one who sees the line of green along the shore of Indian Point. She angles left, cautious of the waves that slop against the bow. Musko stands. "Stay low," Julie warns, and then Musko is over the side, tail sweeping back and forth as he churns away from them and toward the dull green paint streak that is her father's canoe. Laila and Julie paddle hard against the waves, but so much time passes before there are rocks against the green, and a slip of yellow sticking up from the stern, and a pile of cloth on the shore that rises and is a human figure. One arm is up and its hand is against its forehead, shading its eyes. Now a black lump on the waves rises and is a great black dog that splashes to the shore and shakes, spinning around in front of the man who glances at the dog and then continues to watch their canoe with one hand shading his eyes.

"Bit of a wind," Theo Martin comments, steadying the bow.

"It's coming up," Laila agrees, gripping the gunwales and crouching forward. Her mouth tightens as she lifts her left leg over the side. She is stiffer this summer than last. One summer, Julie will lean forward to step out of the canoe, and it will hurt her, too. Like Laila, she will continue to lean forward and step out of the canoe. She will not lament what the years have taken, but embrace what they still hold. She will be like Laila, not like Samuel. She could so easily be Rachel.

Musko springs up and down beside Theo, who grips the fur at the back of his head and gives it a gentle tug. "You're good in a canoe," he says. "Steady as a rock. Jumped over without stirring 'er at all."

"I didn't know you were out here," Julie says.

Her father rubs Musko's ears. "I guess," he mutters.

"Nice thing about Jeremy Bay," Laila observes. "Always somebody going up or down it. You always meet someone. Sometimes someone you know."

"Maybe you'll stop in on the way back?" Julie says.

"Maybe," he mutters, looking away. "I just needed to get away. By myself."

For almost thirty-three years her parents bound her life to theirs. Now, they need their own time. For when he is by himself, Theo is with Alice, his love, his history, and his future. Julie and Tim belong to a murky present whose time has passed for now, but perhaps will come again. No apologies or explanations are offered. This is just the order that things have taken. This is just the way they are. After a year at Meadowbrook Acres, anything, it seems, can happen, and it will be natural.

"It was calm this morning, peaceful," he begins. He turns, facing up the bay. "And I could hear them calling, out there, singing back and forth in the mist, and it was like I could just paddle in the mist and it didn't have to end. It could go on forever."

Fortunately, Rachel is not there to make observations on fairy mists and circles. She would, Julie is sure.

"I love a morning like that," Laila murmurs.

Theo's face lifts and he continues. "It doesn't matter where I am, where I go. I'm always here."

"That's a good way to look at things." Laila nods.

"I got all kinds of plans in my head, for a time." He addresses Laila now. "Going to retire. Do a little carpentry and woodworking business down at Samuel's. Thought of buying a piece of land, there below the orchard, building a cottage there. I could sort of watch the place for him, then."

"Fine place for a cottage," Laila agrees. "Close to your daughter, too," she points out.

He considers this for a moment. "She probably wouldn't stay." His voice is flat; there is no inflection of hope or despair.

It is time for Julie to break into the conversation, for it is hers, after all. "Sometimes I feel like going back to the fly-ins again," she says. "I was excited about teaching then."

"Pretty far," he says. "She never quite understood it."

"It was special," Julie says. "It was who I really was."

"With that Doug fellow."

"Which is when it fell apart."

"You can't go back and make the past happen."

"Then why are you out here?"

Now it is out in the open.

"This is my goodbye day," Theo Martin says. "This is the day when I take it all inside me, and I don't have to come here to be here. Maybe it's a stormy winter day. I can't come here. But I can be here."

"That's a good plan," Laila says. "Any time you want. No matter what."

"No matter what," he affirms.

"I don't have a place to do that," Julie says.

Theo stares at his feet. "Anywhere," he says. "If you don't have a place, it can be anywhere. Just don't get hung up on some one thing or one place; otherwise you'll have to actually touch it or go there. It's like . . ." He hesitates, struggling with the concept. "It's like you carry it, you hold the memory, but you're not trapped by it. You don't have to actually touch it or be there," he repeats.

A smile begins in the left corner of Laila's mouth and spreads across her face. "That's a fine way to put it," she says.

"I like Meadowbrook Acres," Julie says. "I love painting it and putting in little mats and curtains. But it's overwhelming."

"You can put in little mats and curtains and mow lawns and plant gardens anywhere you want," Laila says, "without all the heartache and heartbreak of that place. Maybe you and your dad will build a cottage somewhere together. Maybe you'll fly off somewhere and you can teach and he can fish and teach woodworking or maybe he'll go east and you'll go west, or maybe he'll stay in Waverley and you'll stay here. It don't matter. Just do something and be happy."

"That's just what I figured out today," Theo says. "I want to come here, from time to time, but I don't need to. It doesn't own me like it did."

It is calming now, as evening eases down over Kedge. The lake ripples and puckers in the occasional gust, and flattens to slick oil, colours spilling on the water, blues and coppers and silvers. Julie dips her paddle and the water bubbles against it. She lifts her paddle and the droplets flick, spreading ripples that flatten and fade. They pass, and the lake absorbs their passing. They are gone, and the lake remains.

Rachel's tent and gear are packed and piled on the picnic table at her site when they return. Rachel is seated on the bench, one leg swinging, turning a cigarette pack in her hands. She rises as they approach. "I'll need a ride to my car," she tells Laila. "I'll get the canoe when I come back. I'm going to Wasaya. It's time to be there."

It is Theo who drives her to the picnic grounds near the lake. It is Theo who straps down the canoe and pulls the straps snug. Taggak stands beside him, tail swinging. "We all need a place where we can be," he agrees. "But only when it's time. It can become a trap, so easy."

Julie and Laila wind along the road through Meadow Campground, with Musko pacing from window to window in the backseat, enjoying the smells. Here, a father and two small children are pitching their tent. The father is pacing and tugging lines, a broad grin fixed on his face. The little boy is wriggling the rods into the dirt. "Not like that," the father says in that high, lilting voice parents adopt when their patience is ebbing. "In the pockets." The little girl is clapping her hands and hopping between the tent and the fire pit. "Pockets, po-ckets!" the little girl exclaims. Over there, a middle-aged couple clad in khaki shorts heavy with pockets are assembling a solar panel. She is sorting pages while he tries one piece against another, and then another.

"Think you'll stay on at Meadowbrook?" Laila asks.

Wasaya. Beautiful sunrise. Sunrise Cove. Your future calls you to itself when you and it are ready. It can be a cove or a bay or a lost farm. It can be an old truck and the pine needles under your feet. It can be anything.

Laila knows these things. That is why her life is so rich, wherever she is.

Chapter 35

PASSING

*I*n *the clouded August night, when stars and moon are hidden, three*
figures slink through the shadows, the heavy can gurgling and swishing as
it passes from hand to hand. The first match sparks and sputters, flickering
and gone. The second flares up and Julie holds it aloft. She is surprised to see
her father, but not surprised that the other is Doug. "It's the only way to get
out of this," Doug hisses, gesturing to the base of the house. She touches the
flame to the tinder. "You can't let it control you," Theo says. "Remember:
fire is a good servant but a poor master." "Whatever," mutters Doug. They
shuffle across the lawn and watch from the garage as the fire catches. The
flames rip through the structure, open palms arched against the heavens
and the vapours releasing with a sigh. Snakes ooze from the rock founda-
tion, arching and twisting onto the lawn, bellies scraping the gravel as they
burrow into the fields. Julie and Doug and Theo race ahead of them through
the orchard, to the red jeep that waits below the last McIntoshes. Theo lays
a hand against a trunk. "They did well," he murmurs. Now they are at the
jeep, and Doug's hands twist in his pockets. "The keys," he moans. The snakes
are gliding around them now.

Julie is outside by six that morning, pacing the verandah and studying the rock foundation. Musko trots off, seeking mice and squirrels in
the dew-soaked orchard. Soon the sun will burn through the mist and

the freshness of daybreak will be lost. If she must have dreams, could they not be deer dreams? Deer dreams are light and hopeful; they hint of freedom and reconciliation and Samuel and Rachel skipping along the wagon road to the brook, ten-year-old hopefulness forever uplifting them. Deer dreams are the precursors of pastoral perfection with healed mothers rocking on the verandah while Tina dances—will Tina come back? When has she last thought of Tina?—and her father tending the orchard. Christmas dreams are sweet and sad; they break the heart with yearning. They make you want to paint and put up pretty little curtains and scatter tasteful mats and be caretaker and companion so that Samuel can come home. Snake dreams leave a layer of cellar chill just below the skin. They are damp and heavy, clinging to the dreamer long after the sunrise. Did Grandma Mary have snake dreams? Julie wonders.

Musko lopes up through the orchard and flops on the verandah. He would like a walk with Julie, but there is time, and savouring time is a gift the Creator bestows on dogs. So Musko savours time and Julie paces and tries to think about learning disabilities. Learning disabilities do not reflect a deficit in intelligence, they reflect instead the individual's way of communicating with the world. They describe the learning style: if there is a significant gap between visual and nonvisual scores—there. That brown twist by the hollyhocks. That was a snake. Where did it go? Now, if there is a significant gap between the visual and verbal scores, and the child is strong in visual communication, then we say—why is Musko sniffing the air? What does he smell? Do snakes smell? Where did that hollyhock snake go?—then we say that the child has a learning disability that is verbally based. That is, good with visual information, but not with words. That must make reading and understanding this report extra fun. Why not say the child has a visual learning style? That sounds like a compliment. But perhaps it will not create jobs and provide equipment and programs that may or may not be used, and if used, may or may not help.

They all need friends. Friends from all ages and walks of life to see them strong. And how will you measure and track that, Ms. Martin? How will you ensure that they are meeting their goals? I have this friend Laila. She can just tell these things. She can? That's good to hear. Do you have a sample template for the documentation?

Tina is a poet who sometimes does not choose to speak, but there were no questions on the test to document her gift because she was silent and the test was limited. Tina is a tormented child but no test can measure the depths of her pain and she was silent and the test was limited. Tina is an insightful and spiritual human being but you cannot document that because she was silent and the test was limited.

If Tina were to come back and Julie were her teacher again, what would Julie do differently? She would give her paper and ask her to write and draw and then Julie would have a big folder of paper but no proper documentation because how do you do an analysis of a gift? And then Julie would be looking for a job and Tina would be reading words with a new teacher.

That rustling in the ivy by the shrub—it is wide and zigzagging; it is a little snake fleeing, but why?

So Julie would read with Tina and have coasting parties in the winter to support Tina and build her confidence. That was when the snake dreams started. Perhaps they were going to start anyway.

But they were over. It was all over, and it will be over again. Now. She is a teacher and is thinking about learning disabilities. She could become an educational psychologist and test students and explain to their teachers how to help their children. But the educational psychologists do that now, and their words are filed away, and bless the few readers who take note.

Would she really burn the house down? Burn down the house and free the Hardys? No, they would never be freed by that. It is only the snakes that are freed. Freed to slither around ankles and tires in the orchard. Snake dreams are about betrayal: Is she flushing out the traitors or healing the betrayed? Or are they just the product of a dissatisfied mind? Just? Julie was in the orchard when Doug couldn't find the keys.

The snakes were laughing at it all. Burn us out, they said, and set us free upon the world.

Thinking about learning disabilities does not help.

Julie and Musko walk to the brook in the cool of morning while thrushes call in the woodland and snakes wriggle through the dry hay. As they pass the red pines on the way back from the brook, she sees Samuel's little blue sedan by the back porch. Two figures are pacing around the old Astrakhan tree beyond the west kitchen window.

Julie approaches. Samuel, my father and I would like to build a cabin below your orchard. Actually, my father would like to build a cabin there. I would live in the house, and he would live in the cabin. Or we could both live in the house, no cabin. Would you like us to burn it for you? Get serious, Julie. I do not want to live in the house with your sister, Samuel. That is not my dream. Perhaps you and she could share it, which puts my father and me back in the cabin. You have a family near Waverley, though. You want to stay with them, and dabble in your childhood whenever you want. Actually, you only dabble in your childhood when I am dreaming. Now that says something.

Would you be offended, Samuel, if I terminated the lease and went back to North Ontario? Of course I would miss the place and Musko would, too, and I have been good for the place. But the place has been hard on me.

One man is Samuel; the other is a slightly older, slightly rounder and taller man with a firm chin and clear eyes. "You must be Julie Martin," he says, extending a hand. "I'm Charles. I grew up here."

Samuel is wavering in the background, alternately smiling too brightly and ducking his head away. Change is afoot. Perhaps Rachel is coming back.

"You've done really well here," Charles declares. "From what I hear, you have been an excellent tenant."

An excellent tenant, a builder of futures, a caretaker, and a canoer of shorelines, too.

I even dreamed your great-grandmother, Charles.

"Now that said," Charles continues, "it looks like there are a few changes to be made."

Julie glances at Samuel, who smiles with all his teeth and ducks his head away again.

"The fact is, my wife and I are retiring. From our jobs, that is. But we're not stopping working." Charles laughs, a quick bark of sound. "We," he says, "are going to live here. As proprietors. We are going to turn this place into a bed and breakfast. We, and Samuel, will own the place together. Rachel is not interested. She, once again, has found her niche. Which means she might be joining us any time we choose. It has to be our decision," he confides, "or she'll be buying in and out on a monthly basis. She's very happy on her lake at the moment, and so, I understand, is her furry companion, Taggak. She will be an investor, but closely monitored."

"But you can stay on, if you want," Samuel cuts in. "They won't be here for a while, and even then . . . well, you could help with the renovations. Sure. You'd be good at that. For rent, like."

"My lease," says Julie, for her paint and curtains and mats are suddenly precious.

Charles shrugs. "Leases get terminated all the time. You can't get attached to a place when you're renting."

Julie turns to Samuel. "What about a cabin? Below the orchard? My father would like to build a cabin there. We could look after the place in the winter, or whenever you went away."

Samuel shakes his head. "I don't know. A cabin. Below the orchard. . . ."

"Would look great down there," says Charles. "The cabin, on the edge of the field, like a caretaker's cottage. There was a turkey coop near there, remember?"

"He's a carpenter, isn't he?" says Samuel, getting swept up in the dream. "He could help us put the place back in shape."

"And the money from the land would go into the materials we'll need."

"It's going to be expensive." Samuel sighs.

"We should be ready by next season," Charles calculates.

"Will the income offset the expenses?"

"Eventually. It's a retirement project," Charles explains.

And one day they might break even. It is a dream of the calibre of the snow blower project, without Doug. Julie is embarrassed. They are hopeful. They are seeing their childhood home restored, but without drumming feet on the verandah floor, without the laughter of children on the hill. Strangers will pass through, and they will not see the Christmas tree in the corner, with fragile ornaments and Santa mugs with rolling eyes and all the hope with which the Hardy children started their twisting futures. How much time will pass before they all realize yet again that the house is old and weary, and the dreams have all been dreamed and the future still twists away?

Let them have this. This is what caretakers do. "My father could build such a bannister," Julie says.

"Bannister. Hmm. It has a bannister," says Charles.

And so it begins.

EPILOGUE

Laila holds out a small cooler tight with egg salad sandwiches with cucumber bits, roast beef slices and wedges of cheese, soft chocolate chip cookies for energy, and frozen juice packs that will thaw slowly as Julie travels.

"I thought Musko might like the roast beef," she says.

Musko is already settled in the backseat, head draped over the bag of blankets and pillows. The back of Julie's SUV holds a backpack, six bins, skis, and a bundle of small mats and curtains. Laptop and sleeping bag are wedged into the front passenger seat. The contents of the bins have changed; some items have been discarded and some added, such as a small box of cross-stitched ornaments. Six fit nicely, and so it is six.

Meadowbrook Acres stands on the bend beyond the river, waiting for all the summers that are to come. There, on the turn, is the long white house, neat corners facing the road, the back slashed away to severe edges and the ground tilting away down over the site of the great red barn. There are no feet drumming on the verandah, no children's laughter from the hill, but then again, perhaps there will be no fragile ornaments with fierce little snakes tapping their way out. Perhaps it can simply be a house now. With a caretaker's cottage below the orchard.

In one short year, a cabin has risen below the orchard. Her father has insulated and sanded and hammered and braced. The plank floors of Meadowbrook Acres are oiled and heavy with antique charm, no longer daubed over with cheap paints gleaned from sales. Flimsy veneer panelling has been stripped away and the plaster beneath painstakingly gutted. Ancient newspapers have been scooped up and discarded. Insulation has been snugged between the studs and a clean vapour barrier stretched over it. Fresh drywall has been screwed in, all seams have been filled and sanded, and heritage colours have been smoothed over a thick primer. Wainscoting dignifies the living room and dining room walls for the first time in forty years. Wainscoting had looked tired. It had split the room into too many lines to have wainscoting and all those tall windows. The veneer panelling had been fresh and modern. Then it had been cheap and tacky. One painted this panelling to disguise it, but the tackiness trickled through. Wainscoting, now, wainscoting defines a room. Meadowbrook Acres is stronger for it. And the clients will love it. There will be a few late tourists in September, surely, when the licenses should be in place.

Julie subs and sands and hammers the winter away, and Tina does come back but she is a glimpse in the hallway and there are no coasting parties. Joe Barnes does come back, but there are no deer haunches and no fishing trips.

Charles and his wife arrive in the spring, and Julie retreats to the cabin. It is not her cabin, however, and Meadowbrook Acres is not her care, anymore.

Julie occasionally races through the orchard while the flames burst through the roof that winter, but not often.

The deer do not come.

Musko sprawls and twitches in front of the fridge in the cabin on summer nights; each moment belongs to Musko because he recognizes it.

Samuel stares bewildered at the changes that are bringing him step by step into his childhood home, and then retreats to his family near Waverley.

Taggak and Musko wander the orchard together, when Rachel comes. She rarely stays, however, and spends hours canoeing the shoreline of Wasaya.

Taggak stretches under the porch at Wasaya while Rachel canoes, his body pressed tight to the cool earth. He dreams deep into his youth, and he races free over the ice on a northern lake, all the dogs of his young days bounding beside him.

Nathaniel kayaks the fierce north waters along the mountains. The spray beats his face and he laughs full into an open sky.

Tim manoeuvres expertly through the traffic between his condominium and his bank, his eye on the mirror and his mind on the next resort.

Joe paces the shore above the Narrows, the pine needles soft under his feet.

Laila and Tom continue to live by the side of the road. They do not need to explore the world for the world sweeps past their door and they recognize it and embrace it.

Theo plans and builds against the loneliness in his heart and sometimes goes up to the Park and is with Alice and her loons.

~

Musko rises in the backseat and looks long at the cabin below the orchard, where a man stands in the doorway, one hand raised. Musko's tail begins to swing. He grunts, pawing at the window.

"Well. Maybe not," Laila declares.

Julie feels the release in her heart, and opens the door. Musko lopes down to the cabin and takes up his position beside the man. He rubs Musko's ears and looks up, anxious.

"He wants to stay with you," Julie says. "I guess this is why he came to me in the first place."

"Good place for a dog," Theo agrees, his face clearing. "Good place for a lot of things. When you're ready."

Julie smiles. "Welcome home, Musko," she whispers, and turns back to the SUV.

"So you'll be down at Christmas?" Laila says. "Your dad will like that. Musko can only do so much, you know."

"Probably," says Julie. "It depends on how I do. If I still have what it takes. But next summer, probably, for sure."

A smile begins at the corner of Laila's mouth, and spreads across her face.

And then Julie is on the road, with moose on the highway through New Brunswick ahead, the crush of traffic along the St. Lawrence and into Montreal, the clogged 417 through Ottawa as the workday ends, the great trucks grinding in the night above North Bay, and finally a little plane, and perhaps a little place, for Julie and the Simons of this world.

Her future lies behind her, and she accelerates to meet it.

Printed in Canada